BY PAUL BOWLES

Novels

The Sheltering Sky (1949)
Let It Come Down (1952)
The Spider's House (1955)
Up Above the World (1966)

Collections of Stories

The Delicate Prey (1950)
A Hundred Camels in the Courtyard (1962)
The Time of Friendship (1967)
Things Gone & Things Still Here (1977)

Travel Essays

Yallah (Photographs by Peter W. Haeberlin) (1957)
Their Heads Are Green and Their Hands Are Blue (1963)

Poetry

Two Poems (1933)
Scenes (1968)
The Thicket of Spring (1972)
Next to Nothing (1977)

Texts Taped and Translated from the Moghrebi

A Life Full of Holes (Driss ben Hamed Charhadi) (1964)
Love With A Few Hairs (Mohammed Mrabet) (1968)
The Lemon (Mohammed Mrabet) (1968)
M'Hashish (Mohammed Mrabet) (1970)
The Boy Who Set the Fire (Mohammed Mrabet) (1974)
Look & Move On (Mohammed Mrabet) (1976)
Harmless Poisons, Blameless Sins (Mohammed Mrabet) (1976)
The Big Mirror (Mohammed Mrabet) (1977)

Autobiography

Without Stopping (1972)

PAUL BOWLES

COLLECTED STORIES
1939-1976

Introduction by
GORE VIDAL

BLACK SPARROW PRESS · SANTA BARBARA

1 9 8 5

ACKNOWLEDGEMENT

Grateful acknowledgement is made to the editors of the following periodicals where some of these stories originally appeared: *Antaeus, Art and Literature, Bastard Angel, Big Table, Encounter, Esquire, Harper's Bazaar, Horizon, Life and Letters, The London Magazine, Mademoiselle, New Directions 12, Partisan Review, Penguin New Writing, Prose, Rolling Stone, Transatlantic Review, View, Wake, World Review* and *Zero*.

LIBRARY OF CONGRESS CATALOGING IN PUBLICATION DATA

Bowles, Paul Frederic, 1911-
  The collected stories.

  I. Title.
PZ3.B6826Co [PS3552.0874]   813'.5'4   79-4569
ISBN 0-87685-396-3 (paper edition)
ISBN 0-87685-397-1 (trade cloth edition)

eighth printing

Introduction

"Carson McCullers, Paul Bowles, Tennessee Williams are, at this moment at least, the three most interesting writers in the United States." A quarter century has passed since I wrote that sentence in a piece on contemporary American writing.

Six years ago when I reprinted those words in *Homage to Daniel Says*, I felt obliged to add: "This was written in 1952. McCullers was a good and fashionable novelist of the day (I cannot say that I have any great desire to read her again). Paul Bowles was as little known then as he is now. His short stories are among the best ever written by an American. Tennessee Williams, etc. . . ." All in all, I still see no reason not to support my youthful judgment of Paul Bowles. As a short story writer, he has had few equals in the second half of the twentieth century. Obvious question: If he is so good, why is he so little known?

Great American writers are supposed not only to live in the greatest country in the world (the United States, for those who came in late), but to write about that greatest of all human themes: *The American Experience*. From the beginning of the Republic, this crude America First-ism has flourished. As a result, there is a strong tendency to misrepresent or under-value our three finest novelists: Henry James (who lived in England), Edith Wharton (who lived in France), Vladimir Nabokov (who lived in Switzerland, and who wasn't much of an American anyway despite an unnatural passion for our motels, so lyrically rendered in *Lolita*).

Paul Bowles has lived most of his life in Morocco. He seldom writes about the United States. On the other hand, he has shrewd things to say about Americans confronted with strange cultures and . . . . But, first, let us try to place Paul Bowles.

Born in 1911, he was brought up in New York City and New England. He attended the University of Virginia. When he was seventeen, the Paris-based avant-garde magazine *transition* published some of his poems. Bowles went to Paris, met Gertrude Stein, was influenced by the Surrealists. He quit school to become a writer. Except for Poe, his writing derives not from the usual Anglo-American tradition but from such "exotics" as Valéry, Roussel, Gide and, of course, the expatriate Miss Stein. Later, he was to put to his own uses oral Mexican and Moroccan folk-lore; he listened as much as he read.

I suspect that Bowles's apparent foreignness has limited the number of doctoral theses that ought by now to have been devoted to one whose art far exceeds that of . . . well, name the great American writers of our day (a list that was as different yesterday as it will be tomorrow). For the American Academic, Bowles is still odd man out; he writes as if *Moby Dick* had never been written. Odder still, he is also a distinguished composer of music. In fact, he supported himself for many years by writing incidental music for such Broadway plays as *The Glass Menagerie*. It is curious that at a time when a number of serious critics have expressed the hope that literature might one day take on the attributes of the "highest" of all the arts, music, Bowles has been composing music as well as writing prose. I am certain that the first critic able to deal both with his music and his writing will find that Bowles's life work has been marvelous in a way not accessible to those of us who know only one or the other of the two art forms.

In 1972, Paul Bowles wrote a memoir called, *Without Stopping*. For those able to read between the lines, the book was pleasurable. For anyone else, it must have sounded a bit like Julius Caesar's account of the wars in Gaul. Although there is a good deal of information about various commanders and troop movements, we don't learn much about what the subject had in mind. But there are interesting asides; and the best sort of memoir is entirely to one side of the mere facts of a life.

We learn that Bowles originally wanted to be a writer, not a composer. But at a progressive school he had shown an aptitude for mathematics, cousin germane to music. Nevertheless, he preferred to arrange words rather than notes upon a page until Gertrude Stein read his poems. "She sat back and thought a moment. Then she said: 'Well, the only trouble with all this is that it isn't poetry.'" She found his images false; did not think much of his attempt to write in the Surreal manner, "without conscious intervention." Later, she asked him if he had rewritten the poems. When he said no, "She was triumphant. 'You see,' she cried. 'I told you you were no poet. A real poet, after one conversation, would have gone upstairs and at least tried to recast them, but you haven't even looked at them.'" Bowles stopped writing. He turned to music.

Between 1929 and 1945 he made a name as a composer. He married the odd, brilliant Jane Bowles. She was a writer. He was a composer. Together and separately, they were much admired. During the late thirties and forties they became central figures in the transatlantic (and Pan-American) world of the arts. Although unknown to the general public , the Bowleses were famous among those who were famous; and in some mysterious way the art-grandees wanted, if not the admiration of the Bowleses (seldom bestowed), their tolerance.

They lived in Mexico (the unknown Tennessee Williams made a pilgrimage to their house in Acapulco); they lived in New York, sharing a house with W. H. Auden and Benjamin Britten. After the Second War they moved for good to Tangier where Paul Bowles still lives. Jane Bowles died in Spain in 1973.

In the spring of 1945, Charles Henri Ford asked Bowles to edit an issue of the magazine *View*. The subject was Central and South American culture. Bowles translated a number of Spanish writers; and wrote some texts of his own. In the course of "reading some ethnographic books with texts from the Arapesh or from the Tarahumara given in word-for-word translation . . . the desire came to me to invent my own myths, adopting the point of view of the primitive mind." He resorted to "the old Surrealist method of abandoning conscious control and writing whatever words came from the pen." The first of these stories was written "one rainy Sunday"; it is called "The Scorpion."

The story was well received, and Bowles went on writing. "The subject matter of the myths soon turned from 'primitive' to contemporary. . . . It was through this unexpected little gate that I crept back into the land of fiction writing. Long ago I had decided that the world was too complex for me ever to be able to write fiction; since I failed to understand life, I would not be able to find points of reference which the hypothetical reader might have in common with me." He did not entirely proceed through that small gate until he wrote "A Distant Episode" and found that if life was no more understandable to him than before, prose was. He now possessed the art to depict his dreams.

During the next thirty years Paul Bowles wrote the thirty-nine short stories collected in this volume. They were published originally in three volumes: *The Delicate Prey*, 1950; *The Time of Friendship*, 1967; *Things Gone and Things Still Here*, 1977. Even before the first collection was published, three of the stories caused a great stir in the literary world. "Pages from Cold Point," "The Delicate Prey" and "A Distant Episode" were immediately recognized as being unlike anything else in our literature. I have just re-read the three stories, with some nervousness. After all these years, I wondered if they would still "work." In my youth I had admired D. H. Lawrence's novels. Now, I deeply dislike them. I was relieved to find that Bowles's art is still as disturbing as ever. I was surprised to note how the actual stories differ from my memory of them. I recalled a graphic description of a sixteen-year old boy's seduction of his father on a hot summer night in Jamaica. Over the years, carnal details had built up in my memory like a coral reef. Yet on re-reading "Pages From Cold Point," nothing (and everything) happens. In his memoirs Bowles refers, rather casually, to this story as something he wrote aboard ship from New York to Casablanca: "a long story about a hedonist . . . ." It is a good deal more than that. Both "The Delicate Prey" and "A Distant Episode" create the same sense of strangeness and terror that they did the first time I read them. "The Delicate Prey" turns on a Gidean *acte gratuit*: the slicing off of the boy's penis is not only like the incident on the train in *Les Caves du Vatican* but also presages the driving of a nail through a skull in Bowles's novel *Let It Come Down*. "A Distant Episode" seems to me to be more than ever emblematic of the helplessness of an over-civilized sensibility (the Professor's) when confronted with an alien culture. Captured by North African nomads, his tongue cut out, he is made into a clown, a toy. He is used to make his captors laugh. He *appears* to accept his fate. Something harsh is glimpsed in the lines of a story that is now plainer in its reverberations than it was when written. But then it is no longer news to anyone that the floor to this ramshackle civilization that we have built cannot bear much longer our weight. It was Bowles's genius to suggest the horrors which lie beneath that floor, as fragile, in its way, as the sky that shelters us from a devouring vastness.

The stories fall into rough categories. First: locale. Mexico and North Africa are the principal settings. Landscape is all-important in a Bowles story. Second: how the inhabitants of alien cultures regard the creatures of our civilized world, as in "Under the Sky." Bowles goes even further in a beautiful story called "The Circular Valley" where human life is depicted as it must appear to the anima of a place. This spirit inhabits at will those human beings who visit its valley; feeds on their emotions; alters them during its occupancy. Third: the stories of transference. In "You Are Not I" a madwoman becomes her sane sister. In "Allal," a boy exchanges personality with a snake. The intensity of these stories makes them more like waking dreams than so many words on a page. Identity is transferred in such a way that one wonders which, finally, is which? and what is what? The effect is rather like the Taoist story of the man who dreamed that he was a butterfly. When "he woke up with a start, he did not know whether he was Chuang Chou who had dreamed that he was a butterfly, or whether he was a butterfly dreaming that he was Chuang Chou. Between Chuang Chou and the butterfly there must be some distinction. This is what is called the transformation of things."

There are a number of more or less realistic stories that deal with the plain incomprehension of Americans in contact with the natives of Mexico, North Africa, Thailand. One of the most amusing is "You Have Left Your Lotus Pods on the Bus." An American goes on an excursion with some Buddhist priests. The day is filled with splendid misunderstandings. There is the man at the back of a crowded bus who never stops screaming. He is ignored by everyone except the American who wonders why no one shuts him up. At the end, the priests tell him that the "madman" is an employee of the bus company giving necessary warnings and advice to the driver.

In several stories white ladies respond not-so-ambiguously to dark-skinned youths. Bowles notes the sadism that sexual frustration can cause ("At Paso Rojo"). But where the ordinary writer would leave it at that, Bowles goes deeper into the human case and, paradoxically, he achieves his greatest effects when he concentrates entirely on surfaces. Although he seldom describes a human face, he examines landscape with the precision of a geologist. Bowles himself seems like one of those bright sharp-eyed birds that flit from story to story, staring with eyes that do not blink at desert, hills, sky. He records weather with all the solemnity of a meteorologist. He looks closely at food. As for his human characters, he simply lets them reveal themselves through what they say or do not say. Finally, he is a master of suggesting anxiety (are all the traveller's cheques lost or just mislaid?) and dread (will this desert prove to be the setting for a very special death?). Story after story turns on flight. It is no accident that Bowles called his memoir (with pride?) *Without Stopping*.

Four stories were written to demonstrate that by using "kif-inspired motivations, the arbitrary would be made to seem natural, the diverse elements could be fused, and several people would automatically become one." These pieces strike me as entirely uninhabited, and of no interest. Yet in other stories (inspired perhaps by smaller doses of kif) he does dem-onstrate the essential one-ness of the many as well as the interchangeability not only of personality but of all things. As Webster saw the skull beneath the skin, so Bowles has glimpsed what lies back of our sheltering sky . . . an endless flux of stars so like those atoms which make us up that in our apprehension of this terrible infinity, we experience not only horror but likeness.

Gore Vidal

TABLE OF CONTENTS

Collected Stories of Paul Bowles

Tea on the Mountain

The mail that morning had brought her a large advance from her publishers. At least, it looked large to her there in the International Zone where life was cheap. She had opened the letter at a table of the sidewalk café opposite the Spanish post office. The emotion she felt at seeing the figures on the check had made her unexpectedly generous to the beggars that constantly filed past. Then the excitement had worn off, and she felt momentarily depressed. The streets and the sky seemed brighter and stronger than she. She had of necessity made very few friends in the town, and although she worked steadily every day at her novel, she had to admit that sometimes she was lonely. Driss came by, wearing a spotless mauve *djellaba* over his shoulders and a new fez on his head.

"*Bonjour, mademoiselle,*" he said, making an exaggerated bow. He had been paying her assiduous attention for several months, but so far she had been successful in putting him off without losing his friendship; he made a good escort in the evenings. This morning she greeted him warmly, let him pay her check, and moved off up the street with him, conscious of the comment her action had caused among the other Arabs sitting in the café.

They turned into the rue du Télégraphe Anglais, and walked slowly down the hill. She decided she was trying to work up an appetite for lunch; in the noonday heat it was often difficult to be hungry. Driss had been Europeanized to the point of insisting on apéritifs before his meals; however, instead of having two Dubonnets, for instance, he would take a Gentiane, a Byrrh, a Pernod and an Amer Picon. Then he usually went to sleep and put off eating until later. They stopped at the café facing the Marshan Road, and sat down next to a table occupied by several students from the Lycée Français, who were drinking *limonades* and glancing over their notebooks. Driss wheeled around suddenly and began a casual conversation. Soon they both moved over to the students' table.

She was presented to each student in turn; they solemnly acknowledged her "*Enchantée,*" but remained seated while doing so. Only one, named Mjid, rose from his chair and quickly sat down again, looking worried. He was the one she immediately wanted to get to know, perhaps because he was more serious and soft-eyed, yet at the same time seemed more eager and violent than any of the others. He spoke his stilted theatre-French

15

swiftly, with less accent than his schoolmates, and he punctuated his sentences with precise, tender smiles instead of the correct or expected inflections. Beside him sat Ghazi, plump and Negroid.

She saw right away that Mjid and Ghazi were close friends. They replied to her questions and flattery as one man, Ghazi preferring, however, to leave the important phrases to Mjid. He had an impediment in his speech, and he appeared to think more slowly. Within a few minutes she had learned that they had been going to school together for twelve years, and had always been in the same form. This seemed strange to her, inasmuch as Ghazi's lack of precocity became more and more noticeable as she watched him. Mjid noticed the surprise in her face, and he added:

"Ghazi is very intelligent, you know. His father is the high judge of the native court of the International Zone. You will go to his home one day and see for yourself."

"Oh, but of course I believe you," she cried, understanding now why Ghazi had experienced no difficulty in life so far, in spite of his obvious slow-wittedness.

"I have a very beautiful house indeed," added Ghazi. "Would you like to come and live in it? You are always welcome. That's the way we Tanjaoui are."

"Thank you. Perhaps some day I shall. At any rate, I thank you a thousand times. You are too kind."

"And my father," interposed Mjid suavely but firmly, "the poor man, he is dead. Now it's my brother who commands."

"But, alas, Mjid, your brother is tubercular," sighed Ghazi.

Mjid was scandalized. He began a vehement conversation with Ghazi in Arabic, in the course of which he upset his empty *limonade* bottle. It rolled onto the sidewalk and into the gutter, where an urchin tried to make off with it, but was stopped by the waiter. He brought the bottle to the table, carefully wiped it with his apron, and set it down.

"Dirty Jew dog!" screamed the little boy from the middle of the street.

Mjid heard this epithet even in the middle of his tirade. Turning in his chair, he called to the child: "Go home. You'll be beaten this evening."

"Is it your brother?" she asked with interest.

Since Mjid did not answer her, but seemed not even to have heard her, she looked at the urchin again and saw his ragged clothing. She was apologetic.

"Oh, I'm sorry," she began. "I hadn't looked at him. I see now . . . ."

Mjid said, without looking at her: "You would not need to look at that child to know he was not of my family. You heard him speak. . . ."

"A neighbor's child. A poor little thing," interrupted Ghazi.

Mjid seemed lost in wonder for a moment. Then he turned and

explained slowly to her: "One word we can't hear is tuberculosis. Any other word, syphillis, leprosy, even pneumonia, we can listen to, but not that word. And Ghazi knows that. He wants you to think we have Paris morals here. There I know everyone says that word everywhere, on the boulevards, in the cafés, in Montparnasse, in the Dôme—" he grew excited as he listed these points of interest— "in the Moulin Rouge, in Sacré Coeur, in the Louvre. Some day I shall go myself. My brother has been. That's where he got sick."

During this time Driss, whose feeling of ownership of the American lady was so complete that he was not worried by any conversation she might have with what he considered schoolboys, was talking haughtily to the other students. They were all pimply and bespectacled. He was telling them about the football games he had seen in Málaga. They had never been across to Spain, and they listened, gravely sipped their *limonade*, and spat on the floor like Spaniards.

"Since I can't invite you to my home, because we have sickness there, I want you to make a picnic with me tomorrow," announced Mjid. Ghazi made some inaudible objection which his friend silenced with a glance, whereupon Ghazi decided to beam, and followed the plans with interest.

"We shall hire a carriage, and take some ham to my country villa," continued Mjid, his eyes shining with excitement. Ghazi started to look about apprehensively at the other men seated on the terrace; then he got up and went inside.

When he returned he objected: "You have no sense, Mjid. You say 'ham' right out loud when you know some friends of my father might be here. It would be very bad for me. Not everyone is free as you are."

Mjid was penitent for an instant. He stretched out his leg, pulling aside his silk *gandoura*. "Do you like my garters?" he asked her suddenly.

She was startled. "They're quite good ones," she began.

"Let me see yours," he demanded.

She glanced down at her slacks. She had espadrilles on her feet, and wore no socks. "I'm sorry," she said. "I haven't any."

Mjid looked uncomfortable, and she guessed that it was more for having discovered, in front of the others, a flaw in her apparel, than for having caused her possible embarrassment. He cast a contrite glance at Ghazi, as if to excuse himself for having encouraged a foreign lady who was obviously not of the right sort. She felt that some gesture on her part was called for. Pulling out several hundred francs, which was all the money in her purse, she laid it on the table, and went on searching in her handbag for her mirror. Mjid's eyes softened. He turned with a certain triumph to Ghazi, and permitting himself a slight display of exaltation, patted his friend's cheek three times.

"So it's set!" he exclaimed. "Tomorrow at noon we meet here at the Café du Télégraphe Anglais. I shall have hired a carriage at eleven-thirty at the market. You, dear mademoiselle," turning to her, "will have gone at ten-thirty to the English grocery and bought the food. Be sure to get Jambon Olida, because it's the best."

"The best ham," murmured Ghazi, looking up and down the street a bit uneasily.

"And buy one bottle of wine."

"Mjid, you know this can get back to my father," Ghazi began.

Mjid had had enough interference. He turned to her. "If you like, mademoiselle, we can go alone."

She glanced at Ghazi; his cowlike eyes had veiled with actual tears.

Mjid continued. "It'll be very beautiful up there on the mountain with just us two. We'll take a walk along the top of the mountain to the rose gardens. There's a breeze from the sea all afternoon. At dusk we'll be back at the farm. We'll have tea and rest." He stopped at this point, which he considered crucial.

Ghazi was pretending to read his social correspondence textbook, with his *chechia* tilted over his eyebrows so as to hide his hopelessly troubled face. Mjid smiled tenderly.

"We'll go all three," he said softly.

Ghazi simply said: "Mjid is bad."

Driss was now roaring drunk. The other students were impressed and awed. Some of the bearded men in the café looked over at the table with open disapproval in their faces. She saw that they regarded her as a symbol of corruption. Consulting her fancy little enamel watch, which everyone at the table had to examine and study closely before she could put it back into its case, she announced that she was hungry.

"Will you eat with us?" Ghazi inquired anxiously. It was clear he had read that an invitation should be extended on such occasions; it was equally clear that he was in terror lest she accept.

She declined and rose. The glare of the street and the commotion of the passers-by had tired her. She took her leave of all the students while Driss was inside the café, and went down to the restaurant on the beach where she generally had lunch.

There while she ate, looking out at the water, she thought: "That was amusing, but it was just enough," and she decided not to go on the picnic.

She did not even wait until the next day to stock up with provisions at the English grocery. She bought three bottles of ordinary red wine, two cans of Jambon Olida, several kinds of Huntley and Palmer's biscuits, a bottle of stuffed olives and five hundred grams of chocolates full of liqueurs. The English lady made a splendid parcel for her.

At noon next day she was drinking an *orgeat* at the Café du Télégraphe Anglais. A carriage drove up, drawn by two horses loaded down with sleighbells. Behind the driver, shielded from the sun by the beige canopy of the victoria, sat Ghazi and Mjid, looking serious and pleasant. They got down to help her in. As they drove off up the hill, Mjid inspected the parcel approvingly and whispered: "The wine?"

"All inside," she said.

The locusts made a great noise from the dusty cliffs beside the road as they came to the edge of town. "Our nightingales," smiled Mjid. "Here is a ring for you. Let me see your hand."

She was startled, held out her left hand.

"No, no! The right!" he cried. The ring was of massive silver; it fitted her index finger. She was immensely pleased.

"But you are too nice. What can I give you?" She tried to looked pained and helpless.

"The pleasure of having a true European friend," said Mjid gravely.

"But I'm American," she objected.

"All the better."

Ghazi was looking silently toward the distant Riffian mountains. Prophetically he raised his arm with its silk sleeve blowing in the hot wind, and pointed across the cracked mud fields.

"Down that way," he said softly, "there is a village where all the people are mad. I rode there once with one of my father's assistants. It's the water they drink."

The carriage lurched. They were climbing. Below them the sea began to spread out, a poster blue. The tops of the mountains across the water in Spain rose above the haze. Mjid started to sing. Ghazi covered his ears with his fat dimpled hands.

The summer villa was inhabited by a family with a large number of children. After dismissing the carriage driver and instructing him not to return, since he wanted to walk back down, Mjid took his guests on a tour of inspection of the grounds. There were a good many wells; Ghazi had certainly seen these countless times before, but he stopped as if in amazement at each well as they inspected it, and whispered: "Think of it!"

On a rocky elevation above the farm stood a great olive tree. There they spread the food, and ate slowly. The Berber woman in charge of the farm had given them several loaves of native bread, and olives and oranges. Ghazi wanted Mjid to decline this food.

"A real European picnic is what we should have."

But she insisted they take the oranges.

The opening of the ham was observed in religious silence. It was no time before both cans were consumed. Then they attacked the wine.

"If my father could see us," said Ghazi, draining a tin cup of it. "Ham and wine!"

Mjid drank a cup, making a grimace of distaste. He lay back, his arms folded behind his head. "Now that I've finished, I can tell you that I don't like wine, and everyone knows that ham is filthy. But I hate our severe conventions."

She suspected that he had rehearsed the little speech.

Ghazi was continuing to drink the wine. He finished a bottle all by himself, and excusing himself to his companions, took off his *gandoura*. Soon he was asleep.

"You see?" whispered Mjid. He took her hand and pulled her to her feet. "Now we can go to the rose garden." He led her along the ledge, and down a path away from the villa. It was very narrow; thorny bushes scraped their arms as they squeezed through.

"In America we call walking like this going Indian fashion," she remarked.

"Ah, yes?" said Mjid. "I'm going to tell you about Ghazi. One of his father's women was a Senegalese slave, poor thing. She made Ghazi and six other brothers for her husband, and they all look like Negroes."

"Don't you consider Negroes as good as you?" she asked.

"It's not a question of being as good, but of being as beautiful," he answered firmly.

They had come out into a clearing on the hillside. He stopped and looked closely at her. He pulled his shirt off over his head. His body was white.

"My brother has blond hair," he said with pride. Then confusedly he put the shirt back on and laid his arm about her shoulder. "You are beautiful because you have blue eyes. But even some of us have blue eyes. In any case, you are *magnificent!*" He started ahead again, singing a song in Spanish.

> *"Es pa' mi la más bonita,*
> *La mujer que yo más quiero . . ."*

They came to a cactus fence, with a small gate of twisted barbed wire. A yellow puppy rushed up to the gate and barked delightedly.

"Don't be afraid," said Mjid, although she had given no sign of fear. "You are my sister. He never bites the family." Continuing down a dusty path between stunted palms which were quite dried-up and yellow, they came presently to a primitive bower made of bamboo stalks. In the center was a tiny bench beside a wall, and around the edges several dessicated rose plants grew out of the parched earth. From these he picked two bright red roses, placing one in her hair and the other under his *chechia*, so that it fell like a lock of hair over his forehead. The thick growth of thorny vines climbing over the trellises cast a shadow on the bench. They sat awhile in silence in the shade.

Mjid seemed lost in thought. Finally he took her hand. "I'm thinking," he said in a whisper. "When one is far away from the town, in one's own garden, far from everyone, sitting where it is quiet, one always thinks. Or one plays music," he added.

Suddenly she was conscious of the silence of the afternoon. Far in the distance she heard the forlorn crow of a cock. It made her feel that the sun would soon set, that all creation was on the brink of a great and final sunset. She abandoned herself to sadness, which crept over her like a chill.

Mjid jumped up. "If Ghazi wakes!" he cried. He pulled her arm impatiently. "Come, we'll take a walk!" They hurried down the path, through the gate, and across a bare stony plateau toward the edge of the mountain.

"There's a little valley nearby where the brother of the caretaker lives. We can go there and get some water."

"Way down there?" she said, although she was encouraged by the possibility of escaping from Ghazi for the afternoon. Her mood of sadness had not left her. They were running downhill, leaping from one rock to the next. Her rose fell off and she had to hold it in her hand.

The caretaker's brother was cross-eyed. He gave them some foul-smelling water in an earthen jug.

"Is it from the well?" she inquired under her breath to Mjid.

His face darkened with displeasure. "When you're offered something to drink, even if it's poison, you should drink it and thank the man who offers it."

"Ah," she said. "So it is poison. I thought so."

Mjid seized the jug from the ground between them, and taking it to the edge of the cliff, flung it down with elegant anger. The cross-eyed man protested, and then he laughed. Mjid did not look at him, but walked into the house and began a conversation with some of the Berber women inside, leaving her to face the peasant alone and stammer her dozen words of Arabic with him. The afternoon sun was hot, and the idea of some water to drink had completely filled her mind. She sat down perversely with her back to the view and played with pebbles, feeling utterly useless and absurd. The cross-eyed man continued to laugh at intervals, as if it provided an acceptable substitute for conversation.

When Mjid finally came out, all his ill-humor had vanished. He put out his hand to help her up, and said: "Come, we'll climb back up and have tea at the farm. I have my own room there. I decorated it myself. You'll look at it and tell me if you have as pleasant a room in your house in America for drinking tea." They set off, up the mountain.

The woman at the villa was obsequious. She fanned the charcoal fire and fetched water from the well. The children were playing a mysterious, quiet game at a far end of the enclosure. Mjid led her into the house, through several dim rooms, and finally into one that seemed the last in the series. It was cooler, and a bit darker than the others.

"You'll see," said Mjid, clapping his hands twice. Nothing happened. He called peevishly. Presently the woman entered. She smoothed the mattresses on the floor, and opened the blinds of the one small window, which gave onto the sea. Then she lit several candles which she stuck onto the tile floor, and went out.

His guest stepped to the window. "Can you ever hear the sea here?"

"Certainly not. It's about six kilometers away."

"But it looks as though you could drop a stone into it," she objected, hearing the false inflection of her voice; she was not interested in the conversation, she had the feeling that everything had somehow gone wrong. "What am I doing here? I have no business here. I said I wouldn't come." The idea of such a picnic had so completely coincided with some unconscious desire she had harbored for many years. To be free, out-of-doors, with some young man she did not know—*could* not know—that was probably the important part of the dream. For if she could not know him, he could not know her. She swung the little blind shut and hooked it. A second later she opened it again and looked out at the vast expanse of water growing dim in the twilight.

Mjid was watching her. "You are crazy," he said at last despairingly. "You find yourself here in this beautiful room. You are my guest. You should be happy. Ghazi has already left to go to town. A friend came by with a horse and he got a ride in. You could lie down, sing, drink tea, you could be happy with me . . ." He stopped, and she saw that he was deeply upset.

"What's the matter? What's the matter?" she said very quickly.

He sighed dramatically; perhaps it was a genuine sigh. She thought: "There is nothing wrong. It should have been a man, not a boy, that's all." It did not occur to her to ask herself: "But would I have come if it had been a man?" She looked at him tenderly, and decided that his face was probably the most intense and beautiful she had ever seen. She murmured a word without quite knowing what it was.

"What?" he said.

She repeated it: "Incredible."

He smiled inscrutably.

They were interrupted by the sound of the woman's bare feet slapping the floor. She had a tremendous tray bearing the teapot and its accessories.

While he made the tea, Mjid kept glancing at her as if to assure himself that she was still there. She sat perfectly still on one of the mattresses, waiting.

"You know," he said slowly, "If I could earn money I'd go away tomorrow to wherever I could earn it. I finish school this year anyway, and my brother hasn't the money to send me to a Medersa at Fez. But even if he had it, I wouldn't go. I always stay away from school. Only my brother gets very angry."

"What do you do instead? Go bathing?"

He laughed scornfully, sampled the tea, poured it back into the pot, and sat up on his haunches. "In another minute it will be ready. Bathing? Ah, my friend, it has to be something important for me to risk my brother's anger. I make love those days, all day long!"

"Really? You mean all day?" She was thoughtful.

"All day and most of the night. Oh, I can tell you it's marvelous, magnificent. I have a little room," he crawled over to her and put his hand on her knee, looking up into her face with an eagerness born of faith. "A room my family knows nothing about, in the Casbah. And my little friend is twelve. She is like the sun, soft, beautiful, lovely. Here, take your tea." He sipped from his glass noisily, smacking his lips.

"All day long," she reflected aloud, settling back against the cushions.

"Oh, yes. But I'll tell you a secret. You have to eat as much as you can. But that's not so hard. You're that much hungrier."

"Yes, of course," she said. A little gust of wind blew along the floor and the candles flickered.

"How good it is to have tea and then lie down to rest!" he exclaimed, pouring her more tea and stretching out beside her on the mattress. She made a move as if to spring up, then lay still.

He went on. "It's curious that I never met you last year."

"I wasn't in town very much. Only evenings. And then I was at the beach. I lived on the mountain."

He sat up. "On this mountain here? And I never saw you! Oh, what bad luck!"

She described the house, and since he insisted, told him the rent she had paid. He was ferociously indignant. "For that miserable house that hasn't even a good well? You had to send your Mohammed down the road for water! I know all about that house. My poor friend, you were robbed! If I ever see that dirty bandit I'll smash his face. I'll demand the money you paid him, and we'll make a trip together." He paused. "I mean, I'll give it to you of course, and you can decide what you want to do with it."

As he finished speaking he held up her handbag, opened it, and took out her fountain pen. "It's a beautiful one," he murmured. "Do you have many?"

"It's the only one."

"Magnificent!" He tossed it back in and laid the bag on the floor.

Settling against the pillows he ruminated. "Perhaps some day I shall go to America, and then you can invite me to your house for tea. Each year we'll come back to Morocco and see our friends and bring back cinema stars and presents from New York."

What he was saying seemed so ridiculous to her that she did not bother to answer. She wanted to ask him about the twelve-year-old girl, but she could find no excuse for introducing the subject again.

"You're not happy?" He squeezed her arm.

She raised herself to listen. With the passing of the day the countryside had attained complete silence. From the distance she could hear a faint but clear voice singing. She looked at Mjid.

"The *muezzin*? You can hear it from here?"

"Of course. It's not so far to the Marshan. What good is a country house where you can't hear the *muezzin*? You might as well live in the Sahara."

"Sh. I want to listen."

"It's a good voice, isn't it? They have the strongest voices in the world."

"It always makes me sad."

"Because you're not of the faith."

She reflected a minute and said: "I think that's true." She was about to add: "But your faith says women have no souls." Instead she rose from the mattress and smoothed her hair. The *muezzin* had ceased. She felt quite chilled. "This is over," she said to herself. They stumbled down the dark road into town, saying very little on the way.

He took her to her small hotel. The cable she had vaguely expected for weeks was there. They climbed the stairs to her room, the concierge looking suspiciously after them. Once in the room, she opened the envelope. Mjid had thrown himself onto the bed.

"I'm leaving for Paris tomorrow."

His face darkened, and he shut his eyes for an instant. "You must go away? All right. Let me give you my address." He pulled out his wallet, searched for a piece of paper, and finding none, took a calling card someone had given him, and carefully wrote.

"Fuente Nueva," he said slowly as he formed the letters. "It's my little room. I'll look every day to see if there's a letter."

She had a swift vision of him, reading a letter in a window flooded with sunshine, above the city's terraced roofs, and behind him, in the darkness of the room, with a face wise beyond its years, a complacent child waiting.

He gave her the card. Underneath the address he had written the word

"Incredible," enclosed in quotation marks and underlined twice. She glanced quickly to see his face, but it betrayed nothing.

Below them the town was blue, the bay almost black.

"The lighthouse," said Mjid.

"It's flashing," she observed.

He turned and walked to the door. "Good-bye," he said. "You will come back." He left the door open and went down the stairs. She stood perfectly still and finally moved her head up and down a few times, as if thoughtfully answering a question. Through the open window in the hallway she heard his rapid footsteps on the gravel in the garden. They grew fainter.

She looked at the bed; at the edge, ready to fall to the floor, was the white card where she had tossed it. She wanted more than anything to lie down and rest. Instead, she went downstairs into the cramped little salon and sat in the corner looking at old copies of *L'Illustration*. It was almost an hour before dinner would be served.

New York
1939

The Scorpion

An old woman lived in a cave which her sons had hollowed out of a clay cliff near a spring before they went away to the town where many people live. She was neither happy nor unhappy to be there, because she knew that the end of life was near and that her sons would not be likely to return no matter what the season. In the town there are always many things to do, and they would be doing them, not caring to remember the time when they had lived in the hills looking after the old woman.

At the entrance to the cave at certain times of the year there was a curtain of water-drops through which the old woman had to pass to get inside. The water rolled down the bank from the plants above and dripped onto the clay below. So the old woman accustomed herself to sitting crouched in the cave for long periods of time in order to keep as dry as possible. Outside through the moving beads of water she saw the bare earth lighted by the gray sky, and sometimes large dry leaves went past, pushed by the wind that came from higher parts of the land. Inside where she was the light was pleasant and of a pink color from the clay all around.

A few people used to pass from time to time along the path not far away, and because there was a spring nearby, those travelers who knew that it existed but not just where it was would sometimes come near to the cave before they discovered that the spring was not there. The old woman would never call to them. She would merely watch them as they came near and suddenly saw her. Then she would go on watching as they turned back and went in other directions looking for the water to drink.

There were many things about this life that the old woman liked. She was no longer obliged to argue and fight with her sons to make them carry wood to the charcoal oven. She was free to move about at night and look for food. She could eat everything she found without having to share it. And she owed no one any debt of thanks for the things she had in her life.

One old man used to come from the village on his way down to the valley, and sit on a rock just distant enough from the cave for her to recognize him. She knew he was aware of her presence in the cave there, and although she probably did not know this, she disliked him for not giving

27

some sign that he knew she was there. It seemed to her that he had an unfair advantage over her and was using it in an unpleasant way. She thought up many ideas for annoying him if he should ever come near enough, but he always passed by in the distance, pausing to sit down on the rock for some time, when he would often gaze straight at the cave. Then he would continue slowly on his way, and it always seemed to the old woman that he went more slowly after his rest than before it.

There were scorpions in the cave all year round, but above all during the days just before the plants began to let water drip through. The old woman had a huge bundle of rags, and with this she would brush the walls and ceiling clear of them, stamping quickly on them with her hard bare heel. Occasionally a small wild bird or animal strayed inside the entrance, but she was never quick enough to kill it, and she had given up trying.

One dark day she looked up to see one of her sons standing in the doorway. She could not remember which one it was, but she thought it was the one who had ridden the horse down the dry river bed and nearly been killed. She looked at his hand to see if it was out of shape. It was not that son.

He began to speak: "Is it you?"

"Yes."

"Are you well?"

"Yes."

"Is everything well?"

"Everything."

"You stayed here?"

"You can see."

"Yes."

There was a silence. The old woman looked around the cave and was displeased to see that the man in the doorway made it practically dark in there. She busied herself with trying to distinguish various objects: her stick, her gourd, her tin can, her length of rope. She was frowning with the effort.

The man was speaking again.

"Shall I come in?"

She did not reply.

He backed away from the entrance, brushing the water drops from his garments. He was on the point of saying something profane, thought the old woman, who, even though she did not know which one this was, remembered what he would do.

She decided to speak.

"What?" she said.

He leaned forward through the curtain of water and repeated his question.

"Shall I come in?"

"No."

"What's the matter with you?"

"Nothing."

Then she added: "There's no room."

He backed out again, wiping his head. The old woman thought he would probably go away, and she was not sure she wanted him to. However, there was nothing else he could do, she thought. She heard him sit down outside the cave, and then she smelled tobacco smoke. There was no sound but the dripping of water upon the clay.

A short while later she heard him get up. He stood outside the entrance again.

"I'm coming in," he said.

She did not reply.

He bent over and pushed inside. The cave was too low for him to stand up in it. He looked about and spat on the floor.

"Come on," he said.

"Where?"

"With me."

"Why?"

"Because you have to come."

She waited a little while, and then said suspiciously: "Where are you going?"

He pointed indifferently toward the valley, and said: "Down that way."

"In the town?"

"Farther."

"I won't go."

"You have to come."

"No."

He picked up her stick and held it out to her.

"Tomorrow," she said.

"Now."

"I must sleep," she said, settling back into her pile of rags.

"Good. I'll wait outside," he answered, and went out.

The old woman went to sleep immediately. She dreamed that the town was very large. It went on forever and its streets were filled with people in new clothes. The church had a high tower with several bells that rang all the time. She was in the streets all one day, surrounded by people. She was not sure whether they were all her sons or not. She asked some of them: "Are you my sons?" They could not answer, but she thought that if they had been able to, they would have said: "Yes." Then when it was night she found a house with its door open. Inside there was a light and some women were seated in a corner. They rose when she went in, and said: "You have a room here." She did not want to see it, but they pushed her along until she was in it, and closed the door. She was a little girl and she was crying. The bells of the church were very loud outside, and she imagined they filled the sky. There was an open space in the wall high above her. She could see the stars through it, and they gave light to her room. From the reeds which formed the ceiling a scorpion came crawling. He came slowly down the wall toward her. She stopped crying and watched him. His tail curved up over his back and moved a little from side to side as he crawled. She looked quickly about for something to brush him down with. Since there was nothing in the room she used her hand. But her motions were slow, and the scorpion seized her finger with his pinchers, clinging there tightly although she waved her hand wildly about. Then she realized that he was not going to sting her. A great feeling of happiness went through her. She raised her finger to her lips to kiss the scorpion. The bells stopped ringing. Slowly in the peace which was beginning, the scorpion moved into her mouth. She felt his hard shell and his little clinging legs going across her lips and her tongue. He crawled slowly down her throat and was hers. She woke up and called out.

Her son answered: "What is it?"

"I'm ready."

"So soon?"

He stood outside as she came through the curtain of water, leaning on her stick. Then he began walking a few paces ahead of her toward the path.

"It will rain," said her son.

"Is it far?"

"Three days," he said, looking at her old legs.

She nodded. Then she noticed the old man sitting on the stone. He had an expression of deep surprise on his face, as if a miracle had just occurred. His mouth was open as he stared at the old woman. When they came opposite the rock he peered more intently than ever into her face. She pretended not to notice him. As they picked their way carefully downhill along the stony path, they heard the old man's thin voice behind them, carried by the wind.

"Good-bye."

"Who is that?" said her son.

"I don't know."

Her son looked back at her darkly.

"You're lying," he said.

New York
1944

By the Water

The melting snow dripped from the balconies. People hurried through the little street that always smelled of frying fish. Now and then a stork swooped low, dragging his sticklike legs below him. The small gramophones scraped day and night behind the walls of the shop where young Amar worked and lived. There were few spots in the city where the snow was ever cleared away, and this was not one of them. So it gathered all through the winter months, piling up in front of the shop doors.

But now it was late winter; the sun was warmer. Spring was on the way, to confuse the heart and melt the snow. Amar, being alone in the world, decided it was time to visit a neighboring city where his father had once told him some cousins lived.

Early in the morning he went to the bus station. It was still dark, and the empty bus came in while he was drinking hot coffee. The road wound through the mountains all the way.

When he arrived in the other city it was already dark. Here the snow was even deeper in the streets, and it was colder. Because he had not wanted to, Amar had not foreseen this, and it annoyed him to be forced to wrap his burnous closely about him as he left the bus station. It was an unfriendly town; he could tell that immediately. Men walked with their heads bent forward, and if they brushed against a passer-by they did not so much as look up. Excepting the principal street, which had an arc-light every few meters, there seemed to be no other illumination, and the alleys that led off on either side lay in utter blackness; the white-clad figures that turned into them disappeared straightway.

"A bad town," said Amar under his breath. He felt proud to be coming from a better and larger city, but his pleasure was mingled with anxiety about the night to be passed in this inimical place. He abandoned the idea of trying to find his cousins before morning, and set about looking for a fondouk or a bath where he might sleep until daybreak.

Only a short distance ahead the street-lighting system terminated. Beyond, the street appeared to descend sharply and lose itself in darkness. The snow was uniformly deep here, and not cleared away in patches as it had been nearer the bus station. He puckered his lips and blew his breath

31

ahead of him in little clouds of steam. As he passed over into the unlighted district he heard a few languid notes being strummed on an oud. The music came from a doorway on his left. He paused and listened. Someone approached the doorway from the other direction and inquired, apparently of the man with the oud, if it was "too late."

"No," the musician answered, and he played several more notes.

Amar went over to the door.

"Is there still time?" he said.

"Yes."

He stepped inside the door. There was no light, but he could feel warm air blowing upon his face from the corridor to the right. He walked ahead, letting his hand run along the damp wall beside him. Soon he came into a large dimly lit room with a tile floor. Here and there, at various angles, figures lay asleep, wrapped in gray blankets. In a far corner a group of men, partially dressed, sat about a burning brazier, drinking tea and talking in low tones. Amar slowly approached them, taking care not to step on the sleepers.

The air was oppressively warm and moist.

"Where is the bath?" said Amar.

"Down there," answered one of the men in the group, without even looking up. He indicated the dark corner to his left. And, indeed, now that Amar considered it, it seemed to him that a warm current of air came up from that part of the room. He went in the direction of the dark corner, undressed, and leaving his clothes in a neat pile on a piece of straw matting, walked toward the warmth. He was thinking of the misfortune he had encountered in arriving in this town at nightfall, and he wondered if his clothes would be molested during his absence. He wore his money in a leather pouch which hung on a string about his neck. Feeling vaguely for the purse under his chin, he turned around to look once again at his clothing. No one seemed to have noticed him as he undressed. He went on. It would not do to seem too distrustful. He would be embroiled immediately in a quarrel which could end badly for him.

A little boy rushed out of the darkness toward him, calling: "Follow me, Sidi, I shall lead you to the bath." He was extremely dirty and ragged, and looked rather more like a midget than a child. Leading the way, he chattered as they went down the slippery, warm steps in the dark. "You will call for Brahim when you want your tea? You're a stranger. You have much money. . . ."

Amar cut him short. "You'll get your coins when you come to wake me in the morning. Not tonight."

"But, Sidi! I'm not allowed in the big room. I stay in the doorway and show gentlemen down to the bath. Then I go back to the doorway. I can't wake you."

"I'll sleep near the doorway. It's warmer there, in any case."

"Lazrag will be angry and terrible things will happen. I'll never get home again, or if I do I might be a bird so my parents will not know me. That's what Lazrag does when he gets angry."

"Lazrag?"

"It is his place here. You'll see him. He never goes out. If he did the sun would burn him in one second, like a straw in the fire. He would fall down in the street burned black the minute he stepped out of the door. He was born down here in the grotto."

Amar was not paying strict attention to the boy's babble. They were descending a wet stone ramp, putting one foot before the other slowly in the dark, and feeling the rough wall carefully as they went. There was a sound of splashing water and voices ahead.

"This is a strange *hammam*," said Amar. "Is there a pool full of water?"

"A pool! You've never heard of Lazrag's grotto? It goes on forever, and it's made of deep warm water."

As the boy spoke, they came out onto a stone balcony a few meters above the beginning of a very large pool, lighted beneath where they stood by two bare electric bulbs, and stretching away through the dimness into utter dark beyond. Parts of the roof hung down, "Like gray icicles," thought Amar, as he looked about in wonder. But it was very warm down here. A slight pall of steam lay above the surface of the water, rising constantly in wisps toward the rocky ceiling. A man dripping with water ran past them and dove in. Several more were swimming about in the brighter region near the lights, never straying beyond into the gloom. The plunging and shouting echoed violently beneath the low ceiling.

Amar was not a good swimmer. He turned to ask the boy: "Is it deep?" but he had already disappeared back up the ramp. He stepped backward and leaned against the rock wall. There was a low chair to his right, and in the murky light it seemed to him that a small figure was close beside it. He watched the bathers for a few minutes. Those standing at the edge of the water soaped themselves assiduously; those in the water swam to and fro in a short radius below the lights. Suddenly a deep voice spoke close beside him. He looked down as he heard it say: "Who are you?"

The creature's head was large; its body was small and it had no legs or arms. The lower part of the trunk ended in two flipper-like pieces of flesh. From the shoulders grew short pincers. It was a man, and it was looking up at him from the floor where it rested.

"Who are you?" it said again, and its tone was unmistakably hostile.

Amar hesitated. "I came to bathe and sleep," he said at last.

"Who gave you permission?"

"The man at the entrance."

"Get out. I don't know you."

Amar was filled with anger. He looked down with scorn at the little being, and stepped away from it to join the men washing themselves by the water's edge. But more swiftly than he moved, it managed to throw itself along the floor until it was in front of him, when it raised itself again and spoke.

"You think you can bathe when I tell you to get out?" It laughed shortly, a thin sound, but deep in pitch. Then it moved closer and pushed its head against Amar's legs. He drew back his foot and kicked the head, not very hard, but with enough firmness to send the body off balance. The thing rolled over in silence, making efforts with its neck to keep from reaching the edge of the platform. The men all looked up. An expression of fear was on their faces. As the little creature went over the edge it yelled. The splash was like that of a large stone. Two men already in the water swam quickly to the spot. The others started up after Amar, shouting: "He hit Lazrag!"

Bewildered and frightened, Amar turned and ran back to the ramp. In the blackness he stumbled upward. Part of the wall scraped his bare thigh. The voices behind him grew louder and more excited.

He reached the room where he had left his clothing. Nothing had changed. The men still sat by the brazier talking. Quickly he snatched the pile of garments, and struggling into his burnous, he ran to the door that led into the street, the rest of his clothes tucked under his arm. The man in the doorway with the oud looked at him with a startled face and called after him. Amar ran up the street barelegged toward the center of the town. He wanted to be where there were some bright lights. The few people walking in the street paid him no attention. When he got to the bus station it was closed. He went into a small park opposite, where the iron bandstand stood deep in snow. There on a cold stone bench he sat and dressed himself as unostentatiously as possible, using his burnous as a screen. He was shivering, reflecting bitterly upon his poor luck, and wishing he had not left his own town, when a small figure approached him in the half-light.

"Sidi," it said, "come with me. Lazrag is hunting for you."

"Where to?" said Amar, recognizing the urchin from the bath.

"My grandfather's."

The boy began to run, motioning to him to follow. They went through alleys and tunnels, into the most congested part of the town. The boy did not bother to look back, but Amar did. They finally paused before a small door at the side of a narrow passageway. The boy knocked vigorously. From within came a cracked voice calling: "*Chkoun?*"

"*Annah!* Brahim!" cried the boy.

With great deliberation the old man swung the door open and stood looking at Amar.

"Come in," he finally said; and shutting the door behind them he led them through the courtyard filled with goats into an inner room where a feeble light was flickering. He peered sternly into Amar's face.

"He wants to stay here tonight," explained the boy.

"Does he think this is a *fondouk?*"

"He has money," said Brahim hopefully.

"Money!" the old man cried with scorn. "That's what you learn in the *hammam!* How to steal money! How to take money from men's purses! Now you bring them here! What do you want me to do? Kill him and get his purse for you? Is he too clever for you? You can't get it by yourself? Is that it?" The old man's voice had risen to a scream and he gestured in his mounting excitement. He sat down on a cushion with difficulty and was silent a moment.

"Money," he said again, finally. "Let him go to a *fondouk* or a bath. Why aren't you at the *hammam?*" He looked suspiciously at his grandson.

The boy clutched at his friend's sleeve. "Come," he said, pulling him out into the courtyard.

"Take him to the *hammam!*" yelled the old man. "Let him spend his money there!"

Together they went back into the dark streets.

"Lazrag is looking for you," said the boy. "Twenty men will be going through the town to catch you and take you back to him. He is very angry and he will change you into a bird."

"Where are we going now?" asked Amar gruffly. He was cold and very tired, and although he did not really believe the boy's story, he wished he were out of the unfriendly town.

"We must walk as far as we can from here. All night. In the morning we'll be far away in the mountains, and they won't find us. We can go to your city."

Amar did not answer. He was pleased that the boy wanted to stay with him, but he did not think it fitting to say so. They followed one crooked street downhill until all the houses had been left behind and they were in the open country. The path led down a narrow valley presently, and joined the highway at one end of a small bridge. Here the snow was packed down by the passage of vehicles, and they found it much easier to walk along.

When they had been going down the road for perhaps an hour in the increasing cold, a great truck came rolling by. It stopped just ahead and the driver, an Arab, offered them a ride on top. They climbed up and made a nest of some empty sacks. The boy was very happy to be rushing through the air in the dark night. Mountains and stars whirled by above his head and the truck made a powerful roaring noise as it traveled along the empty highway.

"Lazrag has found us and changed us both into birds," he cried when he could no longer keep his delight to himself. "No one will ever know us again."

Amar grunted and went to sleep. But the boy watched the sky and the trees and the cliffs for a long time before he closed his eyes.

Some time before morning the truck stopped by a spring for water.

In the stillness the boy awoke. A cock crowed in the distance, and then he heard the driver pouring water. The cock crowed again, a sad, thin arc of sound away in the cold murk of the plain. It was not yet dawn. He buried himself deeper in the pile of sacks and rags, and felt the warmth of Amar as he slept.

When daylight came they were in another part of the land. There was no snow. Instead, the almond trees were in flower on the hillsides as they sped past. The road went on unwinding as it dropped lower and lower, until suddenly it came out of the hills upon a spot below which lay a great glittering emptiness. Amar and the boy watched it and said to each other that it must be the sea, shining in the morning light.

The spring wind pushed the foam from the waves along the beach; it rippled Amar's and the boy's garments landward as they walked by the edge of the water. Finally they found a sheltered spot between rocks, and undressed, leaving the clothes on the sand. The boy was afraid to go into the water, and found enough excitement in letting the waves break about his legs, but Amar tried to drag him out further.

"No, no!"

"Come," Amar urged him.

Amar looked down. Approaching him sideways was an enormous crab which had crawled out from a dark place in the rocks. He leapt back in terror, lost his balance, and fell heavily, striking his head against one of the great boulders. The boy stood perfectly still watching the animal make its cautious way toward Amar through the tips of the breaking waves. Amar lay without moving, rivulets of water and sand running down his face. As the crab reached his feet, the boy bounded into the air, and in a voice made hoarse by desperation, screamed: "Lazrag!"

The crab scuttled swiftly behind the rock and disappeared. The boy's face became radiant. He rushed to Amar, lifted his head above a newly breaking wave, and slapped his cheeks excitedly.

"Amar! I made him go away!" he shouted. "I saved you!"

If he did not move, the pain was not too great. So Amar lay still, feeling the warm sunlight, the soft water washing over him, and the cool, sweet wind that came in from the sea. He also felt the boy trembling in his effort to hold his head above the waves, and he heard him saying many times over: "I saved you, Amar."

After a long time he answered: "Yes."

New York
1945

A Distant Episode

The September sunsets were at their reddest the week the Professor decided to visit Aïn Tadouirt, which is in the warm country. He came down out of the high, flat region in the evening by bus, with two small overnight bags full of maps, sun lotions and medicines. Ten years ago he had been in the village for three days; long enough, however, to establish a fairly firm friendship with a café-keeper, who had written him several times during the first year after his visit, if never since. "Hassan Ramani," the Professor said over and over, as the bus bumped downward through ever warmer layers of air. Now facing the flaming sky in the west, and now facing the sharp mountains, the car followed the dusty trail down the canyons into air which began to smell of other things besides the endless ozone of the heights: orange blossoms, pepper, sun-baked excrement, burning olive oil, rotten fruit. He closed his eyes happily and lived for an instant in a purely olfactory world. The distant past returned—what part of it, he could not decide.

The chauffeur, whose seat the Professor shared, spoke to him without taking his eyes from the road. *"Vous êtes géologue?"*

"A geologist? Ah, no! I'm a linguist."

"There are no languages here. Only dialects."

"Exactly. I'm making a survey of variations on Moghrebi."

The chauffeur was scornful. "Keep on going south," he said. "You'll find some languages you never heard of before."

As they drove through the town gate, the usual swarm of urchins rose up out of the dust and ran screaming beside the bus. The Professor folded his dark glasses, put them in his pocket; and as soon as the vehicle had come to a standstill he jumped out, pushing his way through the indignant boys who clutched at his luggage in vain, and walked quickly into the Grand Hotel Saharien. Out of its eight rooms there were two available—one facing the market and the other, a smaller and cheaper one, giving onto a tiny yard full of refuse and barrels, where two gazelles wandered about. He took the smaller room, and pouring the entire pitcher of water into the tin basin, began to wash the grit from his face and ears. The afterglow was nearly gone from the sky, and the pinkness in objects was disappearing, almost as he watched. He lit the carbide lamp and winced at its odor.

39

After dinner the Professor walked slowly through the streets to Hassan Ramani's café, whose back room hung hazardously out above the river. The entrance was very low, and he had to bend down slightly to get in. A man was tending the fire. There was one guest sipping tea. The *qaouaji* tried to make him take a seat at the other table in the front room, but the Professor walked airily ahead into the back room and sat down. The moon was shining through the reed latticework and there was not a sound outside but the occasional distant bark of a dog. He changed tables so he could see the river. It was dry, but there was a pool here and there that reflected the bright night sky. The *qaouaji* came in and wiped off the table.

"Does this café still belong to Hassan Ramani?" he asked him in the Moghrebi he had taken four years to learn.

The man replied in bad French: "He is deceased."

"Deceased?" repeated the Professor, without noticing the absurdity of the word. "Really? When?"

"I don't know," said the *qaouaji*. "One tea?"

"Yes. But I don't understand . . ."

The man was already out of the room, fanning the fire. The Professor sat still, feeling lonely, and arguing with himself that to do so was ridiculous. Soon the *qaouaji* returned with the tea. He paid him and gave him an enormous tip, for which he received a grave bow.

"Tell me," he said, as the other started away. "Can one still get those little boxes made from camel udders?"

The man looked angry. "Sometimes the Reguibat bring in those things. We do not buy them here." Then insolently, in Arabic: "And why a camel-udder box?"

"Because I like them," retorted the Professor. And then because he was feeling a little exalted, he added, "I like them so much I want to make a collection of them, and I will pay you ten francs for every one you can get me."

"*Khamstache*," said the *qaouaji*, opening his left hand rapidly three times in succession.

"Never. Ten."

"Not possible. But wait until later and come with me. You can give me what you like. And you will get camel-udder boxes if there are any."

He went out into the front room, leaving the Professor to drink his tea and listen to the growing chorus of dogs that barked and howled as the moon rose higher into the sky. A group of customers came into the front room and sat talking for an hour or so. When they had left, the *qaouaji* put out the fire and stood in the doorway putting on his burnous. "Come," he said.

Outside in the street there was very little movement. The booths were all closed and the only light came from the moon. An occasional pedestrian passed, and grunted a brief greeting to the *qaouaji*.

"Everyone knows you," said the Professor, to cut the silence between them.

"Yes."

"I wish everyone knew me," said the Professor, before he realized how infantile such a remark must sound.

"*No* one knows you," said his companion gruffly.

They had come to the other side of the town, on the promontory above the desert, and through a great rift in the wall the Professor saw the white endlessness, broken in the foreground by dark spots of oasis. They walked through the opening and followed a winding road between rocks, downward toward the nearest small forest of palms. The Professor thought: "He may cut my throat. But his café—he would surely be found out."

"Is it far?" he asked, casually.

"Are you tired?" countered the *qaouaji*.

"They are expecting me back at the Hotel Saharien," he lied.

"You can't be there and here," said the *qaouaji*.

The Professor laughed. He wondered if it sounded uneasy to the other.

"Have you owned Ramani's café long?"

"I work there for a friend." The reply made the Professor more unhappy than he had imagined it would.

"Oh. Will you work tomorrow?"

"That is impossible to say."

The Professor stumbled on a stone, and fell, scraping his hand. The *qaouaji* said: "Be careful."

The sweet black odor of rotten meat hung in the air suddenly.

"Agh!" said the Professor, choking. "What is it?"

The *qaouaji* had covered his face with his burnous and did not answer. Soon the stench had been left behind. They were on flat ground. Ahead the path was bordered on each side by a high mud wall. There was no breeze and the palms were quite still, but behind the walls was the sound of running water. Also, the odor of human excrement was almost constant as they walked between the walls.

The Professor waited until he thought it seemed logical for him to ask with a certain degree of annoyance: "But where are we going?"

"Soon," said the guide, pausing to gather some stones in the ditch.

"Pick up some stones," he advised. "Here are bad dogs."

"Where?" asked the Professor, but he stooped and got three large ones with pointed edges.

They continued very quietly. The walls came to an end and the bright desert lay ahead. Nearby was a ruined marabout, with its tiny dome only half standing, and the front wall entirely destroyed. Behind it were clumps of stunted, useless palms. A dog came running crazily toward them on three legs. Not until it got quite close did the Professor hear its steady low growl. The *qaouaji* let fly a large stone at it, striking it square in the muzzle. There was a strange snapping of jaws and the dog ran sideways in another direction, falling blindly against rocks and scrambling haphazardly about like an injured insect.

Turning off the road, they walked across the earth strewn with sharp stones, past the little ruin, through the trees, until they came to a place where the ground dropped abruptly away in front of them.

"It looks like a quarry," said the Professor, resorting to French for the word "quarry," whose Arabic equivalent he could not call to mind at the moment. The *qaouaji* did not answer. Instead he stood still and turned his head, as if listening. And indeed, from somewhere down below, but very far below, came the faint sound of a low flute. The *qaouaji* nodded his head slowly several times. Then he said: "The path begins here. You can see it well all the way. The rock is white and the moon is strong. So you can see well. I am going back now and sleep. It is late. You can give me what you like."

Standing there at the edge of the abyss which at each moment looked deeper, with the dark face of the *qaouaji* framed in its moonlit burnous close to his own face, the Professor asked himself exactly what he felt. Indignation, curiosity, fear, perhaps, but most of all relief and the hope that this was not a trick, the hope that the *qaouaji* would really leave him alone and turn back without him.

He stepped back a little from the edge, and fumbled in his pocket for a loose note, because he did not want to show his wallet. Fortunately there was a fifty-franc bill there, which he took out and handed to the man. He knew the *qaouaji* was pleased, and so he paid no attention when he heard him saying: "It is not enough. I have to walk a long way home and there are dogs. . . ."

"Thank you and good night," said the Professor, sitting down with his legs drawn up under him, and lighting a cigarette. He felt almost happy.

"Give me only one cigarette," pleaded the man.

"Of course," he said, a bit curtly, and he held up the pack.

The *qaouaji* squatted close beside him. His face was not pleasant to see. "What is it?" thought the Professor, terrified again, as he held out his lighted cigarette toward him.

The man's eyes were almost closed. It was the most obvious registering of concentrated scheming the Professor had ever seen. When the second cigarette was burning, he ventured to say to the still-squatting Arab:

"What are you thinking about?"

The other drew on his cigarette deliberately, and seemed about to speak. Then his expression changed to one of satisfaction, but he did not speak. A cool wind had risen in the air, and the Professor shivered. The sound of the flute came up from the depths below at intervals, sometimes mingled with the scraping of nearby palm fronds one against the other. "These people are not primitives," the Professor found himself saying in his mind.

"Good," said the *qaouaji*, rising slowly. "Keep your money. Fifty francs is enough. It is an honor." Then he went back into French: "*Ti n'as qu'à discendre, to' droit.*" He spat, chuckled (or was the Professor hysterical?), and strode away quickly.

The Professor was in a state of nerves. He lit another cigarette, and found his lips moving automatically. They were saying: "Is this a situation or a predicament? This is ridiculous." He sat very still for several minutes, waiting for a sense of reality to come to him. He stretched out on the hard, cold ground and looked up at the moon. It was almost like looking straight at the sun. If he shifted his gaze a little at a time, he could make a string of weaker moons across the sky. "Incredible," he whispered. Then he sat up quickly and looked about. There was no guarantee that the *qaouaji* really had gone back to town. He got to his feet and looked over the edge of the precipice. In the moonlight the bottom seemed miles away. And there was nothing to give it scale; not a tree, not a house, not a person. . . . He listened for the flute, and heard only the wind going by his ears. A sudden violent desire to run back to the road seized him, and he turned and looked in the direction the *qaouaji* had taken. At the same time he felt softly of his wallet in his breast pocket. Then he spat over the edge of the cliff. Then he made water over it, and listened intently, like a child. This gave him the impetus to start down the path into the abyss. Curiously enough, he was not dizzy. But prudently he kept from peering to his right, over the edge. It was a steady and steep downward climb. The monotony of it put him into a frame of mind not unlike that which had been induced by the bus ride. He was murmuring "Hassan Ramani" again, repeatedly and in rhythm. He stopped, furious with himself for the sinister overtones the name now suggested to him. He decided he was exhausted from the trip. "And the walk," he added.

He was now well down the gigantic cliff, but the moon, being directly overhead, gave as much light as ever. Only the wind was left behind, above, to wander among the trees, to blow through the dusty streets of Aïn Tadouirt, into the hall of the Grand Hotel Saharien, and under the door of his little room.

It occurred to him that he ought to ask himself why he was doing this irrational thing, but he was intelligent enough to know that since he was doing it, it was not so important to probe for explanations at that moment.

Suddenly the earth was flat beneath his feet. He had reached the bottom sooner than he expected. He stepped ahead distrustfully still, as if he expected another treacherous drop. It was so hard to know in this uniform, dim brightness. Before he knew what had happened the dog was upon him, a heavy mass of fur trying to push him backwards, a sharp nail rubbing down his chest, a straining of muscles against him to get the teeth into his neck. The Professor thought: "I refuse to die this way." The dog fell back; it looked like an Eskimo dog. As it sprang again, he called out, very loud: "Ay!" It fell against him, there was a confusion of sensations and a pain somewhere. There was also the sound of voices very near to him, and he could not understand what they were saying. Something cold and metallic was pushed brutally against his spine as the dog still hung for a second by his teeth from a mass of clothing and perhaps flesh. The Professor knew it was a gun, and he raised his hands, shouting in Moghrebi: "Take away the dog!" But the gun merely pushed him forward, and since the dog, once it was back on the ground, did not leap again, he took a step ahead. The gun kept pushing; he kept taking steps. Again he heard voices, but the person directly behind him said nothing. People seemed to be running about; it sounded that way, at least. For his eyes, he discovered, were still shut tight against the dog's attack. He opened them. A group of men was advancing toward him. They were dressed in the black clothes of the Reguibat. "The Reguiba is a cloud across the face of the sun." "When the Reguiba appears the righteous man turns away." In how many shops and market-places he had heard these maxims uttered banteringly among friends. Never to a Reguiba, to be sure, for these men do not frequent towns. They send a representative in disguise, to arrange with shady elements there for the disposal of captured goods. "An opportunity," he thought quickly, "of testing the accuracy of such statements." He did not doubt for a moment that the adventure would prove to be a kind of warning against such foolishness on his part—a warning which in retrospect would be half sinister, half farcical.

Two snarling dogs came running from behind the oncoming men and threw themselves at his legs. He was scandalized to note that no one paid any attention to this breach of etiquette. The gun pushed him harder as he tried to sidestep the animals' noisy assault. Again he cried: "The dogs! Take them away!" The gun shoved him forward with great force and he fell, almost at the feet of the crowd of men facing him. The dogs were wrenching at his hands and arms. A boot kicked them aside, yelping, and then with increased vigor it kicked the Professor in the hip. Then came a chorus of kicks from different sides, and he was rolled violently about on the earth for a while. During this time he was conscious of hands reaching into his pockets and removing everything from them. He tried to say: "You have all my money; stop kicking me!" But his bruised facial muscles would not work; he felt himself pouting, and that was all. Someone dealt him a terrific blow on the head, and he thought: "Now at least I shall lose consciousness, thank Heaven." Still he went on being aware of the guttural voices he could not understand, and of being bound tightly about the ankles and chest. Then there was black silence that opened like a wound from time to time, to let in the soft, deep notes of the flute playing the same succession of notes again and again. Suddenly he felt excruciating pain everywhere—pain and cold. "So I have been unconscious, after all," he thought. In spite of that, the present seemed only like a direct continuation of what had gone before.

It was growing faintly light. There were camels near where he was lying; he could hear their gurgling and their heavy breathing. He could not bring himself to attempt opening his eyes, just in case it should turn out to be impossible. However, when he heard someone approaching, he found that he had no difficulty in seeing.

The man looked at him dispassionately in the gray morning light. With one hand he pinched together the Professor's nostrils. When the Professor opened his mouth to breathe, the man swiftly seized his tongue and pulled on it with all his might. The Professor was gagging and catching his breath; he did not see what was happening. He could not distinguish the pain of the brutal yanking from that of the sharp knife. Then there was an endless choking and spitting that went on automatically, as though he were scarcely a part of it. The word "operation" kept going through his mind; it calmed his terror somewhat as he sank back into darkness.

The caravan left sometime toward midmorning. The Professor, not unconscious, but in a state of utter stupor, still gagging and drooling blood, was dumped doubled-up into a sack and tied at one side of a camel. The lower end of the enormous amphitheater contained a natural gate in the rocks. The camels, swift *mehara*, were lightly laden on this trip. They passed through single file, and slowly mounted the gentle slope that led up into the beginning of the desert. That night, at a stop behind some low hills, the men took him out, still in a state which permitted no thought, and over the dusty rags that remained of his clothing they fastened a series of curious belts made of the bottoms of tin cans strung together. One after another of these bright girdles was wired about his torso, his arms and legs, even across his face, until he was entirely within a suit of armor that covered him with its circular metal scales. There was a good deal of merriment during this decking-out of the Professor. One man brought out a flute and a younger one did a not ungraceful caricature of an Ouled Naïl executing a cane dance. The Professor was no longer conscious; to be exact, he existed in the middle of the movements made by these other men. When they had finished dressing him the way they wished him to look, they stuffed some food under the tin bangles hanging over his face. Even though he chewed mechanically, most of it eventually fell out onto the ground. They put him back into the sack and left him there.

Two days later they arrived at one of their own encampments. There were women and children here in the tents, and the men had to drive away the snarling dogs they had left there to guard them. When they emptied the Professor out of his sack, there were screams of fright, and it took several hours to convince the last woman that he was harmless, although there had been no doubt from the start that he was a valuable possession. After a few days they began to move on again, taking everything with them, and traveling only at night as the terrain grew warmer.

Even when all his wounds had healed and he felt no more pain, the Professor did not begin to think again; he ate and defecated, and he danced when he was bidden, a senseless hopping up and down that delighted the children, principally because of the wonderful jangling racket it made. And he generally slept through the heat of the day, in among the camels.

Wending its way southeast, the caravan avoided all stationary civilization. In a few weeks they reached a new plateau, wholly wild and with a sparse vegetation. Here they pitched camp and remained, while the *mehara* were turned loose to graze. Everyone was happy here; the weather was cooler and there was a well only a few hours away on a seldom-frequented trail. It was here they conceived the idea of taking the Professor to Fogara and selling him to the Touareg.

It was a full year before they carried out this project. By this time the Professor was much better trained. He could do a handspring, make a series of fearful growling noises which had, nevertheless, a certain element of humor; and when the Reguibat removed the tin from his face they discovered he could grimace admirably while he danced. They also taught him a few basic obscene gestures which never failed to elicit delighted shrieks from the women. He was now brought forth only after especially abundant meals, when there was music and festivity. He easily fell in with their sense of ritual, and evolved an elementary sort of "program" to present when he was called for: dancing, rolling on the ground, imitating certain animals, and finally rushing toward the group in feigned anger, to see the resultant confusion and hilarity.

When three of the men set out for Fogara with him, they took four *mehara* with them, and he rode astride his quite naturally. No precautions were taken to guard him, save that he was kept among them, one man always staying at the rear of the party. They came within sight of the walls at dawn, and they waited among the rocks all day. At dusk the youngest started out, and in three hours he returned with a friend who carried a stout cane. They tried to put the Professor through his routine then and there, but the man from Fogara was in a hurry to get back to town, so they all set out on the *mehara*.

In the town they went directly to the villager's home, where they had coffee in the courtyard sitting among the camels. Here the Professor went into his act again, and this time there was prolonged merriment and much rubbing together of hands. An agreement was reached, a sum of money paid, and the Reguibat withdrew, leaving the Professor in the house of the man with the cane, who did not delay in locking him into a tiny enclosure off the courtyard.

The next day was an important one in the Professor's life, for it was then that pain began to stir again in his being. A group of men came to the house, among whom was a venerable gentleman, better clothed that those others who spent their time flattering him, setting fervent kisses upon his hands and the edges of his garments. This person made a point of going into classical Arabic from time to time, to impress the others, who had not learned a word of the Koran. Thus his conversation would run more or less as follows: "Perhaps at In Salah. The French there are stupid. Celestial vengeance is approaching. Let us not hasten it. Praise the highest and cast thine anathema against idols. With paint on his face. In case the police wish to look close." The others listened and agreed, nodding their heads slowly and solemnly. And the Professor in his stall beside them listened, too. That is, he was *conscious* of the sound of the old man's Arabic. The words penetrated for the first time in many months. Noises, then: "Celestial vengeance is approaching." Then: "It is an honor. Fifty francs is enough. Keep your money. Good." And the *qaouaji* squatting near him at the edge of the precipice. Then "anathema against idols" and more gibberish. He turned over panting on the sand and forgot about it. But the pain had begun. It operated in a kind of delirium, because he had begun to enter into consciousness again. When the man opened the door and prodded him with his cane, he cried out in a rage, and everyone laughed.

They got him onto his feet, but he would not dance. He stood before them, staring at the ground, stubbornly refusing to move. The owner was furious, and so annoyed by the laughter of the others that he felt obliged to send them away, saying that he would await a more propitious time for exhibiting his property, because he dared not show his anger before the elder. However, when they had left he dealt the Professor a violent blow on the shoulder with his cane, called him various obscene things, and went out into the street, slamming the gate behind him. He walked straight to the street of the Ouled Naïl, because he was sure of finding the Reguibat there among the girls, spending the money. And there in a tent he found one of them still abed, while an Ouled Naïl washed the tea glasses. He walked in and almost decapitated the man before the latter had even attempted to sit up. Then he threw his razor on the bed and ran out.

The Ouled Naïl saw the blood, screamed, ran out of her tent into the next, and soon emerged from that with four girls who rushed together into the coffeehouse and told the *qaouaji* who had killed the Reguiba. It was only a matter of an hour before the French military police had caught him at a friend's house, and dragged him off to the barracks. That night the Professor had nothing to eat, and the next afternoon, in the slow sharpening of his consciousness caused by increasing hunger, he walked aimlessly about the courtyard and the rooms that gave onto it. There was no one. In one room a calendar hung on the wall. The Professor watched nervously, like a dog watching a fly in front of its nose. On the white paper were black objects that made sounds in his head. He heard them: "*Grande Epicerie du Sahel. Juin. Lundi, Mardi, Mercredi. . . .*"

The tiny ink marks of which a symphony consists may have been made long ago, but when they are fulfilled in sound they become imminent and mighty. So a kind of music of feeling began to play in the Professor's head, increasing in volume as he looked at the mud wall, and he had the feeling that he was performing what had been written for him long ago. He felt like weeping; he felt like roaring through the little house, upsetting and smashing the few breakable objects. His emotion got no further than this one overwhelming desire. So, bellowing as loud as he could, he attacked the house and its belongings. Then he attacked the door into the street, which resisted for a while and finally broke. He climbed through the opening made by the boards he had ripped apart, and still bellowing and shaking his arms in the air to make as loud a jangling as possible, he began to gallop along the quiet street toward the gateway of the town. A few people looked at him with great curiosity. As he passed the garage, the last building before the high mud archway that framed the desert beyond, a French soldier saw him. "*Tiens,*" he said to himself, "a holy maniac."

Again it was sunset time. The Professor ran beneath the arched gate, turned his face toward the red sky, and began to trot along the Piste d'In Salah, straight into the setting sun. Behind him, from the garage, the soldier took a potshot at him for good luck. The bullet whistled dangerously near the Professor's head, and his yelling rose into an indignant lament as he waved his arms more wildly, and hopped high into the air at every few steps, in an access of terror.

The soldier watched a while, smiling, as the cavorting figure grew smaller in the oncoming evening darkness, and the rattling of the tin became a part of the great silence out there beyond the gate. The wall of the garage as he leaned against it still gave forth heat, left there by the sun, but even then the lunar chill was growing in the air.

New York
1945

The Echo

Aileen pulled out her mirror; the vibration of the plane shook it so rapidly that she was unable to see whether her nose needed powder or not. There were only two other passengers and they were asleep. It was noon; the tropical sun shone violently down upon the wide silver wings and cast sharp reflections on the ceiling. Far below, the uniform green carpet of the jungle moved slowly by. She was sleepy, but she was also excited to be going to a new home. From her handbag she pulled a folded letter which she read again intently, as if to decipher a meaning that did not lie in the sequence of the words. It was in her mother's script:

"Aileen, Sweet—

"I must begin (and finish) this before supper. Prue has gone out for her shower, and that means that by the time she has Luz (the cook) heat the water and can find José (the gardener) to carry it up on the roof to the tank, it will be about an hour. Add to that the time it takes her to do her actual bathing and to dress, and you can see I'll have just about time for a nice chat.

"Perhaps I should begin by saying that Prue and I are sublimely happy here. It is absolute heaven after Washington, as you can pretty well imagine. Prue, of course, never could stand the States, and I felt, after the trouble with your father, that I couldn't face anyone for a while. You know how much importance I have always attached to relaxation. And this is the ideal spot for that.

"Of course I did feel a little guilty about running off down here without seeing you. But I think the trip to Northampton would have sealed my doom. I honestly don't believe I could have stood it. And Prue was nervous about the State Department's passing some new law that would prevent citizens from leaving the U.S. because of the disturbed conditions, and so on. I also felt that the sooner we got down here to Jamonocal the more of a home we could make out of the old place, for you to spend your vacation in. And it *is* going to be beautiful. I won't drag out my reasons for not letting you know beforehand

or it will sound apologetic, and I know I never have to
apologize to you for anything. So I'll leave that and get on. I'm
sure anyway that the eight months passed very quickly up
there for you.

"We have had swarms of men working on the house ever
since last October. Mr. Forbes happened to be in Barranquilla
for a new American project in the interior, and I wanted to be
sure of having him supervise the construction of the cantilever
in the foundation. That man is really a prince. They don't
come much finer. He was up again and again, and gave orders
down to the last detail. I felt guilty about making him work so
hard, but I honestly think he enjoyed himself with us girls. In
any case it seemed silly, when one of the best architects in the
U.S. was right here in Colombia and happened to be an old
friend, not to use him when I needed him. Anyway, the old
house is now the old wing and the new part, which is so exciting I can't wait for you to see it, is built right out over the
gorge. I think there's not likely to be another house like it in the
world, if I do say it myself. The terrace makes me think of an
old cartoon in the *New Yorker* showing two men looking over
the edge of the Grand Canyon, and one is saying to the other:
'Did you ever want to spit a mile, Bill? Now's your chance.'

"We are all installed. The weather has been wonderful, and
if Luz could only learn a little more about what white people
like to eat and how they like it served, the setup would really
be perfect. I know you will enjoy being here with Prue. She
and you have many things in common, even if you do claim to
'remember not liking her much.' That was in Washington and
you were, to put it mildly, at a difficult age. Now, as an adult
(because you really are one by now), you'll be more understanding, I'm sure. She loves books, especially on philosophy
and psychology and other things your poor mother just doesn't
try to follow her in. She has rigged up a kiln and studio in the
old guest house which you probably don't remember. She
works at her ceramics out there all day, and I have all I can do
keeping the house tidy and seeing that the marketing is done.
We have a system by which Luz takes the list to her brother
every afternoon, and he brings the things from town the following day. It just about keeps him fully busy getting up and
down the mountain on his horse. The horse is a lazy old nag
that has done nothing but plod back and forth between house
and the valley all its life, so it doesn't know the meaning of the

word speed. But after all, why hurry, down here?

"I think you will find everything to your liking, and I'm sure you won't require more than five minutes to see that Prue is a dear, and not at all 'peculiar,' as you wrote in your letter. Wire me as soon as you receive this, and let me know just what week you'll be finishing classes. Prue and I will meet you in Barranquilla. I have a list of things I want you to get me in New York. Will wire it to you as soon as I hear. Prue's bath finished. Must close.

Love,
Mother."

Aileen put the letter away, smiling a little, and watched the wings diving in and out of the small thick clouds that lay in the plane's way. There was a slight shock each time they hit one, and the world outside became a blinding whiteness. She fancied jumping out and walking on such solid softness, like a charater in an animated cartoon.

Her mother's letter had put her in mind of a much earlier period in her life: the winter she had been taken to visit Jamonocal. All she could recall in the way of incidents was that she had been placed on a mule by one of the natives, and had felt a painful horror that the animal would walk in the wrong direction, away from the house toward the edge of the gorge. She had no memory of the gorge. Probably she had never seen it, although it was only a few paces from the house, through a short but thick stretch of canebrake. However, she had a clear memory of its presence, of the sensation of enormous void beyond and below that side of the house. And she recalled the distant, hollow sound of water falling from a great height, a constant, soft backdrop of sound that slipped into every moment of the day—between the conversations at mealtimes, in the intervals of play in the garden, and at night between dreams. She wondered if really it were possible to remember all that from the time when she had been only five.

In Panama there was a plane change to be made. It was a clear green twilight, and she took a short walk beyond the airport. Parakeets were fighting in the upper branches of the trees; suddenly they became quiet. She turned back and went inside, where she sat reading until it was time to go aboard.

There was no one there to meet her when she arrived at Barranquilla in the early hours of the morning. She decided to go into town and take a room in the hotel. With her two valises she stepped outside and looked about for a cab. They had all gone to the town with passengers, but a man sitting on a packing case informed her that they would soon be coming back. Then suddenly he said, "You want two ladies?"

"What? No. What do you mean?"

"You want two ladies look for you this night?"

"Where are they?" said Aileen, understanding.

"They want a drink," he answered with an intimate grin.

"Where? Barranquila?"

"No. Here." He pointed down the dark road.

"Where? Can I walk?"

"Sure. I go you."

"No! No thanks. You stay here. Thank you. I can go all right. Where is it? How far?"

"O.K."

"What is it? A bar? What's the name?"

"They got music. La Gloria. You go. You hear music. You look for two ladies. They drinking."

She went inside again and checked the bags with an airline employee who insisted on accompanying her. They strode in silence along the back road. The walls of vegatation on each side sheltered insects that made an occasional violent, dry noise like a wooden ratchet being whirled. Soon there was the sound of drums and trumpets playing Cuban dance music.

"La Gloria," said her escort triumphantly.

La Gloria was a brilliantly lighted mud hut with a thatch-covered veranda giving onto the road. The juke box was outside, where a few drunken Negroes sprawled.

"Are they here?" she said out loud, but to herself.

"La Gloria," he answered, pointing.

As they came opposite the front of the building, she caught a glimpse of a woman in blue jeans, and although instantaneously she knew it was Prue, her mind for some reason failed to accept the fact, and she continued to ask herself, "Are they here or not?"

She turned to go toward the veranda. The record had finished playing. The ditch lay in the dark between the road and the porch. She fell forward into it and heard herself cry out. The man behind her said, *"Cuidado!"* She lay there panting with fury and pain, and said, "Oh! My ankle!" There was an exclamation inside the bar. Her mother's voice cried, "That's Aileen!" Then the juke box began to scratch and roar again. The Negroes remained stationary. Someone helped her up. She was inside the bar in the raw electric glare.

"I'm all right," she said, when she had been eased into a chair.

"But darling, where've you been? We've been waiting for you since eight, and we'd just about given up. Poor Prue's ill."

"Nonsense, I'll recover," said Prue, still seated at the bar. "Been having a touch of the trots, that's all."

"But darling, are you all right? This is absurd, landing here this way."

She looked down at Aileen's ankle.

"Is it all right?"

Prue came over from the bar to shake her hand.

"A dramatic entrance, gal," she said.

Aileen sat there and smiled. She had a curious mental habit. As a child she had convinced herself that her head was transparent, that the thoughts there could be perceived immediately by others. Accordingly, when she found herself in uncomfortable situations, rather than risk the danger of being suspected of harboring uncomplimentary or rebellious thoughts, she had developed a system of refraining from thinking at all. For a while during her childhood this fear of having no mental privacy had been extended to anyone; even persons existing at a distance could have access to her mind. Now she felt open only to those present. And so it was that, finding herself face to face with Prue, she was conscious of no particular emotion save the familiar vague sense of boredom. There was not a thought in her head, and her face made the fact apparent.

Mornings were hard to believe. The primeval freshness, spilled down out of the jungle above the house, was held close to the earth by the mist. Outside and in, it was damp and smelled like a florist's shop, but the dampness was dispelled each day when the stinging sun burned through the thin cape of moisture that clung to the mountain's back. Living there was like living sideways, with the land stretching up on one side and down on the other at the same angle. Only the gorge gave a feeling of perpendicularity; the vertical walls of rock on the opposite side of the great amphitheatre were a reminder that the center of gravity lay below and not obliquely to one side. Constant vapor rose from the invisible pool at the bottom, and the distant, indeterminate calling of water was like the sound of sleep itself.

For a few days Aileen lay in bed listening to the water and the birds, and to the nearby, unfamiliar, domestic sounds. Her mother and Prue both had breakfast in bed, and generally appeared just before the midday meal for a few minutes of conversation until Concha brought the invalid's lunch tray. In the afternoons she thumbed through old magazines and read at murder mysteries. Usually it began to rain about three; the sound at first would be like an augmentation of the waterfall in the distance, and then as its violence increased it came unmistakably nearer—a great roar all around the house that covered every other sound. The black clouds would close in tightly around the mountain, so that it seemed that night would soon arrive. She would ring a small bell for Concha to come and light the oil lamp on the table by the bed. Lying there looking at the wet banana leaves outside the window, with the rain's din everywhere, she felt completely comfortable for the precarious moment. There was no necessity to question the feeling, no need to think—only the subsiding of the rain, the triumphant emergence of the sun into the steaming twilight and an early dinner to look forward to. Each evening after dinner her mother came for a lengthy chat, usually about the servants. The first three nights Prue had come too, carrying a highball, but after that her mother came alone.

Aileen had asked to be put into the old part of the house, rather than into a more comfortable room in the new wing. Her window looked onto the garden, which was a small square of lawn with young banana trees on either side. At the far end was a fountain; behind it was the disordered terrain of the mountainside with its recently cut underbrush and charred stumps, and still further beyond was the high jungle whose frontier had been sliced in a straight line across the slopes many years ago to make the plantation. Here in her room she felt at least that the earth was somewhere beneath her.

When her ankle ceased to pain her, she began going downstairs for lunch, which was served out on the terrace at a table with a beach umbrella stuck in its center. Prue was regularly late in coming from her studio, and she arrived in her blue jeans, which were caked with clay, with smears of dirt across her face. Because Aileen could not bring herself to think what she really felt, which was that Prue was ungracious, ugly and something of an interloper, she remained emotionally unconscious of Prue's presence, which is to say that she was polite but bored, scarcely present in the mealtime conversations. Then, too, Aileen was definitely uncomfortable on the terrace. The emptiness was too near and the balustrade seemed altogether too low for safety. She liked the meals to be as brief as possible, with no unnecessary time spent sipping coffee afterward, but it never would have occurred to her to divulge her reasons. With Prue around she felt constrained to behave with the utmost decorum. Fortunately her ankle provided her with a convenient excuse to get back upstairs to her room.

She soon discovered a tiny patio next to the kitchen where heavy vines with sweet-smelling flowers grew up an arbor that had been placed at one side. The air was full of the humming of hundreds of bees that clung heavily to the petals and moved slowly about in the air. After lunch she would pull a deck chair into the arbor's shade and read until the rain began. It was a stifling, airless spot, but the sound of the bees covered that of the waterfall. One afternoon Prue followed her there and stood with her hands in her hip pockets looking at her.

"How can you take this heat?" she asked Aileen.

"Oh, I love it."

"You do?" She paused. "Tell me, do you really like it here, or do you think it's a bloody bore?"

"Why, I think it's absolutely wonderful."

"Mm. It is."

"Don't you like it?"

Prue yawned. "Oh, I'm all for it. But I keep busy. Wherever I can work, I get on, you know."

"Yes, I suppose so," said Aileen. Then she added, "Are you planning on staying long?"

"What the hell do you mean?" said Prue, leaning backward against the house, her hands still behind her. "I live here."

Aileen laughed shortly. To anyone but Prue it would have sounded like a merry, tinkling laugh, but Prue narrowed her eyes and thrust her jaw forward a bit.

"What's so funny?" she demanded.

"I think you're funny. You're so tied up in knots. You get upset so easily. Perhaps you work too hard out there in your little house."

Prue was looking at her with astonishment.

"God Almighty," she said finally, "your I.Q.'s showing, gal."

"Thank you," said Aileen with great seriousness. "Anyway, I think it's fine that you're happy here, and I hope you go on being happy."

"That's what I came to say to you."

"Then everything's fine."

"I can't make you out," said Prue, frowning.

"I don't know what you're talking about," replied Aileen, fingering the pages of her book impatiently. "It's the most pointless conversation I've ever had."

"That I *don't* think," Prue said, going into the kitchen.

The same evening, when her mother came for her usual after-dinner chat, she looked a little unhappy.

"You don't seem to be getting on very well with Prue," she said reproachfully, as she sat down at the foot of the bed.

"Why, we get on perfectly well. Oh. You're talking about this afternoon, probably."

"Yes, I am, probably. Really, Aileen. You simply can't be rude to a woman her age. She's my guest, and you're my guest, and you've got to be civil to each other. But she's always civil and I have a feeling you're not."

Aileen caught her breath and said, "I'm your guest . . ."

"I invited you here for your vacation and I want things pleasant, and I don't see the slightest reason why they shouldn't be."

Suddenly Aileen cried, "She's a maniac!"

Her mother rose and quickly left the room.

In the quiet days that followed, the incident was not mentioned by any of them. Aileen continued to haunt the little patio after lunch.

There came a morning sweeter than the rest, when the untouched early mist hung inside her bedroom, and the confusion of shrill bird cries came down with perfect clarity from the uncut forest. She dressed quickly and went out. There was a white radiance in the air that she had never seen before. She walked along the path that led by the native huts. There was life stirring within; babies were crying and captive parrots and songbirds laughed and sang. The path swung into a stretch of low trees that had been planted to shield the coffee bushes. It was still almost nocturnal in here; the air was streaked with chill, and the vegetable odors were like invisible festoons drooping from the branches as she walked through. A huge bright spider walked slowly across the path at her feet. She stood still and watched it until it had disappeared in the leaves at one side. She put her hand over her heart to feel how insistently it was beating. And she listened to its sound in her head for a moment, not wanting to break into its rhythm by starting to walk again. Then she began to walk ahead fast, following the path upward toward the lightest part of the sky. When it came out suddenly onto an eminence directly above the plantation, she could barely discern the cluster of roofs through the mist. But here the sound of the waterfall was stronger; she supposed she was near the gorge, although there was no sign of it. The path turned here and went along rough open ground upward. She climbed at a steady gait, breathing slowly and deeply, for perhaps half an hour, and was surprised to find that the jungle had been cut away on all sides in this portion of the mountainside. For a time she thought the sky was growing brighter, and that the sun was about to break through, but as the path leveled out and she was able to see for some distance ahead, she saw that the mist was even thicker up here than down below.

At certain points there was a steep declivity on each side of the path. It was impossible to see how deeply the land fell away. There were a few nearby plants and rocks, the highest fronds of a tree-fern a little beyond, and white emptiness after that. It was like going along the top of a wall high in the air. Then the path would make a wide turn and go sharply upward and she would see a solitary tree above her at one side.

Suddenly she came up against a row of huts. They were less well made than those down at the plantation, and smaller. The mist was full of woodsmoke; there was the smell of pigs. She stood still. A man was singing. Two small naked children came out of the door of one hut, looked at her a moment in terror, and ran quickly back inside. She walked ahead. The singing came from behind the last hut. When she was opposite the hut, she saw that it was enclosed by a tangled but effective fence of barbed wire which left a runway about six feet wide all the way around. A young man appeared from the farther side of the closed-in space. His shirt and pants were tattered; the brown skin showed in many places. He was singing as he walked toward her, and he continued to sing, looking straight into her face with bright, questioning eyes. She smiled and said, *"Buenos días."* He made a beckoning gusture, rather too dramatically. She stopped walking and stood still, looking hesitantly back at the other huts. The young man beckoned again and then stepped inside the hut. A moment later he came out, and still staring fascinatedly at her, made more summoning motions. Aileen stood perfectly quiet, not taking her eyes from his face. He walked slowly over to the fence and grasped the wire with both hands, his eyes growing wider as he pressed the barbs into his palms. And he leaned across, thrusting his head toward her, his eyes fixing hers with incredible intensity. For several seconds they watched each other; then she stepped a little nearer, peering into his face and frowning. At that point with a cry he emptied his mouth of the water he had been holding in it, aiming with force at Aileen's face. Some of it struck her cheek, and the rest the front of her dress. His fingers unclenched themselves from around the wire, and straightening himself, he backed slowly into the hut, watching her face closely all the while.

She stood still an instant, her hand to her cheek. Then she bent down, and picking up a large stone from the path she flung it with all her strength through the door. A terrible cry came from within; it was like nothing she had ever heard. Or yes, she thought as she began to run back past the other huts, it had the indignation and outraged innocence of a small baby, but it was also a grown man's cry. No one appeared as she passed the huts. Soon she was back in the silence of the empty mountainside, but she kept running, and she was astonished to find that she was sobbing as well. She sat down on a rock and calmed herself by watching some ants demolish a bush as they cut away squares of leaf and carried them away in their mouths. The sky was growing brighter now; the sun would soon be through. She went on. By the time she got back to the high spot above the plantation the mist had turned into long clouds that were rolling away down the mountainside into the ravines. She was horrified to see how near she stood to the ugly black edge of the gorge. And the house looked insane down there, leaning out over as if it were trying to see the bottom. Far below the house the vapor rose up from the pool. She followed the sheer sides of the opposite cliff upward with her eye, all the way to the top, a little above the spot where she stood. It made her feel ill, and she stumbled back down to the house with her hand to her forehead, paying no attention to the natives who greeted her from their doorways.

As she ran past the garden a voice called to her. She turned and saw

Prue washing her hands in the fountain's basin. She stood still.

"You're up early. You must feel better," said Prue, drying her hands on her hair. "Your mother's been having a fit. Go in and see her."

Aileen stared at Prue a moment before she said, "I was going in. You don't have to tell me."

"Oh, I thought I did."

"You don't have to tell me anything. I think I can manage all right without your help."

"Help isn't exactly what I'd like to give you," said Prue, putting her hands into her pockets. "A swift kick in the teeth would be more like it. How do you think I like to see your mother worrying about you? First you're sick in bed, then you just disappear into the goddamn jungle. D'you think I like to have to keep talking about you, reassuring her every ten minutes? What the hell d'you think life is, one long coming-out party?"

Aileen stared harder, now with unmasked hatred. "I think," she said slowly, "that life is pretty awful. Here especially. And I think you should look once in the mirror and then jump off the terrace. And I think Mother should have her mind examined."

"I see," said Prue, with dire inflection. She lit a cigarette and strode off to her studio. Aileen went into the house and up to her room.

Less than an hour later, her mother knocked at her door. As she came into the room, Aileen could see she had been crying only a moment before.

"Aileen darling, I've got something to say to you," she began apologetically, "and it just breaks my heart to say it. But I've got to."

She stopped, as though waiting for encouragement.

"Mother, what is it?"

"I think you probably know."

"About Prue, I suppose. No?"

"It certainly is. I don't know how I can ever make it right with her. She told me what you said to her, and I must say I found it hard to believe. How could you?"

"You mean just now in the garden?"

"I don't know where you said it, but I do know this can't go on. So I'm just forced to say this. . . . You'll have to go. I can't be stirred up this way, and I can tell just how it'll be if you stay on."

"I'm not surprised at all," said Aileen, making a show of calm. "When do you want me to leave?"

"This is terribly painful . . . ."

"Oh, stop! It's all right. I've had a vacation and I can get a lot of work done before the term starts. Today? Tomorrow?"

"I think the first of the week. I'll go to Barranquilla with you."

"Would you think I was silly if I had all my meals up here?"

"I think it's a perfect idea, darling, and we can have nice visits together, you and I, between meals."

Now, when the tension should have been over, somehow it was not. During the four nights before she was to leave, Aileen had endless excruciating dreams. She would wake up in the darkness too agonized even to move her hand. It was not fear; she could not recall the dreams. It was rather as if some newly discovered, innermost part of her being were in acute pain. Breathing quickly, she would lie transfixed for long periods listening to the eternal sound of the waterfall, punctuated at great intervals by some slight, nearby nocturnal noise in the trees. Finally, when she had summoned sufficient energy to move, she would change her position in the bed, sigh profoundly, and relax enough to fall back into the ominous world of sleep.

When the final day came, there was a light tapping on her door just after dawn. She got up and unbolted it. Her mother was there, smiling thinly.

"May I come in?"

"Oh. Good morning. Of course. It's early, isn't it?"

Her mother walked across to the window and stood looking down at the misty garden.

"I'm not so well today," she said. "I'm afraid I can't take you to Barranquilla. I'm not up to getting onto a horse today. It's just too much, that three-hour trip to Jamonocal, and then the train and the boat all night. You'll just have to forgive me. I couldn't stand all three. But it won't matter, will it?" she went on, looking up at last. "We'll say good-bye here."

"But, Mother, how can I go alone?"

"Oh, José'll go all the way to Barranquilla with you and be back by Wednesday night. You don't think I'd let you go off by yourself?"

She began to laugh intensely, then stopped suddenly and looked pensive.

"I rather hate to be here two nights without him, but I don't see any other way to get you down there by tomorrow. You can go shipside to Panama. There's usually a seat somewhere. Now, breakfast, breakfast . . ."

Patting Aileen's cheek, she hurried out and downstairs to the kitchen.

The birds' morning song was coming down from the forest; the mist lay ragged in the tops of the great trees up there. Aileen shifted her gaze to the garden at her feet. Suddenly she felt she could not leave; in a sense it was as if she were leaving love behind. She sat down on the bed. "But what is it?" she asked herself desperately. "Not Mother. Not the house. Not the jungle." Automatically she dressed and packed the remaining toilet articles in her overnight case. But the feeling was there, imperious and enveloping in its completeness.

She went downstairs. There was the sound of voices and the clatter of china in the kitchen. Concha and Luz were preparing her breakfast tray. She went out and watched them until everything was ready.

"*Ya se va la señorita?*" said Concha sadly.

She did not answer, but took the tray from her and carried it through the house, out onto the terrace, where she set it on the table. Everything on the terrace was wet with dew and moisture from the gorge. She turned the chair-cushion over and sat down to eat. The sound of the waterfall took her appetite away, but she thought, "This is the last time." She felt choked with emotions, but they were too disparate and confused for her to be able to identify any one of them as outstanding. As she sat there eating intently, she was suddenly aware that someone was watching her. She started up and saw Prue standing in the doorway. She was wearing pajamas and a bathrobe, and in her hand she held a glass of water. She looked very sleepy.

"How are you?" she said, sipping her water.

Aileen stood up.

"We're all up bright and early this morning," Prue went on cheerily.

"I'm—leaving. I've got to go. Excuse me, it's late," mumbled Aileen, glancing about furtively.

"Oh, take your time, gal. You haven't said good-bye to your mother yet. And José is still saddling the nags. You've got a lot of grips with you."

"Excuse me," said Aileen, trying to slip past her through the doorway.

"Well, shake," Prue said, reaching for Aileen's hand.

"Get away!" cried Aileen, struggling to keep clear of her. "Don't touch me!" But Prue had succeeded in grasping one frantic arm. She held it fast.

"A dramatic entrance is enough. We don't have to have the same sort of exit. Say good-bye to me like a human being." She twisted the arm a bit, in spite of herself. Aileen leaned against the door and turned very white.

"Feel faint?" said Prue. She let go of her arm, and holding up her glass of water, flicked some of it into Aileen's face with her fingers.

The reaction was instantaneous. Aileen jumped at her with vicious suddenness, kicking, ripping and pounding all at once. The glass fell to the stone floor; Prue was caught off her guard. Mechanically, with rapid, birdlike fury, the girl hammered at the woman's face and head, as she slowly impelled her away from the doorway and across the terrace.

From Prue's lips came several times the word "God." At first she did very little to defend herself; she seemed half asleep as she moved toward the outer edge beneath the onslaught. Then suddenly she threw herself to the floor. Aileen continued to kick her where she lay doubled over, trying to protect her face.

"Nobody! Nobody! Nobody! Nobody can do that to me!" she cried rhythmically as she kicked.

Her voice rose in pitch and volume; she stopped for an instant, and then, raising her head, she uttered the greatest scream of her life. It came back immediately from the black wall of rock across the gorge, straight through the noise of water. The sound of her own voice ended the episode for her, and she began to walk back across the terrace.

Concha and Luz stood frightened in the doorway; it was as if they had come to watch a terrible storm pass over the countryside. They stepped aside as Aileen walked through.

Outside the stable, José was whistling as he finished saddling the horses. The valises were already strapped on the burro.

Still in the midst of her deep dream, Aileen turned her head toward the house as they rode past. For a brief second, between the leaves, she saw the two figures of her mother and Prue standing side by side on the terrace, the wall of the gorge looming behind. Then the horses turned and began to descend the trail.

New York
1946

Call at Corazón

"But why would you want a little horror like that to go along with us? It doesn't make sense. You know what they're like."

"I know what they're like," said her husband. "It's comforting to watch them. Whatever happens, if I had that to look at, I'd be reminded of how stupid I was ever to get upset."

He leaned further over the railing and looked intently down at the dock. There were baskets for sale, crude painted toys of hard natural rubber, reptile-hide wallets and belts, and a few whole snakeskins unrolled. And placed apart from these wares, out of the hot sunlight, in the shadow of a crate, sat a tiny furry monkey. The hands were folded, and the forehead was wrinkled in sad apprehensiveness.

"Isn't he wonderful?"

"I think you're impossible—and a little insulting," she replied.

He turned to look at her. "Are you serious?" He saw that she was.

She went on, studying her sandaled feet and the narrow deckboards beneath them: "You know I don't really mind all this nonsense, or your craziness. Just let me finish." He nodded his head in agreement, looking back at the hot dock and the wretched tin-roofed village beyond. "It goes without saying I don't mind all that, or we wouldn't be here together. You might be here alone . . . ."

"You don't take a honeymoon alone," he interrupted.

"*You* might." She laughed shortly.

He reached along the rail for her hand, but she pulled it away, saying, "I'm still talking to you. I expect you to be crazy, and I expect to give in to you all along. I'm crazy too, I know. But I wish there were some way I could just once feel that my giving in meant anything to you. I wish you knew how to be gracious about it."

"You think you humor me so much? I haven't noticed it." His voice was sullen.

"I don't *humor* you at all. I'm just trying to live with you on an extended trip in a lot of cramped little cabins on an endless series of stinking boats."

"What do you mean?" he cried excitedly. "You've always said you loved

65

the boats. Have you changed your mind, or just lost it completely?"

She turned and walked toward the prow. "Don't talk to me," she said. "Go and buy your monkey."

An expression of solicitousness on his face, he was following her. "You know I won't buy it if it's going to make you miserable."

"I'll be more miserable if you don't, so please go and buy it." She stopped and turned. "I'd love to have it. I really would. I think it's sweet."

"I don't get you at all."

She smiled. "I know. Does it bother you very much?"

After he had bought the monkey and tied it to the metal post of the bunk in the cabin, he took a walk to explore the port. It was a town made of corrugated tin and barbed wire. The sun's heat was painful, even with the sky's low-lying cover of fog. It was the middle of the day and few people were in the streets. He came to the edge of the town almost immediately. Here between him and the forest lay a narrow, slow-moving stream, its water the color of black coffee. A few women were washing clothes; small children splashed. Gigantic gray crabs scuttled between the holes they had made in the mud along the bank. He sat down on some elaborately twisted roots at the foot of a tree and took out the notebook he always carried with him. The day before, in a bar at Pedernales, he had written: "Recipe for dissolving the impression of hideousness made by a thing: Fix the attention upon the given object or situation so that the various elements, all familiar, will regroup themselves. Frightfulness is never more than an unfamiliar pattern."

He lit a cigarette and watched the women's hopeless attempts to launder the ragged garments. Then he threw the burning stub at the nearest crab, and carefully wrote: "More than anything else, woman requires strict ritualistic observance of the traditions of sexual behavior. That is her definition of love." He thought of the derision that would be called forth should he make such a statement to the girl back on the ship. After looking at his watch, he wrote hurriedly: "Modern, that is, intellectual education, having been devised by males for males, inhibits and confuses her. She avenges . . . ."

Two naked children, coming up from their play in the river, ran screaming past him, scattering drops of water over the paper. He called out to them, but they continued their chase without noticing him. He put his pencil and notebook into his pocket, smiling, and watched them patter after one another through the dust.

When he arrived back at the ship, the thunder was rolling down from the mountains around the harbor. The storm reached the height of its hysteria just as they got under way.

She was sitting on her bunk, looking through the open porthole. The shrill crashes of thunder echoed from one side of the bay to the other as they steamed toward the open sea. He lay doubled up on his bunk opposite, reading.

"Don't lean your head against that metal wall," he advised. "It's a perfect conductor."

She jumped down to the floor and went to the washstand.

"Where are those two quarts of White Horse we got yesterday?"

He gestured. "In the rack on your side. Are you going to drink?"

"I'm going to *have* a drink, yes."

"In this heat? Why don't you wait until it clears, and have it on deck?"

"I want it now. When it clears I won't need it."

She poured the whisky and added water from the carafe in the wall bracket over the washbowl.

"You realize what you're doing, of course."

She glared at him. "What am I doing?"

He shrugged his shoulders. "Nothing, except just giving in to a passing emotional state. You could read, or lie down and doze."

Holding her glass in one hand, she pulled open the door into the passageway with the other, and went out. The noise of the slamming door startled the monkey, perched on a suitcase. It hesitated a second, and hurried under its master's bunk. He made a few kissing sounds to entice it out, and returned to his book. Soon he began to imagine her alone and unhappy on the deck, and the thought cut into the pleasure of his reading. He forced himself to lie still a few minutes, the open book face down across his chest. The boat was moving at full speed now, and the sound of the motors was louder than the storm in the sky.

Soon he rose and went on deck. The land behind was already hidden by the falling rain, and the air smelled of deep water. She was standing alone by the rail, looking down at the waves, with the empty glass in her hand. Pity seized him as he watched, but he could not walk across to her and put into consoling words the emotion he felt.

Back in the cabin he found the monkey on his bunk, slowly tearing the pages from the book he had been reading.

The next day was spent in leisurely preparation for disembarking and changing of boats: in Villalta they were to take a smaller vessel to the opposite side of the delta.

When she came in to pack after dinner, she stood a moment studying the cabin. "He's messed it up, all right," said her husband, "but I found your necklace behind my big valise, and we'd read all the magazines anyway."

"I suppose this represents Man's innate urge to destroy," she said, kicking a ball of crumpled paper across the floor. "And the next time he tries to bite you, it'll be Man's basic insecurity."

"You don't know what a bore you are when you try to be caustic. If you want me to get rid of him, I will. It's easy enough."

She bent to touch the animal, but it backed uneasily under the bunk. She stood up. "I don't mind him. What I mind is you. *He* can't help being a little horror, but he keeps reminding me that you could if you wanted."

Her husband's face assumed the impassivity that was characteristic of him when he was determined not to lose his temper. She knew he would wait to be angry until she was unprepared for his attack. He said nothing, tapping an insistent rhythm on the lid of a suitcase with his fingernails.

"Naturally I don't really mean you're a horror," she continued.

"Why not mean it?" he said, smiling pleasantly. "What's wrong with criticism? Probably I am, to you. I like monkeys because I see them as little model men. You think men are something else, something spiritual or God knows what. Whatever it is, I notice you're the one who's always being disillusioned and going around wondering how mankind can be so bestial. I think mankind is fine."

"Please don't go on," she said. "I know your theories. You'll never convince yourself of them."

When they had finished packing, they went to bed. As he snapped off the light behind his pillow, he said, "Tell me honestly. Do you want me to give him to the steward?"

She kicked off her sheet in the dark. Through the porthole, near the horizon, she could see stars, and the calm sea slipped by just below her. Without thinking she said, "Why don't you drop him overboard?"

In the silence that followed she realized she had spoken carelessly, but the tepid breeze moving with languor over her body was making it increasingly difficult for her to think or speak. As she fell asleep it seemed to her she heard her husband saying slowly, "I believe you would. I believe you would."

The next morning she slept late, and when she went up for breakfast her husband had already finished his and was leaning back, smoking.

"How are you?" he asked brightly. "The cabin steward's delighted with the monkey."

She felt a flush of pleasure. "Oh," she said, sitting down, "did you give it to him? You didn't have to do that." She glanced at the menu; it was the same as every other day. "But I suppose really it's better. A monkey doesn't go with a honeymoon."

"I think you're right," he agreed.

Villalta was stifling and dusty. On the other boat they had grown accustomed to having very few passengers around, and it was an unpleasant surprise to find the new one swarming with people. Their new boat was a two-decked ferry painted white, with an enormous paddle wheel at the stern. On the lower deck, which rested not more than two feet above the surface of the river, passengers and freight stood ready to travel, packed together indiscriminately. The upper deck had a salon and a dozen or so narrow staterooms. In the salon the first-class passengers undid their bundles of pillows and opened their paper bags of food. The orange light of the setting sun flooded the room.

They looked into several of the staterooms.

"They all seem to be empty," she said.

"I can see why. Still, the privacy would be a help."

"This one's double. And it has a screen in the window. This is the best one."

"I'll look for a steward or somebody. Go on in and take over." He pushed the bags out of the passageway where the *cargador* had left them, and went off in search of an employee. In every corner of the boat the people seemed to be multiplying. There were twice as many as there had been a few moments before. The salon was completely full, its floor space occupied by groups of travelers with small children and elderly women, who were already stretched out on blankets and newspapers.

"It looks like Salvation Army headquarters the night after a major disaster," he said as he came back into the stateroom. "I can't find anybody. Anyway, we'd better stay in here. The other cubicles are beginning to fill up."

"I'm not so sure I wouldn't rather be on deck," she announced. "There are hundreds of cockroaches."

"And probably worse," he added, looking at the bunks.

"The thing to do is take those filthy sheets off and just lie on the mattresses." She peered out into the corridor. Sweat was trickling down her neck. "Do you think it's safe?"

"What do you mean?"

"All those people. This old tub."

He shrugged his shoulders.

"It's just one night. Tomorrow we'll be at Cienaga. And it's almost night now."

She shut the door and leaned against it, smiling faintly.

"I think it's going to be fun," she said.

"The boat's moving!" he cried. "Let's go on deck. If we can get out there."

Slowly the old boat pushed across the bay toward the dark east shore. People were singing and playing guitars. On the bottom deck a cow lowed continuously. And louder than all the sounds was the rush of water made by the huge paddles.

They sat on the deck in the middle of a vociferous crowd, leaning against the bars of the railing, and watched the moon rise above the mangrove swamps ahead. As they approached the opposite side of the bay, it looked as if the boat might plow straight into the shore, but a narrow waterway presently appeared, and the boat slipped cautiously in. The people immediately moved back from the railing, crowding against the opposite wall. Branches from the trees on the bank began to rub against the boat, scraping along the side walls of the cabins, and then whipping violently across the deck.

They pushed their way through the throng and walked across the salon to the deck on the other side of the boat; the same thing was happening there.

"It's crazy," she declared. "It's like a nightmare. Whoever heard of going through a channel no wider than the boat! It makes me nervous. I'm going in and read."

Her husband let go of her arm. "You can never enter into the spirit of a thing, can you?"

"You tell me what the spirit is, and I'll see about entering into it," she said, turning away.

He followed her. "Don't you want to go down onto the lower deck? They seem to be going strong down there. Listen." He held up his hand. Repeated screams of laughter came up from below.

"I certainly don't!" she called, without looking around.

He went below. Groups of men were seated on bulging burlap sacks and wooden crates, matching coins. The women stood behind them, puffing on black cigarettes and shrieking with excitement. He watched them closely, reflecting that with fewer teeth missing they would be a handsome people. "Mineral deficiency in the soil," he commented to himself.

Standing on the other side of a circle of gamblers, facing him, was a muscular young native whose visòred cap and faint air of aloofness suggested official position of some sort aboard the boat. With difficulty the traveler made his way over to him, and spoke to him in Spanish.

"Are you an employee here?"

"Yes, sir."

"I am in cabin number eight. Can I pay the supplementary fare to you?"

"Yes, sir."

"Good."

He reached into his pocket for his wallet, at the same time remembering with annoyance that he had left it upstairs locked in a suitcase. The man looked expectant. His hand was out.

"My money is in my stateroom." Then he added, "My wife has it. But if you come up in half an hour I can pay you the fare."

"Yes, sir." The man lowered his hand and merely looked at him. Even though he gave an impression of purely animal force, his broad, somewhat simian face was handsome, the husband reflected. It was surprising when, a moment later, that face betrayed a boyish shyness as the man said, "I am going to spray the cabin for your señora."

"Thank you. Are there many mosquitoes?"

The man grunted and shook the fingers of one hand as if he had just burned them.

"Soon you will see how many." He moved away.

At that moment the boat jolted violently, and there was great merriment among the passengers. He pushed his way to the prow and saw that the pilot had run into the bank. The tangle of branches and roots was a few feet from his face, its complex forms vaguely lighted by the boat's lanterns. The boat backed laboriously and the channel's agitated water rose to deck level and lapped the outer edge. Slowly they nosed along the bank until the prow once more pointed to midstream, and they continued. Then almost immediately the passage curved so sharply that the same thing happened again, throwing him sideways against a sack of something unpleasantly soft and wet. A bell clanged below deck in the interior of the boat; the passengers' laughter was louder.

Eventually they pushed ahead, but now the movement became painfully slow as the sharpness of the curves in the passage increased. Under the water the stumps groaned as the boat forced its sides against them. Branches cracked and broke, falling onto the forward and upper decks. The lantern at the prow was swept into the water.

"This isn't the regular channel," muttered a gambler, glancing up.

Several travelers exclaimed, "What?" almost in unison.

"There's a pile of passages through here. We're picking up cargo at Corazón."

The players retreated to a square inner arena which others were forming by shifting some of the crates. The husband followed them. Here they were comparatively safe from the intruding boughs. The deck was better lighted here, and this gave him the idea of making an entry in his notebook. Bending over a carton marked *Vermifugo Santa Rosalia*, he wrote: "November 18. We are moving through the blood stream of a giant. A very dark night." Here a fresh collision with the land knocked him over, knocked over everyone who was not propped between solid objects.

A few babies were crying, but most of them still slept. He slid down to the deck. Finding his position fairly comfortable, he fell into a dozing state which was broken irregularly by the shouting of the people and the jolting of the boat.

When he awoke later, the boat was quite stationary, the games had ceased, and the people were asleep, a few of the men continuing their conversation in small groups. He lay still, listening. The talk was all about places; they were comparing the unpleasant things to be found in various parts of the republic: insects, weather, reptiles, diseases, lack of food, high prices.

He looked at his watch. It was half past one. With difficulty he got to his feet, and found his way to the stairs. Above, in the salon, the kerosene lamps illumined a vast disorder of prostrate figures. He went into the corridor and knocked on the door marked with an eight. Without waiting for her to answer, he opened the door. It was dark inside. He heard a muffled cough nearby, and decided that she was awake.

"How are the mosquitoes? Did my monkey man come and fix you up?" he asked.

She did not answer, so he lit a match. She was not in the bunk on the left. The match burned his thumb. With the second one, he looked at the right-hand bunk. A tin insecticide sprayer lay there on the mattress; its leak had made a large circle of oil on the bare ticking. The cough was repeated. It was someone in the next cabin.

"Now what?" he said aloud, uncomfortable at finding himself upset to this degree. A suspicion seized him. Without lighting the hanging lamp, he rushed to open her valises, and in the dark felt hurriedly through the flimsy pieces of clothing and the toilet articles. The whisky bottles were not there.

This was not the first time she had gone on a solitary drinking bout, and it would be easy to find her among the passengers. However, being angry, he decided not to look for her. He took off his shirt and trousers and lay down on the left-hand bunk. His hand touched a bottle standing on the floor by the head of the bunk. He raised himself enough to smell it; it was beer and the bottle was half full. It was hot in the cabin, and he drank the remaining warm, bitter liquid with relish and rolled the bottle across the room.

The boat was not moving, but voices shouted out here and there. An occasional bump could be felt as a sack of something heavy was heaved aboard. He looked through the little square window with the screen in it. In the foreground, dimly illumined by the boat's lanterns, a few dark men, naked save for their ragged underdrawers, stood on a landing made in the mud and stared toward the boat. Through the endless intricacies of roots and trunks behind them he saw a bonfire blazing, but it was far back in the swamp. The air smelled of stagnant water and smoke.

Deciding to take advantage of the relative silence, he lay down and tried to sleep; he was not surprised, however, by the difficulty he found in relaxing. It was always hard to sleep when she was not there in the room. The comfort of her presence was lacking, and there was also the fear of being awakened by her return. When he allowed himself to, he would quickly begin to formulate ideas and translate them into sentences whose recording seemed the more urgent because he was lying comfortably in the dark. Sometimes he thought about her, but only as an unclear figure whose character lent flavor to a succession of backdrops. More often he reviewed the day just completed, seeking to convince himself that it had carried him a bit further away from his childhood. Often for months at a time the strangeness of his dreams persuaded him that at last he had turned the corner, that the dark place had finally been left behind, that he was out of hearing. Then, one evening as he fell asleep, before he had time to refuse, he would be staring closely at a long-forgotten object—a plate, a chair, a pin-cushion—and the accustomed feeling of infinite futility and sadness would recur.

The motor started up, and the great noise of the water in the paddle wheel recommenced. They pushed off from Corazón. He was pleased. "Now I shan't hear her when she comes in and bangs around," he thought, and fell into a light sleep.

He was scratching his arms and legs. The long-continued, vague malaise eventually became full consciousness, and he sat up angrily. Above the sounds made by the boat he could hear another sound, one which came through the window: an incredibly high and tiny tone, tiny but constant in pitch and intensity. He jumped down from the berth and went to the window. The channel was wider here, and the overhanging vegetation no longer touched the sides of the boat. In the air, nearby, far away, everywhere, was the thin wail of mosquito wings. He was aghast, and completely delighted by the novelty of the phenomenon. For a moment he watched the tangled black wilderness slip past. Then with the itching he remembered the mosquitoses inside the cabin. The screen did not reach quite to the top of the window; there was ample space for them to crawl in. Even there in the dark as he moved his fingers along the frame to find the handle he could feel them; there were that many.

Now that he was fully awake, he lighted a match and went to her bunk. Of course she was not there. He lifted the Flit gun and shook it. It was empty, and as the match went out, he saw that the spot on the mattress had spread even further.

"Son of a bitch!" he whispered, and going back to the window he tugged the screen vigorously upward to close the crack. As he let go of it, it fell out into the water, and almost immediately he became conscious of the soft caress of tiny wings all about his head. In his undershirt and trousers he rushed out into the corridor. Nothing had changed in the salon. Almost everyone was asleep. There were screen doors giving onto the deck. He inspected them: they appeared to be more firmly installed. A few mosquitoes brushed against his face, but it was not the horde. He edged in between two women who were sleeping sitting with their backs against the wall, and stayed there in acute discomfort until again he dozed. It was not long before he opened his eyes to find the dim light of dawn in the air. His neck ached. He arose and went out onto the deck, to which most of the people from the salon had already crowded.

The boat was moving through a wide estuary dotted with clumps of plants and trees that rose out of the shallow water. Along the edges of the small islands stood herons, so white in the early gray light that their brightness seemed to come from inside them.

It was half past five. At this moment the boat was due in Cienaga, where it was met on its weekly trip by the train that went into the interior. Already a thin spit of land ahead was being identified by eager watchers. Day was coming up swiftly; sky and water were the same color. The deck reeked of the greasy smell of mangoes as people began to breakfast.

And now at last he began to feel pangs of anxiety as to where she might be. He determined to make an immediate and thorough search of the boat. She would be instantly recognizable in any group. First, he looked methodically through the salon, then he exhausted the possibilities on the upper decks. Then he went downstairs, where the gambling had already begun again. Toward the stern, roped to two flimsy iron posts, stood the cow, no longer bellowing. Nearby was an improvised lean-to, probably the crew's quarters. As he passed the small door, he peered through the low transom above it, and saw her lying beside a man on the floor. Automatically he walked on; then he turned and went back. The two were asleep, and half-clothed. In the warm air that came through the screened transom there was the smell of whisky that had been drunk and whisky that had been spilled.

He went upstairs, his heart beating violently. In the cabin, he closed her two valises, packed his own, set them all together by the door and laid the raincoats on top of them. He put on his shirt, combed his hair carefully, and went on deck. Cienaga was there ahead, in the mountains' morning shadow: the dock, a line of huts against the jungle behind, and the railway station to the right beyond the village.

As they docked, he signaled the two urchins who were waving for his attention, screaming, "*Equipajes!*" They fought a bit with one another until he made them see his two fingers held aloft. Then to make them certain, he pointed at each of them in turn, and they grinned. Still grinning, they stood beside him with the bags and coats, and he was among the first of the upper-deck passengers to get on land. They went down the street to the station with the parrots screaming at them from each thatched gable along the way.

On the crowded, waiting train, with the luggage finally in the rack, his heart beat harder than ever, and he kept his eyes painfully on the long dusty street that led back to the dock. At the far end, as the whistle blew, he thought he saw a figure in white running among the dogs and children toward the station, but the train started up as he watched, and the street was lost to view. He took out his notebook, and sat with it on his lap, smiling at the shining green landscape that moved with increasing speed past the window.

New York
1946

Under the Sky

Inland from the sea on the dry coastal plain lay the town, open, spread out under the huge high sky. People who lived outside in the country, and even some of the more educated town-dwellers, called the town "the Inferno" because nowhere in the region was the heat so intense. No other place around was quite so shadowless and so dusty; it seemed that the clouds above shrank upwards to their farthest possible positions. Many miles above, and to all sides, they hung there in their massive patterns, remote and motionless. In the spring, during the nights, the lightning constantly jumped from one cloud to another, revealing unexpected distances between them. Then, if anyone ever looked at the sky, he was surprised to see how each flash revealed a seemingly more distant portion of the heavens to which still more clouds had receded. But people in the town seldom turned their heads upward. They knew at what time of the year the rains would come, and it was unnecessary to scan those vast regions in order to say what day that would be. When the wind had blown hard for two weeks so that the dust filled the wide empty streets, and the lightning grew brighter each night until finally there was a little thunder, they could be sure the water would soon fall.

Once a year when the lightning was in the sky Jacinto left his village in the mountains and walked down to the town, carrying with him all the things his family had made since his last trip. There were two days of walking in the sierra where it was cool; the third day the road was through the hot lands, and this was the day he preferred, because the road was flat and he could walk faster and leave the others behind. He was taller and prouder than they, and he refused to bend over in order to be able to trot uphill and downhill as they did. In the mountains he labored to keep up with them, but on the plain he strode powerfully ahead and sometimes arrived at the market before sunset.

Now he stood in the public square with a small paper parcel in his hand. He had arrived the day before. Instead of sitting in the sidestreet near the fountain and discussing the sales with the others from his village, he walked into the municipal garden and sat down on a concrete bench marked "1936." He looked up and down the walk. No one paid him any attention. He was barefoot, so the shoeshine boys passed him by.

Tearing open the paper packet he emptied the dried leaves into his left hand. With his right he picked out all the little round, black berries and tossed them away. Then he crushed the leaves and slowly rolled them into five thin cigarettes. This took all his attention for a half hour.

A voice beside him said: "That's pretty."

He looked up. It was a town-dweller; he had never seen him before, so he did not answer.

"All for you?" said the other in the silken town voice that Jacinto had learned to distrust.

"I bought it. I made them," said Jacinto.

"But I like *grifas* too," smiled the stranger. He was poorly dressed and had black teeth.

Jacinto covered the cigarettes completely with one big hand which he placed on the seat of the bench. The stranger pointed to a soldier sleeping on another bench near the iron bandstand.

"He wants one and I want one. You should be more careful. It's three months now for possessing marijuana. Don't you know?"

"No," said Jacinto. "I don't know." Then he slowly handed over two of the cigarettes. The man took them.

"So long," he said.

Jacinto stood up full of fury, and with the other three cigarettes still in his hand, he walked out into the plaza and down the long street that led to the station. It was nearly time for the daily train from the north. Sometimes crazy people got off, who would give a man enough money for two good meals, just for carrying a bundle into the town for them. There was a cemetery behind the roundhouse where some of the railroad employees went to smoke the weed. He remembered it from the preceding year; he had met an inspector there who had taken him to see a girl. She had proved to be ugly—one side of her face was mottled with blue and purple.

At the station the train had already arrived. The people trying to get on were fighting with those who were trying to get off. He wondered why with all those open windows everyone insisted on going through the two little doors at the ends of the cars. It would have been very simple the other way, but these people were too stupid to think of it. His defeat at the hands of the townsman still bothered him; he wanted to have a gun so he could pull it out and shout: "I am the father of all of you!" But it was not likely that he ever would have a gun.

Without approaching the platform where so many people were moving about, he stood and impassively watched the confusion. From the crowd three strange-looking people suddenly emerged. They all had very white skin and yellow hair. He knew, of course, that they were from a faraway place because everyone knows that when people look as strange as that they are from the capital or even farther. There were two women and one man, and as they approached him, he noticed that they were speaking a language which only they could understand. Each one carried a leather bag covered with small squares of colored paper stuck on at different angles. He stepped back, keeping his eyes on the face of the younger woman. He could not be sure whether he found her beautiful or revolting. Still he continued to look at her as she passed, holding on to the man's arm. The other woman noticed him, and smiled faintly as she went by.

He turned angrily and walked toward the tracks. He was angry at her stupidity—for thinking he could have enough money to pay her as much as she would surely want. He walked on until he came to the cemetery. It was empty save for the gray lizards that scurried from the path at his feet. In the farthest corner there was a small square building with a white stone woman on top. He sat in the shade of the little building and took out his cigarettes.

The train whistled; it was starting on its trip to the sea where the people eat nothing but fish and travel on top of the water. He drew in the first few breaths very slowly and deliberately, holding the smoke in his lungs until he felt it burning the edges of his soul. After a few minutes the feeling began to take shape. From the back of his head it moved down to his shoulder. It was as if he were wearing a tight metal garment. At that instant he looked at the sky and saw far above him the tiny black dots that were vultures, moving ever so slowly in circles as they surveyed the plain in the afternoon sunlight. Beyond them stood the clouds, deep and monumental. "Ay!" he sighed, shutting his eyes, and it occurred to him that this was what the dead people, who were lying on all sides of him, looked at day after day. This was all they could see—the clouds, and the vultures, which they did not need to fear, hidden safely as they were, deep in holy ground.

He continued to smoke, going deeper and deeper into delight. Finally he lay back and murmured: "Now I am dead too." When he opened his eyes it was still the same day, and the sun was very low in the sky. Some men were talking nearby. He listened; they were trainmen come to smoke, discussing wages and prices of meals. He did not believe any of the figures they so casually mentioned. They were lying to impress one another, and they did not even believe each other. He smoked half of the second cigarette, rose, stretched, and jumped over the cemetery wall, going back to the station by a roundabout path in order not to have to speak to the trainmen. Those people, when they smoked, always wanted more and more company; they would never let a fellow smoker go quietly on his way.

He went to the cantina by the station, and standing in the street, watched the railway employees playing billiards inside. As night approached, the lightning became increasingly visible. He walked up the long street toward the center of town. Men were playing marimbas in the doorways and in front of the houses—three or four together, and sometimes only one, indolently. The marimbas and the marijuana were the only good things in the town, reflected Jacinto. The women were ugly and dirty, and the men were all thieves and drunkards. He remembered the three people at the station. They would be in the hotel opposite the plaza. He walked a little faster, and his eyes, bloodshot from lack of sleep and too much of the drug, opened a bit wider.

After he had eaten heartily in the market sitting by the edge of the fountain, he felt very well. By the side wall of the cathedral were all the families from the mountains, some already asleep, the others preparing for the night. Almost all the stalls in the market were dark; a few figures still stood in front of the cold fruit-juice stand. Jacinto felt in his pocket for the stub and the whole cigarette, and keeping his fingers around them, walked across to the park. The celestial fireworks were very bright, but there was no thunder. Throughout the town sounded the clink and purr of the marimbas, some near and some far away. A soft breeze stirred the branches of the few lemon trees in the park. He walked along thoughtfully until he came to a bench directly opposite the entrance of the hotel, and there he sat down and brazenly began to smoke his stub. After a few minutes it was easier for him to believe that one of the two yellow-haired women would come out. He flicked away the butt, leaned back and stared straight at the hotel. The manager had put a square loudspeaker over the entrance door, and out of it came a great crackling and hissing that covered the sound of the marimbas. Occasionally a few loud notes of band music rose above the chaos, and from time to time there seemed to be a man's voice speaking behind the noise. Jacinto was annoyed: the women would want to stay inside where they could hear the sound better.

A long time went by. The radio was silenced. The few voices in the park disappeared down the streets. By the cathedral everyone was asleep. Even the marimbas seemed to have stopped, but when the breeze occasionally grew more active, it brought with it, swelling and dying, long marimba trills from a distant part of the town.

It grew very late. There was no sound but the lemon leaves rubbing together and the jet of water splashing into the basin in the center of the market. Jacinto was used to waiting. And halfway through the night a woman stepped out of the hotel, stood for a moment looking at the sky, and walked across the street to the park. From his bench in the dark he watched her as she approached. In the lightning he saw that it was not the younger one. He was disappointed. She looked upward again before moving into the shade of the lemon trees, and in a moment she sat down on the next bench and lighted a cigarette. He waited a few minutes. Then he said: "Señorita."

The yellow-haired woman cried: "Oh!" She had not seen him. She jumped up and stood still, peering toward his bench.

He moved to the end of the seat and calmly repeated the word. "Señorita."

She walked uncertainly toward him, still peering. He knew this was a ruse. She could see him quite clearly each second or so, whenever the sky lighted up. When she was near enough to the bench, he motioned for her to sit down beside him. As he had suspected, she spoke his tongue.

"What is it?" she asked. The talk in the strange language at the station had only been for show, after all.

"Sit down, señorita."

"Why?"

"Because I tell you to."

She laughed and threw away her cigarette.

"That's not a reason," she said, sitting down at the other end of the bench. "What are you doing here so late?" She spoke carefully and correctly, like a priest. He answered this by saying: "And you, what are you looking for?"

"Nothing."

"Yes. You are looking for something," he said solemnly.

"I was not sleeping. It is very hot."

"No. It is not hot," said Jacinto. He was feeling increasingly sure of himself, and he drew out the last cigarette and began to smoke it. "What are you doing here in this town?" he asked her after a moment.

"Passing on my way south to the border," she said, and she told him how she was traveling with two friends, a husband and wife, and how she often took a walk when they had gone to bed.

Jacinto listened as he drew in the smoke and breathed it out. Suddenly he jumped up. Touching her arm, he said: "Come to the market."

She arose, asking: "Why?" and walked with him across the park. When they were in the street, he took her wrist fiercely and pressing it, said between his teeth: "Look at the sky."

She looked up wonderingly, a little fearfully. He went on in a low, intense voice: "As God is my witness, I am going into the hotel and kill the man who came here with you."

Her eyes grew large. She tried to wrest her arm away, but he would not let it go, and he thrust his face into hers. "I have a pistol in my pocket and I am going to kill that man."

"But why?" she whispered weakly, looking up and down the empty street.

"I want his wife."

The woman said: "It is not possible. She would scream."

"I know the proprietor," said Jacinto, rolling his eyes and grinning. The woman seemed to believe him. Now he felt that a great thing was about to happen.

"And you," he said, twisting her arm brutally, "you do not scream."

"No."

Again he pointed to the sky.

"God is my witness. You can save the life of your friend. Come with me."

She was trembling violently, but as they stumbled through the street and he let go of her for an instant, she began to run. With one bound he had overtaken her, and he made her stop and look at the sky again as he went through his threats once more. She saw his wide, red-veined eyes in a bright flash of lightning, and his utterly empty face. Mechanically she allowed him to push her along through the streets. He did not let go of her again.

"You are saving your friend's life," he said. "God will reward you."

She was sobbing as she went along. No one passed them as they moved unsteadily on toward the station. When they were nearly there they made a great detour past the edge of town, and finally came to the cemetery.

"This is a holy place," he murmured, swiftly crossing himself. "Here you are going to save your friend's life."

He took off his shirt, laid it on the stony ground, and pushed her down. There was nothing but the insistent, silent flashing in the sky. She kept her eyes shut, but she shuddered at each flash, even with her lids closed. The wind blew harder, and the smell of the dust was in her nostrils.

He took her back as far as the park and there he let go of her. Then he said: "Good night, señorita," and walked away very quickly. He was happy because she had not asked for any money.

The next year when he came down to the town he waited at the station four afternoons to see the train come in. The last afternoon he went to the cemetery and sat near the small square building that had the stone woman on top of it. On the ground the dust blew past. The enormous clouds hung in the sky and the vultures were there high above him. As he smoked he recalled the yellow-haired woman. After a time he began to weep, and rolled over onto the earth, clutching the pebbles as he sobbed. An old woman of the town, who came every day to her son's grave, passed near to him. Seeing him, she shook her head and murmured to herself: "He has lost his mother."

Southampton
1946

Pages from Cold Point

Our civilization is doomed to a short life: its component parts are too heterogeneous. I personally am content to see everything in the process of decay. The bigger the bombs, the quicker it will be done. Life is visually too hideous for one to make the attempt to preserve it. Let it go. Perhaps some day another form of life will come along. Either way, it is of no consequence. At the same time, I am still a part of life, and I am bound by this to protect myself to whatever extent I am able. And so I am here. Here in the Islands vegetation still has the upper hand, and man has to fight even to make his presence seen at all. It is beautiful here, the trade winds blow all year, and I suspect that bombs are extremely unlikely to be wasted on this unfrequented side of the island, if indeed on any part of it.

I was loath to give up the house after Hope's death. But it was the obvious move to make. My university career always having been an utter farce (since I believe no reason inducing a man to "teach" can possibly be a valid one), I was elated by the idea of resigning, and as soon as her affairs had been settled and the money properly invested, I lost no time in doing so.

I think that week was the first time since childhood that I had managed to recapture the feeling of there being a content in existence. I went from one pleasant house to the next, making my adieux to the English quacks, the Philosophy fakirs, and so on—even to those colleagues with whom I was merely on speaking terms. I watched the envy in their faces when I announced my departure by Pan American on Saturday morning; and the greatest pleasure I felt in all this was in being able to answer, "Nothing," when I was asked, as invariably I was, what I intended to do.

When I was a boy people used to refer to Charles as "Big Brother C.," although he is only a scant year older than I. To me now he is merely "Fat Brother C.," a successful lawyer. His thick, red face and hands, his back-slapping joviality, and his fathomless hypocritical prudery, these are the qualities which make him truly repulsive to me. There is also the fact that he once looked not unlike the way Racky does now. And after all, he still is my big brother, and disapproves openly of everything I do. The loathing I feel for him is so strong that for years I have not been able to swallow a morsel of food or a drop of liquid in his presence without making a prodigious effort. No one knows this but me—certainly not Charles, who would be the last one I should tell about it. He came up on the late train two nights before I left. He got quickly to the point—as soon as he was settled with a highball.

"So you're off for the wilds," he said, sitting forward in his chair like a salesman.

"If you can call it the wilds," I replied. "Certainly it's not wild like Mitichi." (He has a lodge in northern Quebec.) "I consider it really civilized."

He drank and smacked his lips together stiffly, bringing the glass down hard on his knee.

"And Racky. You're taking him along?"

"Of course."

"Out of school. Away. So he'll see nobody but you. You think that's good."

I looked at him. "I do," I said.

"By God, if I could stop you legally, I would!" he cried, jumping up and putting his glass on the mantel. I was trembling inwardly with excitement, but I merely sat and watched him. He went on. "You're not fit to have custody of the kid!" he shouted. He shot a stern glance at me over his spectacles.

"You think not?" I said gently.

Again he looked at me sharply. "D'ye think I've forgotten?"

I was understandably eager to get him out of the house as soon as I could. As I piled and sorted letters and magazines on the desk, I said: "Is that all you came to tell me? I have a good deal to do tomorrow and I must get some sleep. I probably shan't see you at breakfast. Agnes'll see that you eat in time to make the early train."

All he said was: "God! Wake up! Get wise to yourself! You're not fooling anybody, you know."

That kind of talk is typical of Charles. His mind is slow and obtuse; he constantly imagines that everyone he meets is playing some private game of deception with him. He is so utterly incapable of following the functioning of even a moderately evolved intellect that he finds the will to secretiveness and duplicity everywhere.

"I haven't time to listen to that sort of nonsense," I said, preparing to leave the room.

But he shouted, "You don't want to listen! No! Of course not! You just want to do what you want to do. You just want to go on off down there and live as you've a mind to, and to hell with the consequences!" At this point I heard Racky coming downstairs. C. obviously heard nothing and he raved on. "But just remember, I've got your number all right, and if there's any trouble with the boy I'll know who's to blame."

I hurried across the room and opened the door so he could see that Racky was there in the hallway. That stopped his tirade. It was hard to know whether Racky had heard any of it or not. Although he is not a quiet young person, he is the soul of discretion, and it is almost never possible to know any more about what goes on inside his head than he intends one to know.

I was annoyed that C. should have been bellowing at me in my own house. To be sure, he is the only one from whom I would accept such behavior, but then, no father likes to have his son see him take criticism meekly. Racky simply stood there in his bathrobe, his angelic face quite devoid of expression, saying: "Tell Uncle Charley good night for me, will you? I forgot."

I said I would, and quickly shut the door. When I thought Racky was back upstairs in his room, I bade Charles good night. I have never been able to get out of his presence fast enough. The effect he has on me dates from an early period in our lives, from days I dislike to recall.

Racky is a wonderful boy. After we arrived, when we found it impossible to secure a proper house near any town where he might have the company of English boys and girls his own age, he showed no sign of chagrin, although he must have been disappointed. Instead, as we went out of the renting office into the glare of the street, he grinned and said: "Well, I guess we'll have to get bikes, that's all."

The few available houses near what Charles would have called "civilization" turned out to be so ugly and so impossibly confining in atmosphere that we decided immediately on Cold Point, even though it was across the island and quite isolated on its seaside cliff. It was beyond a doubt one of the most desirable properties on the island, and Racky was as enthusiastic about its splendors as I.

"You'll get tired of being alone out there, just with me," I said to him as we walked back to the hotel.

"Aw, I'll get along all right. When do we look for the bikes?"

At his insistence we bought two the next morning. I was sure I should not make much use of mine, but I reflected that an extra bicycle might be convenient to have around the house. It turned out that the servants all had their own bicycles, without which they would not have been able to get to and from the village of Orange Walk, eight miles down the shore. So for a while I was forced to get astride mine each morning before breakfast and pedal madly along beside Racky for a half hour. We would ride through the cool early air, under the towering silk-cotton trees near the house, and out to the great curve in the shoreline where the waving palms bend landward in the stiff breeze that always blows there. Then we would make a wide turn and race back to the house, loudly discussing the degrees of our desires for the various items of breakfast we knew were awaiting us there on the terrace. Back home we would eat in the wind, looking out over the Caribbean, and talk about the news in yesterday's local paper, brought to us by Isiah each morning from Orange Walk. Then Racky would disappear for the whole morning on his bicycle, riding furiously along the road in one direction or the other until he had discovered an unfamiliar strip of sand along the shore that he could consider a new beach. At lunch he would describe it in detail to me, along with a recounting of all the physical hazards involved in hiding the bicycle in among the trees, so that natives passing along the road on foot would not spot it, or in climbing down unscalable cliffs that turned out to be much higher than they had appeared at first sight, or in measuring the depth of the water preparatory to diving from the rocks, or in judging the efficacy of the reef in barring sharks and barracuda. There is never any element of bragadoccio in Racky's relating of his exploits—only the joyous excitement he derives from telling how he satisfies his inexhaustible curiosity. And his mind shows its alertness in all directions at once. I do not mean to say that I expect him to be an "intellectual." That is no affair of mine, nor do I have any particular interest in whether he turns out to be a thinking man or not. I know he will always have a certain boldness of manner and a great purity of spirit in judging values. The former will prevent his becoming what I call a "victim": he never will be brutalized by realities. And his unerring sense of balance in ethical considerations will shield him from the paralyzing effects of present-day materialism.

For a boy of sixteen Racky has an extraordinary innocence of vision. I do not say this as a doting father, although God knows I can never even think of the boy without that familiar overwhelming sensation of delight and gratitude for being vouchsafed the privilege of sharing my life with him. What he takes so completely as a matter of course, our daily life here together, is a source of never-ending wonder to me; and I reflect upon it a good part of each day, just sitting here being conscious of my great good fortune in having him all to myself, beyond the reach of prying eyes and malicious tongues. (I suppose I am really thinking of C. when I write that.) And I believe that a part of the charm of sharing Racky's life with him consists precisely in his taking it all so utterly for granted. I have never asked him whether he likes being here—it is so patent that he does, very much. I think if he were to turn to me one day and tell me how happy he is here, that somehow, perhaps, the spell might be broken. Yet if he were to be thoughtless and inconsiderate, or even unkind to me, I feel that I should be able only to love him the more for it.

I have reread that last sentence. What does it mean? And why should I even imagine it could mean anything more than it says?

Still, much as I may try, I can never believe in the gratuitous, isolated fact. What I must mean is that I feel that Racky already has been in some way inconsiderate. But in what way? Surely I cannot resent his bicycle treks; I cannot expect him to want to stay and sit talking with me all day. And I never worry about his being in danger; I know he is more capable than most adults of taking care of himself, and that he is no more likely than any native to come to harm crawling over the cliffs or swimming in the bays. At the same time there is no doubt in my mind that something about our existence annoys me. I must resent some detail in the pattern, whatever that pattern may be. Perhaps it is just his youth, and I am envious of the lithe body, the smooth skin, the animal energy and grace.

For a long time this morning I sat looking out to sea, trying to solve that small puzzle. Two white herons came and perched on a dead stump east of the garden. They stayed a long time there without stirring. I would turn my head away and accustom my eyes to the bright sea-horizon, then I would look suddenly at them to see if they had shifted position, but they would always be in the same attitude. I tried to imagine the black stump without them—a purely vegetable landscape—but it was impossible. All the while I was slowly forcing myself to accept a ridiculous explanation of my annoyance with Racky. It had made itself manifest to me only yesterday, when instead of appearing for lunch, he sent a young colored boy from Orange Walk to say that he would be lunching in the village. I could not help noticing that the boy was riding Racky's bicycle. I had been waiting lunch a good half hour for him, and I had Gloria serve immediately as the boy rode off, back to the village. I was curious to know in what sort of place and with whom Racky could be eating, since Orange Walk, as far as I know, is inhabited exclusively by Negroes, and I was sure Gloria would be able to shed some light on the matter, but I could scarcely ask her. However, as she brought on the dessert, I said: "Who was that boy that brought the message from Mister Racky?"

She shrugged her shoulders. "A young lad of Orange Walk. He's named Wilmot."

When Racky returned at dusk, flushed from his exertion (for he never rides casually), I watched him closely. His behavior struck my already suspicious eye as being one of false heartiness and a rather forced good humor. He went to his room early and read for quite a while before turning off his light. I took a long walk in the almost day-bright moonlight, listening to the songs of the night insects in the trees. And I sat for a while in the dark on the stone railing of the bridge across Black River. (It is really only a brook that rushes down over the rocks from the mountain a few miles inland, to the beach near the house.) In the night it always sounds louder and more important than it does in the daytime. The music of the water over the stones relaxed my nerves, although why I had need of such a thing I find it difficult to understand, unless I was really upset by Racky's not having come home for lunch. But if that were true it would be absurd, and moreover, dangerous—just the sort of the thing the parent of an adolescent has to beware of and fight against, unless he is indifferent to the prospect of losing the trust and affection of his offspring permanently. Racky must stay out whenever he likes, with whom he likes, and for as long as he likes, and I must not think twice about it, much less mention it to him, or in any way give the impression of prying. Lack of confidence on the part of a parent is the one unforgivable sin.

Although we still take our morning dip together on arising, it is three weeks since we have been for the early spin. One morning I found that Racky had jumped onto his bicycle in his wet trunks while I was still swimming, and gone by himself, and since then there has been an unspoken agreement between us that such is to be the procedure; he will go alone. Perhaps I held him back; he likes to ride so fast.

Young Peter, the smiling gardener from Saint Ives Cove, is Racky's special friend. It is amusing to see them together among the bushes, crouched over an ant-hill or rushing about trying to catch a lizard, almost of an age the two, yet so disparate—Racky with his tan skin looking almost white in contrast to the glistening black of the other. Today I know I shall be alone for lunch, since it is Peter's day off. On such days they usually go together on their bicycles into Saint Ives Cove, where Peter keeps a small rowboat. They fish along the coast there, but they have never returned with anything so far.

Meanwhile I am here alone, sitting on the rocks in the sun, from time to time climbing down to cool myself in the water, always conscious of the house behind me under the high palms, like a large glass boat filled with orchids and lilies. The servants are clean and quiet, and the work seems to be accomplished almost automatically. The good, black servants are another blessing of the islands; the British, born here in this paradise, have no conception of how fortunate they are. In fact, they do nothing but complain. One must have lived in the United States to appreciate the wonder of this place. Still, even here ideas are changing each day. Soon the people will decide that they want their land to be a part of today's monstrous world, and once that happens, it will be all over. As soon as you have that desire, you are infected with the deadly virus, and you begin to show the symptoms of the disease. You live in terms of time and money, and you think in terms of society and progress. Then all that is left for you is to kill the other people who think the same way, along with a good many of those who do not, since that is the final manifestation of the malady. Here for the moment at any rate, one has a feeling of staticity—existence ceases to be like those last few seconds in the hour-glass when what is left of the sand suddenly begins to rush through to the bottom all at once. For the moment, it seems suspended. And if it seems, it is. Each wave at my feet, each bird-call in the forest at my back, does *not* carry me one step nearer the final disaster. The disaster is certain, but it will suddenly have happened, that is all. Until then, time stays still.

I am upset by a letter in this morning's mail: The Royal Bank of Canada requests that I call in person at its central office to sign the deposit slips and other papers for a sum that was cabled from the bank in Boston. Since the central office is on the other side of the island, fifty miles away, I shall have to spend the night over there and return the following day. There is no point in taking Racky along. The sight of "civilization" might awaken a longing for it in him; one never knows. I am sure it would have in me when I was his age. And if that should once start, he would merely be unhappy, since there is nothing for him but to stay here with me, at least for the next two years, when I hope to renew the lease, or, if things in New York pick up, buy the place. I am sending word by Isiah when he goes home into Orange Walk this evening, to have the McCoigh car call for me at seven-thirty tomorrow morning. It is an enormous old open Packard, and Isiah can save the ride out to work here by piling his bicycle into the back and riding with McCoigh.

The trip across the island was beautiful, and would have been highly enjoyable if my imagination had not played me a strange trick at the very outset. We stopped in Orange Walk for gasoline, and while that was being seen to, I got out and went to the corner store for some cigarettes. Since it was not yet eight o'clock, the store was still closed, and I hurried up the side street to the other little shop which I thought might be open. It was, and I bought my cigarettes. On the way back to the corner I noticed a large black woman leaning with her arms on the gate in front of her tiny house, staring into the street. As I passed by her, she looked straight into my face and said something with the strange accent of the island. It was said in what seemed an unfriendly tone, and ostensibly was directed at me, but I had no notion what it was. I got back into the car and the driver started it. The sound of the words had stayed in my head, however, as a bright shape outlined by darkness is likely to stay in the mind's eye, in such a way that when one shuts one's eyes one can see the exact contour of the shape. The car was already roaring up the hill toward the overland road when I suddenly reheard the very words. And they were: "Keep your boy at home, mahn." I sat perfectly rigid for a moment as the open countryside rushed past. Why should I think she had said that? Immediately I decided that I was giving an arbitrary sense to a phrase I could not have understood even if I had been paying strict attention. And then I wondered why my subconscious should have chosen that sense, since now that I whispered the words over to myself they failed to connect with any anxiety to which my mind might have been disposed. Actually I have never given a thought to Racky's wanderings about Orange Walk. I can find no such preoccupation no matter how I put the question to myself. Then, could she really have said those words? All the way through the mountains I pondered the question, even though it was obviously a waste of energy. And soon I could no longer hear the sound of her voice in my memory: I had played the record over too many times, and worn it out.

Here in the hotel a gala dance is in progress. The abominable orchestra, comprising two saxophones and one sour violin, is playing directly under my window in the garden, and the serious-looking couples slide about on the waxed concrete floor of the terrace, in the light of strings of paper lanterns. I suppose it is meant to look Japanese.

At this moment I wonder what Racky is doing there in the house with only Peter and Ernest the watchman to keep him company. I wonder if he is asleep. The house, which I am accustomed to think of as smiling and benevolent in its airiness, could just as well be in the most sinister and remote regions of the globe, now that I am here. Sitting here with the absurd orchestra bleating downstairs, I picture it to myself, and it strikes me as terribly vulnerable in its isolation. In my mind's eye I see the moonlit point with its tall palms waving restlessly in the wind, its dark cliffs licked by the waves below. Suddenly, although I struggle against the sensation, I am inexpressibly glad to be away from the house, helpless there, far on its point of land, in the silence of the night. Then I remember that the night is seldom silent. There is the loud sea at the base of the rocks, the droning of the thousands of insects, the occasional cries of the night birds—all the familiar noises that make sleep so sound. And Racky is there surrounded by them as usual, not even hearing them. But I feel profoundly guilty for having left him, unutterably tender and sad at the thought of him, lying there alone in the house with the two Negroes the only human beings within miles. If I keep thinking of Cold Point I shall be more and more nervous.

I am not going to bed yet. They are all screaming with laughter down there, the idiots; I could never sleep anyway. The bar is still open. Fortunately it is on the street side of the hotel. For once I need a few drinks.

Much later, but I feel no better; I may be a little drunk. The dance is over and it is quiet in the garden, but the room is too hot.

As I was falling asleep last night, all dressed, and with the overhead light shining sordidly in my face, I heard the black woman's voice again, more clearly even than I did in the car yesterday. For some reason this morning there is no doubt in my mind that the words I heard are the words she said. I accept that and go on from there. Suppose she did tell me to keep Racky home. It could only mean that she, or someone else in Orange Walk, has had a childish altercation with him; although I must say it is hard to conceive of Racky's entering into any sort of argument or feud with those people. To set my mind at rest (for I do seem to be taking the whole thing with great seriousness), I am going to stop in the village this afternoon before going home, and try to see the woman. I am extremely curious to know what she could have meant.

I had not been conscious until this evening when I came back to Cold Point how powerful they are, all those physical elements that go to make up its atmosphere: the sea and wind-sounds that isolate the house from the road, the brilliancy of the water, sky and sun, the bright colors and strong odors of the flowers, the feeling of space both outside and within the house. One naturally accepts these things when one is living here. This afternoon when I returned I was conscious of them all over again, of their existence and their strength. All of them together are like a powerful drug; coming back made me feel as though I had been disintoxicated and were returning to the scene of my former indulgences. Now at eleven it is as if I had never been absent an hour. Everything is the same as always, even to the dry palm branch that scrapes against the window screen by my night table. And indeed, it is only thirty-six hours since I was here; but I always expect my absence from a place to bring about irremediable changes.

Strangely enough, now that I think of it, I feel that something *has* changed since I left yesterday morning, and that is the general attitude of the servants—their collective aura, so to speak. I noticed that difference immediately upon arriving back, but was unable to define it. Now I see it clearly. The network of common understanding which slowly spreads itself through a well-run household has been destroyed. Each person is by himself now. No unfriendliness, however, that I can see. They all behave with the utmost courtesy, excepting possibly Peter, who struck me as looking unaccustomedly glum when I encountered him in the kitchen after dinner. I meant to ask Racky if he had noticed it, but I forgot and he went to bed early.

In Orange Walk I made a brief stop on the pretext to McCoigh that I wanted to see the seamstress in the side street. I walked up and back in front of the house where I had seen the woman, but there was no sign of anyone.

As for my absence, Racky seems to have been perfectly content, having spent most of the day swimming off the rocks below the terrace. The insect sounds are at their height now, the breeze is cooler than usual, and I shall take advantage of these favorable conditions to get a good long night's rest.

Today has been one of the most difficult days of my life. I arose early, we had breakfast at the regular time, and Racky went off in the direction of Saint Ives Cove. I lay in the sun on the terrace for a while, listening to the noises of the household's regime. Peter was all over the property, collecting dead leaves and fallen blossoms in a huge basket and carrying them off to the compost heap. He appeared to be in an even fouler humor than last night. When he came near to me at one point on his way to another part of the garden I called to him. He set the basket down and stood looking at me; then he walked across the grass toward me slowly—reluctantly, it seemed to me.

"Peter, is everything all right with you?"

"Yes, sir."

"No trouble at home?"

"Oh, no, sir."

"Good."

"Yes, sir."

He went back to his work. But his face belied his words. Not only did he seem to be in a decidedly unpleasant temper; out here in the sunlight he looked positively ill. However, it was not my concern, if he refused to admit it.

When the heavy heat of the sun reached the unbearable point for me, I got out of my chair and went down the side of the cliff along the series of steps cut there into the rock. A level platform is below, and a diving board, for the water is deep. At each side, the rocks spread out and the waves break over them, but by the platform the wall of rock is vertical and the water merely hits against it below the springboard. The place is a tiny amphitheatre, quite cut off in sound and sight from the house. There too I like to lie in the sun; when I climb out of the water I often remove my trunks and lie stark naked on the springboard. I regularly make fun of Racky because he is embarrassed to do the same. Occasionally he will do it, but never without being coaxed. I was spread out there without a stitch on, being lulled by the slapping of the water, when an unfamiliar voice very close to me said: "Mister Norton?"

I jumped with nervousness, nearly fell off the springboard, and sat up, reaching at the same time, but in vain, for my trunks, which were lying on the rock practically at the feet of a middle-aged mulatto gentleman. He was in a white duck suit, and wore a high collar with a black tie, and it seemed to me that he was eyeing me with a certain degree of horror.

My next reaction was one of anger at being trespassed upon in this way. I rose and got the trunks, however, donning them calmly and saying nothing more meaningful than: "I didn't hear you come down the steps."

"Shall we go up?" said my caller. As he led the way, I had a definite premonition that he was here on an unpleasant errand. On the terrace we sat down, and he offered me an American cigarette which I did not accept.

"This is a delightful spot," he said, glancing out to sea and then at the end of his cigarette, which was only partially aglow. He puffed at it.

I said, "Yes," waiting for him to go on; presently he did.

"I am from the constabulary of this parish. The police, you see." And seeing my face, "This is a friendly call. But still it must be taken as a warning, Mister Norton. It is very serious. If anyone else comes to you about this it will mean trouble for you, heavy trouble. That's why I want to see you privately this way and warn you personally. You see."

I could not believe I was hearing his words. At length I said faintly: "But what about?"

"This is not an official call. You must not be upset. I have taken it upon myself to speak to you because I want to save you deep trouble."

"But I *am* upset!" I cried, finding my voice at last. "How can I help being upset, when I don't know what you're talking about?"

He moved his chair close to mine, and spoke in a very low voice.

"I have waited until the young man was away from the house so we could talk in private. You see, it is about him."

Somehow that did not surprise me. I nodded.

"I will tell you very briefly. The people here are simple country folk. They make trouble easily. Right now they are all talking about the young man you have living here with you. He is your son, I hear." His inflection here was sceptical.

"Certainly he's my son."

His expression did not change, but his voice grew indignant. "Whoever he is, that is a bad young man."

"What do you mean?" I cried, but he cut in hotly: "He may be your son; he may not be. I don't care who he is. That is not my affair. But he is bad through and through. We don't have such things going on here, sir. The people in Orange Walk and Saint Ives Cove are very cross now. You don't know what these folk do when they are aroused."

I thought it my turn to interrupt. "Please tell me why you say my son is bad. What has he done?" Perhaps the earnestness in my voice reached him, for his face assumed a gentler aspect. He leaned still closer to me and almost whispered.

"He has no shame. He does what he pleases with all the young boys, and the men too, and gives them a shilling so they won't tell about it. But they talk. Of course they talk. Every man for twenty miles up and down the coast knows about it. And the women too, they know about it." There was a silence.

I had felt myself preparing to get to my feet for the last few seconds because I wanted to go into my room and be alone, to get away from that scandalized stage whisper. I think I mumbled "Good morning" or "Thank you," as I turned away and began walking toward the house. But he was still beside me, still whispering like an eager conspirator into my ear: "Keep him home, Mister Norton. Or send him away to school, if he is your son. But make him stay out of these towns. For his own sake."

I shook hands with him and went to lie on my bed. From there I heard his car door slam, heard him drive off. I was painfully trying to formulate an opening sentence to use in speaking to Racky about this, feeling that the opening sentence would define my stand. The attempt was merely a sort of therapeutic action, to avoid thinking about the thing itself. Every attitude seemed impossible. There was no way to broach the subject. I suddenly realized that I should never be able to speak to him directly about it. With the advent of this news he had become another person—an adult, mysterious and formidable. To be sure, it did occur to me that the mulatto's story might not be true, but automatically I rejected the doubt. It was as if I wanted to believe it, almost as if I had already known it, and he had merely confirmed it.

Racky returned at midday, panting and grinning. The inevitable comb appeared and was used on the sweaty, unruly locks. Sitting down to lunch, he exclaimed: "Gosh! Did I find a swell beach this morning! But what a job to get to it!" I tried to look unconcerned as I met his gaze; it was as if our positions had been reversed, and I were hoping to stem his rebuke. He prattled on about thorns and vines and his machete. Throughout the meal I kept telling myself: "Now is the moment. You must say something." But all I said was: "More salad? Or do you want dessert now?" So the lunch passed and nothing happened. After I had finished my coffee I went into my bedroom and looked at myself in the large mirror. I saw my eyes trying to give their reflected brothers a little courage. As I stood there I heard a commotion in the other wing of the house: voices, bumpings, the sound of a scuffle. Above the noise came Gloria's sharp voice, imperious and excited: "No, mahn! Don't strike him!" And louder: "Peter, mahn, no!"

I went quickly toward the kitchen, where the trouble seemed to be, but on the way I was run into by Racky, who staggered into the hallway with his hands in front of his face.

"What is it, Racky?" I cried.

He pushed past me into the living room without moving his hands away from his face; I turned and followed him. From there he went into his own room, leaving the door open behind him. I heard him in his bathroom running the water. I was undecided what to do. Suddenly Peter appeared in the hall doorway, his hat in his hand. When he raised his head, I was surprised to see that his cheek was bleeding. In his eyes was a strange, confused expression of transient fear and deep hostility. He looked down again.

"May I please talk with you, sir?"

"What was all the racket? What's been happening?"

"May I talk with you outside, sir?" He said it doggedly, still not looking up.

In view of the circumstances, I humored him. We walked slowly up the cinder road to the main highway, across the bridge, and through the forest while he told me his story. I said nothing.

At the end he said: "I never wanted to, sir, even the first time, but after the first time I was afraid, and Mister Racky was after me every day."

I stood still, and finally said: "If you had only told me this the first time it happened, it would have been much better for everyone."

He turned his hat in his hands, studying it intently. "Yes, sir. But I didn't know what everyone was saying about him in Orange Walk until today. You know I always go to the beach at Saint Ives Cove with Mister Racky on my free days. If I had known what they were all saying I wouldn't have been afraid, sir. And I wanted to keep on working here. I needed the money." Then he repeated what he had already said three times. "Mister Racky said you'd see about it that I was put in the jail. I'm a year older than Mister Racky, sir."

"I know, I know," I said impatiently; and deciding that severity was what Peter expected of me at this point I added: "You had better get your things together and go home. You can't work here any longer, you know."

The hostility in his face assumed terrifying proportions as he said: "If you killed me I would not work any more at Cold Point, sir."

I turned and walked briskly back to the house, leaving him standing there in the road. It seems he returned at dusk, a little while ago, and got his belongings.

In his room Racky was reading. He had stuck some adhesive tape on his chin and over his cheekbone.

"I've dismissed Peter," I announced. "He hit you, didn't he?"

He glanced up. His left eye was swollen, but not yet black.

"He sure did. But I landed him one, too. And I guess I deserved it anyway."

I rested against the table. "Why?" I asked nonchalantly.

"Oh, I had something on him from a long time back that he was afraid I'd tell you."

"And just now you threatened to tell me?"

"Oh, no! He said he was going to quit the job here, and I kidded him about being yellow."

"Why did he want to quit? I thought he liked the job."

"Well, he did, I guess, but he didn't like me." Racky's candid gaze betrayed a shade of pique. I still leaned against the table.

I persisted. "But I thought you two got on fine together. You seemed to."

"Nah. He was just scared of losing his job. I had something on him. He was a good guy, though; I liked him all right." He paused. "Has he gone yet?" A strange quaver crept into his voice as he said the last words, and I understood that for the first time Racky's heretofore impeccable histrionics were not quite equal to the occasion. He was very much upset at losing Peter.

"Yes, he's gone," I said shortly. "He's not coming back, either." And as Racky, hearing the unaccustomed inflection in my voice, looked up at me suddenly with faint astonishment in his young eyes, I realized that this was the moment to press on, to say: "What did you have on him?" But as if he had arrived at the same spot in my mind a fraction of a second earlier, he proceeded to snatch away my advantage by jumping up, bursting into loud song, and pulling off all his clothes simultaneously. As he stood before me naked, singing at the top of his lungs, and stepped into his swimming trunks, I was conscious that again I should be incapable of saying to him what I must say.

He was in and out of the house all afternoon: some of the time he read in his room, and most of the time he was down on the diving board. It is strange behavior for him; if I could only know what is in his mind. As evening approached, my problem took on a purely obsessive character. I walked to and fro in my room, always pausing at one end to look out the window over the sea, and at the other end to glance at my face in the mirror. As if that could help me! Then I took a drink. And another. I thought I might be able to do it at dinner, when I felt fortified by the whisky. But no. Soon he will have gone to bed. It is not that I expect to confront him with any accusations. That I know I never can do. But I must find a way to keep him from his wanderings, and I must offer a reason to give him, so that he will never suspect that I know.

We fear for the future of our offspring. It is ludicrous, but only a little more palpably so than anything else in life. A length of time has passed; days which I am content to have known, even if now they are over. I think that this period was what I had always been waiting for life to offer, the recompense I had unconsciously but firmly expected, in return for having been held so closely in the grip of existence all these years.

That evening seems long ago only because I have recalled its details so many times that they have taken on the color of legend. Actually my problem already had been solved for me then, but I did not know it. Because I could not perceive the pattern, I foolishly imagined that I must cudgel my brains to find the right words with which to approach Racky. But it was he who came to me. That same evening, as I was about to go out for a solitary stroll which I thought might help me hit upon a formula, he appeared at my door.

"Going for a walk?" he asked, seeing the stick in my hand.

The prospect of making an exit immediately after speaking with him made things seem simpler. "Yes," I said, "But I'd like to have a word with you first."

"Sure. What?" I did not look at him because I did not want to see the watchful light I was sure was playing in his eyes at this moment. As I spoke I tapped with my stick along the designs made by the tiles in the floor. "Racky, would you like to go back to school?"

"Are you kidding? You know I hate school."

I glanced up at him. "No, I'm not kidding. Don't look so horrified. You'd probably enjoy being with a bunch of fellows your own age." (That was not one of the arguments I had meant to use.)

"I might like to be with guys my own age, but I don't want to have to be in school to do it. I've had school enough."

I went to the door and said lamely: "I thought I'd get your reactions."

He laughed. "No, thanks."

"That doesn't mean you're not going," I said over my shoulder as I went out.

On my walk I pounded the highway's asphalt with my stick, stood on the bridge having dramatic visions which involved such eventualities as our moving back to the States, Racky's having a bad spill on his bicycle and being paralyzed for some months, and even the possibility of my letting events take their course, which would doubtless mean my having to visit him now and then in the governmental prison with gifts of food, if it meant nothing more tragic and violent. "But none of these things will happen," I said to myself, and I knew I was wasting precious time; he must not return to Orange Walk tomorrow.

I went back toward the point at a snail's pace. There was no moon and very little breeze. As I approached the house, trying to tread lightly on the cinders so as not to awaken the watchful Ernest and have to explain to him that it was only I, I saw that there were no lights in Racky's room. The house was dark save for the dim lamp on my night table. Instead of going in, I skirted the entire building, colliding with bushes and getting my face sticky with spider webs, and went to sit a while on the terrace where there seemed to be a breath of air. The sound of the sea was far out on the reef, where the breakers sighed. Here below, there were only slight watery chugs and gurgles now and then. It was unusually low tide. I smoked three cigarettes mechanically, having ceased even to think, and then, my mouth tasting bitter from the smoke, I went inside.

My room was airless. I flung my clothes onto a chair and looked at the night table to see if the carafe of water was there. Then my mouth opened. The top sheet of my bed had been stripped back to the foot. There on the far side of the bed, dark against the whiteness of the lower sheet, lay Racky asleep on his side, and naked.

I stood looking at him for a long time, probably holding my breath, for I remember feeling a little dizzy at one point. I was whispering to myself, as my eyes followed the curve of his arm, shoulder, back, thigh, leg: "A child. A child." Destiny, when one perceives it clearly from very near, has no qualities at all. The recognition of it and the consciousness of the vision's clarity leave no room on the mind's horizon. Finally I turned off the light and softly lay down. The night was absolutely black.

He lay perfectly quiet until dawn. I shall never know whether or not he was really asleep all that time. Of course he couldn't have been, and yet he lay so still. Warm and firm, but still as death. The darkness and silence were heavy around us. As the birds began to sing, I sank into a soft, enveloping slumber; when I awoke in the sunlight later, he was gone.

I found him down by the water, cavorting alone on the springboard; for the first time he had discarded his trunks without my suggesting it. All day we stayed together around the terrace and on the rocks, talking, swimming, reading, and just lying flat in the hot sun. Nor did he return to his room when night came. Instead after the servants were asleep, we brought three bottles of champagne in and set the pail on the night table.

Thus it came about that I was able to touch on the delicate subject that still preoccupied me, and profiting by the new understanding between us, I made my request in the easiest, most natural fashion.

"Racky, would you do me a tremendous favor if I asked you?"

He lay on his back, his hands beneath his head. It seemed to me his regard was circumspect, wanting in candor.

"I guess so," he said. "What is it?"

"Will you stay around the house for a few days—a week, say? Just to please me? We can take some rides together, as far as you like. Would you do that for me?"

"Sure thing," he said, smiling.

I was temporizing, but I was desperate.

Perhaps a week later—(it is only when one is not fully happy that one is meticulous about time, so that it may have been more or less)—we were having breakfast. Isiah stood by, in the shade, waiting to pour us more coffee.

"I noticed you had a letter from Uncle Charley the other day," said Racky. "Don't you think we ought to invite him down?"

My heart began to beat with great force.

"Here? He'd hate it here," I said casually. "Besides, there's no room. Where would he sleep?" Even as I heard myself saying the words, I knew that they were the wrong ones, that I was not really participating in the conversation. Again I felt the fascination of complete helplessness that comes when one is suddenly a conscious on-looker at the shaping of one's fate.

"In my room," said Racky. "It's empty."

I could see more of the pattern at that moment than I had ever suspected existed. "Nonsense," I said. "This is not the sort of place for Uncle Charley."

Racky appeared to be hitting on an excellent idea. "Maybe if I wrote and invited him," he suggested, motioning to Isiah for more coffee.

"Nonsense," I said again, watching still more of the pattern reveal itself, like a photographic print becoming constantly clearer in a tray of developing solution.

Isiah filled Racky's cup and returned to the shade. Racky drank slowly, pretending to be savoring the coffee.

"Well, it won't do any harm to try. He'd appreciate the invitation," he said speculatively.

For some reason, at this juncture I knew what to say, and as I said it, I knew what I was going to do.

"I thought we might fly over to Havana for a few days next week."

He looked guardedly interested, and then he broke into a wide grin. "Swell!" he cried. "Why wait till next week?"

The next morning the servants called "Good-bye" to us as we drove up the cinder road in the McCoigh car. We took off from the airport at six that evening. Racky was in high spirits; he kept the stewardess engaged in conversation all the way to Camagüey.

He was delighted also with Havana. Sitting in the bar at the Nacional, we continued to discuss the possibility of having C. pay us a visit at the island. It was not without difficulty that I eventually managed to persuade Racky that writing him would be inadvisable.

We decided to look for an apartment right there in Vedado for Racky. He did not seem to want to come back here to Cold Point. We also decided that living in Havana he would need a larger income than I. I am already having the greater part of Hope's estate transferred to his name in the form of a trust fund which I shall administer until he is of age. It was his mother's money, after all.

We bought a new convertible, and he drove me out to Rancho Boyeros in it when I took my plane. A Cuban named Claudio with very white teeth, whom Racky had met in the pool that morning, sat between us.

We were waiting in front of the landing field. An official finally unhooked the chain to let the passengers through. "If you get fed up, come to Havana," said Racky, pinching my arm.

The two of them stood together behind the rope, waving to me, their shirts flapping in the wind as the plane started to move.

The wind blows by my head; between each wave there are thousands of tiny licking and chopping sounds as the water hurries out of the crevices and holes; and a part-floating, part-submerged feeling of being in the water haunts my mind even as the hot sun burns my face. I sit here and I read, and I wait for the pleasant feeling of repletion that follows a good meal, to turn slowly, as the hours pass along, into the even more delightful, slightly stirring sensation deep within, which accompanies the awakening of the appetite.

I am perfectly happy here in reality, because I still believe that nothing very drastic is likely to befall this part of the island in the near future.

MS Ferncape
(*New York-Casablanca*)
1947

How Many Midnights

How many midnights, she wondered, had she raised the shade, opened the big window, and leaned out to gaze across the gently stirring city toward the highest towers? Over there behind a certain unmistakable group of them was his building, and at the very top of the building was his apartment, six flights up. In the summer she would look out over the rooftops at some length and sigh, and during the hottest weeks she moved her bed over, directly under the window. Then she would turn off all the lights and sit on the bed combing her hair in the glowing dimness of the city night, or sometimes even by moonlight, which of course was perfect. In the winter however she had to content herself with a moment of looking and a flash of imagining before she bounded across the room into bed.

It was winter now. She was walking crosstown, east, along one of the late Forties. This part of town always had seemed vaguely mysterious to her because of its specially constructed buildings that did not quite touch the pavement. All the buildings just north of the Grand Central were built that way, to absorb the shock, Van had told her; and there were long stretches of grillwork in the sidewalks through which, particularly at night, one could see another world beneath: railway tracks and sometimes a slowly moving train. When it snowed, as it was doing now, the snow filtered down through the grills and covered the ties; then they were even more apparent.

Van worked here in this neighborhood: he was manager of a large bookshop and lending library on Madison Avenue. And he lived in the neighborhood as well, only farther over east, between Third and Second Avenues. His place was not ideal, either as to actual physical comfort or as to locality (since the immediate district was clearly a slum), but with her help he had made it livable, and she used to tell him: "New York and Paris are like that: no clear demarcation of neighborhoods."

In any case, they already had signed a sublease for a place near Gramercy Park which was to be free the first of March. This was of prime importance because they planned to marry on Valentine's Day. They were by no means sentimental souls, either one of them, and for that very reason it seemed to June a little daring to announce to their friends during cocktails: "It's to be Valentine's Day."

Her father, who always was to be counted on to do the thoughtful thing, was staking them to two weeks in Bermuda. "God knows why," Van said. "He hates my guts."

"I don't know how you can say a thing like that about Dad," objected June. "He's never been anything but the essence of politeness with you."

"That's right," said Van, but impenitently.

She crossed Lexington Avenue. The entire sky looked as though it were being illumined from above by gray-violet neons. The tops of the buildings were lost in the cloud made by the falling snow. And the harbor sounds, instead of coming from the river ahead, came from above, as if the tugs were making their careful way around the tips of the towers. "This is the way New York was meant to be," she thought—not the crowded fire-escape, open-hydrant, sumac-leaved summer. Just this quiet, damp, neutral weather when the water seemed all around. She stood still a moment in the middle of the block, listening to the fog horns; there was a whole perspective of them. In the remotest background was a very faint, smothered one that said: "Mmmmm! Mmmmm!" "It must be on the Sound," she thought. She started to walk again.

In her coat pocket she had the keys, because this was to be a special night. Not that there had been any overt reference to that: there was no need for it. It had been implicit in their conversation yesterday afternoon when she had stopped in at the bookshop to see him. They had stood a few minutes talking in the back of the store among the desks, and then he had slipped her the keys. That was surely the most exciting single thing that ever had happened between them—the passage of the keys from his hand to hers. By the gesture he gave up what she knew was most dear to him: his privacy. She did not want him to think that she was in any way unaware of this, and she said in a low voice: "You can trust me with them, I think," laughing immediately afterward so that her remark should not sound ridiculous. He had kissed her and they had gone out for ten minutes to have coffee.

Sitting at the counter he had told how he had caught a man stealing books the night before. (The bookshop was open at night; because of the location it seemed they did almost as much business in the evening as they did during the day.) Van had just finished arranging a display of new books in one of the show windows, and was standing outside in the street looking in. He had noticed a man wearing a long overcoat, standing by the technical books. "I had my eye on him from the beginning. It's a type, you know. You get to spot them. He looked at me right through the window. I suppose he thought I was just another man in the street. I had on *my* overcoat, too." And the man had taken a quick glance around the store to be sure that no one was watching him, had reached up, snatched down a book and dropped it inside his coat. Van had gone quickly to the corner, tapped the traffic policeman on the shoulder and said: "Would you mind coming into my store for a minute? I want you to arrest a man." They had caught him, and when they had opened his coat they found he already had taken three books.

Van always said: "You see some funny things in a bookshop," and often they were really funny. But this story struck June as remotely sinister rather than amusing. Not because it had to do with a theft, certainly. It was not the first case of booklifting he had related to her. Perhaps it was because more than anything else she hated being watched behind her back, and involuntarily she put herself in the place of the thief, with whom she felt that Van had not been quite fair. It seemed to her that he might have gone in and said to him: "I've been watching you. I've seen everything you've been doing. Now, I give you one last chance. Put back whatever you've taken and get the hell out, and don't come back in here." To spring on the man out of the dark after spying on him did seem a little unfair. But she knew she was being absurd. Van could never be unfair with anyone; this was his way of handling the affair, and it was typical of him: he never would argue. She never knew even when he was angry with her until after it was all over, and he told her, smiling: "Gee, I was burned up last Friday."

She crossed Third Avenue. Up to now the snow had been melting as fast as it fell, but the air was getting colder, and the sidewalk began to show silver. The keys jingled in her coat pocket; she pulled off her glove and felt for them. They also were cold. When she had left her house, she had said to her parents: "I'm going out with Van. I'll probably be rather late." They had merely said: "Yes." But she thought she had intercepted a look of mutual understanding between them. It was all right: in ten more days they would be married. She had climbed up the six steep flights of stairs on a good many evenings during the past two years, just to spend an hour or so with him, but never, she reflected with an obscure sort of pride, had anything ever occurred between them which was not what her parents would call "honorable."

She had arrived at the apartment house; it had a gray-stone façade and a good deal of wrought iron around the entrance door. A woman who looked like a West Indian of some sort came out. Noticing that June was carrying a potted plant under her arm, she held the door partially open for her. June thanked her and went in. It was a rubber plant she had bought for Van's apartment. He was inclined to be indifferent about flowers, and, she feared, about decoration in general. She always had hoped to develop aesthetic appreciation in him, and she considered that she had made re-markable progress during the past year. Practically all the adornments in his apartment were objects either of her buying or her choosing.

She knew just how many steps there were to each flight of stairs: nineteen for the first and fifteen for the others. The halls were tiled in black and white, like a bathroom, and tonight, to add to that impression, the stairs and floors were thoroughly wet with the melting snow people had tracked in; the air smelled of wet doormats, wet rubbers, wet clothing. On the third floor a huge perambulator of black leatherette nearly blocked the passage-way between the stairs. She frowned at it and thought of the fire regula-tions.

Because she did not want to be out of breath she mounted the stairs slowly. Not that Van would be there when she arrived—it was still too early—but being out of breath always created in her a false kind of excite-ment which she particularly wanted to avoid tonight. She turned the key in the lock and stepped inside. It gave her a strange sensation to push open the door all by herself and stand there in the hall alone, smelling the special odor of the place: an amalgam in which she imagined she detected furniture polish, shaving cream and woodsmoke. Woodsmoke there surely was, because he had a fireplace. It was she who had persuaded him to have it installed. And it had not been nearly so expensive to build as he had imagined it was going to be, because since this was the top floor the chimney had only to be built up through the roof. Many times he had said to her: "That was one sensible idea you had," as though the others had not been just as good! They had cut down the legs of all the living-room furniture so that it nestled nearer the floor and made the room seem spacious; they had painted each wall a different shade of gray, adding the occasional wall brackets of ivy; they had bought the big glass coffee table. All these things had made the place pleasanter, and they had all been her ideas.

She shut the door and went into the kitchen. It was a little chilly in the apartment; she lit the gas oven. Then she unwrapped the wet brown paper from around the rubber plant, and set the pot upright on the table. The plant leaned somewhat to one side. She tried to make it stand straight, but it would not. The icebox motor was purring. She took out two trays of ice and dumped the cubes into a bowl. Reaching up to the top shelf of the cabinet she brought down an almost full bottle of Johnny Walker, and set it, along with two highball glasses, onto the big lacquer tray. The room suddenly seemed terribly close; she turned off the oven. Then she scurried about looking for newspapers with which to lay a fire. There were only a few, but she found some old magazines in the kitchen. She rolled the newspapers into thin little logs and set them at various angles across the andirons. Underneath she pushed crumpled pages of the magazines, and on top she put what kindling wood there was. The logs she decided to leave until the kindling already was burning. When the fire was laid, but not lighted, she looked out the window. The snow was coming down thicker than it had been when she came in. She drew the heavy woolen curtains; they covered one entire wall, and they too had been her idea. Van had wanted to have Venetian blinds made. She had tried to make him see how hideous they would be, but although he had agreed that the black-and-white curtains were smart, he never would admit that Venetian blinds were ugly. "Maybe you're right, for this room," he said. "For every room in the world," she had wanted to declare, but she decided against it, since after all, he had given in.

It wasn't that Van had really bad taste. He had an innate sensitivity and a true intelligence which became manifest whenever he talked about the books he had read (and he read a good many during odd moments at the bookshop). But his aesthetic sense had never been fully awakened. Naturally she never mentioned it—she merely made small suggestions which he was free to take or to leave as he saw fit. And usually, if she let her little hints fall at strategic moments, he would take them.

On the mantel were two enormous plaster candelabra covered with angels; she had brought them herself all the way from Matamoros Izúcar in Mexico. Actually she had packed six of them, and all had broken except these two which did not quite match, one of them being somewhat taller than the other. (These were among the few things about which Van was still a bit recalcitrant: he could not be sure he liked them, even yet.) Each one held six candles. She went to a drawer in the desk and got out a dozen long yellow tapers. Often she brought him a dozen at a time. "Where am I supposed to put the damned things?" he would complain. She got a knife from the kitchen and began to scrape the bottoms of the candles to make them fit the holders. "In the middle of this operation he's going to arrive," she said to herself. She wanted the place to be perfect before he got there. Nervously she tossed the paraffin scrapings into the fireplace. She had a feeling that he would not just come up; it would be more like him to ring from the vestibule downstairs. At least, she hoped he would do that. The time it would take him to get up the six flights might make a great difference in the way the room would look. She fitted the last candle into the bright holder and sighed with relief. They were slow-burning ones; she decided to light them now before returning the candelabra to the mantel. Up there they looked beautiful. She stepped back to admire their splendor, and for a moment watched the slowly moving interplay of shadows on the wall. She switched off the electric lights in the room. With the fireplace aglow the effect would be breathtaking.

Impetuously she determined to do a very daring thing. It might possibly annoy Van when he first saw it, but she would do it anyway. She rushed to the other side of the room and feverishly began to push the divan across the floor toward the fireplace. It would be so snug to be right in front of the blaze, especially with the snow outside. The cushions fell off and a caster got entangled with the long wool of the goatskin rug she had given him for his birthday. She got the rug out of the way and continued to manipulate the divan. It looked absurd out there in the middle of the room, and she swung one end around so that it lay at right angles to the fireplace, against the wall. After she had piled the cushions back she stepped aside to observe it, and decided to leave it there. Then the other pieces had to be arranged. The whole room was in disorder at this point.

"I know he's going to open that door this minute," she thought. She turned the overhead light back on and quickly began to shift chairs, lamps and tables. The last piece to be moved was a small commode that she had once helped him sandpaper. As she carried it across the room its one little drawer slid out and fell on the floor. All the letters Van had received in the past months were there, lying in a fairly compact heap at her feet. "Damnation!" she said aloud, and as she said it, the hideous metallic sound of the buzzer in the kitchen echoed through the apartment. She let go of the commode and rushed out to press the button that opened the door downstairs onto the street. Then, without pressing it, she ran back into the living room and knelt on the floor, quickly gathering up the letters and dumping them into the drawer. But they had been piled carefully into that small space before the accident, and now they were not; as a result the drawer was overfull and would not close. Again she spoke aloud. "Oh, my God!" she said. And she said that because for no reason at all it had occurred to her that Van might think she had been reading his correspondence. The main thing now was to get the commode over into the corner; then she might be able to force the drawer shut. As she lifted it, the buzzer pealed again, with insistence. She ran into the kitchen, and this time pressed the answer button with all her might. Swiftly she hurried back and carried the commode into the corner. Then she tried to close the drawer and found it an impossibility. In a burst of inspiration she turned the little piece of furniture around so that the drawer opened toward the wall. She stepped to the fireplace and touched a match to the paper logs. By now he would got only about to the fourth floor; there were three more.

She turned off the lights once again, went into the hall and looked at herself briefly in the mirror, put out the light there, and moved toward the entrance door. With her hand on the knob, she held her breath, and found that her heart was beating much too fast. It was just what she had not wanted. She had hoped to have him step into a little world of absolute calm. And now because of that absurd drawer she was upset. Or perhaps it was the dragging around of all that furniture. She opened the door a crack and listened. A second later she stepped out into the hall, and again she listened. She walked to the stairs. "Van?" she called, and immediately she was furious with herself.

A man's voice answered from two floors below. "Riley?" he yelled.

"What?" she cried.

"I'm looking for Riley."

"You've rung the wrong bell," she shouted, enunciating the words very distinctly in spite of her raised voice.

She went in and shut the door, holding onto the knob and leaning her forehead against the panel for a moment. Now her heart was beating even more violently. She returned to the commode in the corner. "I might as well fix it once and for all right now," she thought. Otherwise her mind would be on it every instant. She turned it around, took out all the letters and carefully replaced them in four equal piles. Even then the drawer shut with difficulty, but it did close. When that was done, she went to the window and pulled back the curtain. It seemed to be growing much colder. The wind had risen; it was blowing from the east. The sky was no longer violet. It was black. She could see the snow swirling past the street lamp below. She wondered if it were going to turn into a blizzard. Tomorrow was Sunday; she simply would stay on. There would be a terrible moment in the morning, of course, when her parents arose and found she had not come in, but she would not be there to see it, and she could make it up with them later. And what an ideal little vacation it would make: a night and day up there in the snow, isolated from everything, shut away from everyone but Van. As she watched the street, she gradually became convinced that the storm would last all night. She looked back into the room. It gave her keen pleasure to contrast its glow with the hostile night outside. She let the curtain fall and went to the fireplace. The kindling was at the height of its blazing and there was no more; she piled two small logs on top of it. Soon they were crackling with such energy that she thought it wise to put the screen across in front of them. She sat on the divan looking at her legs in the blended firelight and candleglow. Smiling, she leaned back against the cushions. Her heart was no longer racing. She felt almost calm. The wind whined outside; to her it was inevitably a melancholy sound. Even tonight.

Suddenly she decided that it would be inexcusable not to let her parents know she was staying the night. She went into the bedroom and lay on the bed, resting the telephone on her stomach. It moved ridiculously while she dialed. Her mother, not her father, answered. "Thank God," she said to herself, and she let her head fall back upon the pillows. Her mother had been asleep; she did not sound too pleased to have been called to the telephone. "You're all right, I hope," she said. They spoke of the storm. "Yes, it's awful out," said June. "Oh, no, I'm at Van's. We have a fire. I'm going to stay. All night." There was a short silence. "Well, I think you're very foolish," she heard her mother say. And she went on. June let her talk a bit. Then she interrupted, letting a note of impatience sound in her voice. "I can't very well discuss it now. You understand." Her mothers's voice was shrill. "No, I *don't* understand!" she cried. She was taking it more seriously than June had expected. "I can't talk now," said June. "I'll see you tomorrow." She said good night and hung up, lying perfectly still for a moment. Then she lifted the telephone and set it on the night table, but still she did not move. When she had heard herself say: "We have a fire," a feeling of dread had seized her. It was as if in giving voice to the pretense she thereby became conscious of it. Van had not yet arrived; why then had she taken care to speak as though he had? She could only have been trying to reassure herself. Again her heart had begun to beat heavily. And finally she did what she had been trying not even to think of doing ever since she had arrived: she looked at her watch.

It was a little after midnight. There was absolutely no doubt about it; already he was quite late. He no longer could arrive without going into explanations. Something must have happened, and it only could be something bad. "Ridiculous!" she cried in anger, jumping up and going out into the kitchen. The ice cubes had melted a good deal; she poured the cold water into the sink between her spread fingers, and shook the cubes around the bowl petulantly, trying to stem the resentment she felt rising up inside her. "It will be interesting to know what his excuse will be," she said to herself. She decided that when he arrived her only possible behavior would be to pretend not to have noticed his lateness.

She dropped some of the ice cubes into one of the glasses, poured in some Scotch, stirred it, and went into the living room with it. The fire was burning triumphantly; the whole room danced in flamelight. She sat on the couch and downed her drink, a little too quickly for a young woman completely at her ease, which was what she was trying to be. When she had finished the last drop, she forced herself to sit without moving for ten minutes by her watch. Then she went out and made herself another drink, a little stronger. This one she drank walking thoughtfully around and around the center of the room. She was fighting against an absurd impulse to put on her coat and go into the street to look for him. "Old woman," she said to herself. Old people always had that reaction—they always expected tragedies. As she came to the end of her second drink she succeeded in convincing herself that the mathematical probabilities of Van's having met with his first serious accident on this particular evening were extremely slight. This moral certitude engendered a feeling of lightheartedness, which expressed itself in the desire for a third drink. She had only just begun this one when an even sharper anguish seized her. If it was not likely that he had had an accident, it was utterly unthinkable that he should have let some unforeseen work detain him until this late; he would have telephoned her anyway. It was even more inconceivable that their rendezvous should have slipped his mind. The final, remaining possibility therefore was that he had deliberately avoided it, which of course was absurd. She tossed another log onto the fire. Again she went to the window and peered between the curtains down into the empty street. The wind had become a gale. She felt each blast against her face through the closed window. Listening for sounds of traffic, she heard none; even the boats seemed to have been silenced. Only the rushing of the wind was left—that and the occasional faint hissing of the fine snow against the glass. She burst into tears; she did not know whether it was out of self-pity, anger and humiliation, loneliness, or just plain nervousness.

As she stood there in the window with the tears covering her sight, it occurred to her how ironic it would be if he should come and find her like this: slightly drunk, sobbing, with her make-up surely in a state of complete ruin. A sound behind her ended her weeping instantly. She let go of the curtain and turned to face the room: through her tears she could see nothing but quivering webs of light. She squeezed her lids tightly together: one of the logs had broken in two. The smaller half lay on the hearth smoking. She went over and kicked it into the fire. Then she tiptoed into the hall to the entrance door and slipped the chain on. As soon as she had done that she was terrified. It was nothing less than a symbol of fear—she realized it as she looked at the brass links stretching across from jamb to door. But once having put it up, she did not have the courage to take it down again.

Still on tiptoe, she returned to the living room and lay on the divan, burying her face in the cushions. She was not crying any longer—she felt too empty and frightened to do anything but lie quite still. But after a while she sat up and looked slowly about the room. The candles had burned down half way; she looked at them, at the ivy trailing down from the little pots on the wall, at the white goatskin by her feet, at the striped curtains. They were all hers. "Van, Van," she said under her breath. Unsteadily she rose and made her way to the bathroom. The glaring light hurt her eyes. Hanging on the inside of the door was Van's old flannel bathrobe. It was too big for her, but she got into it and rolled the sleeves back, turning up the collar and pulling the belt tightly about her waist. In the living room she lay down again on the divan among the cushions. From time to time she rubbed her cheek against the wool of the sleeve under her face. She stared into the fire.

Van was in the room. It was daylight out—a strange gray dawn. She sat up, feeling light-headed. "Van," she said. He was moving slowly across the floor toward the window. And the curtains had been drawn back. There was the rectangle of dim white sky, with Van going toward it. She called to him again. If he heard her he paid no attention. She sat back, watching. Now and then he shook his head slowly from side to side; the gesture made her feel like crying again, but not for herself this time. It was quite natural that he should be there, shuffling slowly across the room in the pale early light, shaking his head from one side to the other. Suddenly she said to herself that he was looking for something, that he might find it, and she began to shiver sitting up there in the cold. "He *has* found it," she thought, "but he's pretending he hasn't because he knows I'm watching him." And even as the idea formed itself in her mind she saw him reach up and swing himself through the window. She screamed, jumped down from the couch and ran across the room. When she got to the window there was nothing to see but the vast gray panorama of a city at dawn, spitefully clear in every tiniest detail. She stood there looking out, seeing for miles up and down the empty streets. Or were they canals? It was a foreign city.

The sputtering of a candle as it went out roused her. Several of them had already burned out. The shadows on the ceiling were wavering like bats. The room was cold and the curtains across the closed window moved inward with the force of the wind. She lay perfectly still. In the fireplace she heard the powdery, faintly metallic sound of a cooling ember as it fell. For a long time she remained unmoving. Then she sprang up, turned on all the lights, went into the bedroom and stood for a moment looking at the telephone. The sight of it calmed her a little. She took off the bathrobe and opened the closet door to hang it up. She knew his luggage by heart; his small overnight valise was missing. Slowly her mouth opened. She did not think to put her hand over it.

She slipped on her coat and unhooked the chain on the entrance door. The hall outside was full of scurrying draughts. Down the six flights she ran, one after the other, until she was at the front door. The snow had drifted high, completely covering the steps. She went out. It was bitter cold in the wind, but only a stray flake fell now and then. She stood there. The street did not tell her what to do. She began to wade through the deep snow, eastward. A taxi, moving cautiously down Second Avenue, its chains clanking rhythmically, met her at the corner. She hailed it, got in.

"Take me to the river," she said, pointing.

"What street?"

"Any street that goes down all the way."

Almost immediately they were there. She got out, paid the driver, walked slowly to the end of the pavement, and stood watching. The dawn was really breaking now, but it was very different from the one she had seen through the window. The wind took her breath away, the water out there was alive. Against the winter sky across the river there were factories. The lights of a small craft moved further down in midstream. She clenched her fists. A terrible anguish had taken possession of her. She was trembling, but she did not feel the cold. Abruptly she turned around. The driver was standing in the street blowing into his cupped hands. And he was looking at her intently.

"You're not waiting for me, are you?" she said. (Was that her voice?)

"Yes, *Ma'am*," he said with force.

"I didn't tell you to." (With her whole life falling to pieces before her, how was it that her voice rang with such asperity, such hard self-assurance?)

"That's right." He put his gloves back on. "Take your time," he said.

She turned her back on him and watched the changing water. Suddenly she felt ridiculous. She went over to the cab, got in, and gave her home address.

The doorman was asleep when she rang, and even after she was inside she had to wait nearly five minutes for the elevator boy to bring the car up from the basement. She tiptoed through the apartment to her room, shutting the door behind her. When she had undressed she opened the big window without looking out, and got into bed. The cold wind blew through the room.

Tangier
1947

The Circular Valley

The abandoned monastery stood on a slight eminence of land in the middle of a vast clearing. On all sides the ground sloped gently downward toward the tangled, hairy jungle that filled the circular valley, ringed about by sheer, black cliffs. There were a few trees in some of the courtyards, and the birds used them as meeting-places when they flew out of the rooms and corridors where they had their nests. Long ago bandits had taken whatever was removable out of the building. Soldiers had used it once as headquarters, had, like the bandits, built fires in the great windy rooms so that afterward they looked like ancient kitchens. And now that everything was gone from within, it seemed that never again would anyone come near the monastery. The vegetation had thrown up a protecting wall; the first storey was soon quite hidden from view by small trees which dripped vines to lasso the cornices of the windows. The meadows roundabout grew dank and lush; there was no path through them.

At the higher end of the circular valley a river fell off the cliffs into a great cauldron of vapor and thunder below; after this it slid along the base of the cliffs until it found a gap at the other end of the valley, where it hurried discreetly through with no rapids, no cascades—a great thick black rope of water moving swiftly downhill between the polished flanks of the canyon. Beyond the gap the land opened out and became smiling; a village nestled on the side hill just outside. In the days of the monastery it was there that the friars had got their provisions, since the Indians would not enter the circular valley. Centuries ago when the building had been constructed the Church had imported the workmen from another part of the country. These were traditional enemies of the tribes thereabouts, and had another language; there was no danger that the inhabitants would communicate with them as they worked at setting up the mighty walls. Indeed, the construction had taken so long that before the east wing was completed the workmen had all died, one by one. Thus it was the friars themselves who had closed off the end of the wing with blank walls, leaving it that way, unfinished and blind-looking, facing the black cliffs.

Generation after generation, the friars came, fresh-cheeked boys who grew thin and gray, and finally died, to be buried in the garden beyond the courtyard with the fountain. One day not long ago they had all left the monastery; no one knew where they had gone, and no one thought to ask. It was shortly after this that the bandits and then the soldiers had come. And now, since the Indians do not change, still no one from the village went up through the gap to visit the monastery. The Atlájala lived there; the friars had not been able to kill it, had given up at last and gone away. No one was surprised, but the Atlájala gained in prestige by their departure. During the centuries the friars had been there in the monastery, the Indians had wondered why it allowed them to stay. Now, at last, it had driven them out. It always had lived there, they said, and would go on living there because the valley was its home, and it could never leave.

In the early morning the restless Atlájala would move through the halls of the monastery. The dark rooms sped past, one after the other. In a small patio, where eager young trees had pushed up the paving stones to reach the sun, it paused. The air was full of small sounds: the movements of butterflies, the falling to the ground of bits of leaves and flowers, the air following its myriad courses around the edges of things, the ants pursuing their endless labors in the hot dust. In the sun it waited, conscious of each gradation in sound and light and smell, living in the awareness of the slow, constant disintegration that attacked the morning and transformed it into afternoon. When evening came, it often slipped above the monastery roof and surveyed the darkening sky: the waterfall would roar distantly. Night after night, along the procession of years, it had hovered here above the valley, darting down to become a bat, a leopard, a moth for a few minutes or hours, returning to rest immobile in the center of the space enclosed by the cliffs. When the monastery had been built, it had taken to frequenting the rooms, where it had observed for the first time the meaningless gestures of human life.

And then one evening it had aimlessly become one of the young friars. This was a new sensation, strangely rich and complex, and at the same time unbearably stifling, as though every other possibility besides that of being enclosed in a tiny, isolated world of cause and effect had been removed forever. As the friar, it had gone and stood in the window, looking out at the sky, seeing for the first time, not the stars, but the space between and beyond them. Even at that moment it had felt the urge to leave, to step outside the little shell of anguish where it lodged for the moment, but a faint curiosity had impelled it to remain a little longer and partake a little futher of the unaccustomed sensation. It held on; the friar raised his arms to the sky in an imploring gesture. For the first time the Atlája sensed opposition, the thrill of a struggle. It was delicious to feel the young man striving to free himself of its presence, and it was immeasurably sweet to remain there. Then with a cry the friar had rushed to the other side of the room and seized a heavy leather whip hanging on the wall. Tearing off his clothing he had begun to carry out a ferocious self-beating. At the first blow of the lash the Atlájala had been on the point of letting go, but then it realized that the immediacy of that intriguing inner pain was only made more manifest by the impact of the blows from without, and so it stayed and felt the young man grow weak under his own lashing. When he had finished and said a prayer, he crawled to his pallet and fell asleep weeping, while the Atlájala slipped out obliquely and entered into a bird which passed the night sitting in a great tree on the edge of the jungle, listening intently to the night sounds, and uttering a scream from time to time.

Thereafter the Atlájala found it impossible to resist sliding inside the bodies of the friars; it visited one after the other, finding an astonishing variety of sensation in the process. Each was a separate world, a separate experience, because each had different reactions when he became conscious of the other being within him. One would sit and read or pray, one would go for a long troubled walk in the meadows, around and around the building, one would find a comrade and engage in an absurd but bitter quarrel, a few wept, some flagellated themselves or sought a friend to wield the lash for them. Always there was a rich profusion of perceptions for the Atlájala to enjoy, so that it no longer occurred to it to frequent the bodies of insects, birds and furred animals, nor even to leave the monastery and move in the air above. Once it almost got into difficulties when an old friar it was occupying suddenly fell back dead. That was a hazard it ran in the frequenting of men: they seemed not to know when they were doomed, or if they did know, they pretended with such strength not to know, that it amounted to the same thing. The other beings knew beforehand, save when it was a question of being seized unawares and devoured. And that the Atlájala was able to prevent: a bird in which it was staying was always avoided by the hawks and eagles.

When the friars left the monastery, and, following the government's orders, doffed their robes, dispersed and became workmen, the Atlájala was at a loss to know how to pass its days and nights. Now everything was as it had been before their arrival: there was no one but the creatures that always had lived in the circular valley. It tried a giant serpent, a deer, a bee: nothing had the savor it had grown to love. Everything was the same as before, but not for the Atlájala; it had known the existence of man, and now there were no men in the valley—only the abandoned building with its empty rooms to make man's absence more poignant.

Then one year bandits came, several hundred of them in one stormy afternoon. In delight it tried many of them as they sprawled about cleaning their guns and cursing, and it discovered still other facets of sensation: the hatred they felt for the world, the fear they had of the soldiers who were pursuing them, the strange gusts of desire that swept through them as they sprawled together drunk by the fire that smoldered in the center of the floor, and the insufferable pain of jealousy which the nightly orgies seem to awaken in some of them. But the bandits did not stay long. When they had left, the soldiers came in their wake. It felt very much the same way to be a soldier as to be a bandit. Missing were the strong fear and the hatred, but the rest was almost identical. Neither the bandits nor the soldiers appeared to be at all conscious of its presence in them; it could slip from one man to another without causing any change in their behavior. This surprised it, since its effect on the friars had been so definite, and it felt a certain disappointment at the impossibility of making its existence known to them.

Nevertheless, the Atlájala enjoyed both bandits and soldiers immensely, and was even more desolate when it was left alone once again. It would become one of the swallows that made their nests in the rocks beside the top of the waterfall. In the burning sunlight it would plunge again and again into the curtain of mist that rose from far below, sometimes uttering exultant cries. It would spend a day as a plant louse, crawling slowly along the under side of the leaves, living quietly in the huge green world down there which is forever hidden from the sky. Or at night, in the velvet body of a panther, it would know the pleasure of the kill. Once for a year it lived in an eel at the bottom of the pool below the waterfall, feeling the mud give slowly before it as it pushed ahead with its flat nose; that was a restful period, but afterward the desire to know again the mysterious life of man had returned—an obsession of which it was useless to try to rid itself. And now it moved restlessly through the ruined rooms, a mute presence, alone, and thirsting to be incarnate once again, but in man's flesh only. And with the building of highways through the country it was inevitable that people should come once again to the circular valley.

A man and a woman drove their automobile as far as a village down in a lower valley; hearing about the ruined monastery and the waterfall that dropped over the cliffs into the great amphitheatre, they determined to see these things. They came on burros as far as the village outside the gap, but there the Indians they had hired to accompany them refused to go any farther, and so they continued alone, upward through the canyon and into the precinct of the Atlájala.

It was noon when they rode into the valley; the black ribs of the cliffs glistened like glass in the sun's blistering downward rays. They stopped the burros by a cluster of boulders at the edge of the sloping meadows. The man got down first, and reached up to help the woman off. She leaned forward, putting her hands on his face, and for a long moment they kissed. Then he lifted her to the ground and they climbed hand in hand up over the rocks. The Atlájala hovered near them, watching the woman closely: she was the first ever to have come into the valley. The two sat beneath a small tree on the grass, looking at one another, smiling. Out of habit, the Atlájala entered into the man. Immediately, instead of existing in the midst of the sunlit air, the bird calls and the plant odors, it was conscious only of the woman's beauty and her terrible imminence. The waterfall, the earth, and the sky itself receded, rushed into nothingness, and there were only the woman's smile and her arms and her odor. It was a world more suffocating and painful than the Atlájala had thought possible. Still, while the man spoke and the woman answered, it remained within.

"Leave him. He doesn't love you."

"He would kill me."

"But I love you. I need you with me."

"I can't. I'm afraid of him."

The man reached out to pull her to him; she drew back slightly, but her eyes grew large.

"We have today," she murmured, turning her face toward the yellow walls of the monastery.

The man embraced her fiercely, crushing her against him as though the act would save his life. "No, no, no. It can't go on like this," he said. "No."

The pain of his suffering was too intense; gently the Atlájala left the man and slipped into the woman. And now it would have believed itself to be housed in nothing, to be in its own spaceless self, so completely was it aware of the wandering wind, the small flutterings of the leaves, and the bright air that surrounded it. Yet there was a difference: each element was magnified in intensity, the whole sphere of being was immense, limitless. Now it understood what the man sought in the woman, and it knew that he suffered because he never would attain that sense of completion he sought. But the Atlájala, being one with the woman, had attained it, and being aware of possessing it, trembled with delight. The woman shuddered as her lips met those of the man. There on the grass in the shade of the tree their joy reached new heights; the Atlájala, knowing them both, formed a single channel between the secret springs of their desires. Throughout, it remained within the woman, and began vaguely to devise ways of keeping her, if not inside the valley, at least nearby, so that she might return.

In the afternoon, with dreamlike motions, they walked to the burros and mounted them, driving them through the deep meadow grass to the monastery. Inside the great courtyard they halted, looking hesitantly at the ancient arches in the sunlight, and at the darkness inside the doorways.

"Shall we go in?" said the woman.

"We must get back."

"I want to go in," she said. (The Atlájala exulted.) A thin gray snake slid along the ground into the bushes. They did not see it.

The man looked at her perplexedly. "It's late," he said.

But she jumped down from her burro by herself and walked beneath the arches into the long corridor within. (Never had the rooms seemed so real as now when the Atlájala was seeing them through her eyes.)

They explored all the rooms. Then the woman wanted to climb up into the tower, but the man took a determined stand.

"We must go back now," he said firmly, putting his hand on her shoulder.

"This is our only day together, and you think of nothing but getting back."

"But the time . . . ."

"There is a moon. We won't lose the way."

He would not change his mind. "No."

"As you like," she said. "I'm going up. You can go back alone if you like."

The man laughed uneasily. "You're mad." He tried to kiss her.

She turned away and did not answer for a moment. Then she said: "You want me to leave my husband for you. You ask everything from me, but what do you do for me in return? You refuse even to climb up into a little tower with me to see the view. Go back alone. Go!"

She sobbed and rushed toward the dark stairwell. Calling after her, he followed, but stumbled somewhere behind her. She was as sure of foot as if she had climbed the many stone steps a thousand times before, hurrying up through the darkness, around and around.

In the end she came out at the top and peered through the small apertures in the cracking walls. The beams which had supported the bell had rotted and fallen; the heavy bell lay on its side in the rubble, like a dead animal. The waterfall's sound was louder up here; the valley was nearly full of shadow. Below, the man called her name repeatedly. She did not answer. As she stood watching the shadow of the cliffs slowly overtake the farthest recesses of the valley and begin to climb the naked rocks to the east, an idea formed in her mind. It was not the kind of idea which she would have expected of herself, but it was there, growing and inescapable. When she felt it complete there inside her, she turned and went lightly back down. The man was sitting in the dark near the bottom of the stairs, groaning a little.

"What is it?" she said.

"I hurt my leg. Now are you ready to go or not?"

"Yes," she said simply. "I'm sorry you fell."

Without saying anything he rose and limped after her out into the courtyard where the burros stood. The cold mountain air was beginning to flow down from the tops of the cliffs. As they rode through the meadow she began to think of how she would broach the subject to him. (It must be done before they reached the gap. The Atlájala trembled.)

"Do you forgive me?" she asked him.

"Of course," he laughed.

"Do you love me?"

"More than anything in the world."

"Is that true?"

He glanced at her in the failing light, sitting erect on the jogging animal.

"You know it is," he said softly.

She hesitated.

"There is only one way, then," she said finally.

"But what?"

"I'm afraid of him. I won't go back to him. You go back. I'll stay in the village here." (Being that near, she would come each day to the monastery.) "When it is done, you will come and get me. Then we can go somewhere else. No one will find us."

The man's voice sounded strange. "I don't understand."

"You do understand. And that is the only way. Do it or not, as you like. It is the only way."

They trotted along for a while in silence. The canyon loomed ahead, black against the evening sky.

Then the man said, very clearly: "Never."

A moment later the trail led out into an open space high above the swift water below. The hollow sound of the river reached them faintly. The light in the sky was almost gone; in the dusk the landscape had taken on false contours. Everthing was gray—the rocks, the bushes, the trail—and nothing had distance or scale. They slowed their pace.

His words still echoed in her ears.

"I won't go back to him!" she cried with sudden vehemence. "You can go back and play cards with him as usual. Be his good friend the same as always. I won't go. I can't go on with both of you in the town." (The plan was not working; the Atlájala saw it had lost her, yet it still could help her.)

"You're very tired," he said softly.

He was right. Almost as he said the words, that unaccustomed exhilaration and lightness she had felt ever since noon seemed to leave her; she hung her head wearily, and said: "Yes, I am."

At the same moment the man uttered a sharp, terrible cry; she looked up in time to see his burro plunge from the edge of the trail into the grayness below. There was a silence, and then the faraway sound of many stones sliding downward. She could not move or stop the burro; she sat dumbly, letting it carry her along, an inert weight on its back.

For one final instant, as she reached the pass which was the edge of its realm, the Atlájala alighted tremulously within her. She raised her head and a tiny exultant shiver passed through her; then she let it fall forward once again.

Hanging in the dim air above the trail, the Atlájala watched her indistinct figure grow invisible in the gathering night. (If it had not been able to hold her there, still it had been able to help her.)

A moment later it was in the tower, listening to the spiders mend their webs that she had damaged. It would be a long, long time before it would bestir itself to enter into another being's awareness. A long, long time— perhaps forever.

Fez
1948

At Paso Rojo

When old Señora Sanchez died, her two daughters Lucha and Chalía decided to visit their brother at his ranch. Out of devotion they had agreed never to marry while their mother lived, and now that she was gone and they were both slightly over forty there seemed just as little likelihood of a wedding in the family as there ever had. They would probably not admit this even to themselves, however. It was with complete understanding of his two sisters that Don Federico suggested they leave the city and go down to Paso Rojo for a few weeks.

Lucha arrived in black crêpe. To her, death was one of the things that happen in life with a certain regularity, and it therefore demanded outward observance. Otherwise her life was in no way changed, save that at the ranch she would have to get used to a whole new staff of servants.

"Indians, poor things, animals with speech," she said to Don Federico the first night as they sat having coffee. A barefooted girl had just carried the dessert dishes out.

Don Federico smiled. "They are good people," he said deliberately. Living at the ranch so long had lowered his standards, it was said, for even though he had always spent a month or so of each year in the capital, he had grown increasingly indifferent to the social life there.

"The ranch is eating his soul little by little," Lucha used to say to Señora Sanchez.

Only once the old lady had replied. "If his soul is to be eaten, then let the ranch do it."

She looked around the primitive dining room with its dry decorations of palm leaves and branches. "He loves it here because everything is his," she thought, "and some of the things could never have been his if he had not purposely changed to fit them." That was not a completely acceptable thought. She knew the ranch had made him happy and tolerant and wise; to her it seemed sad that he could not have been those things without losing his civilized luster. And that he certainly had lost. He had the skin of a peasant—brown and lined everywhere. He had the slowness of speech of men who have lived for long periods of time in the open. And the inflections of his voice suggested the patience that can come from talking to

121

animals rather than to human beings. Lucha was a sensible woman; still, she could not help feeling a certain amount of regret that her little brother, who at an earlier point in his life had been the best dancer among the members of the country club, should have become the thin, sad-faced, quiet man who sat opposite her.

"You've changed a great deal," she suddenly said, shaking her head from side to side slowly.

"Yes. You change here. But it's a good place."

"Good, yes. But so sad," she said.

He laughed. "Not sad at all. You get used to the quiet. And then you find it's not quiet at all. But you never change much, do you? Chalía's the one who's different. Have you noticed?"

"Oh, Chalía's always been crazy. She doesn't change either."

"Yes. She is very much changed." He looked past the smoking oil lamp, out into the dark. "Where is she? Why doesn't she take coffee?"

"She has insomnia. She never takes it."

"Maybe our nights will put her to sleep," said Don Federico.

Chalía sat on the upper veranda in the soft night breeze. The ranch stood in a great clearing that held the jungle at bay all about, but the monkeys were calling from one side to the other, as if neither clearing nor ranch house existed. She had decided to put off going to bed—that way there was less darkness to be borne in case she stayed awake. The lines of a poem she had read on the train two days before were still in her mind: "*Aveces la noche.* . . . Sometimes the night takes you with it, wraps you up and rolls you along, leaving you washed in sleep at the morning's edge." Those lines were comforting. But there was the terrible line yet to come: "And sometimes the night goes on without you." She tried to jump from the image of the fresh sunlit morning to a completely alien idea: the waiter at the beach club in Puntarenas, but she knew the other thought was waiting there for her in the dark.

She had worn riding breeches and a khaki shirt open at the neck, on the trip from the capital, and she had announced to Lucha her intention of going about in those clothes the whole time she was at Paso Rojo. She and Lucha had quarreled at the station.

"Everyone knows Mamá has died," said Lucha, "and the ones who aren't scandalized are making fun of you."

With intense scorn in her voice Chalía had replied, "You have asked them, I suppose."

On the train as it wound through the mountains toward *tierra caliente* she had suddenly said, apropos of nothing: "Black doesn't become me." Really upsetting to Lucha was the fact that in Puntarenas she had gone off and bought some crimson nail polish which she had painstakingly applied herself in the hotel room.

"You can't, Chalía!" cried her sister, wide-eyed. "You've never done it before. Why do you do it now?"

Chalía had laughed immoderately. "Just a whim!" she had said, spreading her decorated hands in front of her.

Loud footsteps came up the stairs and along the veranda, shaking it slightly. Her sister called: "Chalía!"

She hesitated an instant, then said, "Yes."

"You're sitting in the dark! Wait. I'll bring out a lamp from your room. What an idea!"

"We'll be covered with insects," objected Chalía, who, although her mood was not a pleasant one, did not want it disturbed.

"Federico says no!" shouted Lucha from inside. "He says there are no insects! None that bite, anyway!"

Presently she appeared with a small lamp which she set on a table against the wall. She sat down in a nearby hammock and swung herself softly back and forth, humming. Chalía frowned at her, but she seemed not to notice.

"What heat!" exclaimed Lucha finally.

"Don't exert yourself so much," suggested Chalía.

They were quiet. Soon the breeze became a strong wind, coming from the direction of the distant mountains; but it too was hot, like the breath of a great animal. The lamp flickered, threatened to go out. Lucha got up and turned it down. As Chalía moved her head to watch her, her attention was caught by something else, and she quickly shifted her gaze to the wall. Something enormous, black and swift had been there an instant ago; now there was nothing. She watched the spot intently. The wall was faced with small stones which had been plastered over and whitewashed indifferently, so that the surface was very rough and full of large holes. She rose suddenly and approaching the wall, peered at it closely. All the holes, large and small, were lined with whitish funnels. She could see the long, agile legs of the spiders that lived inside, sticking out beyond some of the funnels.

"Lucha, this wall is full of monsters!" she cried. A beetle flew near to the lamp, changed its mind and lighted on the wall. The nearest spider darted forth, seized it and disappeared into the wall with it.

"Don't look at them," advised Lucha, but she glanced about the floor near her feet apprehensively.

Chalía pulled her bed into the middle of the room and moved a small table over to it. She blew out the lamp and lay back on the hard mattress. The sound of the nocturnal insects was unbearably loud—an endless, savage scream above the noise of the wind. All the vegetation out there was dry. It made a million scraping sounds in the air as the wind swept through it. From time to time the monkeys called to each other from the different sides. A night bird scolded occasionally, but its voice was swallowed up in the insistent insect song and the rush of wind across the hot countryside. And it was absolutely dark.

Perhaps an hour later she lit the lamp by her bed, rose, and in her nightgown went to sit on the veranda. She put the lamp where it had been before, by the wall, and turned her chair to face it. She sat watching the wall until very late.

At dawn the air was cool, full of the sound of continuous lowing of cattle, nearby and far. Breakfast was served as soon as the sky was completely light. In the kitchen there was a hubbub of women's voices. The dining room smelled of kerosene and oranges. A great platter heaped with thick slices of pale pineapple was in the center of the table. Don Federico sat at the end, his back to the wall. Behind him was a small niche, bright with candles, and the Virgin stood there in a blue and silver gown.

"Did you sleep well?" said Don Federico to Lucha.

"Ah, wonderfully well!"

"And you?" to Chalía.

"I never sleep well," she said.

A hen ran distractedly into the room from the veranda and was chased out by the serving girl. Outside the door a group of Indian children stood guard around a square of clothesline along which was draped a red assortment of meat: strips of flesh and loops of internal organs. When a vulture swooped low, the children jumped up and down, screaming in chorus, and drove it into the air again. Chalía frowned at their noise. Don Federico smiled.

"This is all in your honor," he said. "We killed a cow yesterday. Tomorrow all that will be gone."

"Not the vultures!" exclaimed Lucha.

"Certainly not. All the cowboys and servants take some home to their families. And they manage to get rid of quite a bit of it themselves.

"You're too generous," said Chalía. "It's bad for them. It makes them dissatisfied and unhappy. But I suppose if you didn't give it to them, they'd steal it anyway."

Don Federico pushed back his chair.

"No one here has ever stolen anything from me." He rose and went out.

After breakfast while it was still early, before the sun got too high in the sky, he regularly made a two-hour tour of the ranch. Since he preferred to pay unexpected visits to the vaqueros in charge of the various districts, he did not always cover the same regions. He was explaining this to Lucha as he untethered his horse outside the high barbed-wire fence that enclosed the house. "Not because I hope to find something wrong. But this is the best way always to find everything right."

Like Chalía, Lucha was skeptical of the Indian's ability to do anything properly. "A very good idea," she said. "I'm sure you are much too lenient with those boys. They need a strong hand and no pity."

Above the high trees that grew behind the house the red and blue macaws screamed, endlessly repeating their elliptical path in the sky. Lucha looked up in their direction and saw Chalía on the upper porch, tucking a khaki shirt into her breeches.

"Rico, wait! I want to go with you," she called, and rushed into her room.

Lucha turned back to her brother. "You won't take her? She couldn't! With Mamá . . ."

Don Federico cut her short, so as not to hear what would have been painful to him. "You both need fresh air and exercise. Come, both of you."

Lucha was silent a moment, looking aghast into his face. Finally she said, "I couldn't," and moved away to open the gate. Several cowboys were riding their horses slowly up from the paddock toward the front of the house. Chalía appeared on the lower porch and hurried to the gate, where Lucha stood looking at her.

"So you're going horseback riding," said Lucha. Her voice had no expression.

"Yes. Are you coming? I suppose not. We should be back soon; no, Rico?"

Don Federico disregarded her, saying to Lucha: "It would be good if you came."

When she did not reply, but went through the gate and shut it, he had one of the cowboys dismount and help Chalía onto his horse. She sat astride the animal beaming down at the youth.

"Now, you can't come. You have no horse!" she cried, pulling the reins taut violently so that the horse stood absolutely still.

"Yes, señora. I shall go with the señores." His speech was archaic and respectful, the speech of the rustic Indian. Their soft, polite words always annoyed her, because she believed, quite erroneously, that she could detect mockery underneath. "Like parrots who've been taught two lines of Gongora!" she would laugh, when the subject was being discussed. Now she was further nettled by hearing herself addressed as señora. "The idiot!" she thought. "He should know that I'm not married." But when she looked down at the cowboy again she noticed his white teeth and his very young face. She smiled, saying, "How hot it is already," and undid the top button of her shirt.

The boy ran to the paddock and returned immediately, riding a larger and more nervous horse. This was a joke to the other cowboys, who started ahead, laughing. Don Federico and Chalía rode side by side, and the boy went along behind them, by turns whistling a tune and uttering soothing words to his skittish horse.

The party went across the mile or so of open space that lay between the house and the jungle. Then the high grass swept the riders' legs as the horses went downward to the river, which was dry save for a narrow stream of water in the middle. They followed the bed downstream, the vegetation increasing in height along the banks as they progressed. Chalía had enameled her fingernails afresh before starting out and was in a good humor. She was discussing the administration of the ranch with Don Federico. The expenses and earning capacity interested her particularly, although she had no clear idea of the price of anything. She had worn an enormous soft straw sombrero whose brim dropped to her shoulders as she rode. Every few minutes she turned around and waved to the cowboy who still remained behind, shouting to him: "Muchacho! You're not lost yet?"

Presently the river was divided into two separate beds by a large island which loomed ahead of them, its upper reaches a solid wall of branches and vines. At the foot of the giant trees among some gray boulders was a score or so of cows, looking very small indeed as they lay hunched up in the mud or ambled about seeking the thickest shade. Don Federico galloped ahead suddenly and conferred loudly with the other vaqueros. Almost simultaneously Chalía drew in her reins and brought her horse to a halt. The boy was quickly abreast of her. As he came up she called to him: "It's hot, isn't it?"

The men rode on ahead. He circled around her. "Yes, señora. But that is because we are in the sun. There"—he indicated the island—"it is shady. Now they are almost there."

She said nothing, but took off her hat and fanned herself with the brim. As she moved her hand back and forth she watched her red nails. "What an ugly color," she murmured.

"What, señora?"

"Nothing." She paused. "Ah, what heat!"

"Come, señora. Shall we go on?"

Angrily she crumpled the crown of the sombrero in her fist. "I am not señora," she said distinctly, looking at the men ahead as they rode up to the cows and roused them from their lethargy. The boy smiled. She went on. "I am señorita. That is not the same thing. Or perhaps you think it is?"

The boy was puzzled; he was conscious of her sudden emotion, but he had no idea of its cause. "Yes, señorita," he said politely, without conviction. And he added, with more assurance, "I am Roberto Paz, at your orders."

The sun shone down upon them from above and was reflected by the mica in the stones at their feet. Chalía undid another button of her shirt.

"It's hot. Will they come back soon?"

"No, señorita. They return by the road. Shall we go?" He turned his horse toward the island ahead.

"I don't want to be where the cows are," said Chalía with petulance. "They have *garrapatas*. The *garrapatas* get under your skin."

Roberto laughed indulgently. "The *garrapatas* will not molest you if you stay on your horse, señorita."

"But I want to get down and rest. I'm so tired!" The discomfort of the heat became pure fatigue as she said the words; this made it possible for the annoyance she felt with him to transform itself into a general state of self-pity and depression that came upon her like a sudden pain. Hanging her head she sobbed: "*Ay, madre mía!* My poor mamá!" She stayed that way a moment, and her horse began to walk slowly toward the trees at the side of the river bed.

Roberto glanced perplexedly in the direction the others had taken. They had all passed out of sight beyond the head of the island; the cows were lying down again. "The señorita should not cry."

She did not reply. Since the reins continued slack, her horse proceeded at a faster pace toward the forest. When it had reached the shade at the edge of the stream, the boy rode quickly to her side. "Señorita!" he cried.

She sighed and looked up at him, her hat still in her hand. "I'm very tired," she repeated. "I want to get down and rest."

There was a path leading into the forest. Roberto went ahead to lead the way, hacking at stray vines and bushes with his machete. Chalía followed, sitting listlessly in the saddle, calmed by the sudden entrance into the green world of silence and comparative coolness.

They rode slowly upward through the forest for a quarter of an hour or so without saying anything to each other. When they came to a gate Roberto opened it without dismounting and waited for Chalía to pass through. As she went by him she smiled and said: "How nice it is here."

He replied, rather curtly, she thought: "Yes, Señorita."

Ahead, the vegetation thinned, and beyond lay a vast, open, slightly undulating expanse of land, decorated here and there, as if by intent, with giant white-trunked ceiba trees. The hot wind blew across this upland terrain, and the cry of cicadas was in the air. Chalía halted her horse and jumped down. The tiny thistlelike plants that covered the ground crackled under her boots. She seated herself carefully in the shade at the very edge of the open land.

Roberto tied the two horses to a tree and stood looking at her with the alert, hostile eyes of the Indian who faces what he does not understand.

"Sit down. Here," she said.

Stonily he obeyed, sitting with his legs straight on the earth in front of him, his back very erect. She rested her hand on his shoulder. "*Qué calor*," she murmured.

She did not expect him to answer, but he did, and his voice sounded remote. "It is not my fault, señorita."

She slipped her arm around his neck and felt the muscles grow tense. She rubbed her face over his chest; he did not move or say anything. With her eyes shut and her head pressing hard against him, she felt as if she were hanging to consciousness only by the ceaseless shrill scream of the cicadas. She remained thus, leaning ever more heavily upon him as he braced himself with his hands against the earth behind him. His face had become an impenetrable mask; he seemed not to be thinking of anything, not even to be present.

Breathing heavily, she raised her head to look at him, but found she did not have the courage to reach his eyes with her gaze. Instead she watched his throat and finally whispered, "It doesn't matter what you think of me. It's enough for me to hold you like this."

He turned his head stiffly away from her face, looking across the landscape to the mountains. Gruffly he said, "My brother could come by this place. We must go back to the river."

She tried to bury her face in his chest, to lose herself once more in the delicious sensation. Without warning, he moved quickly and stood up, so that she tumbled forward with her face against the ground.

The surprise of her little fall changed her mood instantly. She sprang up, dashed blindly for the nearer of the two horses, was astride it in an instant, and before he could cry, "It's the bad horse!" had pounded the animal's flanks with her heels. It raised its head wildly; with a violent bound it began to gallop over the countryside. At the first movement she realized dimly that there had been a change, that it was not the same horse, but in her excitement she let her observation stop there. She was delighted to be moving swiftly across the plain against the hot wind. Roberto was left behind.

"*Idiota!*" she screamed into the air. "*Idiota! Idiota!*" with all her might. Ahead of her a tremendous vulture, panic-stricken at the approaching hoof sounds, flapped clumsily away into the sky.

The saddle, having been strapped on for less vigorous action, began to slip. She gripped the pommel with one hand, and seizing her shirt with the other gave it a convulsive tug that ripped it completely open. A powerful feeling of exultation came to her as she glanced down and saw her own skin white in the sunlight.

In the distance to one side, she dimly saw some palm trees reaching above a small patch of lower vegetation. She shut her eyes: the palms looked like shiny green spiders. She was out of breath from the jolting. The sun was too hot. The saddle kept slipping further; she could not right it. The horse showed no sign of being aware of her existence. She pulled on the reins as hard as she could without falling over backward, but it had no effect on the horse, which continued to run at top speed, following no path and missing some of the trees by what seemed no more than inches.

"Where shall I be in an hour?" she asked herself. "Dead, perhaps?" The idea of death did not frighten her the way it did some people. She was afraid of the night because she could not sleep; she was not afraid of life and death because she did not feel implicated to any extent in either one. Only other people lived and died, had their lives and deaths. She, being inside herself, existed merely as herself and not as a part of anything else. People, animals, flowers and stones were objects, and they all belonged to the world outside. It was their juxtapositions that made hostile or friendly patterns. Sometimes she looked at her own hands and feet for several minutes, trying to fight off an indefinite sensation they gave her of belonging also to the world outside. But this never troubled her deeply. The impressions were received and accepted without question; at most she could combat them when they were too strong for her comfort.

Here in the hot morning sun, being pulled forward through the air, she began to feel that almost all of her had slipped out of the inside world, that only a tiny part of her was still she. The part that was left was full of astonishment and disbelief; the only discomfort now lay in having to accept the fact of the great white tree trunks that continued to rush by her.

She tried several times to make herself be elsewhere: in her rose garden at home, in the hotel dining room at Puntarenas, even as a last resort which might prove feasible since it too had been unpleasant, in her bed back at the ranch, with the dark around her.

With a great bound, the horse cleared a ditch. The saddle slipped completely around and hung underneath. Having no pommel to cling to, she kept on as best she could, clutching the horse's flanks with her legs and always pulling on the reins. Suddenly the animal slowed down and stepped briskly into a thicket. There was a path of sorts; she suspected it was the same one they had used coming from the river. She sat listlessly, waiting to see where the horse would go.

Finally it came out into the river bed as she had expected, and trotted back to the ranch. The sun was directly overhead when they reached the paddock. The horse stood outside, waiting to be let in, but it seemed that no one was around. Making a great effort, she slid down to the ground and found she had difficulty in standing because her legs were trembling so. She was furious and ashamed. As she hobbled toward the house she was strongly hoping Lucha would not see her. A few Indian girls appeared to be the only people about. She dragged herself upstairs and shut herself in her room. The bed had been pushed back against the wall, but she did not have the force to pull it out into the center where she wanted it.

When Don Federico and the others returned, Lucha, who had been reading downstairs, went to the gate. "Where's Chalía?" she cried.

"She was tired. One of the boys brought her back a while ago," he said. "It's just as well. We went halfway to Cañas."

Chalía had her lunch in bed and slept soundly until late in the afternoon. When she emerged from her room onto the veranda, a woman was dusting the rocking chairs and arranging them in a row against the wall.

"Where's my sister?" demanded Chalía.

"Gone to the village in the truck with the señor," the woman replied, going to the head of the stairs and beginning to dust them one by one, as she went down backward.

Chalía seated herself in a chair and put her feet up on the porch railing, reflecting as she did so that if Lucha had been there she would have disapproved of the posture. There was a bend in the river—the only part of it that came within sight of the house—just below her, and a portion of the bank was visible to her through the foliage from where she sat. A large breadfruit tree spread its branches out almost to the opposite side of the stream. There was a pool at the turn, just where the tree's trunk grew out of the muddy bank. An Indian sauntered out of the undergrowth and calmly removed his trousers, then his shirt. He stood there a moment, stark naked, looking at the water, before he walked into it and began to splash and swim. When he had finished bathing he stood again on the bank, smoothing his blue-black hair. Chalía was puzzled, knowing that few Indians would be so immodest as to bathe naked in full view of the upstairs veranda. With a sudden strange sensation as she watched him, she realized it was Roberto and that he was wholly conscious of her presence at that moment.

"He knows Rico is gone and that no one can see him from downstairs," she thought, resolving to tell her brother when he came home. The idea of vengeance upon the boy filled her with a delicious excitement. She watched his deliberate movements as he dressed. He sat down on a rock with only his shirt on and combed his hair. The late afternoon sun shone through the leaves and gave his brown skin an orange cast. When finally he had gone away without once glancing up at the house, she rose and went into her room. Maneuvering the bed into the middle of the floor once more, she began to walk around it; her mood was growing more and more turbulent as she circled about the room.

She heard the truck door slam, and a moment later, voices downstairs. With her finger to her temple, where she always put it when her heart was beating very fast, she slipped out onto the veranda and downstairs. Don Federico was in the commissary, which he opened for a half hour each morning and evening. Chalía stepped inside the door, her mouth already open, feeling the words about to burst from her lungs. Two children were pushing their copper coins along the counter, pointing at the candy they wanted. By the lamp a woman was looking at a bolt of goods. Don Federico was on a ladder, getting down another bolt. Chalía's mouth closed slowly. She looked down at her brother's desk by the door beside her, where he kept his ledgers and bills. In an open cigar box almost touching her hand was a pile of dirty bank notes. She was back in the room before she knew it. She shut the door and saw that she had four ten-colon notes in her hand. She stuffed them into her breeches pocket.

At dinner they made fun of her for having slept all the afternoon, telling her that now she would lie awake again all night.

She was busy eating. "If I do, so much the worse," she said, without looking up.

"I've arranged a little concert after dinner," said Don Federico. Lucha was ecstatic. He went on: "The cowboys have some friends here, over from Bagaces, and Raul has finished building his marimba."

The men and boys began to assemble soon after dinner. There was laughter, and guitars were strummed in the dark on the terrace. The two sisters went to sit at the end near the dining room, Don Federico was in the middle with the vaqueros, and the servants were ranged at the kitchen end. After several solo songs by various men with guitars, Raul and a friend began to play the marimba. Roberto was seated on the floor among the cowboys who were not performing.

"Suppose we all dance," said Don Federico, jumping up and seizing Lucha. They moved about together at one end of the terrace for a moment, but no one else stirred.

"*A bailar!*" Don Federico shouted, laughing.

Several of the girls started to dance timidly in couples, with loud giggling. None of the men would budge. The marimba players went on pounding out the same piece over and over again. Don Federico danced with Chalía, who was stiff from her morning ride; soon she excused herself and left. Instead of going upstairs to bed she crossed onto the front veranda and sat looking across the vast moonlit clearing. The night was thick with eternity. She could feel it there, just beyond the gate. Only the monotonous, tinkling music kept the house within the confines of time, saved it from being engulfed. As she listened to the merrymaking progress, she had the impression that the men were taking more part in it. "Rico has probably opened them a bottle of rum," she thought with fury.

At last it sounded as though everyone were dancing. Her curiosity having risen to a high pitch, she was about to rise and return to the terrace, when a figure appeared at the other end of the veranda. She needed no one to tell her it was Roberto. He was walking soundlessly toward her; he seemed to hesitate as he came up to her, then he squatted down by her chair and looked up at her. She had been right: he smelled of rum.

"Good evening, señorita."

She felt impelled to remain silent. Nevertheless, she said, "Good evening." She put her hand into her pocket, saying to herself that she must do this correctly and quickly.

As he crouched there with his face shining in the moonlight, she bent forward and passed her hand over his smooth hair. Keeping her fingers on the back of his neck, she leaned still further forward and kissed his lips. The rum was very strong. He did not move. She began to whisper in his ear, very low: "Roberto, I love you. I have a present for you. Forty *colones*. Here."

He turned his head swiftly and said out loud, "Where?"

She put the bills into his hand, still holding his head, and whispered again: "Sh! Not a word to anyone. I must go now. I'll give you more tomorrow night." She let go of him.

He rose and went out the gate. She went straight upstairs to bed, and as she went to sleep the music was still going on.

Much later she awoke and lit her lamp. It was half past four. Day would soon break. Feeling full of an unaccustomed energy, Chalía dressed, extinguished the lamp and went outdoors, shutting the gate quickly behind her. In the paddock the horses stirred. She walked by it and started along the road to the village. It was a very silent hour: the night insects had ceased their noises and the birds had not yet begun their early-morning twitter. The moon was low in the sky, so that it remained behind the trees most of the time. Ahead of her Venus flared like a minor moon. She walked quickly, with only a twinge of pain now and then in her hip.

Something dark lying in the road ahead of her made her stop walking. It did not move. She watched it closely, stepping cautiously toward it, ready to run the other way. As her eyes grew accustomed to its form, she saw that it was a man lying absolutely still. And as she drew near, she knew it was Roberto. She touched his arm with her foot. He did not respond. She leaned over and put her hand on his chest. He was breathing deeply, and the smell of liquor was almost overpowering. She straightened and kicked him lightly in the head. There was a tiny groan from far within. This also, she said to herself, would have to be done quickly. She felt wonderfully light and powerful as she slowly maneuvered his body with her feet to the right-hand side of the road. There was a small cliff there, about twenty feet high. When she got him to the edge, she waited a while, looking at his features in the moonlight. His mouth was open a little, and the white teeth peeked out from behind the lips. She smoothed his forehead a few times and with a gentle push rolled him over the edge. He fell very heavily, making a strange animal sound as he hit.

She walked back to the ranch at top speed. It was getting light when she arrived. She went into the kitchen and ordered her breakfast, saying: "I'm up early." The entire day she spent around the house, reading and talking to Lucha. She thought Don Federico looked preoccupied when he set out on his morning tour of inspection, after closing the commissary. She thought he still did when he returned; she told him so at lunch.

"It's nothing," he said. "I can't seem to balance my books."

"And you've always been such a good mathematician," said Chalía.

During the afternoon some cowboys brought Roberto in. She heard the commotion in the kitchen and the servants' cries of "*Ay, Dios!*" She went out to watch. He was conscious, lying on the floor with all the other Indians staring at him.

"What's the matter?" she said.

One of the cowboys laughed. "Nothing of importance. He had too much—" the cowboy made a gesture of drinking from a bottle, "and fell off the road. Nothing but bruises, I think."

After dinner Don Federico asked Chalía and Lucha into his little private office. He looked drawn, and he spoke more slowly than usual. As Chalía entered she saw that Roberto was standing inside the door. He did not look at her. Lucha and Chalía sat down; Don Federico and Roberto remained standing.

"This is the first time anyone has done this to me," said Don Federico, looking down at the rug, his hands locked behind him. "Roberto has stolen from me. The money is missing. Some of it is in his pocket still, more than his monthly wages. I know he has stolen it because he had no money yesterday and because," he turned to Chalía, "because he can account for having it only by lying. He says you gave it to him. Did you give Roberto any money yesterday?"

Chalía looked puzzled. "No," she said. "I thought of giving him a *colon* when he brought me back from the ride yesterday morning. But then I thought it would be better to wait until we were leaving to go back to the city. Was it much? He's just a boy."

Don Federico said: "It was forty *colones*. But that's the same as forty *centavos*. Stealing . . ."

Chalía interrupted him. "Rico!" she exclaimed. "Forty *colones!* That's a great deal! Has he spent much of it? You could take it out of his wages little by little." She knew her brother would say what he did say, a moment later.

"Never! He'll leave tonight. And his brother with him."

In the dim light Chalía could see the large purple bruise on Roberto's forehead. He kept his head lowered and did not look up, even when she and Lucha rose and left the room at a sign from their brother. They went upstairs together and sat down on the veranda.

"What barbarous people they are!" said Lucha indignantly. "Poor Rico may learn some day how to treat them. But I'm afraid one of them will kill him first."

Chalía rocked back and forth, fanning herself lazily. "With a few more lessons like this he may change," she said. "What heat!"

They heard Don Federico's voice below by the gate. Firmly it said, "*Adiós.*" There were muffled replies and the gate was closed. Don Federico joined his sisters on the veranda. He sat down sadly.

"I didn't like to send them away on foot at night," he said, shaking his head. "But that Roberto is a bad one. It was better to have him go once and for all, quickly. Juan is good, but I had to get rid of him too, of course."

"*Claro, claro,*" said Lucha absently. Suddenly she turned to her brother full of concern. "I hope you remembered to take away the money you said he still had in his pocket."

"Yes, yes," he assured her, but from the tone of his voice she knew he had let the boy keep it.

Don Federico and Lucha said good night and went to bed. Chalía sat up a while, looking vaguely at the wall with the spiders in it. Then she yawned and took the lamp into her room. Again the bed had been pushed back against the wall by the maid. Chalía shrugged her shoulders, got into the bed where it was, blew out the lamp, listened for a few minutes to the

At Paso Rojo

night sounds, and went peacefully to sleep, thinking of how surprisingly little time it had taken her to get used to life at Paso Rojo, and even, she had to admit now, to begin to enjoy it.

Oche Rios, Jamaica
1947

Pastor Dowe at Tacaté

Pastor Dowe delivered his first sermon in Tacaté on a bright Sunday morning shortly after the beginning of the rainy season. Almost a hundred Indians attended, and some of them had come all the way from Balaché in the valley. They sat quietly on the ground while he spoke to them for an hour or so in their own tongue. Not even the children became restive; there was the most complete silence as long as he kept speaking. But he could see that their attention was born of respect rather than of interest. Being a conscientious man he was troubled to discover this.

When he had finished the sermon, the notes for which were headed "Meaning of Jesus," they slowly got to their feet and began wandering away, quite obviously thinking of other things. Pastor Dowe was puzzled. He had been assured by Dr. Ramos of the University that his mastery of the dialect was sufficient to enable his prospective parishioners to follow his sermons, and he had had no difficulty conversing with the Indians who had accompanied him up from San Gerónimo. He stood sadly on the small thatch-covered platform in the clearing before his house and watched the men and women walking slowly away in different directions. He had the sensation of having communicated absolutely nothing to them.

All at once he felt he must keep the people here a little longer, and he called out to them to stop. Politely they turned their faces toward the pavilion where he stood, and remained looking at him, without moving. Several of the smaller children were already playing a game, and were darting about silently in the background. The pastor glanced at his wrist watch and spoke to Nicolás, who had been pointed out to him as one of the most intelligent and influential men in the village, asking him to come up and stand beside him.

Once Nicolás was next to him, he decided to test him with a few questions. "Nicolás," he said in his dry, small voice, "what did I tell you today?"

Nicolás coughed and looked over the heads of the assembly to where an enormous sow was rooting in the mud under a mango tree. Then he said: "Don Jesucristo."

137

"Yes," agreed Pastor Dowe encouragingly. *"Bai,* and Don Jesucristo what?"

"A good man," answered Nicolás with indifference.

"Yes, yes, but what more?" Pastor Dowe was impatient; his voice rose in pitch.

Nicolás was silent. Finally he said, "Now I go," and stepped carefully down from the platform. The others again began to gather up their belongings and move off. For a moment Pastor Dowe was furious. Then he took his notebook and his Bible and went into the house.

At lunch Mateo, who waited on table, and whom he had brought with him from Ocosingo, stood leaning against the wall smiling.

"Señor," he said, "Nicolás says they will not come again to hear you without music."

"Music!" cried Pastor Dowe, setting his fork on the table. "Ridiculous! What music? We have no music."

"He says the father at Yalactín used to sing."

"Ridiculous!" said the pastor again. "In the first place I can't sing, and in any case it's unheard of! *Inaudito!*"

"Sí, verdad?" agreed Mateo.

The pastor's tiny bedroom was breathlessly hot, even at night. However, it was the only room in the little house with a window on the outside; he could shut the door onto the noisy patio where by day the servants invariably gathered for their work and their conversations. He lay under the closed canopy of his mosquito net, listening to the barking of the dogs in the village below. He was thinking about Nicolás. Apparently Nicolás had chosen for himself the role of envoy from the village to the mission. The pastor's thin lips moved. "A troublemaker," he whispered to himself. "I'll speak with him tomorrow."

Early the next morning he stood outside Nicolás's hut. Each house in Tacaté had its own small temple: a few tree trunks holding up some thatch to shelter the offerings of fruit and cooked food. The pastor took care not to go near the one that stood near by; he already felt enough like a pariah, and Dr. Ramos had warned him against meddling of that sort. He called out.

A little girl about seven years old appeared in the doorway of the house. She looked at him wildly for a moment with huge round eyes before she squealed and disappeared back into the darkness. The pastor waited and called again. Presently a man came around the hut from the back and told him that Nicolás would return. The pastor sat down on a stump. Soon the little girl stood again in the doorway; this time she smiled coyly. The pastor looked at her severely. It seemed to him she was too old to run about naked. He turned his head away and examined the thick red petals of a banana blossom hanging nearby. When he looked back she had come out and was standing near him, still smiling. He got up and walked toward the road, his head down, as if deep in thought. Nicolás entered through the gate at the moment, and the pastor, colliding with him, apologized.

"Good," grunted Nicolás. "What?"

His visitor was not sure how he ought to begin. He decided to be pleasant.

"I am a good man," he smiled.

"Yes," said Nicolás. "Don Jesucristo is a good man."

"No, no, no!" cried Pastor Dowe.

Nicolás looked politely confused, but said nothing.

Feeling that his command of the dialect was not equal to this sort of situation, the pastor wisely decided to begin again. "Hachakyum made the world. Is that true?"

Nicolás nodded in agreement, and squatted down at the pastor's feet, looking up at him, his eyes narrowed against the sun.

"Hachakyum made the sky," the pastor began to point, "the mountains, the trees, those people there. Is that true?"

Again Nicolás assented.

"Hachakyum is good. Hachakyum made you. True?" Pastor Dowe sat down again on the stump.

Nicolás spoke finally, "All that you say is true."

The pastor permitted himself a pleased smile and went on. "Hachakyum made everything and everyone because He is mighty and good."

Nicolás frowned. "No!" he cried. "That is not true! Hachakyum did not make everyone. He did not make you. He did not make guns or Don Jesucristo. Many things He did not make!"

The pastor shut his eyes a moment, seeking strength. "Good," he said at last in a patient voice. "Who made the other things? Who made me? Please tell me."

Nicolás did not hesitate. "Metzabok."

"But who is Metzabok?" cried the pastor, letting an outraged note show in his voice. The word for God he had always known only as Hachakyum.

"Metzabok makes all the things that do not belong here," said Nicolás.

The pastor rose, took out his handkerchief and wiped his forehead. "You hate me," he said, looking down at the Indian. The word was too strong, but he did not know how to say it any other way.

Nicolás stood up quickly and touched the pastor's arm with his hand. "No. That is not true. You are a good man. Everyone likes you."

Pastor Dowe backed away in spite of himself. The touch of the brown hand was vaguely distasteful to him. He looked beseechingly into the Indian's face and said, "But Hachakyum did not make me?"

"No."

There was a long pause.

"Will you come next time to my house and hear me speak?"

Nicolás looked uncomfortable.

"Everyone has work to do," he said.

"Mateo says you want music," began the pastor.

Nicolás shrugged. "To me it is not important. But the others will come if you have music. Yes, that is true. They like music."

"But *what* music?" cried the pastor in desperation.

"They say you have a *bitrola*."

The pastor looked away, thinking: "There is no way to keep anything from these people." Along with all his other household goods and the things left behind by his wife when she died, he had brought a little portable phonograph. It was somewhere in the storeroom piled with the empty valises and cold-weather garments.

"Tell them I will play the *bitrola*," he said, going through the gate.

The little girl ran after him and stood watching him as he walked up the road.

On his way through the village the pastor was troubled by the reflection that he was wholly alone in this distant place, alone in his struggle to bring the truth to its people. He consoled himself by recalling that it is only in each man's own consciousness that the isolation exists; objectively man is always a part of something.

When he arrived home he sent Mateo to the storeroom to look for the portable phonograph. After a time the boy brought it out, dusted it and stood by while the pastor opened the case. The crank was inside. He took it out and wound the spring. There were a few records in the compartment at the top. The first he examined were "Let's Do It," "Crazy Rhythm," and "Strike up the Band," none of which Pastor Dowe considered proper accompaniments to his sermons. He looked further. There was a recording of Al Jolson singing "Sonny Boy" and a cracked copy of "She's Funny That Way." As he looked at the labels he remembered how the music on each disc had sounded. Unfortunately Mrs. Dowe had disliked hymn music; she had called it "mournful."

"So here we are," he sighed, "without music."

Mateo was astonished. "It does not play?"

"I can't play them this music for dancing, Mateo."

"*Cómo no, señor!* They will like it very much!"

"No, Mateo!" said the pastor forcefully, and he put on "Crazy Rhythm" to illustrate his point. As the thin metallic tones issued from the instrument, Mateo's expression changed to one of admiration bordering on beatitude. "*Qué bonito!*" he said reverently. Pastor Dowe lifted the tone

arm and the hopping rhythmical pattern ceased.

"It cannot be done," he said with finality, closing the lid.

Nevertheless on Saturday he remembered that he had promised Nicolás there would be music at the service, and he decided to tell Mateo to carry the phonograph out to the pavilion in order to have it there in case the demand for it should prove to be pressing. This was a wise precaution, because the next morning when the villagers arrived they were talking of nothing but the music they were to hear.

His topic was "The Strength of Faith," and he had got about ten minutes into the sermon when Nicolás, who was squatting directly in front of him, quietly stood up and raised his hand. Pastor Dowe frowned and stopped talking.

Nicolás spoke: "Now music, then talk. Then music, then talk. Then music." He turned around and faced the others. "That is a good way." There were murmurs of assent, and everyone leaned a bit farther forward on his haunches to catch whatever musical sounds might issue from the pavilion.

The pastor sighed and lifted the machine onto the table, knocking off the Bible that lay at the edge. "Of course," he said to himself with a faint bitterness. The first record he came to was "Crazy Rhythm." As it started to play, an infant nearby, who had been singsonging a series of meaningless sounds, ceased making its parrotlike noises, remaining silent and transfixed as it stared at the platform. Everyone sat absolutely quiet until the piece was over. Then there was a hubbub of approbation. "Now more talk," said Nicolás, looking very pleased.

The pastor continued. He spoke a little haltingly now, because the music had broken his train of thought, and even by looking at his notes he could not be sure just how far he had got before the interruption. As he continued, he looked down at the people sitting nearest him. Beside Nicolás he noticed the little girl who had watched him from the doorway, and he was gratified to see that she was wearing a small garment which managed to cover her. She was staring at him with an expression he interpreted as one of fascinated admiration.

Presently, when he felt that his audience was about to grow restive (even though he had to admit that they never would have shown it outwardly) he put on "Sonny Boy." From the reaction it was not difficult to guess that this selection was finding less favor with its listeners. The general expression of tense anticipation at the beginning of the record soon relaxed into one of routine enjoyment of a less intense degree. When the piece was finished, Nicolás got to his feet again and raised his hand solemnly, saying: "Good. But the other music is more beautiful."

The pastor made a short summation, and, after playing "Crazy Rhythm" again, he announced that the service was over.

In this way "Crazy Rhythm" became an integral part of Pastor Dowe's weekly service. After a few months the old record was so badly worn that he determined to play it only once at each gathering. His flock submitted to this show of economy with bad grace. They complained, using Nicolás as emissary.

"But the music is old. There will be no more if I use it all," the pastor explained.

Nicolás smiled unbelievingly. "You say that. But you do not want us to have it."

The following day, as the pastor sat reading in the patio's shade, Mateo again announced Nicolás, who had entered through the kitchen and, it appeared, had been conversing with the servants there. By now the pastor had learned fairly well how to read the expressions on Nicolás's face; the one he saw there now told him that new exactions were at hand.

Nicolás looked respectful. "Señor," he said, "we like you because you have given us music when we asked you for it. Now we are all good friends. We want you to give us salt."

"Salt?" exclaimed Pastor Dowe, incredulous. "What for?"

Nicolás laughed good-naturedly, making it clear that he thought the pastor was joking with him. Then he made a gesture of licking. "To eat," he said.

"Ah, yes," murmured the pastor, recalling that among the Indians rock salt is a scarce luxury.

"But we have no salt," he said quickly.

"Oh, yes, señor. There." Nicolás indicated the kitchen.

The pastor stood up. He was determined to put an end to this haggling, which he considered a demoralizing element in his official relationship with the village. Signaling for Nicolás to follow, he walked into the kitchen, calling as he entered, "Quintina, show me our salt."

Several of the servants, including Mateo, were standing in the room. It was Mateo who opened a low cupboard and disclosed a great stack of grayish cakes piled on the floor. The pastor was astonished. "So many kilos of salt!" he exclaimed. *"Cómo se hace?"*

Mateo calmly told him it had been brought with them all the way from Ocosingo. "For us," he added, looking about at the others.

Pastor Dowe seized upon this, hoping it was meant as a hint and could be recognized as one. "Of course," he said to Nicolás. "This is for my house."

Nicolás looked unimpressed. "You have enough for everyone in the village," he remarked. "In two Sundays you can get more from Ocosingo. Everyone will be very happy all the time that way. Everyone will come

each time you speak. You give them salt and make music."

Pastor Dowe felt himself beginning to tremble a little. He knew he was excited and so he was careful to make his voice sound natural.

"I will decide, Nicolás," he said. "Good-bye."

It was clear that Nicolás in no way regarded these words as a dismissal. He answered, "Good-bye," and leaned back against the wall calling, "Marta!" The little girl, of whose presence in the room the pastor now became conscious, moved out from the shadows of a corner. She held what appeared to him to be a large doll, and was being very solicitous of it. As the pastor stepped out into the bright patio, the picture struck him as false, and he turned around and looked back into the kitchen, frowning. He remained in the doorway in an attitude of suspended action for a moment, staring at little Marta. The doll, held lovingly in the child's arms, and swaddled in a much-used rag, was making spasmodic movements.

The pastor's ill-humor was with him; probably he would have shown it no matter what the circumstances. "What is it?" he demanded indignantly. As if in answer the bundle squirmed again, throwing off part of the rag that covered it, and the pastor saw what looked to him like a comic-strip caricature of Red Riding Hood's wolf peering out from under the grand-mother's nightcap. Again Pastor Dowe cried, "What is it?"

Nicolás turned from his conversation, amused, and told Marta to hold it up and uncover it so the señor could see it. This she did, pulling away the wrapping and exposing to view a lively young alligator which, since it was being held more or less on its back, was objecting in a routine fashion to the treatment by rhythmically paddling the air with its little black feet. Its rather long face seemed, however, to be smiling.

"Good heavens!" cried the pastor in English. The spectacle struck him as strangely scandalous. There was a hidden obscenity in the sight of the mildly agitated little reptile with its head wrapped in a rag, but Marta was still holding it out toward him for his inspection. He touched the smooth scales of its belly with his fingers, and withdrew his hand, saying, "Its jaws should be bound. It will bite her."

Mateo laughed. "She is too quick," and then said it in dialect to Nicolás, who agreed, and also laughed. The pastor patted Marta on the head as she returned the animal to her bosom and resumed cradling it tenderly.

Nicolás's eyes were on him. "You like Marta?" he asked seriously.

The pastor was thinking about the salt. "Yes, yes," he said with the false enthusiasm of the preoccupied man. He went to his bedroom and shut the door. Lying on the narrow bed in the afternoon was the same as lying on it at night: there was the same sound of dogs barking in the vil-lage. Today there was also the sound of wind going past the window. Even the canopy of mosquito netting swayed a little from time to time as the air came into the room. The pastor was trying to decide whether or not to give in to Nicolás. When he got very sleepy, he thought: "After all, what principle am I upholding in keeping it from them? They want music. They want salt. They will learn to want God." This thought proved relaxing to him, and he fell asleep to the sound of the dogs barking and the wind shrilling past the window.

During the night the clouds rolled down off the mountains into the valley, and when dawn came they remained there, impaled on the high trees. The few birds that made themselves heard sounded as though they were singing beneath the ceiling of a great room. The wet air was thick with wood smoke, but there was no noise from the village; a wall of cloud lay between it and the mission house.

From his bed, instead of the wind passing the window, the pastor heard the slow drops of water falling upon the bushes from the eaves. He lay still awhile, lulled by the subdued chatter of the servant's voices in the kitchen. Then he went to the window and looked out into the grayness. Even the nearest trees were invisible; there was a heavy odor of earth. He dressed, shivering as the damp garments touched his skin. On the table lay a newspaper:

BARCELONA BOMBARDEADO POR DOSCIENTOS AVIONES

As he shaved, trying to work up a lather with the tepid water Quintina had brought him, full of charcoal ashes, it occurred to him that he would like to escape from the people of Tacaté and the smothering feeling they gave him of being lost in antiquity. It would be good to be free from that infinite sadness even for a few hours.

He ate a larger breakfast than usual and went outside to the sheltered platform, where he sat down in the dampness and began to read the seventy-eighth Psalm, which he had thought of using as the basis of a sermon. As he read he looked out at the emptiness in front of him. Where he knew the mango tree stood he could see only the white void, as if the land dropped away at the platform's edge for a thousand feet or more.

"He clave the rocks in the wilderness, and gave them drink as out of the great depths." From the house came the sound of Quintina's giggling. "Mateo is probably chasing her around the patio," thought the pastor; wisely he had long since given up expecting any Indian to behave as he considered an adult should. Every few seconds on the other side of the pavilion a turkey made its hysterical gobbling sound. The pastor spread his Bible out on the table, put his hands to his ears, and continued to read: "He caused an east wind to blow in the heaven: and by His power He brought in the south wind."

"Passages like that would sound utterly pagan in the dialect," he caught himself thinking. He unstopped his ears and reflected: "But to their ears *everything* must have a pagan sound. Everything I say is transformed on the way to them into something else," This was a manner of thinking that Pastor Dowe had always taken pains to avoid. He fixed his eyes on the text with determination, and read on. The giggling in the house was louder; he could hear Mateo too now. "He sent divers sorts of flies among them; . . . and frogs, which destroyed them." The door into the patio was opened and the pastor heard Mateo coughing as he stood looking out. "He certainly has tuberculosis," said the pastor to himself, as the Indian spat repeatedly. He shut his Bible and took off his glasses, feeling about on the table for their case. Not encountering it, he rose, and taking a step forward, crushed it under his heel. Compassionately, he stooped down and picked it up. The hinges were snapped and the metal sides under their artificial leather covering were bent out of shape. Mateo could have hammered it back into a semblance of its form, but Pastor Dowe preferred to think: "All things have their death." He had had the case eleven years. Briefly he summed up its life: the sunny afternoon when he had bought it on the little side street in downtown Havana; the busy years in the hills of southern Brazil; the time in Chile when he had dropped the case, with a pair of dark glasses in it, out the bus window, and everyone in the bus had got out and helped him look for it; the depressing year in Chicago when for some reason he had left it in a bureau drawer most of the time and had carried his glasses loose in his coat pocket. He remembered some of the newspaper clippings he had kept in the case, and many of the little slips of paper with ideas jotted down on them. He looked tenderly down at it, thinking: "And so this is the place and time, and these are the circumstances of its death." For some reason he was happy to have witnessed this death; it was comforting to know exactly how the case had finished its existence. He still looked at it with sadness for a moment. Then he flung it out into the white air as if the precipice were really there. With his Bible under his arm he strode to the door and brushed past Mateo without saying a word. But as he walked into his room it seemed to him that Mateo had looked at him in a strange fashion, as if he knew something and were waiting to see when the pastor would find out, too.

Back in his suffocating little room the pastor felt an even more imperious need to be alone for a time. He changed his shoes, took his cane and went out into the fog. In this weather there was only one path practicable, and that led downward through the village. He stepped ahead over the stones with great caution, for although he could discern the ground at his feet and the spot where he put the tip of his cane each time, beyond that on all sides was mere whiteness. Walking along thus, he reflected, was like trying to read a text with only one letter visible at a time. The wood smoke was sharp in the still air.

For perhaps half an hour Pastor Dowe continued this way, carefully putting one foot before the other. The emptiness around him, the lack of all visual detail, rather than activating his thought, served to dull his perceptions. His progress over the stones was laborious but strangely relaxing. One of the few ideas that came into his head as he moved along was that it would be pleasant to pass through the village without anyone's noticing him, and it seemed to him that it might be managed; even at ten feet he would be invisible. He could walk between the huts and hear the babies crying, and when he came out at the other end no one would know he had been there. He was not sure where he would go then.

The way became suddenly rougher as the path went into a zigzagging descent along the steep side of a ravine. He had reached the bottom before he raised his head once. "Ah," he said, standing still. The fog was now above him, a great gray quilt of cloud. He saw the giant trees that stood around him and heard them dripping slowly in a solemn, uneven chorus onto the wild coca leaves beneath.

"There is no place such as this on the way to the village," thought the pastor. He was mildly annoyed, but more astonished, to find himself standing by these trees that looked like elephants and were larger than any other trees he had seen in the region. Automatically he turned around in the path and started back up the slope. Beside the overpowering sadness of the landscape, now that it was visible to him, the fog up there was a comfort and a protection. He paused for a moment to stare back at the fat, spiny tree trunks and the welter of vegetation beyond. A small sound behind him made him turn his head.

Two Indians were trotting down the path toward him. As they came up they stopped and looked at him with such expectancy on their dark little faces that Pastor Dowe thought they were going to speak. Instead the one ahead made a grunting sound and motioned to the other to follow. There was no way of effecting a detour around the pastor, so they brushed violently against him as they went by. Without once looking back they hurried on downward and disappeared among the green coca leaves.

This unlikely behavior on the part of the two natives vaguely intrigued him; on an impulse he determined to find an explanation for it. He started after them.

Soon he had gone beyond the spot where he had turned back a moment ago. He was in the forest; the plant odor was almost unbearable—a smell of living and dead vegetation in a world where slow growth and slow death are simultaneous and inseparable. He stopped once and listened for footsteps. Apparently the Indians had run on ahead of him; nevertheless he continued on his way. Since the path was fairly wide and well broken in, it was only now and then that he came into contact with a hanging tendril or a projecting branch.

The posturing trees and vines gave the impression of having been arrested in furious motion, and presented a monotonous successsion of tortured tableaux vivants. It was as if, for the moment while he watched, the desperate battle for air had been suspended and would be resumed only when he turned away his head. As he looked, he decided that it was precisely this unconfirmable quality of surreptitiousness which made the place so disquieting. Now and then, high above his head, a blood-colored butterfly would float silently through the gloom from one tree trunk to another. They were all alike; it seemed to him that it must be always the same insect. Several times he passed the white grillwork of great spider webs flung between the plants like gates painted on the dark wall behind. But all the webs looked uninhabited. The large, leisurely drops of water still continued to fall from above; even if it had been raining hard, the earth could not have been wetter.

The pastor was astigmatic, and since he was beginning to be dizzy from watching so many details, he kept his eyes looking straight ahead as he walked, deviating his gaze only when he had to avoid the plant life that had grown across the path. The floor of the forest continued flat. Suddenly he became aware that the air around him was reverberating with faint sounds. He stood still, and recognized the casual gurgle a deep stream makes from time to time as it moves past its banks. Almost immediately ahead of him was the water, black and wide, and considering its proximity, incredibly quiet in its swift flowing. A few paces before him a great dead tree, covered with orange fungus, lay across the path. The pastor's glance followed the trunk to the left; at the small end, facing him, sat the two Indians. They were looking at him with interest, and he knew they had been waiting for him. He walked over to them, greeted them. They replied solemnly, never taking their shining eyes from his face.

As if they had rehearsed it, they both rose at the same instant and walked to the water's edge, where they stood looking down. Then one of them glanced back at the pastor and said simply, "Come." As he made his way around the log he saw that they were standing by a long bamboo raft which was beached on the muddy bank. They lifted it and dropped one end into the stream.

"Where are you going?" asked the pastor. For reply they lifted their short brown arms in unison and waved them slowly in the direction of downstream. Again the one who had spoken before said, "Come." The pastor, his curiosity aroused, looked suspiciously at the delicate raft, and back at the two men. At the same time he felt that it would be pleasanter to be riding with them than to go back through the forest. Impatiently he again demanded, "Where are you going? Tacaté?"

"Tacaté," echoed the one who up to this point had not spoken.

"Is it strong?" queried the pastor, stooping to push lightly on a piece of bamboo. This was merely a formality; he had perfect faith in the Indians' ability to master the materials of the jungle.

"Strong," said the first. "Come."

The pastor glanced back into the wet forest, climbed onto the raft, and sat doubled up on its bottom in the stern. The two quickly jumped aboard and pushed the frail craft from the bank with a pole.

Then began a journey which almost at once Pastor Dowe regretted having undertaken. Even as the three of them shot swiftly ahead, around the first bend in the stream, he wished he had stayed behind and could be at this moment on his way up the side of the ravine. And as they sped on down the silent waterway he continued to reproach himself for having come along without knowing why. At each successive bend in the tunnel-like course, he felt farther from the world. He found himself straining in a ridiculous effort to hold the raft back: it glided far too easily along the top of the black water. Farther from the world, or did he mean farther from God? A region like this seemed outside God's jurisdiction. When he had reached that idea he shut his eyes. It was an absurdity, manifestly impossible—in any case, inadmissible—yet it had occurred to him and was remaining with him in his mind. "God is always with me," he said to himself silently, but the formula had no effect. He opened his eyes quickly and looked at the two men. They were facing him, but he had the impression of being invisible to them; they could see only the quickly dissipated ripples left behind on the surface of the water, and the irregular arched ceiling of vegetation under which they had passed.

The pastor took his cane from where it was lying hidden, and gesticulated with it as he asked, "Where are we going?" Once again they both pointed vaguely into the air, over their shoulders, as if the question were of no interest, and the expression on their faces never changed. Loath to let even another tree go past, the pastor mechanically immersed his cane in the water as though he would stop the constant forward thrusting of the raft; he withdrew it immediately and laid it dripping across the bottom. Even that much contact with the dark stream was unpleasant to him. He tried to tell himself that there was no reason for his sudden spiritual collapse, but at the same time it seemed to him that he could feel the innermost fibers of his consciousness in the process of relaxing. The journey downstream was a monstrous letting go, and he fought against it with all his power. "Forgive me, O God, I am leaving You behind. Forgive me for leaving You behind." His nails pressed into his palms as he prayed.

And so he sat in agonized silence while they slid ahead through the forest and out into a wide lagoon where the gray sky was once more visible. Here the raft went much more slowly, and the Indians propelled it gently with their hands toward the shore where the water was shallow. Then one of them poled it along with the bamboo stick. The pastor did not notice the great beds of water hyacinth they passed through, or the silken sound they made as they rubbed against the raft. Out here under the low-hanging clouds there was occasionally a bird cry or a sudden rustle in the high grass by the water's edge. Still the pastor remained sunk within himself, feeling, rather than thinking: "Now it is done. I have passed over into the other land." And he remained so deeply preoccupied with this emotional certainty that he was not aware of it when they approached a high escarpment rising sheer from the lagoon, nor of when they drew up onto the sand of a small cove at one side of the cliff. When he looked up the two Indians were standing on the sand, and one of them was saying, "Come." They did not help him get ashore; he did this with some difficulty, although he was conscious of none.

As soon as he was on land they led him along the foot of the cliff that curved away from the water. Following a tortuous track beaten through the undergrowth they came out all at once at the very foot of the wall of rock.

There were two caves—a small one opening to the left, and a wider, higher one to the right. They halted outside the smaller. "Go in," they said to the pastor. It was not very light inside, and he could see very little. The two remained at the entrance. "Your god lives here," said one. "Speak with him."

The pastor was on his knees. "O Father, hear my voice. Let my voice come through to you. I ask it in Jesus' name . . . ." The Indian was calling to him, "Speak in our tongue." The pastor made an effort, and began a halting supplication in the dialect. There were grunts of satisfaction outside. The concentration demanded in order to translate his thoughts into the still unfamiliar language served to clear his mind somewhat. And the comforting parallel between this prayer and those he offered for his congregation helped to restore his calm. As he continued to speak, always with fewer hesitations, he felt a great rush of strength going through him. Confidently he raised his head and went on praying, his eyes on the wall in front of him. At the same moment he heard the cry: "Metzabok hears you now. Say more to him."

The pastor's lips stopped moving, and his eyes saw for the first time the red hand painted on the rock before him, and the charcoal, the ashes, the flower petals and the wooden spoons strewn about. But he had no sensation of horror; that was over. The important thing now was that he felt strong and happy. His spiritual condition was a physical fact. Having prayed to Metzabok was also a fact, of course, but his deploring of it was in purely mental terms. Without formulating the thought, he decided that forgiveness would be forthcoming when he asked God for it.

To satisfy the watchers outside the cave he added a few formal phrases to his prayer, rose, and stepped out into the daylight. For the first time he noticed a certain animation in the features of the two little men. One said, "Metzabok is very happy." The other said, "Wait." Whereupon they both hurried over to the larger of the two apertures and disappeared inside. The pastor sat on a rock, resting his chin on the hand that held the head of his cane. He was still suffused with the strange triumphant sensation of having returned to himself.

He heard them muttering for a quarter of an hour or so inside the cave. Presently they came out, still looking very serious. Moved by curiosity, the pastor risked a question. He indicated the larger cave with a finger and said, "Hachakyum lives there?" Together they assented. He wanted to go further and ask if Hachakyum approved of his having spoken with Metzabok, but he felt the question would be imprudent; besides, he was certain the answer would be in the affirmative.

They arrived back in the village at nightfall, after having walked all the way. The Indians' gait had been far too swift for Pastor Dowe, and they had stopped only once to eat some sapotes they had found under the trees. He asked to be taken to the house of Nicolás. It was raining lightly when they reached the hut. The pastor sat down in the doorway beneath the overhanging eaves of cane. He felt utterly exhausted; it had been one of the most tiring days of his life, and he was not home yet.

His two companions ran off when Nicolás appeared. Evidently he already knew of the visit to the cave. It seemed to the pastor that he had never seen his face so full of expression or so pleasant. "*Utz, utz,*" said Nicolás. "Good, good. You must eat and sleep."

After a meal of fruit and maize cakes, the pastor felt better. The hut was filled with wood smoke from the fire in the corner. He lay back in a low hammock which little Marta, casually pulling on a string from time to time, kept in gentle motion. He was overcome with a desire to sleep, but his host seemed to be in a communicative mood, and he wanted to profit by it. As he was about to speak, Nicolás approached, carrying a rusty tin biscuit box. Squatting beside the hammock he said in a low voice: "I will show you my things." The pastor was delighted; this bespoke a high degree of friendliness. Nicolás opened the box and took out some sample-size squares of printed cloth, an old vial of quinine tablets, a torn strip of newspaper, and four copper coins. He gave the pastor time to examine each carefully. At the bottom of the box were a good many orange and blue feathers which Nicolás did not bother to take out. The pastor realized that he was seeing the treasures of the household, that these items were rare objects of art. He looked at each thing with great seriousness handing it back with a verbal expression of admiration. Finally he said: "Thank you," and fell back into the hammock. Nicolás returned the box to the women sitting in the corner. When he came back over to the pastor he said: "Now we sleep."

"Nicolás," asked the pastor, "is Metzabok bad?"

"*Bai*, señor. Sometimes very bad. Like a small child. When he does not get what he wants right away, he makes fires, fever, wars. He can be very good, too, when he is happy. You should speak with him every day. Then you will know him."

"But you never speak with him."

"*Bai*, we do. Many do, when they are sick or unhappy. They ask him to take away the trouble. I never speak with him," Nicolás looked pleased, "because Hachakyum is my good friend and I do not need Metzabok. Besides, Metzabok's home is far—three hours' walk. I can speak with Hachakyum here." The pastor knew he meant the little altar outside. He nodded and fell asleep.

The village in the early morning was a chaos of shrill sounds: dogs, parrots and cockatoos, babies, turkeys. The pastor lay still in his hammock awhile listening, before he was officially wakened by Nicolás. "We must go now, señor," he said. "Everyone is waiting for you."

The pastor sat up, a little bit alarmed. "Where?" he cried.

"You speak and make music today."

"Yes, yes." He had quite forgotten it was Sunday.

The pastor was silent, walking beside Nicolás up the road to the mission. The weather had changed, and the early sun was very bright. "I have been fortified by my experience," he was thinking. His head was clear; he felt amazingly healthy. The unaccustomed sensation of vigor gave him a strange nostalgia for the days of his youth. "I must always have felt like this then. I remember it," he thought.

At the mission there was a great crowd—many more people than he had ever seen attend a sermon at Tacaté. They were chatting quietly, but when he and Nicolás appeared there was an immediate hush. Mateo was standing in the pavilion waiting for him, with the phonograph open. With a pang the pastor realized he had not prepared a sermon for his flock. He went into the house for a moment, and returned to seat himself at the table in the pavilion, where he picked up his Bible. He had left his few notes in the book, so that it opened to the seventy-eighth Psalm. "I shall read them that," he decided. He turned to Mateo. "Play the *disco*," he said. Mateo put on "Crazy Rhythm." The pastor quickly made a few pencil alterations in the text of the psalm, substituting the names of minor local deities, like Usukun and Sibanaa for such names as Jacob and Ephraim, and local place names for Israel and Egypt. And he wrote the word Hachakyum each time the word God or the Lord appeared. He had not finished when the record stopped. "Play it again," he commanded. The audience was delighted, even though the sound was abominably scratchy. When the music was over for the second time, he stood and began to paraphrase the psalm in a clear voice. "The children of Sibanaa, carrying bows to shoot, ran into the forest to hide when the enemy came. They did not keep their promises to Hachakyum, and they would not live as He told them to live." The audience was electrified. As he spoke, he looked down and saw the child Marta staring up at him. She had let go of her baby alligator, and it was crawling with a surprising speed toward the table where he sat. Quintina, Mateo, and the two maids were piling up the bars of salt on the ground to one side. They kept returning to the kitchen for more. He realized that what he was saying doubtless made no sense in terms of his listeners' religion, but it was a story of the unleashing of divine displeasure upon an unholy people, and they were enjoying it vastly. The alligator, trailing its rags, had crawled to within a few inches of the pastor's feet, where it remained quiet, content to be out of Marta's arms.

Presently, while he was still speaking, Mateo began to hand out the salt, and soon they all were running their tongues rhythmically over the large rough cakes, but continuing to pay strict attention to his words. When he was about to finish, he motioned to Mateo to be ready to start the record again the minute he finished; on the last word he lowered his arm as a signal, and "Crazy Rhythm" sounded once more. The alligator began to crawl hastily toward the far end of the pavilion. Pastor Dowe bent down and picked it up. As he stepped forward to hand it to Mateo, Nicolás rose from the ground, and taking Marta by the hand, walked over into the pavilion with her.

"Señor," he said, "Marta will live with you. I give her to you."

"What do you mean?" cried the pastor in a voice which cracked a little. The alligator squirmed in his hand.

"She is your wife. She will live here."

Pastor Dowe's eyes grew very wide. He was unable to say anything for a moment. He shook his hands in the air and finally he said: "No" several times.

Nicolás' face grew unpleasant. "You do not like Marta?"

"Very much. She is beautiful." The pastor sat down slowly on his chair. "But she is a little child."

Nicolás frowned with impatience. "She is already large."

"No, Nicolás. No. No."

Nicolás pushed his daughter forward and stepped back several paces, leaving her there by the table. "It is done," he said sternly. "She is your wife. I have given her to you."

Pastor Dowe looked out over the assembly and saw the unspoken approval in all the faces. "Crazy Rhythm" ceased to play. There was silence. Under the mango tree he saw a woman toying with a small, shiny object. Suddenly he recognized his glasses case; the woman was stripping the leatheroid fabric from it. The bare aluminum with its dents flashed in the sun. For some reason even in the middle of this situation he found himself thinking: "So I was wrong. It is not dead. She will keep it, the way Nicolás has kept the quinine tablets."

He looked down at Marta. The child was staring at him quite without expression. Like a cat, he reflected.

Again he began to protest. "Nicolás," he cried, his voice very high, "this is impossible!" He felt a hand grip his arm, and turned to receive a warning glance from Mateo.

Nicolás had already advanced toward the pavilion, his face like a thundercloud. As he seemed about to speak, the pastor interrupted him quickly. He had decided to temporize. "She may stay at the mission today," he said weakly.

"She is your wife," said Nicolás with great feeling. "You cannot send her away. You must keep her."

"*Diga que sí,*" Mateo was whispering. "Say yes, señor."

"Yes," the pastor heard himself saying. "Yes. Good." He got up and walked slowly into the house, holding the alligator with one hand and pushing Marta in front of him with the other. Mateo followed and closed the door after them.

"Take her into the kitchen, Mateo," said the pastor dully, handing the little reptile to Marta. As Mateo went across the patio leading the child by the hand, he called after him. "Leave her with Quintina and come to my room."

He sat down on the edge of his bed, staring ahead of him with unseeing eyes. At each moment his predicament seemed to him more terrible. With relief he heard Mateo knock. The people outdoors were slowly leaving. It cost him an effort to call out, "*Adelante.*" When Mateo had come in, the pastor said, "Close the door."

"Mateo, did you know they were going to do this? That they were going to bring that child here?"

"*Sí, señor.*"

"You knew it! But why didn't you say anything? Why didn't you tell me?"

Mateo shrugged his shoulders, looking at the floor. "I didn't know it would matter to you," he said. "Anyway, it would have been useless."

"Useless? Why? You could have stopped Nicolás," said the pastor, although he did not believe it himself.

Mateo laughed shortly. "You think so?"

"Mateo, you must help me. We must oblige Nicolás to take her back."

Mateo shook his head. "It can't be done. These people are very severe. They never change their laws."

"Perhaps a letter to the administrator at Ocosingo . . ."

"No, señor. That would make still more trouble. You are not a Catholic." Mateo shifted on his feet and suddenly smiled thinly. "Why not let her stay? She doesn't eat much. She can work in the kitchen. In two years she will be very pretty."

The pastor jumped, and made such a wide and vehement gesture with his hands that the mosquito netting, looped above his head, fell down about his face. Mateo helped him disentangle himself. The air smelled of dust from the netting.

"You don't understand anything!" shouted Pastor Dowe, beside himself. "I can't talk to you! I don't want to talk to you! Go out and leave me alone." Mateo obediently left the room.

Pounding his left palm with his right fist, over and over again, the pastor stood in his window before the landscape that shone in the strong sun. A few women were still eating under the mango tree; the rest had gone back down the hill.

He lay on his bed throughout the long afternoon. When twilight came he had made his decision. Locking his door, he proceeded to pack what personal effects he could into his smallest suitcase. His Bible and notebooks went on top with his toothbrush and atabrine tablets. When Quintina came to announce supper he asked to have it brought to his bed, taking care to slip the packed valise into the closet before he unlocked the door for her to enter. He waited until the talking had ceased all over the house, until he knew everyone was asleep. With the small bag not too heavy in one hand he tiptoed into the patio, out through the door into the fragrant night, across the open space in front of the pavilion, under the mango tree and down the path leading to Tacaté. Then he began to walk fast, because he wanted to get through the village before the moon rose.

There was a chorus of dogs barking as he entered the village street. He began to run, straight through to the other end. And he kept running even then, until he had reached the point where the path, wider here, dipped beneath the hill and curved into the forest. His heart was beating rapidly from the exertion. To rest, and to try to be fairly certain he was not being followed, he sat down on his little valise in the center of the path. There he remained a long time, thinking of nothing, while the night went on and the moon came up. He heard only the light wind among the leaves and vines. Overhead a few bats reeled soundlessly back and forth. At last he took a deep breath, got up, and went on.

New York
1946

You Are Not I

You are not I. No one but me could possibly be. I know that, and I know where I have been and what I have done ever since yesterday when I walked out the gate during the train wreck. Everyone was so excited that no one noticed me. I became completely unimportant as soon as it was a question of cut people and smashed cars down there on the tracks. We girls all went running down the bank when we heard the noise, and we landed against the cyclone fence like a lot of monkeys. Mrs. Werth was chewing on her crucifix and crying her eyes out. I suppose it hurt her lips. Or maybe she thought one of her daughters was on the train down there. It was really a bad accident; anyone could see that. The spring rains had dissolved the earth that kept the ties firm, and so the rails had spread a little and the train had gone into the ditch. But how everyone could get so excited I still fail to understand.

I always hated the trains, hated to see them go by down there, hated to see them disappear way off up the valley toward the next town. It made me angry to think of all those people moving from one town to another, without any right to. Whoever said to them: "You may go and buy your ticket and make the trip this morning to Reading. You will go past twenty-three stations, over forty bridges, through three tunnels, and still keep going, if you want to, even after you get to Reading"? No one. I know that. I know there is no chief who says things like that to people. But it makes it pleasanter for me when I imagine such a person does exist. Perhaps it would be only a tremendous voice speaking over a public-address system set up in all the main streets.

When I saw the train down there helpless on its side like an old worm knocked off a plant, I began to laugh. But I held on to the fence very hard when the people started to climb out the windows bleeding.

I was up in the courtyard, and there was the paper wrapper off a box of Cheese Tid Bits lying on the bench. Then I was at the main gate, and it was open. A black car was outside at the curb, and a man was sitting in front smoking. I thought of speaking to him and asking him if he knew who I was, but I decided not to. It was a sunny morning full of sweet air and birds, I followed the road around the hill, down to the tracks. Then I

157

walked up the tracks feeling excited. The dining car looked strange lying on its side with the window glass all broken and some of the cloth shades drawn down. A robin kept whistling in a tree above. "Of course," I said to myself. "This is just in man's world. If something real should happen, they would stop singing." I walked up and down along the cinder bed beside the track, looking at the people lying in the bushes. Men were beginning to carry them up toward the front end of the train where the road crosses the tracks. There was a woman in a white uniform, and I tried to keep from passing close to her.

I decided to go down a wide path that led through the blackberry bushes, and in a small clearing I found an old stove with a lot of dirty bandages and handkerchiefs in the rubbish around the base of it. Underneath everything was a pile of stones. I found several round ones and some others. The earth here was very soft and moist. When I got back to the train there seemed to be a lot more people running around. I walked close to the ones who were lying side by side on the cinders, and looked at their faces. One was a girl and her mouth was open. I dropped one of the stones in and went on. A fat man also had his mouth open. I put in a sharp stone that looked like a piece of coal. It occurred to me that I might not have enough stones for them all, and the cinders were too small. There was one old woman walking up and down wiping her hands on her skirt very quickly, over and over again. She had on a long black silk dress with a design of blue mouths stamped all over it. Perhaps they were supposed to be leaves but they were formed like mouths. She looked crazy to me and I kept clear of her. Suddenly I noticed a hand with rings on the fingers sticking out from under a lot of bent pieces of metal. I tugged at the metal and saw a face. It was a woman and her mouth was closed. I tried to open it so I could get a stone in. A man grabbed me by the shoulder and pulled at me. He looked angry. "What are you doing?" he yelled. "Are you crazy?" I began to cry and said she was my sister. She did look a little like her, and I sobbed and kept saying: "She's dead. She's dead." The man stopped looking so angry and pushed me along toward the head of the train, holding my arm tightly with one hand. I tried to jerk away from him. At the same time I decided not to say anything more except "She's dead" once in a while. "That's all right," the man said. When we got to the front end of the train he made me sit down on the grass embankment alongside a lot of other people. Some of them were crying, so I stopped and watched them.

It seemed to me that life outside was like life inside. There was always somebody to stop people from doing what they wanted to do. I smiled when I thought that this was just the opposite of what I had felt when I was still inside. Perhaps what we want to do is wrong, but why should they always be the ones to decide? I began to consider this as I sat there pulling the little new blades of grass out of the ground. And I thought that for once *I* would decide what was right, and do it.

It was not very long before several ambulances drove up. They were for us, the row of people sitting on the bank, as well as for the ones lying around on stretchers and overcoats. I don't know why, since the people weren't in pain. Or perhaps they were. When a great many people are in pain together they aren't so likely to make a noise about it, probably because no one listens. Of course I was in no pain at all. I could have told anyone that if I had been asked. But no one asked me. What they did ask me was my address, and I gave my sister's address because it is only a half hour's drive. Besides, I stayed with her for quite a while before I went away, but that was years ago, I think. We all drove off together, some lying down inside the ambulances, and the rest of us sitting on an uncomfortable bench in one that had no bed. The woman next to me must have been a foreigner; she was moaning like a baby, and there was not a drop of blood on her that I could see, anywhere. I looked her all over very carefully on the way, but she seemed to resent it, and turned her face the other way, still crying. When we got to the hospital we were all taken in and examined. About me they just said: "Shock," and asked me again where I lived. I gave them the same address as before, and soon they took me out again and put me into the front seat of a sort of station wagon, between the driver and another man, an attendant, I suppose. They both spoke to me about the weather, but I knew enough not to let myself be trapped that easily. I know how the simplest subject can suddenly twist around and choke you when you think you're quite safe. "She's dead," I said once, when we were halfway between the two towns. "Maybe not, maybe not," said the driver, as if he were talking to a child. I kept my head down most of the time, but I managed to count the gas stations as we went along.

When we arrived at my sister's house the driver got out and rang the bell. I had forgotten that the street was so ugly. The houses were built one against the other, all alike, with only a narrow cement walk between. And each one was a few feet lower than the other, so that the long row of them looked like an enormous flight of stairs. The children were evidently allowed to run wild over all the front yards, and there was no grass anywhere in sight, only mud.

My sister came to the door. The driver and she spoke a few words, and then I saw her look very worried very suddenly. She came out to the car and leaned in. She had new glasses, thicker than the others. She did not seem to be looking at me. Instead she said to the driver: "Are you *sure* she's all right?"

"Absolutely," he answered. "I wouldn't be telling you if she wasn't. She's just been examined all over up at the hospital. It's just shock. A good rest will fix her up fine." The attendant got out, to help me out and up the steps, although I could have gone perfectly well by myself. I saw my sister looking at me out of the corner of her eye the same as she used to. When I was on the porch I heard her whisper to the attendant: "She don't look well yet to *me*." He patted her arm and said: "She'll be fine. Just don't let her get excited."

"That's what they always said," she complained, "but she just *does*."

The attendant got into the car. "She ain't hurt at *all*, lady." He slammed the door.

"Hurt!" exclaimed my sister, watching the car. It drove off and she stood following it with her eyes until it got to the top of the hill and turned. I was still looking down at the porch floor because I wasn't sure yet what was going to happen. I often feel that something is about to happen, and when I do, I stay perfectly still and let it go ahead. There's no use wondering about it or trying to stop it. At this time I had no particular feeling that a special event was about to come out, but I did feel that I would be more likely to do the right thing if I waited and let my sister act first. She stood where she was, in her apron, breaking off the tips of the pussywillow stems that stuck out of the bush beside her. She still refused to look at me. Finally she grunted: "Might as well go on inside. It's cold out here." I opened the door and walked in.

Right away I saw she had had the whole thing rebuilt, only backward. There was always a hall and a living room, except that the hall used to be on the left-hand side of the living room and now it was on the right. That made me wonder why I had failed to notice that the front door was now at the right end of the porch. She had even switched the stairs and fireplace around into each other's places. The furniture was the same, but each piece had been put into the position exactly opposite to the way it had been before. I decided to say nothing and let her do the explaining if she felt like it. It occurred to me that it must have cost her every cent she had in the bank, and still it looked exactly the same as it had when she began. I kept my mouth shut, but I could not help looking around with a good deal of curiosity to see if she had carried out the reversal in every detail.

I went into the living room. The three big chairs around the center table were still wrapped in old sheets, and the floor lamp by the pianola had the same torn cellophane cover on its shade. I began to laugh, everything looked so comical backward. I saw her grab the fringe of the portiere and look at me hard. I went on laughing.

The radio next door was playing an organ selection. Suddenly my sister said: "Sit down, Ethel. I've got something to do. I'll be right back." She went into the kitchen through the hall and I heard the back door open.

I knew already where she was going. She was afraid of me, and she wanted Mrs. Jelinek to come over. Sure enough, in a minute they both came in, and my sister walked right into the living room this time. She looked angry now, but she had nothing to say. Mrs. Jelinek is sloppy and fat. She shook hands with me and said: "Well, well, old-timer!" I decided not to talk to her either because I distrust her, so I turned around and lifted the lid of the pianola. I tried to push down some keys, but the catch was on and they were all stiff and wouldn't move. I closed the lid and went over to see out the window. A little girl was wheeling a doll carriage along the sidewalk down the hill; she kept looking back at the tracks the wheels made when they left a wet part of the pavement and went onto a dry patch. I was determined not to let Mrs. Jelinek gain any advantage over me, so I kept quiet. I sat down in the rocker by the window and began to hum.

Before long they started to talk to each other in low voices, but of course I heard everything they said. Mrs. Jelinek said: "I thought they was keeping her." My sister said: "I don't know. So did I. But the man kept telling me she was all right. Huh! She's just the same." "Why, sure," said Mrs. Jelinek. They were quiet a minute.

"Well, I'm not going to put up with it!" said my sister, suddenly. "I'm going to tell Dr. Dunn what I think of him."

"Call the Home," urged Mrs. Jelinek.

"I certainly am," my sister answered. "You stay here. I'll see if Kate's in." She meant Mrs. Schultz, who lives on the other side and has a telephone. I did not even look up when she went out. I had made a big decision, and that was to stay right in the house and under no condition let myself be taken back there. I knew it would be difficult, but I had a plan I knew would work if I used all my will power. I have great will power.

The first important thing to do was to go on keeping quiet, not to speak a word that might break the spell I was starting to work. I knew I would have to concentrate deeply, but that is easy for me. I knew it was going to be a battle between my sister and me, but I was confident that my force of character and superior education had fitted me for just such a battle, and that I could win it. All I had to do was to keep insisting inside myself, and things would happen the way I willed it. I said this to myself as I rocked. Mrs. Jelinek stood in the hall doorway with her arms folded, mostly looking out the front door. By now life seemed much clearer and more purposeful than it had in a long, long time. This way I would have what I wanted. "No one can stop you," I thought.

It was a quarter of an hour before my sister came back. When she walked in she had both Mrs. Schultz and Mrs. Schultz's brother with her, and all three of them looked a little frightened. I knew exactly what had happened even before she told Mrs. Jelinek. She had called the Home and complained to Dr. Dunn that I had been released, and he had been very much excited and told her to hold on to me by all means because I had not been discharged at all but had somehow *got out*. I was a little shocked to hear it put that way, but now that I thought of it, I had to admit to myself that that was just what I had done.

I got up when Mrs. Schultz's brother came in, and glared at him hard.

"Take it easy, now, Miss Ethel," he said, and his voice sounded nervous. I bowed low to him: at least he was polite.

"'Lo, Steve," said Mrs. Jelinek.

I watched every move they made. I would have died rather than let the spell be broken. I felt I could hold it together only by a great effort. Mrs. Schultz's brother was scratching the side of his nose, and his other hand twitched in his pants pocket. I knew he would give me no trouble. Mrs. Schultz and Mrs. Jelinek would not go any further than my sister told them to. And she herself was terrified of me, for although I had never done her any harm, she had always been convinced that some day I would. It may be that she knew now what I was about to do to her, but I doubt it, or she would have run away from the house.

"When they coming?" asked Mrs. Jelinek.

"Soon's they can get here," said Mrs. Schultz.

They all stood in the doorway.

"I see they rescued the flood victims, you remember last night on the radio?" said Mrs. Schultz's brother. He lit a cigarette and leaned back against the banisters.

The house was very ugly, but I already was getting ideas for making it look better. I have excellent taste in decoration. I tried not to think of those things, and said over and over inside my head: "Make it work."

Mrs. Jelinek finally sat down on the couch by the door, pulled her skirt around her legs and coughed. She still looked red in the face and serious. I could have laughed out loud when I thought of what they were really waiting to see if they had only known it.

I heard a car door slam outside. I looked out. Two of the men from the Home were coming up the walk. Somebody else was sitting at the wheel, waiting. My sister went quickly to the front door and opened it. One of the men said: "Where is she?" They both came in and stood a second looking at me and grinning.

"Well, hel-*lo!*" said one. The other turned and said to my sister: "No trouble?" She shook her head. "It's a wonder you couldn't be more careful," she said angrily. "They get out like that, how do *you* know what they're going to do?"

The man grunted and came over to me. "Wanna come with us? I know somebody who's waiting to see you."

I got up and walked slowly across the room, looking at the rug all the way, with one of the men on each side of me. When I got to the doorway beside my sister I pulled my hand out of the pocket of my coat and looked at it. I had one of my stones in my hand. It was very easy. Before either of them could stop me I reached out and stuffed the stone into her mouth. She screamed just before I touched her, and just afterward her lips were bleeding. But the whole thing took a very long time. Everybody was standing perfectly still. Next, the two men had hold of my arms very tight and I was looking around the room at the walls. I felt that my front teeth were broken. I could taste blood on my lips. I thought I was going to faint. I wanted to put my hand to my mouth, but they held my arms. "This is the turning point," I thought.

I shut my eyes very hard. When I opened them everything was different and I knew I had won. For a moment I could not see very clearly, but even during that moment I saw myself sitting on the divan with my hands in front of my mouth. As my vision cleared, I saw that the men were holding my sister's arms, and that she was putting up a terrific struggle. I buried my face in my hands and did not look up again. While they were getting her out the front door, they managed to knock over the umbrella stand and smash it. It hurt her ankle and she kicked pieces of porcelain back into the hall. I was delighted. They dragged her along the walk to the car, and one man sat on each side of her in the back. She was yelling and showing her teeth, but as they left the city limits she stopped, and began to cry. All the same, she was really counting the service stations along the road on the way back to the Home, and she found there was one more of them than she had thought. When they came to the grade crossing near the spot where the train accident had happened, she looked out, but the car was over the track before she realized she was looking out the wrong side.

Driving in through the gate, she really broke down. They kept promising her ice cream for dinner, but she knew better than to believe them. As she walked through the main door between the two men she stopped on the threshold, took out one of the stones from her coat pocket and put it into her mouth. She tried to swallow it, but it choked her, and they rushed her down the hall into a little waiting room and made her give it up. The strange thing, now that I think about it, was that no one realized she was not I.

They put her to bed, and by morning she no longer felt like crying: she was too tired.

It's the middle of the afternoon and raining torrents. She is sitting on her bed (the very one I used to have) in the Home, writing all this down on paper. She never would have thought of doing that up until yesterday, but now she thinks she has become me, and so she does everthing I used to do.

The house is very quiet. I am still in the living room, sitting on the divan. I could walk upstairs and look into her bedroom if I wanted to. But it is such a long time since I have been up there, and I no longer know how the rooms are arranged. So I prefer to stay down here. If I look up I can see the square window of colored glass over the stairs. Purple and orange, an hourglass design, only the light never comes in very much because the house next door is so close. Besides, the rain is coming down hard here, too.

New York
1948

The Delicate Prey

There were three Filala who sold leather in Tabelbala—two brothers and the young son of their sister. The two older merchants were serious, bearded men who liked to engage in complicated theological discussions during the slow passage of the hot hours in their *hanoute* near the market-place; the youth naturally occupied himself almost exclusively with the black-skinned girls in the small *quartier réservé*. There was one who seemed more desirable than the others, so that he was a little sorry when the older men announced that soon they would all leave for Tessalit. But nearly every town has its *quartier*, and Driss was reasonably certain of being able to have any lovely resident of any *quartier*, whatever her present emotional entanglements; thus his chagrin at hearing of the projected departure was short-lived.

The three Filala waited for the cold weather before starting out for Tessalit. Because they wanted to get there quickly they chose the westernmost trail, which is also the one leading through the most remote regions, contiguous to the lands of the plundering Reguibat tribes. It was a long time since the uncouth mountain men had swept down from the *hammada* upon a caravan; most people were of the opinion that since the war of the Sarrho they had lost the greater part of their arms and ammunition, and, more important still, their spirit. And a tiny group of three men and their camels could scarcely awaken the envy of the Reguibat, traditionally rich with loot from all Rio de Oro and Mauretania.

Their friends in Tabelbala, most of them other Filali leather merchants, walked beside them sadly as far as the edge of the town; then they bade them farewell, and watched them mount their camels to ride off slowly toward the bright horizon.

"If you meet any Reguibat, keep them ahead of you!" they called.

The danger lay principally in the territory they would reach only three or four days' journey from Tabelbala; after a week the edge of the land haunted by the Reguibat would be left entirely behind. The weather was cool save at midday. They took turns sitting guard at night; when Driss stayed awake he brought out a small flute whose piercing notes made the older uncle frown with annoyance, so that he asked him to go and sit at

165

some distance from the sleeping-blankets. All night he sat playing whatever sad songs he could call to mind; the bright ones in his opinion belonged to the *quartier*, where one was never alone.

When the uncles kept watch, they sat quietly, staring ahead of them into the night. There were just the three of them.

And then one day a solitary figure appeared, moving toward them across the lifeless plain from the west. One man on a camel; there was no sign of any others, although they scanned the wasteland in every direction. They stopped for a while; he altered his course slightly. They went ahead; he changed it again. There was no doubt that he wanted to speak with them.

"Let him come," grumbled the older uncle, glaring about the empty horizon once more. "We each have a gun."

Driss laughed. To him it seemed absurd even to admit the possibility of trouble from one lone man.

When finally the figure arrived within calling distance, it hailed them in a voice like a muezzin's: "*S'l'm aleikoum!*" They halted, but did not dismount, and waited for the man to draw nearer. Soon he called again; this time the older uncle replied, but the distance was still too great for his voice to carry, and the man did not hear his greeting. Presently he was close enough for them to see that he did not wear Reguiba attire. They muttered to one another: "He comes from the north, not the west." And they all felt glad. However, even when he came up beside them they remained on the camels, bowing solemnly from where they sat, and always searching in the new face and in the garments below it for some false note which might reveal the possible truth—that the man was a scout for the Reguibat, who would be waiting up on the *hammada* only a few hours distant, or even now moving parallel to the trail, closing in upon them in such a manner that they would not arrive at a point within visibility until after dusk.

Certainly the stranger himself was no Reguiba; he was quick and jolly, with light skin and very little beard. It occurred to Driss that he did not like his small, active eyes which seemed to take in everything and give out nothing, but this passing reaction became only a part of the general initial distrust, all of which was dissipated when they learned that the man was a Moungari. Moungar is a holy place in that part of the world, and its few residents are treated with respect by the pilgrims who go to visit the ruined shrine nearby.

The newcomer took no pains to hide the fear he had felt at being alone in the region, or the pleasure it gave him to be now with three other men. They all dismounted and made tea to seal their friendship, the Moungari furnishing the charcoal.

During the third round of glasses he made the suggestion that since he was going more or less in their direction he accompany them as far as Taoudeni. His bright black eyes darting from one Filali to the other, he explained that he was an excellent shot, that he was certain he could supply them all with some good gazelle meat en route, or at least an *aoudad*. The Filala considered; the oldest finally said: "Agreed." Even if the Moungari turned out to have not quite the hunting prowess he claimed for himself, there would be four of them on the voyage instead of three.

Two mornings later, in the mighty silence of the rising sun, the Moungari pointed at the low hills that lay beside them to the east: *"Timma.* I know this land. Wait here. If you hear me shoot, then come, because that will mean there are gazelles."

The Moungari went off on foot, climbing up between the boulders and disappearing behind the nearest crest. "He trusts us," thought the Filala. "He has left his *mehari,* his blankets, his packs." They said nothing, but each knew that the others were thinking the same as he, and they all felt warmly toward the stranger. They sat waiting in the early morning chill while the camels grumbled.

It seemed unlikely that there would prove to be any gazelles in the region, but if there should be any, and the Moungari were as good a hunter as he claimed to be, then there was a chance they would have a *mechoui* of gazelle that evening, and that would be very fine.

Slowly the sun mounted in the hard blue sky. One camel lumbered up and went off, hoping to find a dead thistle or a bush between the rocks, something left over from a year when rain might have fallen. When it had disappeared, Driss went in seach of it and drove it back to the others, shouting: *"Hut!"*

He sat down. Suddenly there came a shot, a long empty interval, and then another shot. The sounds were fairly distant, but perfectly clear in the absolute silence. The older brother said: "I shall go. Who knows? There may be many gazelles."

He clambered up the rocks, his gun in his hand, and was gone.

Again they waited. When the shots sounded this time, they came from two guns.

"Perhaps they have killed one!" Driss cried.

"Yemkin. With Allah's aid," replied his uncle, rising and taking up his gun. "I want to try my hand at this."

Driss was disappointed: he had hoped to go himself. If only he had got up a moment ago, it might have been possible, but even so it was likely that he would have been left behind to watch the *mehara.* In any case, now it was too late; his uncle had spoken.

"Good."

His uncle went off singing a song from Tafilalet: it was about date-palms and hidden smiles. For several minutes Driss heard snatches of the song, as the melody reached the high notes. Then the sound was lost in the enveloping silence.

He waited. The sun began to be very hot. He covered his head with his burnous. The camels looked at each other stupidly, craning their necks, baring their brown and yellow teeth. He thought of playing his flute, but it did not seem the right moment: he was too restless, too eager to be up there with his gun, crouching behind the rocks, stalking the delicate prey. He thought of Tessalit and wondered what it would be like. Full of blacks and Touareg, certainly more lively than Tabelbala, because of the road that passed through it. There was a shot. He waited for others, but no more came this time. Again he imagined himself there among the boulders, taking aim at a fleeing beast. He pulled the trigger, the animal fell. Others appeared, and he got them all. In the dark the travelers sat around the fire gorging themselves with the rich roasted flesh, their faces gleaming with grease. Everyone was happy, and even the Moungari admitted that the young Filali was the best hunter of them all.

In the advancing heat he dozed, his mind playing over a landscape made of soft thighs and small hard breasts rising like sand dunes; wisps of song floated like clouds in the sky, and the air was thick with the taste of fat gazelle meat.

He sat up and looked around quickly. The camels lay with their necks stretched along the ground in front of them. Nothing had changed. He stood up, uneasily scanned the stony landscape. While he had slept, a hostile presence had entered into his consciousness. Translating into thought what he already sensed, he cried out. Since first he had seen those small, active eyes he had felt mistrust of their owner, but the fact that his uncles had accepted him had pushed suspicion away into the dark of his mind. Now, unleashed in his slumber, it had bounded back. He turned toward the hot hillside and looked intently between the boulders, into the black shadows. In memory he heard again the shots up among the rocks, and he knew what they had meant. Catching his breath in a sob, he ran to mount his *mehari*, forced it up, and already had gone several hundred paces before he was aware of what he was doing. He stopped the animal to sit quietly a moment, glancing back at the campsite with fear and indecision. If his uncles were dead, then there was nothing to do but get out into the open desert as quickly as possible, away from the rocks that could hide the Moungari while he took aim.

And so, not knowing the way to Tessalit, and without sufficient food or water, he started ahead, lifting one hand from time to time to wipe away the tears.

For two or three hours he continued that way, scarcely noticing where the *mehari* walked. All at once he sat erect, uttered an oath against himself, and in a fury turned the beast around. At that very moment his uncles might be seated in the camp with the Moungari, preparing a *mechoui* and a fire, sadly asking themselves why their nephew had deserted them. Or perhaps one would already have set out in search of him. There would be no possible excuse for his conduct, which had been the result of an absurd terror. As he thought about it, his anger against himself mounted: he had behaved in an unforgivable manner. Noon had passed; the sun was in the west. It would be late when he got back. At the prospect of the inevitable reproaches and the mocking laughter that would greet him, he felt his face grow hot with shame, and he kicked the *mehari's* flanks viciously.

A good while before he arrived at the camp he heard singing. This surprised him. He halted and listened: the voice was too far away to be identified, but Driss felt certain it was the Moungari's. He continued around the side of the hill to a spot in full view of the camels. The singing stopped, leaving silence. Some of the packs had been loaded back onto the beasts, preparatory to setting out. The sun had sunk low, and the shadows of the rocks were stretched out along the earth. There was no sign that they had caught any game. He called out, ready to dismount. Almost at the same instant there was a shot from very nearby, and he heard the small rushing sound of a bullet go past his head. He seized his gun. There was another shot, a sharp pain in his arm, and his gun slipped to the ground.

For a moment he sat there holding his arm, dazed. Then swiftly he leapt down and remained crouching among the stones, reaching out with his good arm for the gun. As he touched it, there was a third shot, and the rifle moved along the ground a few inches toward him in a small cloud of dust. He drew back his hand and looked at it: it was dark and blood dripped from it. At that moment the Moungari bounded across the open space between them. Before Driss could rise the man was upon him, had pushed him back down to the ground with the barrel of his rifle. The untroubled sky lay above; the Moungari glanced up at it defiantly. He straddled the supine youth, thrusting the gun into his neck just below the chin, and under his breath he said: "Filali dog!"

Driss stared up at him with a certain curiosity. The Moungari had the upper hand; Driss could only wait. He looked at the face in the sun's light, and discovered a peculiar intensity there. He knew the expression: it comes from hashish. Carried along on its hot fumes, a man can escape very far from the world of meaning. To avoid the malevolent face he rolled his eyes from side to side. There was only the fading sky. The gun was choking him a little. He whispered: "Where are my uncles?"

The Moungari pushed harder against his throat with the gun, leaned partially over and with one hand ripped away his *serouelles*, so that he lay naked from the waist down, squirming a little as he felt the cold stones beneath him.

Then the Moungari drew forth rope and bound his feet. Taking two steps to his head, he abruptly faced in the other direction, and thrust the gun into his navel. Still with one hand he slipped the remaining garments off over the youth's head and lashed his wrists together. With an old barber's razor he cut off the superfluous rope. During this time Driss called his uncles by name, loudly, first one and then the other.

The man moved and surveyed the young body lying on the stones. He ran his finger along the razor's blade; a pleasant excitement took possession of him. He stepped over, looked down, and saw the sex that sprouted from the base of the belly. Not entirely conscious of what he was doing, he took it in one hand and brought his other arm down with the motion of a reaper wielding a sickle. It was swiftly severed. A round, dark hole was left, flush with the skin; he stared a moment, blankly. Driss was screaming. The muscles all over his body stood out, moved.

Slowly the Mourgari smiled, showing his teeth. He put his hand on the hard belly and smoothed the skin. Then he made a small vertical incision there, and using both hands, studiously stuffed the loose organ in until it disappeared.

As he was cleaning his hands in the sand, one of the camels uttered a sudden growling gurgle. The Moungari leapt up and wheeled about savagely, holding his razor high in the air. Then, ashamed of his nervousness, feeling that Driss was watching and mocking him, (although the youth's eyes were unseeing with pain) he kicked him over on to his stomach where he lay making small spasmodic movements. And as the Moungari followed these with his eyes, a new idea came to him. It would be pleasant to inflict an ultimate indignity upon the young Filali. He threw himself down; this time he was vociferous and leisurely in his enjoyment. Eventually he slept.

At dawn he awoke and reached for his razor, lying on the ground nearby. Driss moaned faintly. The Moungari turned him over and pushed the blade back and forth with a sawing motion into his neck until he was certain he had severed the windpipe. Then he rose, walked away, and finished the loading of the camels he had started the day before. When this was done he spent a good while dragging the body over to the base of the hill and concealing it there among the rocks.

In order to transport the Filala's merchandise to Tessalit (for in Taoudeni there would be no buyers) it was necessary to take their *mehara* with him. It was nearly fifty days later when he arrived. Tessalit is a small town. When the Mourgari began to show the leather around, an old Filali

living there, whom the people called Ech Chibani, got wind of his presence. As a prospective buyer he came to examine the hides, and the
Moungari was unwise enough to let him see them. Filali leather is unmistakable, and only the Filala buy and sell it in quantity. Ech Chibani knew
the Moungari had come by it illicitly, but he said nothing. When a few
days later another caravan arrived from Tabelbala with friends of the three
Filala who asked after them and showed great distress on hearing that they
never had arrived, the old man went to the Tribunal. After some difficulty
he found a Frenchman who was willing to listen to him. The next day the
Commandant and two subordinates paid the Moungari a visit. They asked
him how he happened to have the three extra *mehara*, which still carried
some of their Filali trappings; his replies took a devious turn. The
Frenchmen listened seriously, thanked him, and left. He did not see the
Commandant wink at the others as they went out into the street. And so
he remained sitting in his courtyard, not knowing that he had been judged
and found guilty.

The three Frenchmen went back to the Tribunal where the newly
arrived Filali merchants were sitting with Ech Chibani. The story had an
old pattern; there was no doubt at all about the Moungari's guilt. "He is
yours," said the Commandant. "Do what you like with him."

The Filala thanked him profusely, held a short conference with the aged
Chibani, and strode out in a group. When they arrived at the Moungari's
dwelling he was making tea. He looked up, and a chill moved along his
spine. He began to scream his innocence at them; they said nothing, but at
the point of a rifle bound him and tossed him into a corner, where he
continued to babble and sob. Quietly they drank the tea he had been
brewing, made some more, and went out at twilight. They tied him to one
of the *mehara*, and mounting their own, moved in a silent procession (silent
save for the Moungari) out through the town gate into the infinite waste-
land beyond.

Half the night they continued, until they were in a completely unfrequented region of the dessert. While he lay raving, bound to the camel,
they dug a well-like pit, and when they had finished they lifted him off,
still trussed tightly, and stood him in it. Then they filled all the space
around his body with sand and stones, until only his head remained above
the earth's surface. In the faint light of the new moon his shaved pate
without its turban looked rather like a rock. And still he pleaded with
them, calling upon Allah and Sidi Ahmed Ben Moussa to witness his
innocence. But he might have been singing a song for all the attention they
paid to his words. Presently they set off for Tessalit; in no time they were
out of hearing.

When they had gone the Moungari fell silent, to wait through the cold hours for the sun that would bring first warmth, then heat, thirst, fire, visions. The next night he did not know where he was, did not feel the cold. The wind blew dust along the ground into his mouth as he sang.

SS Saturnia
(New York-Gibraltar)
1948

Señor Ong and Señor Ha

At the end of the town's long street a raw green mountain cut across the sky at a forty-five degree angle, its straight slope moving violently from the cloudy heights down into the valley where the river ran. In the valley, although the land was fertile, there were no farms or orchards, because the people of the town were lazy and did not want to bother clearing away the rocks that strewed the ground. And then, it was always too hot for that sort of work, and everybody had malaria there, so that long ago the town had fallen into its little pattern of living off the Indians who came down from the mountains with food and went back with cheap cloth, machetes and things like mirrors or empty bottles. Life always had been easy; although no one in the town was rich, still, no one ever went hungry. Almost every house had some papayas and a mango tree beside it, and there were plenty of avocados and pineapples to be had in the market for next to nothing.

Some of this had changed when the government had begun the building of the great dam up above. No one seemed to know exactly where the dam was; they were building it somewhere up in the mountains; already the water had covered several villages, and now after six years the construction was still going on. This last was the important part, because it meant that when the Indians came down from above they now brought with them not only food but money. Thus it had come about that certain people in the town had suddenly found themselves rich. They could scarcely believe it themselves, but there was the money, and still the Indians went on coming down and leaving more and more of it on the counters of their shops. They did not know what to do with all these unexpected pesos. Most of them bought huge radios which they kept going from early morning until night, all tuned in full strength to Tapachula, so that when they walked the length of the main street they were never out of earshot of the program and could follow it without a break. But still they had money. Pepe Jimenez had brought a bright new automobile in the capital, but by the time he had arrived back in town with it, after driving it over the sixty miles of trail from Mapastenango, it was no longer an object

to excite admiration, and he felt that he had made an unwise purchase.
Even the main street was too bumpy and muddy for him to drive it up and
down, and so it stood rusting in front of Mi Esperanza, the bar by the
bridge. When they came out of school Nicho and his companions would
play in it, pretending it was a fort. But then a group of larger boys from
the upper end of the town had come one day and appropriated the car for
their own games, so that the boys who lived by the river no longer dared
to approach it.

Nicho lived with his aunt in a small house whose garden ended in a
wilderness of plants and vines; just below them rushed the river, dashing
sideways from boulder to boulder in its shallow mist-filled canyon. The
house was clean and simple, and they lived quietly. Nicho's aunt was a
woman of too easygoing a nature. Being conscious of this, she felt that one
way of giving her dead sister's child the proper care was to attempt to instil
discipline in him; the discipline consisted in calling him by his true name,
which was Dionisio.

Nor did she have any conception of discipline as far as her own living
was concerned, so that the boy was not astonished when the day came that
she said to him: "Dionisio, you will have to stop going to school. We have
no more money. Don Anastasio will hire you at ten pesos a month to work
in his store, and you can get the noonday meal there too. *Lástima*, but
there is no money!"

For a week Nicho sat in the shop learning the prices of the articles that
Don Anastasio sold, and then one evening when he went home he found a
strange-looking man in the house, sitting in the other rocking chair opposite his aunt. The man looked a little like some of the Indians that came
down from the furthest and highest mountains, but his skin was lighter,
he was plumper and softer-seeming, and his eyes were almost shut. He
smiled at the boy, but not in a way that Nicho thought very friendly, and
shook hands without getting up from his chair. That night his aunt looked
really quite happy, and as they were getting ready for bed she said to him:
"Señor Ong is coming to live with us. You will not have to work any
more. God has been good to us."

But it occured to Nicho that if Señor Ong was to live with them, he
would prefer to go on working at Don Anastasio's, in order not to be
around the house and so have to see Señor Ong so much. Tactfully he
said: "I like Don Anastasio." His aunt looked at him sharply. "Señor Ong
does not want you to work. He is a proud man, and rich enough to feed us
both. It is nothing for him. He showed me his money."

Nicho was not at all pleased, and he went to sleep slowly, his mind full
of misgivings. He was afraid that one day he would fight with Señor Ong.
And besides, what would his friends say? Señor Ong was such a strange-

looking man. But the very next morning he arrived from the Hotel Paraiso with three boys whom Nicho knew, and each boy carried a large bag on his head. From the garden he watched them accept the generous tips Señor Ong gave them and then run off to school without waiting to see whether Nicho wanted to speak to them or not. "Very bad," he said to himself as he kicked a stone around and around the bare earth floor of the garden. A little while later he went down to the river and sat on top of the highest boulder watching the milky water that churned beneath him. One of his five cockatoos was screaming from the tangle of leaves on the banks. "*Callate!*" he yelled at it; his own ill-humor annoyed him as much as Señor Ong's arrival.

And everything turned out much as he had feared—only worse. Two days later, one of the boys from the upper end of the street said to him in passing: "*Hola, Chale!*" He replied to the greeting automatically and walked on, but a second later he said to himself: "*Chale?* But that means Chinaman! Chink!" Of course. Señor Ong must be a Chinaman. He turned to look at the boy, and thought of hitting him in the back with a stone. Then he hung his head and walked on slowly. Nothing would do any good.

Little by little the joke spread, and soon even his own friends called him *Chale* when they met him, and although it was really he who had become less friendly, he imagined that they all were avoiding him, that no one wanted to see him any more, and he spent most of his time playing by the river. The water's sound was deafening, but at the same time it made him feel a little bit better.

Neither Señor Ong nor his aunt paid much attention to him, save for their constant mealtime demands that he eat. "Now that we have more food than we need, you don't want to eat it," said his aunt angrily. "Eat, Dionisio," smiled Señor Ong. "*Bien,*" said Nicho, full of resentment, but in a tone of mock-resignation, and pulled off a small piece of tortilla which he chewed very slowly.

There seemed to be no question of his returning to school; at least, the subject was never mentioned, for which he was most grateful, since he had no desire to be back in the midst of his friends just to hear them call him *Chale.* The name by itself would have been bearable if only it had not implied the ridicule of his home life; his powerlessness to change that condition seemed much more shameful than any state of affairs for which he himself might have been at fault. And so he spent his days down by the river, jumping like a goat across the rocks, throwing stones to frighten the vultures away from the carcasses the water left for them, finding deep pools to swim in, and following the river downstream to lie idly naked on the rocks in the hot sun. No matter how pleasant to him Señor Ong might be—and already he had given him candy on several occasions, as well as a metal pencil with red lead in it—he could not bring himself to accept his being a part of the household. And then there were the singular visits of strange, rich townspeople, persons whom his aunt never had known, but who now appeared to find it quite natural to come to the house, stay for five or ten minutes talking to Señor Ong, and then go away again without so much as asking after his aunt, who always made a point of being in the back of the house or in the garden when they came. He could not understand that at all. It was still her house. Or perhaps not! Maybe she had given it to Señor Ong. Women often were crazy. He did not dare ask her. Once he was able to bring himself to inquire about the people, who kept coming in increasing numbers. She had answered: "They are friends of Señor Ong," and had looked at him with an expression which seemed to say: "Is that enough for you, busybody?" He was more than ever convinced that there was something more to know about the visitors. Then he met Luz, and being no longer alone, he ceased for a time to think about them.

When, one windy day, he had first seen her standing on the bridge, her bright head shining against the black mountains behind, he had stopped walking and stood perfectly still in order to look more carefully: he thought there was a mistake in his seeing. Never would he have believed it possible for anyone to look that way. Her hair was a silky white helmet on the top of her head, her whole face was white, almost as if she had covered it with paint, her brows and lashes, and even her eyes, were light to the point of not existing. Only her pale pink lips seemed real. She clutched the railing of the bridge tightly, an expression of intense preoccupation—or perhaps faint pain—on her face as she peered out from beneath her inadequate white brows. And her head moved slowly up and down as if it were trying to find an angle of vision which would be bearable for those feeble eyes that suffered behind their white lashes.

A few weeks back he merely would have stood looking at this apparition; now he watched intently until the girl, who was about his own age, seemed on the point of pitching forward into the road, and then he hurried toward her and firmly took her arm. An instant she drew back, squinting into his face.

"Who?" she said, confused.

"Me. What's the matter?"

She relaxed, let herself be led along. "Nothing," she answered after a moment. Nicho walked with her down the path to the river. When they got to the shade, the heavy lines in her forehead disappeared. "The sun hurts your eyes?" he asked her, and she said that it did. Under a giant breadfruit tree there were clean gray rocks; they sat down and he began a series of questions. She answered placidly; her name was Luz; she had come with her sister only two days ago from San Lucas; she would stay on with her grandfather here because her parents were having quarrels at home. All her replies were given while she gazed out across the landscape, yet Nicho was sure she could not see the feathery trees across the river or the mountains beyond. He asked her: "Why don't you look at me when you talk to me?"

She put her hand in front of her face. "My eyes are ugly."

"It's not true!" he declared with indignation. Then, "They're beautiful," he added, after looking at them carefully for a moment.

She saw that he was not making fun of her, and straightway decided that she liked him more than any boy she had ever known.

That night he told his aunt about Luz, and as he described the colors in her face and hair he saw her look pleased. "*Una hija del sol!*" she exclaimed. "They bring good luck. You must invite her here tomorrow. I shall prepare her a good *refresco de tamarindo.*" Nicho said he would, but he had no intention of subjecting his friend to his aunt's interested scrutiny. And while he was not at all astonished to hear that albinos had special powers, he thought it selfish of his aunt to want to profit immediately by those which Luz might possess.

The next day when he went to the bridge and found Luz standing there, he was careful to lead her through a hidden lane down to the water, so that she might remain unseen as they passed near the house. The bed of the river lay largely in the shadows cast by the great trees that grew along its sides. Slowly the two children wandered downstream, jumping from rock to rock. Now and then they startled a vulture, which rose at their approach like a huge cinder, swaying clumsily in the air while they walked by, to realight in the same spot a moment later. There was a particular place that he wanted to show her, where the river widened and had sandy shores, but it lay a good way downstream, so that it took them a long time to get there. When they arrived, the sun's light was golden and the insects had begun to call. On the hill, invisible behind the thick wall of trees, the soldiers were having machine-gun practice: the blunt little berries of sound came in clusters at irregular intervals. Nicho rolled his trouser legs up high above his knees and waded well out into the shallow stream. "Wait!" he called to her. Bending, he scooped up a handful of sand from the river bed. His attitude as he brought it back for her to see was so triumphant that she caught her breath, craned her neck to see it before he had arrived. "What is it?" she asked.

"Look! Silver!" he said, dropping the wet sand reverently into her outstretched palm. The tiny grains of mica glistened in the late sunlight.

"*Qué precioso!*" she cried in delight. They sat on some roots by the water.

When the sand was drier, she poured it carefully into the pocket of her dress.

"What are you going to do with it?" he asked her.

"Give it to my grandfather."

"No, no!" he exclaimed. "You don't give away silver. You hide it. Don't you have a place where you hide things?"

Luz was silent; she never had thought of hiding anything. "No," she said presently, and she looked at him with admiration.

He took her hand. "I'll give you a special place in my garden where you can hide everything you want. But you must never tell anyone."

"Of course not." She was annoyed that he should think her so stupid. For a while she had been content just to sit there with Nicho beside her; now she was impatient to get back and deposit the treasure. He tried to persuade her to stay a little longer, saying that there would be time enough if they returned later, but she had stood up and would not sit down again. They climbed upstream across the boulders, coming suddenly upon a pool where two young women stood thigh-deep washing clothes, naked save for the skirts wrapped round their waists, long full skirts that floated gently in the current. The women laughed and called out a greeting. Luz was scandalized.

"They should be ashamed!" she cried. "In San Lucas if a woman did that, everyone would throw stones at her until she was buried under them!"

"Why?" said Nicho, thinking that San Lucas must be a very wicked town.

"Because they would," she answered, still savoring the shock and shame she had felt at the sight of the golden breasts in the sunlight.

When they got back to town they turned into the path that led to Nicho's house, and while they were still in the jungle end of the garden, Nicho stopped and indicated a dead tree whose trunk had partially decayed. With the gesture of a conspirator he pulled aside the fringed curtain of vines that hung down across most of it, revealing several dark holes. Reaching into one of them, he pulled out a bright tin can, flicked off the belligerent ants that raced wildly around it, and held it forth for her.

"Put it in here," he whispered.

It took a while to transfer all the sand from her pocket to the can; when it was done he replaced it inside the dark trunk and let the vines fall straight again to cover the place. Then he conducted Luz quickly up through the garden, around the house, into the street. His aunt, having caught sight of them, called: "Dionisio!" But he pretended not to have heard her and pushed Luz ahead of him nervously. He was suddenly in terror lest Luz see Señor Ong; that was something which must be avoided at any cost.

"Dionisio!" She was still calling; she had come out and was standing in front of the door, looking down the street after them, but he did not turn around. They reached the bridge. It was out of sight of the house.

"*Adiós,*" he said.

"*Hasta mañana,*" she answered, peering up at him with her strange air of making a great effort. He watched her walk up the street, moving her head from side to side as if there were a thousand things to see, when in reality there were only a few pigs and some chickens roaming about.

At the evening meal his aunt eyed him reproachfully. He avoided her gaze; she did not mention his promise to bring Luz to the house for *refrescos.* That night he lay on his mat watching the phosphorescent beetles. His room gave on the patio; it had only three walls. The fourth side was wide open. Branches of the lemon tree reached in and rubbed against the wall above his head; up there, too, was a huge unfolding banana leaf which was pushing its way further into the room each day. Now the patio was dizzy with the beetles' sharp lights. Crawling on the plants or flying frantically between them, they flashed their signals on and off with maddening insistence. In the neighboring room his aunt and Señor Ong occupied the bed of the house, enjoying the privacy of quarters that were closed in on all four sides. He listened: the wind was rising. Nightly it appeared and played on the leaves of the trees, dying away again before dawn. Tomorrow he would take Luz down to the river to get more silver. He hoped Señor Ong had not been spying when he had uncovered the holes in the tree trunk. The mere thought of such a possibility set him to worrying, and he twisted on his mat from one side to the other.

Presently he decided to go and see if the silver was still there. Once he had assured himself either that it was safe or that it had been stolen, he would feel better about it. He sat up, slipped into his trousers, and stepped out into the patio. The night was full of life and motion; leaves and branches touched, making tiny sighs. Singing insects droned in the trees overhead; everywhere the bright beetles flashed. As he stood there feeling the small wind wander over him he became aware of other sounds in the direction of the *sala.* The light was on there, and for a moment he thought that perhaps Señor Ong had a late visitor, since that was the room where he received his callers. But he heard no voices. Avoiding the lemon tree's sharp twigs, he made his way soundlessly to the closed doors and peered between them.

There was a square niche in the *sala* wall across which, when he had first arrived, Señor Ong had tacked a large calendar. This bore a colored picture of a smiling Chinese girl. She wore a blue bathing suit and white fur-topped boots, and she sat by a pool of shiny pink tiles. Over her head in a luminous sky a gigantic four-motored plane bore down upon her, and further above, in a still brighter area of the heavens, was the benevolent face of Generalissimo Chiang. Beneath the picture were the words: ABARROTES FINOS. Sun Man Ngai, Huixtla, Chis. The calendar was the one object Señor Ong had brought with him that Nicho could wholeheartedly admire; he knew every detail of the picture by heart. Its presence had transformed the *sala* from a dull room with two old rocking chairs and a table to a place where anything might happen if one waited long enough. And now as he peeked through the crack, he saw with a shock that Señor Ong had removed the calendar from its place on the wall, and laid it on the table. He had a hammer and a chisel and he was pounding and scratching the bottom of the niche. Occasionally he would scoop out the resulting plaster and dust with his fat little hands, and dump it in a neat pile on the table. Nicho waited for a long time without daring to move. Even when the wind blew a little harder and chilled his naked back he did not stir, for fear of seeing Señor Ong turn around and look with his narrow eyes toward the door, the hammer in one hand, the chisel in the other. Besides, it was important to know what he was doing. But Señor Ong seemed to be in no hurry. Almost an hour went by, and still tirelessly he kept up his methodical work, pausing regularly to take out the debris and pile it on the table. At last Nicho began to feel like sneezing; in a frenzy he turned and ran through the patio to his room, scratching his chest against the branches on the way. The emotion engendered by his flight had taken away his desire to sneeze, but he lay down anyway for fear it might return if he went back to the door. In the midst of wondering about Señor Ong he fell asleep.

The next morning when he went into the *sala* the pretty Chinese girl covered the niche as usual. He stood still listening: his aunt and Señor Ong were talking in the next room. Quickly he pulled out the thumbtack in the lower left-hand corner of the calendar and reached in. He could feel nothing there. Disappointed, he fastened it back and went out into the garden. In the tree his treasure was undisturbed, but now that he suspected Señor Ong of having a treasure too, the little can of sand seemed scarcely worth his interest.

He went to the bridge and waited for Luz. When she came they walked to the river below the garden and sat beside the water. Nicho's mind was full of the image of Señor Ong bending over the niche with his tools, and his fancy was occupied with speculation as to what exactly he had been doing. He was uncertain whether or not to share his secret with Luz. He hoped she would not talk about her silver this morning; to forestall inquiries about it he mentioned curtly that he had looked at it only a half hour ago and that it was intact. Luz sat regarding him perplexedly; he seemed scarcely the same person as yesterday. Finally she said, as he continued to fix his gaze on the black pebbles at his feet: "What's the matter with you today?"

"Nothing." He grasped her arm to belie his word; the gesture betrayed him into beginning the confidence. "Listen. In my house there's a lot of gold hidden." He told her everything: Señor Ong's arrival, his own dislike of him, the visits of the town's rich shopkeepers to the house, and finally the suspicious behavior of Señor Ong in the *sala* the night before. She listened, blinking rapidly all the while. And when he had finished she agreed with him that it was probably gold hidden there in the niche, only she was inclined to think that it belonged to his aunt, and that Señor Ong had stolen it from her. This idea had not occurred to Nicho, and he did not really believe it. Nevertheless, it pleased him. "I'll get it and give it back to her," he declared. "Of course," said Luz solemnly, as if there were no alternative. They sat a while without speaking. Up in the garden all the cockatoos were screaming at once. The prospect of stealing back the gold in order to return it to his aunt excited him. But there were dangers. He began to describe the hideousness of Señor Ong's person and character, extemporaneously adding details. Luz shivered and looked apprehensively toward the shadowy path. "*Hay que tener mucho cuidado,*" she murmured. Then suddenly she wanted to go home.

Now there was only one thing to wait for: Señor Ong's absence from the house. In Tlaltepec there lived a Chinese man whom he usually visited each week, going on the early bus in the morning and returning in time for the midday meal. Three days went by. People came to the house and went away again, but Señor Ong sat quietly in the *sala* without once going into the street. Each day Nicho and Luz met on the bridge and sat by the river discussing the treasure with an excitement that steadily grew. "*Ay, qué maravilla!*" she would exclaim, holding her hands far apart. "This much gold!" Nicho would nod in agreement; all the same he had a feeling that when he saw the treasure he would be disappointed.

Finally the morning came when Señor Ong kissed Nicho's aunt on the cheek and went out of the house carrying a newspaper under his arm. "Where is he going?" Nicho asked innocently.

"Tlaltepec." His aunt was scrubbing the floor of the *sala*.

He went into the patio and watched a humming-bird buzz from one to another of the *huele-de-noche's* white flowers. When his aunt had finished in the *sala* she shut the door and started on the floor of the bedroom. In agitation he tiptoed into the room and over to the calendar, whose two lower corners he unfastened from the wall. Again the niche was empty. Its floor consisted of four large flower-decorated tiles. Without touching them he could tell which was the loose one. He lifted it up and felt underneath. It was a paper packet, not very large, and, which was worse, soft to the touch. He pulled out a fat manila envelope, replaced the tile and the calendar, and walked softly out through the patio, into the garden to his tree.

In the large envelope were a lot of little envelopes, and in some of the little envelopes there was a small quantity of odorless white powder. The other little envelopes were empty, held together by a rubber band. That was all there was. Nicho had expected a disappointment, but scarcely so complete a one as this. He was furious: Señor Ong had played a joke on him, had replaced the gold with this worthless dust, just out of deviltry. But when he thought about it, he decided that Señor Ong could not have guessed that he knew about the niche, so that after all this powder must be the real treasure. Also he felt it unlikely that it belonged to his aunt, in which case Señor Ong would be even more angry to find it gone. He took out two of the small empty envelopes, and from each of the others he poured a tiny bit of powder, until these two also contained about the same amount. Then he replaced both empty and full envelopes in the larger folder, and seeing that his aunt was in the kitchen, went back to the *sala* with it. Señor Ong would never notice the two missing envelopes or the powder that Nicho had poured into them. Once back in the garden he hid the two tiny packets under the tin can full of sand, and wandered down to the bridge.

It was too early to expect Luz. A thin gray curtain of rain came drifting up the valley. In another few minutes it would have arrived. The green mountainside at the end of the street glared in the half light. Don Anastasio came walking jauntily down the main street, and turned in at the side street where Nicho's house was. Obeying a blind impulse, he called to him: "*Muy buenos, Don Anastasio!*" The old man wheeled about; he seemed none too pleased to see Nicho. "Good day," he replied, and then he hurried on. Nicho ran from the bridge and stood at the entrance of the street watching him. Sure enough, he was about to go into Nicho's house.

"Don Anastasio!" he shouted, beginning to run toward him.

Don Anastasio stopped walking and stood still, his face screwed up in annoyance. Nicho arrived out of breath. "You wanted to see Señor Ong? He's gone out."

Don Anastasio did not look happy now, either. "Where?" he said heavily.

"I think to Mapastenango, perhaps," said Nicho, trying to sound vague, and wondering if that could be counted as a lie.

"*Qué malo!*" grunted Don Anastasio. "He won't be back today, then."

"I don't know."

There was a silence.

"Can I do anything for you?" faltered Nicho.

"No, no," said Don Anastasio hastily; then he stared down at him. During the week when Nicho had been working at his store, he had had occasion to notice that the boy was unusually quick. "That is," he added slowly, "I don't suppose—did Señor Ong . . . ?"

"Just a minute," said Nicho, feeling that he was about to discover the secret and at the same time become master of the situation. "Wait here," he added firmly. At the moment Don Anastasio showed no inclination to do anything else. He stood watching Nicho disappear around the corner of the house.

In a minute the boy returned panting, and smiled at Don Anastasio. "Shall we go to the bridge?" he said.

Again Don Anastasio acquiesced, looking furtively up and down the long street as they came out into it. They stood on the bridge leaning over the water below, and Nicho brought one of the little envelopes out of his pocket, glancing up at Don Anastasio's face at the same time. Yes! He had been right! He saw the features fixed in an expression of relief, pleasure and greedy anticipation. But only for an instant. By the time he was handing over the packet to Don Anastasio, the old man's face looked the same as always.

"*Muy bien, muy bien,*" he grumbled. The first small drops of rain alighted softly on their heads, but neither noticed them. "Do I pay you or Señor Ong?" said Don Anastasio, pocketing the envelope.

Nicho's heart beat harder for a few seconds: Señor Ong must not know of this. But he could not ask Don Anastasio not to tell him. He cleared his throat and said: "Me." But his voice sounded feeble.

"Aha!" said Don Anastasio, smiling a little; and he ruffled Nicho's hair in paternal fashion. Finding it wet, he looked up vacantly at the sky. "It's raining," he commented, a note of surprise in his voice.

"*Sí, señor,*" assented Nicho weakly.

"How much?" said Don Anastasio, looking at him very hard. In the valley the thunder groaned faintly.

Nicho felt he must answer immediately, but he had no idea what to say. "Is a peso all right?"

Don Anastasio stared at him even harder; he felt that the old man's eyes would cut through him in another instant. Then Don Anastasio's countenance changed suddenly, and he said: "A peso. Good." And he handed him a silver coin. "Next week you come to my store with another envelope. I'll give you an extra twenty centavos for making the trip. And— sssst!" He put his fingers to his lips, rolling his eyes upward. "Ssst!" He patted Nicho on the shoulder, looking very pleased, and went up the street.

Señor Ong came back earlier than usual, wet through, and in rather a bad humor. Nicho never had paid any attention to the conversations that passed between his aunt and Señor Ong. Now from the kitchen he listened, and heard him say: "I have no confidence in Ha. They tell me he was in town here two days ago. Of course he swears he was in Tlaltepec all the time."

"Three thousand pesos thrown into the street!" declared his aunt savagely. "I told you so then. I told you he would go on selling here as well as in Tlaltepec. *Yo te lo dije, hombre!*"

"I am not sure yet," said Señor Ong, and Nicho could imagine his soft smile as he said the words. Now that he had stolen from him he disliked him more than ever; in a sense he almost wished Señor Ong might discover the theft and accuse him, thereby creating the opportunity for him to say: "Yes, I stole from you, and I hate you." But he knew that he himself would do nothing to hasten such a moment. He went out through the rain to his tree. The earth's dark breath rose all around him, hung in the wet air. He took out the can of sand and dropped the peso into it.

It rained all day and through the night; Nicho did not see Luz until the following day. Then he adopted a mysterious, baffled air and conducted her to the tree.

"Look!" he cried, showing her the tin can. "The silver has made a peso!"

Luz was convinced and delighted, but she did not seem really surprised. "*Qué bueno!*" she murmured.

"Do you want to take it?" He held up the coin. But he was careful to keep his hand over the envelope in the tree's hollow.

"No, no! Leave it! Maybe it will make more. Put it back! Put it back!"

He was a little crestfallen to find that she took his miracle so nearly for granted. They stamped their feet to knock off the ants that were beginning to climb up their legs.

"And the gold?" she whispered. "Did you get it back for your aunt? Was it heavy? What did Señor Ong say?"

"There was nothing there at all," said Nicho, feeling uncomfortable without knowing why.

"Oh." She was disappointed.

They took a long walk down the river, and came upon an enormous iguana sunning himself on a rock above a pool. Nicho threw a stone, and the monster lumbered away into the leaves. Luz clutched his arm tightly as it disappeared from sight; there was the heavy sound of its body dragging through the underbrush. All at once Nicho shook himself free, pulling off his shirt and trousers, and gave a running leap into the pool. He splashed about, beating wildly at the water with his arms and legs, yelling loudly all the while. With an uncertain gait Luz approached the edge, where she sat down and watched him. Presently she said: "Find some more silver." She did not seem at all shocked by his nudity. He sank to the bottom and scrabbled about, touching only rock. Up again, he shouted: "There isn't any!" Her white head followed his movements as he cavorted around the pool. When he came out, he sat on the opposite side, letting the sun dry him. Behind the hill the machine-gun practice was again in progress.

"In San Lucas do you think they'd throw stones at me?" he shouted.

"Why?" she called. "No, no! *Claro que no!* For boys it's all right."

The next few days were sunny, and they came each afternoon to the pool.

One morning, the other little envelope in his pocket, Nicho went into the center of town to Don Anastasio's shop. The old man seemed very glad to see him. He opened the envelope behind the counter and looked carefully at its contents. Then he handed Nicho a peso and a half.

"I have no change," said Nicho.

"The *tostón* is for you," said Don Anastasio gruffly. "There's a cinema tonight. Come back next week. Don't forget."

Nicho ran down the street, wondering when he would have the chance to fill another envelope for Don Anastasio. It was about time for Señor Ong to make a trip to Tlaltepec.

A moment before he got to the bridge a tall woman stepped out of a shop and confronted him. She had very large eyes and a rather frightening face.

"*Hola, chico!*"

"*Sí, señora.*" He stood still and stared at her.

"Have you got something for me?"

"Something for you?" he repeated blankly.

"A little envelope?" She held out two pesos. Nicho looked at them and said: "*No, señora.*"

Her face became more frightening. "Yes. Yes. You have," she insisted, moving toward him. He glanced up and down the street: there was no one. The shop seemed to be empty. It was the hot hour of the day. He was suddenly terrified by her face. "Tomorrow," he cried, ducking to one side in order to dart past her. But she caught hold of his neck. "Today," she said roughly; her long fingernails were pushing into his skin. "*Sí, señora.*" He did not dare look up at her. "On the bridge," she grated. "This afternoon."

"*Sí, señora.*"

She let go and he walked on, sobbing a little with anger and shame for having been afraid.

In the *sala* Señor Ong and his aunt were talking excitedly. He did not go in, but climbed into a hammock in the patio and listened. Don Anastasio's name was mentioned. Nicho's heart skipped ahead: something had happened!

"Now I am almost sure," Señor Ong said slowly. "It is two weeks since he has been here, and Saenz tells me he is perfectly happy. That means only one thing: Ha must be supplying him directly."

"Of course," said his aunt bitterly. "You needn't have waited two weeks to know that. Three thousand pesos dropped into the river. What a waste! *Qué idota, tú!*"

Señor Ong paid no attention to her. "There's also the Fernandez woman," he mused. "She should have been around a few days ago. I know she has no money, but so far she has always managed to scrape together something."

"That old hag!" said his aunt contemptuously. "With her face now, she'll be lucky if she can raise twenty, not to speak of fifty."

"She can raise it," said Señor Ong with confidence in his voice. "The question is, has Ha already found her and is he giving it to her for less?"

"Don't ask *me* all these questions!" cried his aunt with impatience. "Go to Tlaltepec and ask the old man himself!"

"When I go there," said Señor Ong in a quiet, deadly voice, "it will not be to ask him anything."

At that moment a knock came at the front door; his aunt immediately left the room, shutting the door behind her, and went through the patio into the kitchen. For a few minutes Nicho could hear only the confused sound of low voices talking in the *sala*. Presently someone closed the front door. The visitor was gone.

Before the midday meal Nicho went out into the garden and tossed the two silver coins Don Anastasio had given him into the can of sand. It gave him pleasure to think of showing them to Luz; her credulity made him feel clever and superior. He determined never to tell her about the powder. All through lunch he thought about the tall woman he was to meet on the bridge. When the meal was over, Señor Ong did something unusual: he took up his hat and said: "I am going to see Saenz and have a talk with him." And he went out. Nicho watched him disappear into the main street; then he went into the house and saw his aunt shut herself into the bedroom for her siesta. Without hesitating he walked straight to the niche in the *sala* and took out the big yellow envelope. He knew he was doing a dangerous thing, but he was determined to do it anyway. Quickly he slipped two fat little envelopes into his pocket. He left one in his tree, and with the other he went out and stood on the bridge to wait for the woman. She was not long in spotting him from the shop. As she came toward him, her haggard face seemed to darken the afternoon. He held the little white envelope out to her even as she approached, as if to keep her at a certain distance from him. Frowning mightily, she reached for it, snatched it from his fingers like a furious bird, and violently pushed it inside her bodice. With the other hand she put two pesos into his still outstretched palm; and then she strode away without saying a word. He decided to remain on the bridge, hoping that Luz would appear presently.

When she came, he suddenly did not want to take her to the tree, or even to the river. Instead, grasping her hand, he said: "I have an idea." This was not true: as yet he had no idea, but he felt the need of doing something new, important.

"What idea?"

"Let's take a trip!"

"A trip! Where to?"

They started up the street hand in hand.

"We can take a bus," he said.

"But where?"

"No importa adonde."

Luz was not convinced the idea was sound; her mind was encumbered with visions of her older sister's stern face when she returned. Nevertheless he could see that she would go. As they came to where the houses and shops began, he let go of her hand for fear of meeting one of his friends. He had never walked on the street with her. The sun's light was intense, but a gigantic white cloud was rising slowly up from behind the mountains in front of them. He turned to look at her pale shining head. Her eyes were painful, squinting slits in her face. Surely no one else in the world had such beautiful hair. Glancing at the cloud he whispered to her: "The sun will go in soon."

At the central plaza there was a bus half full of people. From time to time the driver, who stood leaning against its red tin body, shouted: "Tlaltepec! Tlaltepec!" No sooner had they got aboard and taken seats near the back alongside the windows than Luz, in an access of apprehensiveness, asked to get out. But he held her arm and said, hurriedly inventing: *"Oye,* I wanted to go to Tlaltepec because we have something very important to do there. We have to save somebody's life." She listened attentively to his story: the monstrous Señor Ong was going to kill old Señor Ha for not having kept his promise to stay in Tlaltepec. As he recounted the tale, and recalled the wording of Señor Ong's threat, he began to believe the story himself. "When I go there it will not be to ask him anything." The old man would be given no opportunity to explain, no chance to defend himself. As the bus moved out of the plaza, he was as convinced as Luz that they were off to Tlaltepec on an heroic mission.

Tlaltepec was below, in a closed valley with mountains on all sides. The great white cloud, its brilliant edges billowing outward, climbed higher into the sky; as into a cave, the bus entered the precinct of its shadow. Here suddenly everything was green. Scraps of bird-song came in through the open windows, sharp above the rattling of the ancient vehicle.

"*Ay, el pobrecito!*" sighed Luz from time to time.

They came into Tlaltepec, stopped in the plaza. The passengers got out and quickly dispersed in different directions. The village was very quiet. Bright green grass grew in the middle of the streets. A few silent Indians sat around the plaza against the walls. Nicho and Luz walked up the main street, awed by the hush that enveloped the village. The cloud had covered the sky; now it was slowly pulled down like a curtain over the other side of the valley. A sad little churchbell began to ring behind them in the plaza. They turned into a small shop marked *Farmacia Moderna*. The man sitting inside knew Señor Ha: he was the only Chinese in the village. "He lives opposite the convent, in the last house." In Tlaltepec everything was nearby. The bell was still tolling from the plaza. In front of the ruined convent was an open square of sward; basketball posts had been put up at each end, but now they were broken. Before the last house stood a large tree laden with thousands of lavender flowers. In the still air they fell without cease, like silent tears, onto the damp earth beneath.

Nicho knocked on the door. A servant girl came and looked at the two children indifferently, went away. In a moment Señor Ha appeared. He was not quite so old as they had expected; his angular face was expressionless, but he looked closely at both of them. Nicho had hoped he would ask them into the house: he wanted to see if Señor Ha had a calendar like the one at home in the *sala*, but no such hospitality was forthcoming. Luz sat down on the stone step below them and picked up some of the blossoms that had fallen from the tree while Nicho told Señor Ha who he was and why he had come. Señor Ha stood quite still. Even when Nicho said: "And he is going to kill you," his hard little eyes remained in exactly the same position. Nothing in his face moved; he looked at Nicho as though he had not heard a word. For a moment Nicho thought that perhaps he understood nothing but Chinese, but then Señor Ha said, very clearly: "What lies!" And he shut the door.

They walked back to the plaza without saying anything, and sat down on an iron bench to wait for the bus. A warm, mistlike rain moved downward through the air, falling so softly that it was inaudible even in the stillness of the deserted plaza. At one point while they waited Nicho got up and went to the main street in search of some candy. As he came out of the shop, a little man carrying a briefcase walked quickly past and crossed the street. It was Señor Ha.

While they sat eating the candy a battered sedan came out of the main street and bumped across the plaza; on the edge of its back seat, leaning forward talking to the driver, was Señor Ha. They stared. The car turned into the road that led up the mountainside toward the town, and disappeared in the twilight.

"He's going to tell Señor Ong!" cried Nicho suddenly. He let his mouth stay open and fixed on the ground.

Luz squeezed his arm. "You don't care," she declared. "They're only Chinamen. You're not afraid of them."

He looked blankly at her. Then with scorn he answered: "No!"

They talked very little on the ride up in the rain. It was night by the time they arrived in the town. Wet and hungry, they went down the street toward the bridge, still without speaking. As they crossed the river Nicho turned to her and said: "Come and have dinner at my house."

"My sister . . . ."

But he pulled her roughly along with him. Even as he opened the front door and saw his aunt and Señor Ong sitting inside, he knew that Señor Ha had not been there.

"Why are you so late?" said his aunt. "You're wet." Then she saw Luz. "Shut the door, *niña*," she said, looking pleased.

While they ate in the covered part of the patio, Señor Ong continued with what he apparently had been saying earlier in the evening. ". . . She looked directly at me without saying a word."

"Who?" said his aunt, smiling at Luz.

"The Fernandez woman. This afternoon." Señor Ong's voice was edged with impatience. "For me that is proof enough. She's getting it somewhere else."

His aunt snorted. "Still you're looking for proof! *Niña*, take more meat." She piled extra food on Luz's plate.

"Yes, there's no doubt now," Señor Ong continued.

"What beautiful hair! *Ay, Dios!*" She smoothed the top of the girl's head. Nicho was ashamed: he knew that he had invited her to dinner because he had been afraid to come home alone, and he knew that his aunt was touching her hair only in order to bring herself good luck. He sighed miserably and glanced at Luz; she seemed perfectly content as she ate.

Suddenly there were several loud knocks on the front door. Señor Ong rose and went into the *sala*. There was a silence. A man's voice said: "*Usted se llama Narciso Ong?*" All at once there followed a great deal of noise; feet scuffled and furniture scraped on the tile floor. Nicho's aunt jumped up and ran into the kitchen where she began to pray very loudly. In the *sala* there was grunting and wheezing, and then as the racket grew less intense, a man said: "*Bueno.* I have it. A hundred grams, at least, right in his pocket. That's all we needed, my friend. *Vámonos.*"

Nicho slid down from his chair and stood in the doorway. Two men in wet brown ponchos were pushing Señor Ong out the front door. But he did not seem to want to go. He twisted his head and saw Nicho, opened his mouth to speak to him. One of the men hit him in the side of the face with his fist. "Not in front of the boy," said Señor Ong, wriggling his jaw back and forth to see if it was all right. "Not in front of the boy," he said again thickly. The other man slammed the door shut. The *sala* was empty. There was no sound but his aunt's wailing voice in the kitchen, crying aloud to God. He turned to look at Luz, who was sitting perfectly still.

"Do you want to go home?" he said to her.

"Yes." She got up. His aunt came out of the kitchen wringing her hands. Going over to Luz she laid her hand briefly on the white hair, still muttering a prayer.

"*Adiós, niña.* Come back tomorrow," she said.

There was still a light rain falling. A few insects sang from the wet leaves as the two silent children passed along the way to the house where Luz lived. When they rapped on the door it was opened immediately. A tall thin girl stood there. Without speaking she seized Luz with one arm and pulled her violently inside, closing the door with the other.

When Nicho got home and went into the *sala*, his first thought was that Señor Ong had returned, but the next instant he felt that he was in the middle of a bad dream. Señor Ha was sitting there talking with his aunt. She looked up tearfully. "Go to bed," she commanded.

Señor Ha reached out from his chair as Nicho passed and caught his arm—caught it very tightly. "*Ay!*" said Nicho in spite of himself. "One moment," said Señor Ha, still looking at Nicho's aunt, and never for a second relaxing his grip. "Perhaps this one knows." And without turning his face toward Nicho he said: "The police have taken Señor Ong to prison. He will not come back here. He hid something in this house. Where is it?"

It seemed as though the hard fingers would cut through his skin. His aunt looked up at him hopefully. He felt suddenly very important.

"There," he said, pointing to the calendar.

Señor rose and yanked the pretty girl from the wall. In an instant he had the yellow envelope in his hand. As he examined its contents, he said: "Is there any more?"

"No," said Nicho, thinking of the envelope lying in the safety of his tree out there in the rainy night. Señor Ha began to twist his arm, but the thought of his secret made him feel strong; his pain and his hatred flowed into that feeling of strength. He stood stiffly and let Señor Ha hurt him. A moment later Señor Ha let go of him and gave him a violent push that sent him halfway across the room. "Go to bed," he said.

When Nicho had gone out and closed the door, Señor Ha turned to the aunt. "Tomorrow I shall come back with my clothes," he said. "It is not good to have a boy around the house doing nothing; he gets into trouble. From now on he will deliver it; there will be no one coming to the house."

"But if the police catch him . . ." she objected.

"There will be no trouble with them. It is all arranged. Fortunately I had nearly three thousand pesos on hand." He picked up his briefcase and went to the door. She looked after him with frank admiration and sighed deeply. "You won't stay tonight?" She said the words timidly, and they sounded strangely coquettish.

"No. The car is outside waiting for me. Tomorrow." He opened the door. Rising, she went and took his hand, pressing it warmly between her two hands. "Tomorrow," he repeated.

When the car had driven away and she could no longer hear it, she closed the door, turned off the light, and went out into the patio, where she got into a hammock and lay swinging gently back and forth.

"An intelligent man," she said to herself. "What good luck!" She stopped swinging a moment. "Good luck! Of course! Dionisio must bring her to the house again one day very soon."

The town went on being prosperous, the Indians kept coming down from the heights with money, the thick jungle along the way to Mapas- tenango was hacked away, the trail widened and improved. Nicho bought a packet of little envelopes. Far down the river he found another hollow tree. Here he kept his slowly increasing store of treasure; during the very first month he picked up enough money on the side to buy Luz a lipstick and a pair of dark glasses with red and green jewels all around the rims.

Fez
1947

A Thousand Days for Mokhtar

Mokhtar lived in a room not far from his shop, overlooking the sea. There was a tiny window in the wall above his sleeping-mattress, through which, if he stood on tiptoe, he could see the waves pounding against the rocks of the breakwater far below. The sound came up, too, especially on nights when the Casbah was wrapped in rain and its narrow streets served only for the passage of unexpected gusts of wind. On these nights the sound of the waves was all around, even though he kept the window shut. Throughout the year there were many such nights, and it was precisely at such times that he did not feel like going home to be alone in his little room. He had been by himself ten years now, ever since his wife had died; his solitude never weighed on him when the weather was clear and the stars shone in the sky. But a rainy night put him in mind of the happy hours of his life, when in just such nocturnal wind and storm he and his great-eyed bride would pull the heavy blinds shut and live quietly in each other's company until dawn. These things he could not think about; he would go to the Café Ghazel and play dominoes hour after hour with anyone who came along, rather than return to his room.

Little by little the other men who sat regularly in the café had come to count on Mokhtar's appearance. "It's beginning to rain: Si Mokhtar will be along soon. Save him the mat next to you." And he never disappointed them. He was pleasant and quiet; the latter quality made him a welcome addition to a game, since the café's habitués considered each other far too talkative.

Sitting in the Café Ghazel tonight Mokhtar was unaccountably uneasy. He was disturbed by the bonelike sound of the dominoes as they were shuffled on the tables. The metallic scraping of the old phonograph in the inner room bothered him, and he looked up with an unreasoning annoyance at each new arrival who came in through the door, heralded by blasts of wet wind. Often he glanced out the window beside him at the vast blackness of the sea lying below at the foot of the city. On the other side of the glass, just at the edge of the cliff, a few tall stalks of bamboo caught the light from inside, stood out white against the blackness beyond, bending painfully before the gale.

193

"They'll break," murmured Mokhtar.

"What?" said Mohammed Slaoui.

Mokhtar laughed, but said nothing. As the evening continued, his discomfort increased. In the inner room they had stopped the phonograph and were singing a strident song. Some of the men around him joined in the noise. He could no longer hear the wind. As that round of dominoes came to an end, he rose precipitately and said: "Good night," not caring how strange his sudden departure might seem to the others.

Outside in the street it was scarcely raining at all, but the wind raged upward from the shore below, bringing with it the bloodlike smell of the sea; the crashing waves seemed very near, almost at his feet. He looked down as he walked along. At each mound of garbage there were cats; they ran across in front of him constantly from one pile to another. As Mokhtar reached his door and pulled out his key, he had the feeling that he was about to perform an irrevocable act, that stepping inside would be a gesture of finality.

"What is happening?" he asked himself. "Am I going to die?" He would not be afraid of that; still, he would like to know it a few moments in advance, if possible. He flexed his arms and legs before opening the door: there was no pain anywhere, everything appeared to be in good condition. "It's my head," he decided. But his head felt clear, his thoughts moved forward in orderly fashion. Nevertheless, these discoveries did not reassure him; he knew something was wrong. He bolted the door behind him and began to mount the stairs in the dark. More clearly than anything else at the moment he sensed that this conviction of having entered into a new region of his life was only in the nature of a warning. "Don't go on," he was being told. "Doing what?" he asked himself as he undressed. He had no secrets, no involvements, no plans for the future, no responsibilities. He merely lived. He could not heed the warning because he could not understand it. And yet there was no doubt that it was there in his room, and it made itself most strongly felt when he lay down. The wind shook the blinds. The rain had begun to fall again; it showered violently on the panes of glass over the corridor, and rattled down the drainpipe from the roof. And the unappeased roaring of the waves went on, down at the base of the ramparts. He considered the sadness, the coldness of the damp blanket; he touched the straw-covered wall with his finger. In the black night he groaned: "Al-lah!" and fell asleep.

But even in sleep he went on worrying; his dreams were a chaotic, relentless continuation of his waking state. The same accent of implicit warning was present in the sequences of streets and shops which unrolled before his eyes. He was at the entrance to the public market. A great many people were inside, where they had gone to get out of the rain. Although it was mid-morning, the day was so dark that all the stalls were blazing with electric lights. "If only she could have seen this," he said to himself, thinking of how much pleasure it would have given his wife. "Poor girl, in her day it was always dark here." And Mokhtar wondered if really he had the right to go on living and watching the world change, without her. Each month the world had changed a little more, had gone a little farther away from what it had been when she had known it.

"Also, since she is not here to eat it, what am I doing buying meat?" He was standing before the stall of his friend Abdallah ben Bouchta, looking at the cuts that were displayed on the slab of white marble in front of him. And all at once he was embroiled in a quarrel with Bouchta. He felt himself seizing the old man by the throat; he felt his fingers pressing with increasing force: he was choking Bouchta and he was glad to be doing it. The violence of the act was a fulfillment and a relief. Bouchta's face grew black, he fell, and his glazed eyes stared like the eyes in a sheep's head served on a platter for the feast of Aïd el Kébir.

Mokhtar awoke, horrified. The wind was still blowing, carrying with it, above the town, wisps of the voice of the muezzin who at that moment was calling from the Jaamâa es Seghira. But the warnings had ceased, and this was comforting enough to make more sleep possible.

The morning was gray and cheerless. Mokhtar rose at the usual hour, made his daily visit to the great mosque for a few moments of prayer and a thorough wash, and proceeded through the rain to his shop. There were few people in the streets. The memory of his dream weighed upon him, saddening him even more than the prospect of a day of infrequent sales. As the morning progressed he thought often of his old friend; he was consumed with the desire to pass by the market, just to assure himself that Bouchta was there as always. There was no reason why he should not be, but once Mokhtar had seen him with his own eyes he would be content.

A little before noon he boarded up the front of his shop and set out for the market. When his eyes became accustomed to the dim inner light of the building, the first person he saw was Bouchta standing behind the counter in his stall, chopping and slicing the meat the same as any other day. Feeling immensely relieved, Mokhtar wandered over to the counter and spoke to him. Perhaps the note of excessive cordiality in his voice surprised Bouchta, for he glanced up with a startled expression in his face, and seeing Mokhtar, said shortly: "*Sbahalkheir.*" Then he resumed hacking at a piece of meat for a customer. His rather unfriendly look was lost on Mokhtar, who was so pleased to see him there that he was momentarily unable to perceive anything but that one fact. However, when Bouchta, on completing the sale, turned to him and said abruptly: "I'm busy this morning," Mokhtar stared at him, and again felt his fear stir within him.

"Yes, Sidi?" he said pleasantly.

Bouchta glared. "Twenty-two douro would be a more welcome offering than your foolish smile," he said.

Mokhtar looked confused. "Twenty-two douro, Sidi?"

"Yes. The twenty-two douro you never paid me for the lamb's head at last Aïd el Kébir."

Mokhtar felt the blood leap upward in him like a fire. "I paid you for that the following month."

"*Abaden!* Never!" cried Bouchta excitedly. "I have eyes and a head too! I remember what happens! You can't take advantage of me the way you did of poor old Tahiri. I'm not that old yet!" And he began to call out unpleasant epithets, brandishing his cleaver.

People had stopped in their tracks and were following the conversation with interest. As Mokhtar's anger mounted, he suddenly heard, among the names that Bouchta was calling him, one which offended him more than the rest. He reached across the counter and seized Bouchta's *djellaba* in his two hands, pulling on the heavy woolen fabric until it seemed that it would surely be ripped off the old man's back.

"Let go of me!" shouted Bouchta. The people were crowding in to see whatever violence might result. "Let go of me!" he kept screaming, his face growing steadily redder.

At this point the scene was so much like his dream that Mokhtar, even while he was enjoying his own anger and the sight of Bouchta as he became the victim of such a senseless rage, was suddenly very much frightened. He let go of the *djellaba* with one hand, and turning to the onlookers said loudly: "Last night I dreamed that I came here and killed this man, who is my friend. I do not want to kill him. I am not going to kill him. Look carefully. I am not hurting him."

Bouchta's fury was reaching grotesque proportions. With one hand he was trying to pry Mokhtar's fingers from his garment, and with the other, which held the cleaver, he was making crazy gyrations in the air. All the while he jumped quickly up and down, crying: "Let go! Let go! *Khlass!*"

"At any moment he is going to hit me with the cleaver," thought Mokhtar, and so he seized the wrist that held it, pulling Bouchta against the counter. For a moment they struggled and panted, while the slabs of meat slid about under their arms and fell heavily onto the wet floor. Bouchta was strong, but he was old. Suddenly he relaxed his grasp on the cleaver and Mokhtar felt his muscles cease to push. The crowd murmured. Mokhtar let go of both the wrist and the *djellaba*, and looked up. Bouchta's face was an impossible color, like the sides of meat that hung behind him. His mouth opened and his head slowly tilted upward as if he were looking at the ceiling of the market. Then, as if someone had pushed him from behind, he fell forward onto the marble counter and lay still, his nose in a shallow puddle of pinkish water. Mokhtar knew he was dead, and he was a little triumphant as he shouted to everyone: "I dreamed it! I dreamed it! I told you! Did I kill him? Did I touch him? You saw!" the crowd agreed, nodding.

"Get the police!" cried Mokhtar. "I want everyone to be my witness." A few people moved away quietly, not wishing to be involved. But most of them stayed, quite ready to give the authorities their version of the strange phenomenon.

In court the Cadí proved to be unsympathetic. Mokhtar was bewildered by his lack of friendliness. The witnesses had told the story exactly as it had happened; obviously they all were convinced of Mokhtar's innocence.

"I have heard from the witnesses what happened in the market," said the Cadí impatiently, "And from those same witnesses I know you are an evil man. It is impossible for the mind of an upright man to bring forth an evil dream. Bouchta died as a result of your dream." And as Mokhtar attempted to interrupt: "I know what you are going to say, but you are a fool, Mokhtar. You blame the wind, the night, your long solitude. Good. For a thousand days in our prison here you will not hear the wind, you will not know whether it is night or day, and you will never lack the companionship of your fellow-prisoners."

The Cadí's sentence shocked the inhabitants of the town, who found it of an unprecedented severity. But Mokhtar, once he had been locked up. was persuaded of its wisdom. For one thing, he was not unhappy to be in prison, where each night, when he had begun to dream that he was back in his lonely room, he could awaken to hear on all sides of him the comforting snores of the other prisoners. His mind no longer dwelled upon the earlier happy hours of his life, because the present hours were happy ones as well. And then, the very first day there, he had suddenly remembered with perfect clarity that, although he had intended to do so, he never had paid Bouchta the twenty-two douro for the lamb's head, after all.

Tangier
1948

The Fourth Day Out
From Santa Cruz

Ramón signed on at Cádiz. The ship's first call was at Santa Cruz de Tenerife, a day and a half out. They put in at night, soon after dark. Floodlights around the harbor illumined the steep bare mountains and made them grass-green against the black sky. Ramón stood at the rail, watching. "It must have been raining here," he said to a member of the crew standing beside him. The man grunted, looking not at the green slopes unnaturally bright in the electric glare, but at the lights of the town ahead. "Very green," went on Ramón, a little less certainly; the man did not even grunt in reply.

As soon as the ship was anchored, scores of Hindu shopkeepers came aboard with laces and embroidered goods for the passengers who might not be going ashore. They stayed on the first-class deck, not bothering to go down below to third-class where Ramón was scullery boy in the passengers' *cocina*. The work so far did not upset him; he had held more exacting and tiring jobs in Cádiz. There was sufficient food, and although it was not very good, nevertheless it was better than what was taken out to the third-class passengers. It had never occurred to Ramón to want privacy in his living quarters, so that he was unmoved by the necessity of sharing a cabin with a dozen or so shipmates. Still, he had been acutely unhappy since leaving Cádiz. Except for the orders they gave him in the kitchen, the sailors behaved as if he did not exist. They covered his bunk with their dirty clothes, and lay on it, smoking, at night when he wanted to sleep. They failed to include him in any conversation, and so far no one had even made an allusion, however deprecatory, to his existence. For them it appeared that he simply was not present. To even the least egocentric man such a state of affairs can become intolerable. In his sixteen years Ramón had not been in a similar situation; he had been maltreated but not wholly disregarded.

Most of the crew stood at the prow smoking, pointing out bars to one another, as they scanned the waterfront. Partly out of perversity born of his grievance, and partly because he wanted to be by himself for a spell, Ramón walked to the stern and leaned heavily against the rail, looking down into

the darkness below. He could hear an automobile horn being blown continuously as it drove along the waterfront. The hills behind backed up the sound, magnified it as they threw it across the water. From the other side came the dim roar of the sea's waves against the breakwater. He was a little homesick, and as he stood there he became angry as well. It was inadmissible that this state of affairs should continue. A day and a half was too long; he was determined to force a change immediately, and to his undisciplined young mind· kept recurring the confused image of a fight—a large-scale struggle with the entire crew, in which he somehow finished as the sole victor.

It is pleasant to walk by the sea-wall of a foreign port at night, with the autumn wind gently pushing at your back. Ramón was in no hurry; he stopped before each café and listened to the guitars and shouting, without, however, allowing himself to be detained by the women who called to him from the darker doorways. Having had to clean up the galley after an extra meal had been served to sixty workmen who had just come aboard here at Santa Cruz, bound for South America, he had been the last to get off the ship, and so he was looking for his shipmates. At the Café del Teide he found several of them seated at a table sharing a bottle of rum. They saw him come in, but they gave no sign of recognition. There was no empty chair. He walked toward the table, slowed down a bit as he approached it, and then continued walking toward the back of the café. The man behind the bar called out to him: "You were looking for something?" Ramón turned around and sat down suddenly at a small table. The waiter came and served him, but he scarcely noticed what he was drinking. He was watching the table with the six men from his ship. Like one fascinated, he let his eyes follow each gesture: the filling of the little glasses, the tossing down the liquor, the back of the hand wiping the mouth. And he listened to their words punctuated by loud laughter. Resentment began to swell in him; he felt that if he sat still any longer he would explode. Pushing back in his chair, he jumped up and strode dramatically out into the street. No one noticed his exit.

He began to walk fast through the town, paying no attention to where he was going. His eyes fixed on an imaginary horizon, he went through the *plaza*, along the wide Paseo de Ronda, and into the tiny streets that lie behind the cathedral. The number of people in the streets increased as he walked away from the center of town, until when he had come to what seemed an outlying district, where the shops were mere stalls, he was forced to saunter along with the crowd. As he slowed down his gait, he felt less nervous. Gradually he took notice of the merchandise for sale, and of the people around him. It suddenly occurred to him that he would like to buy a large handkerchief. Outside certain booths there were wires strung up;

from these hung, clipped by their corners, a great many of the squares of cloth, their bright colors showing in the flare of the carbide lamps. As Ramón stopped to choose one at the nearest booth he became aware that in the next booth a girl with a laughing face was also buying a bandana. He waited until she had picked out the one she wanted, and then he stepped quickly over to the shopkeeper and pointing down at the package he was making, said: "Have you another handkerchief exactly like that?" The girl paid no attention to him and put her change into her purse. "Yes," said the shopkeeper, reaching out over the counter to examine the bandanas. The girl picked up her little packet wrapped in newspaper, turned away, and walked along the street. "No, you haven't!" cried Ramón, and he hurried after her so as not to lose sight of her in the crowd. For some distance he trailed her along the thoroughfare, until she turned into a side street that led uphill. It smelled here of drains and there was very little light. He quickened his pace for fear she would go into one of the buildings before he had had the opportunity to talk to her. Somewhere in the back of his mind he hoped to persuade her to go with him to the Café del Teide. As he overtook her, he spoke quietly without turning his head: "Señorita." To his surprise she stopped walking and stood still on the pavement. Although she was very near to him, he could not see her face clearly.

"What do you want?"

"I wanted to talk to you."

"Why?"

He could not answer.

"I thought . . ." he stammered.

"What?"

There was a silence, and then as she laughed Ramón remembered her face: open and merry, but not a child's face. In spite of the confidence its recalled image inspired in him, he asked: "Why do you laugh?"

"Because I think you're crazy."

He touched her arm and said boldly: "You'll see if I'm crazy."

"I'll see nothing. You're a sailor. I live here"; she pointed to the opposite side of the street. "If my father sees you, you'll have to run all the way to your ship." Again she laughed. To Ramón her laugh was music, faintly disturbing.

"I don't want to bother you. I only wanted to talk to you," he said, timid again.

"Good. Now you've talked. *Adiós.*" She began to walk on. So did Ramón, close behind her. She did not speak. A moment later, he remarked triumphantly: "You said you lived back there!"

"It was a lie," she said in a flat voice. "I always lie."

"Ah. You always lie," echoed Ramón with great seriousness.

They came to a street light at the foot of a high staircase. The sidewalk became a series of stone steps leading steeply upward between the houses. As they slowly ascended, the air changed. It smelled of wine, food cooking, and burning eucalyptus leaves. Up above the city here, life was more casual. People leaned over the balconies, sat in dark doorways chatting, stood in the streets like islands among the moving dogs and children.

The girl stopped and leaned against the side of a house. She was a little out of breath from the climb.

"Tired?" he asked.

Instead of replying she turned swiftly and darted inside the doorway beside her. For a few seconds Ramón was undecided whether or not to follow her. By the time he had tiptoed into the dimly lit passageway she had disappeared. He walked through into the courtyard. Some ragged boys who were running about stopped short and stared at him. A radio was playing guitar music above. He looked up. The building was four stories high; there were lights in almost all the windows.

On his way back to the waterfront a woman appeared from the shadows of the little park by the cathedral and took his arm. He looked at her; she was being brazenly coy, with her head tilted at a crazy angle as she repeated: "I like sailors." He let her walk with him to the Café del Teide. Once inside, he was disappointed to see that his shipmates were gone. He bought the woman a *manzanilla* and walked out on her as she began to drink it. He had not said a word to her. Outside, the night seemed suddenly very warm. He came to the Blanco y Negro; a band was playing inside. Two or three of the men from the ship were on the dark dance floor, trying to instil a bit of life into the tired girls that hung to them. He did not even have a drink here, but hurried back to the ship. His bunk was piled with newspapers and bundles, but the cabin was empty, and he had several hours in the dark in which to brood and doze, before the others arrived. The boat sailed at dawn.

They skirted the island next day—not close enough to see the shore, but within sight of the great conical mountain, which was there all day beside them in the air, clear in distant outline. For two days the ship continued on a southwest course. The sea grew calm, a deep blue, and the sun blazed brighter in the sky. The crew had ceased gathering on the poopdeck, save in the early evening and at night, when they lay sprawled all over it, singing in raucous voices while the stars swayed back and forth over their heads.

For Ramón life continued the same. He could see no difference in the crew's attitude toward him. It still seemed to him that they lived without him. The magazines that had been bought at Santa Cruz were never passed around the cabin. Afternoons when the men sat around the table in the third-class *comedor*, the stories that were recounted could never be interpreted by any gesture in their telling as being directed at a group that included him. And he certainly knew better than to attempt to tell any himself. He still waited for a stroke of luck that might impose him forcibly upon their consciousness.

In the middle of the fourth morning out from Santa Cruz he poked his head from the galley and noticed several of the men from his cabin gathered along the railing at the stern. The sun was blinding and hot, and he knew something must be keeping them there. He saw one man pointing aft. Casually he wandered out across the deck to within a few feet of the group, searching the sea and the horizon for some object—something besides the masses of red seaweed that constantly floated by on top of the dark water.

"It's getting nearer!"

"*Qué fuerza!*"

"It's worn out!"

"*Claro!*"

Ramón looked over their heads, and between them when they changed position from time to time. He saw nothing. He was almost ready to be convinced that the men were baiting him, in the hope of being able to amuse themselves when his curiosity should be aroused to the point of making him ask: "What is it?" And so he was determined to be quiet, to wait and see.

Suddenly he did see. It was a small yellow and brown bird flying crookedly after the boat, faltering as it repeatedly fell back toward the water between spurts of desperate energy.

"A thousand miles from land!"

"It's going to make it! Look! Here it comes!"

"No!"

"Next time."

At each wild attempt to reach the deck, the bird came closer to the men, and then, perhaps from fear of them, it fluttered down toward the boiling sea, missing the wake's maelstrom by an ever closer margin. And when it seemed that this time it surely would be churned under into the white chaos of air and water, it would surge feebly upward, its head turned resolutely toward the bright mass of the ship that moved always in front of it.

Ramón was fascinated. His first thought was to tell the men to step back a little from the rail so that the bird might have the courage to land. As he opened his mouth to suggest this, he thought better of it, and was immediately thankful for having remained quiet. He could imagine the ridicule that would have been directed at him later: in the cabin, at mealtime, evenings on the deck . . . Someone would have invented a shameful little ditty about Ramón and his bird. He stood watching, in a growing agony of suspense.

"Five pesetas it goes under!"

"Ten it makes it!"

Ramón wheeled about and ran lightly across to the galley. Almost immediately he came out again. In his arms he carried the ship's mascot, a heavy tomcat that blinked stupidly in the sudden glare of the sun. This time he walked directly back to the railing where the others stood. He set the animal down at their feet.

"What are you doing?" said one.

"Watch," said Ramón.

They were all quiet a moment. Ramón held the cat's flanks and head steady, waiting for it to catch sight of the fluttering bird. It was difficult to do. No matter how he directed its head it showed no sign of interest. Still they waited. As the bird came up to the level of the deck at a few feet from the boat, the cat's head suddenly twitched, and Ramón knew the contact had been made. He took his hands away. The cat stood perfectly still, the end of its tail moving slightly. It took a step closer to the edge, watching each movement of the bird's frantic efforts.

"Look at that!"

"He sees it."

"But the bird doesn't see him."

"If it touches the boat, the ten pesetas still go."

The bird rose in the air, flew faster for a moment until it was straight above their heads. They looked upward into the flaming sun, trying to shade their eyes. It flew still farther forward, until, if it had dropped, it would have landed a few feet ahead of them on the deck. The cat, staring up into the air, ran quickly across the deck so that it was directly below the bird, which slowly let itself drop until it seemed that they could reach out and take it. The cat made a futile spring into the air. They all cried out, but the bird was too high. Suddenly it rose much higher; then it stopped flying. Swiftly they passed beneath it as it remained poised an instant in the air. When they had turned their heads back it was a tiny yellow thing falling slowly downward, and almost as quickly they lost sight of it.

At the noonday meal they talked about it. After some argument the bets were paid. One of the oilers went to his cabin and brought out a bottle of cognac and a set of little glasses which he put in front of him and filled, one after the other.

"Have some?" he said to Ramón.

Ramón took a glass, and the oiler passed the rest around to the others.

Tangier
1949

Doña Faustina

1

No one could understand why Doña Faustina had bought the inn. It stood on one of the hairpin curves in the old highway leading up from the river valley to the town, but the route had been made useless by the building of the new paved road. Now it was impossible to reach the inn except by climbing up a stony path over the embankment and walking several hundred feet down the old road which, no longer kept in repair, already was being washed away by the rains and strangled by the shiny vegetation of that lowland region.

On Sundays the people used to walk out from the town, the women carrying parasols and the men guitars (for this was before the days of the radio, when almost everyone knew how to make a little music); they would get as far as the great breadfruit tree and look up the road at the faded façade of the building, more than half hidden by young bamboo and banana plants, stare a few seconds, and turn around to go back. "Why does she leave the sign up?" they would say. "Does she think anyone would ever spend the night there now?" And they were quite right: no one went near the inn any more. Only the people of the town knew that it existed, and they had no need of it.

There remained the mystery of why she had bought it. As usual when there is something townspeople cannot understand, they invented a whole series of unpleasant explanations for Doña Faustina's behavior. The earliest and most common one, which was that she had decided to transform the place into a house of ill-repute, soon fell to pieces, for there was absolutely nothing to substantiate such a theory. No one had been seen to go near the inn for weeks, except Doña Faustina's younger sister Carlota who arrived from Jalapa, and the old servants José and Elena, who went to market each morning and minded their business strictly enough to satisfy even the most vicious gossips. As for Carlota, she appeared occasionally at Mass, dressed in black. It was said that she had taken their father's death very much to heart, and would probably not remove the mourning, ever.

The other suppositions evolved by the people of the town in their effort to bring light to the mystery proved as unlikely as the first. It was rumored that Doña Faustina was giving asylum to Chato Morales, a bandit whom the police of the region had been trying for months to capture, but he was caught soon afterward in a distant part of the province. Then it was said that the inn was a depository for a drug ring; this also proved to be false. The leaders of the ring, having been arrested, divulged their secrets, and the cache proved to be in a room above the Farmácia Ideal. There were darker hints to the effect that Carlota might be luring lone voyagers to the inn, where they met the fate that traditionally befalls such solitary visitors to lonely inns. But people did not take such suggestions seriously. The opinion grew that Doña Faustina had merely gone a little mad, and that her madness, having taken an antisocial turn, had induced her to retire to the outskirts of town where she could live without ever seeing anyone. To be sure, this theory was contested by certain younger members of the community who claimed that she was no more crazy than they, that on the contrary she was extremely crafty. They said that having a great deal of money she had bought the inn because of the ample lands which surrounded it, and that there in the privacy of the plant-smothered gardens and orchards she had devised all kinds of clever ways of hiding her riches. The older citizens of the town took no stock in this, however, since they clearly remembered both her husband and her father, neither of whom had evinced any unusual prowess in collecting money. And she had bought the inn for practically nothing. "Where would she have got the pesos?" they said sceptically. "Out of the trees, perhaps?"

2

Once when a child disappeared from the town (small children were often stolen in those days and taken off to distant places where they were made to work), the parents insisted that the police search the inn. Doña Faustina, who was a large woman in the prime of life, met the little policeman at the door and refused to let him in. Indeed, she was so brusque with him and glared at him with such malignity that he felt obliged to go back to the *comisaría* and get reinforcements. When he and the three extra men returned to the inn, they made a complete but unrewarding search of the place, followed at every step by Doña Faustina, who did not cease to shower them with insults until they had left the premises. But they returned to town with a story. The rooms were a shambles, they said, the furniture was broken, there was rubbish and garbage everywhere in the corridors, the railing of the second-story balcony had given way and been replaced by a single strand of barbed wire, and the place looked generally as though innumerable picnic parties had been held there over a period of years. This report helped to fortify people in their belief that Doña Faustina had more or less lost her mind, and for a time the town ceased thinking about her.

Some time afterward it was noted that she and her sister had taken to making trips to neighboring towns; they had been seen in such widely separated places as Tlacotalpam and Zempoala. But even these peregrinations failed to elicit true interest. Heads were shaken, sympathetically or otherwise, and it was remarked that Doña Faustina was growing less and less sane, but that was all.

When the mistresses of the house were absent they did not return for three or four days, and José and Elena remained alone to guard the property, not even venturing forth to the town for marketing until the two reappeared. On their return the sisters would take an old covered carriage that went each day to the station to await the train. They would pile their numerous bundles and baskets in and drive as far as the curve, where they would get down, the driver helping them up the embankment with their effects and then leaving them to get to the house in whatever way they could. Carlota would go and bring up José to help carry the things, but Doña Faustina always insisted on carrying the heaviest baskets herself. A few trips would be made back and forth through the undergrowth, and then the abandoned road would be quiet again until the old servants went to market the next morning.

In another fortnight or so they would set out once more, always to a new place; necessarily this led them farther and farther afield. Someone even claimed to have seen them once in Vera Cruz, although, given the number of false stories which were circulated about the two women, there was no particular reason to believe this.

Before the house had been made into an inn it had been a prosperous *finca*, with terraced lands planted with fruit trees, leading downward rather steeply for a mile or so to a high bluff above the river. For fifty years or more the land had been totally neglected, so that now it was hard to find the avocado and mango trees in the tangle of new, eager parasites which had sprung up on every side and often reached above even the tallest of the older trees. Lianas looped down from the branches, climbing plants stretched up to clutch at them, and a person could not stray more than fifty feet down one of the orchard paths from the house without coming face to face with an impenetrable curtain of leaves. And now no one really knew how far it was from the house to the river, because the borders of the property gave on even thicker jungle.

3

Not even José would have known the tank existed, if he had not strayed a bit farther down than usual one afternoon, to see if he could find some *zapotes*. In the deep silence of the undergrowth there, far beneath the regions where the sun could reach, he had heard a heavy splash not far distant, as though a boulder had been flung into deep water. He had listened intently, but there had been no other sound. The next afternoon during siesta time he went back to the same spot carrying a machete, and laboriously hacked his way through the stubborn vegetation. It was nearly twilight when he caught sight of the water ahead. Finally he stood near the edge of the tank. The stagnant water gave off a heavy odor, and insects hovered in swarms in the still air above it. And as he watched, it seemed to him that there was a faint movement down in the brown depths; for some reason the water was not completely motionless. For a while he stood there staring downward, lost in contemplation; then, as the light was fading, he turned and started back, resolving without knowing why he did so, to say nothing about the tank to Elena when he returned to the house.

Several times in the course of the following months José returned there, always with the hope of discovering what had made the splash. Even a man diving into the tank could scarcely have caused such a noise. There was a stone-paved ramp at the far end (the tank doubtless had been built to bathe cattle) and on two occasions he found the ramp partially wet, which merely added to his perplexity. The second time he noticed this, he began to cut his way through the vines along the edge, in order to examine the ramp closely. And half-way along he found the path. Someone had cleared a narrow but practicable passage to the tank from some point back near the house. Abandoning his project, he followed the path and came out in a corner of what had once been a rose garden, on a lower terrace between the door to the laundry and the ruined stables. As he stood blinking in the sunlight, Doña Faustina appeared coming down the short flight of steps outside the laundry door. By its handle she carried a basket with a newspaper tucked over the top. Automatically old José walked toward her to take the basket from her. Evidently she had not been expecting to see him, for when she looked up and realized he was near her, her face took on an extraordinary expression. But all she said was: "What are you doing down here? Go to the kitchen." Then she stepped to a stone bench under an arbor near her and sat down, putting the basket on the bench beside her.

As he went on up towards the house José thought he had never seen his *patrona* look quite so fierce. She was always severe, and often forbidding, but not to the point of being able to frighten him as she had today. It was as if a demon had peered out at him for a moment from beneath her heavy lids.

"It must be true," he thought. "Doña Faustina is going mad. What will become of Elena and me?"

This time when he got to the kitchen he took Elena into a corner and whispered to her, telling her his fears, and of how strange the señora had looked in the garden. Elena crossed herself. "Oh, God," she murmured. But he did not mention the tank to her, either now or later. He did not even want to think about it, because he suspected that in some way it was connected with Doña Faustina's madness, and being the only one who knew about it gave him a certain feeling of security which he would have lost had he shared the knowledge with Elena.

4

One cold evening of *llovizna*, as the mealy fog slowly turned to water and drenched the countryside, there was a knock at the entrance door. Doña Faustina, who spent much of her time pottering about in the basement where the baths and laundry were, heard it from there, and straightway mounted the stairs, her face dark with fury. Carlota stood in the *comedor*, undecided as to whether she should answer. The knocking was repeated as Doña Faustina reached her.

"Again the police?" said Carlota a bit fearfully.

"*Ya veremos,*" muttered Doña Faustina. And she went out and stood behind the door, calling out in a loud voice: "Who?"

There was no answer.

"Don't open it," whispered Carlota, who stood behind her.

Doña Faustina made an impatient gesture to silence her sister. They waited several minutes, but the knock did not come again. There was only the irregular dripping of the water from the balcony above on to the ground.

"Stay here," said Doña Faustina, and she went through the *comedor*, down the stairs and into the laundry again. Here she gathered up all the refuse that strewed the floor and the washtubs, and packing it into two large baskets, continued out the side door which gave on the grape arbor. From here, descending the steps slowly, she disappeared into the darkness of the rose garden.

Within a half-hour she was back in the entrance hall where Carlota still stood listening by the door.

"Nothing," said Carlota in answer to Doña Faustina's questioning gesture. Doña Faustina's beckoned to her. They went into the *comedor* and whispered together. One candle flame cowered behind a pitcher on the newpaper-covered sideboard.

"It's not the police," said Doña Faustina. "Your room has a key. Go immediately. Lock the door and go to bed."

"But you . . . ?"

"I'm not afraid."

Left alone in the *comedor*, Doña Faustina poured herself a glass of water and drank it. Then she took the candle and went up the long staircase to her room. She closed the door and set the candle down. By her sagging bed, around which Elena had draped the patched mosquito-net, stood a man. Swiftly he stepped over to her, and putting one arm around her neck tightly, stuffed a crumpled cloth into her mouth. She swung her arms about wildly, and managed to hit him once in the face, but almost immediately he had tied her wrists together. There was no further struggle. He propelled her roughly to the bed, yanked aside the netting and pushed her down. She looked at him: he was a tall young man, a *mestizo* probably, and badly dressed. As he moved about the room looking into the crates and boxes that lay in wild disorder about the floor, he snorted with distaste. Finally he overturned a chair in anger and with a scornful gesture swept all the empty bottles and piles of newspapers off the bureau onto the floor. He approached the bed again and looked at Doña Faustina in the wavering light. Then, to her surprise (although it cannot be said to her annoyance) he lay down and had his way with her quietly, impersonally. A few minutes later he sat up and pulled the cloth out of her mouth. She lay perfectly still and looked up at him. Finally she said: "What do you want here? I have no money."

"Who knows if you have or not?"

"I tell you there is none."

"We'll see."

He got up. Again he spent a quarter of an hour or so searching the room, scuffing piles of refuse under the tables, kicking the furniture over to examine the under part, emptying drawers of their dust and litter. He lit a small cigar and returned to the bed. His oblique eyes looked almost closed in the light of the candle.

"Where is it?" he said.

"There is none. But I have something more precious."

"What?" He looked at her with scornful disbelief. What could be more precious than money?

"Untie my hands."

He gave her the use of one hand, holding the other arm firmly while she fumbled in her clothing. In a moment she drew forth a small parcel done up in newspaper, and handed it to him. He placed it on the bed and bound her hands together. Then in a gingerly fashion he lifted the parcel and smelled of it. It was soft, and slightly wet.

"What is it?"

"Open it, *hombre*. Eat it. You know what it is."

Suspiciously he removed the outer layer of paper and held the contents close to the candle.

"What is this?" he cried.

"*Ya sabes, hombre,*" she said calmly. "*Cómelo.*"

"What is it?" he said again, trying to sound stern; but there was fear in his voice.

"Eat it, son. You don't have the chance every day."

"Where did you get it?"

"Ah!" Doña Faustina looked mysterious and wise, and gave no further answer.

"What do I want of it?" said the young man presently, looking down at the little object in his hand.

"Eat it! Eat it and have the power of two," she said cajolingly.

"*Brujerías!*" he exclaimed, still without putting the thing down.

A moment later he added, speaking slowly: "I don't like witchcraft. I don't like it."

"Bah!" Doña Faustina snorted. "Don't be stupid, son. Don't ask questions. Eat it, and go on your way with the force of two. Who will ever know? Tell me that! Who?"

This argument appeared to weigh with the young man. Suddenly he lifted the thing to his mouth and bit into it as if it had been a plum. While he ate he looked once at Doña Faustina darkly. When he had finished, he walked around the room tentatively for a moment, his head slightly on one side. Doña Faustina watched him closely.

"How do you feel?" she inquired.

"*Bien,*" he said.

"Two," she reminded him. "Now you have the power of two."

As if inspired by the fortifying suggestion, he walked to the bed, threw himself down on it and lay with her again briefly. This time she kissed his forehead. When it was over he rose, and without undoing the rope that bound her hands, without saying a word, he went out of the door and down the stairs. A minute or so later she heard the front door close. At the same time the candle, which had burned down to its base, began to flicker wildly, and soon the room was in darkness.

5

All night Doña Faustina lay perfectly still on her bed, sleeping now and then, and during the periods of wakefulness listening to the slow dripping of the mist outside her windows. In the morning Carlota, still fearful, opened her door a crack, and apparently finding everything in the corridors in a normal state went to Doña Faustina's room.

"*Ay, Dios!*" she cried when she saw Doña Faustina lying with her clothing partially ripped away and her hands lashed together. "Oh, God! Oh, God!"

But Doña Faustina was calm. As Carlota undid the rope, she said: "He did no harm. But I had to give him the heart."

Carlota looked at her sister with horror.

"You're mad?" she cried. "The police will be here any minute."

"No, no," Doña Faustina reassured her, and she was right: no police arrived to search the house again. Nothing happened. At the end of two weeks they made another trip, and a little while later still another. Two days after they had returned from this one, Doña Faustina called Carlota into her room and said to her: "There will be a child."

Carlota sat down slowly on the bed.

"How terrible!"

Doña Faustina smiled. "No, no. It's perfect. Think. It will have the power of thirty-seven."

But Carlota did not seem convinced. "We don't know about those things," she said. "It may be a vengeance."

"No, no, no," said Doña Faustina, shaking her head. "But now we must be more careful than ever."

"No more trips?" said Carlota hopefully.

"I shall think about it."

A few days later they were both in the rose garden sitting on a bench.

"I have thought," said Doña Faustina. "And there will be no more trips."

"Good," replied Carlota.

Toward the end of the year Doña Faustina was confined to bed, awaiting the birth of the child. She lay back comfortably in the crooked old bed, and had Elena come and sweep out the room for the first time in many months. Even when the floor was clean, the room still reeked of the garbage that had lain there for so long. Carlota had bought a tiny crib in the town; the purchase had awakened interest in their activities on the part of the townspeople.

When the time arrived, Elena and Carlota were both in the room to assist at the birth. Doña Faustina did not scream once. The baby was washed and laid beside her in the bed.

"A boy," said Elena, smiling down at her.

"Of course," said Doña Faustina, beginning to nurse him.

Elena went down to the kitchen to tell José the good news. He shook his head gloomily.

"Something bad in all his," he muttered.

"In all what?" said Elena sharply.

"Who is the father?" said José, looking up.

"That is Doña Faustina's secret," Elena replied smugly, rather as if it had been her own.

"Yes. I think so too," said José meaningfully. 'I think there is no father, if you want to know. I think she got the child from the Devil."

Elena was scandalized. "Shameless!" she cried. "How can you say such a thing?"

"I have reasons," said José darkly. And he would say no more.

Things went smoothly at the inn. Several months passed. The baby had been named Jesus Maria and was in perfect health—"*un torito*," said Elena, "a real little bull."

"Of course," Doña Faustina had replied on that occasion. "He has the power of thirty-seven . . . ." Exactly then Carlota had been taken with a violent fit of coughing which managed to cover the rest of the sentence. But Elena had noticed nothing.

The rainy season had finished again, and the bright days of sunlight and green leaves had come. José went in search of fruit once more, wandering down through the garden, crouching over most of the time to creep beneath the hanging walls of vines and tendrils. Again one day he cut his way to the tank, and stood on the edge of it looking toward the ramp, and this time he saw the monster just as it slid forward and disappeared beneath the surface of the water. His mouth dropped open. Only one word came out: "*Caimán!*"

He stood still for several minutes looking down at the dark water. Then he edged along the side of the tank to the place where the path had been the year before. It had completely disappeared. No one had been to the tank in many months; there was no indication that such a corridor had ever existed there in the mass of vegetation. He returned the way he had come.

It was a scandal, thought José , that such a beast should be living on Doña Faustina's property, and he determined to speak to her about it immediately. He found her in the kitchen talking with Elena. From his face she saw that something was wrong, and fearful perhaps that he was going to say just what he did say a moment later, she tried to get him out of the room.

"Come upstairs. I want you to do something for me," she said, walking over to him and pulling him by the arm.

But José's excitement was too great. He did not even notice that she was touching him. "Señora!" he cried. "There is a crocodile in the garden!"

Doña Faustina looked at him with black hatred. "What are you saying?" she said sofly and with a certain concern in her voice, as if the old man needed to be treated with gentleness.

"An enormous *caimán!* I saw it!"

Elena looked at him apprehensively. "He's ill," she whispered to Doña Faustina. José heard her. "Ill!" he laughed scornfully. "Come with me and wait a little. I'll show you who's ill! Just come!"

"You say in the garden?" repeated Doña Faustina incredulously. "But where?"

"In the great tank, señora."

"Tank? What tank?"

"The señora doesn't know about the tank? There's a tank down below in the orchard. *Sí, sí, sí,*" he insisted, seeing Elena's face. "I've been there many times. It's not far. Come."

Inasmuch as Elena seemed to be on the point of removing her apron and, accepting his invitation, Doña Faustina changed her tactics. "Stop this nonsense!" she shouted. "If you're ill, José, go to bed. Or are you drunk?" She stepped close to him and sniffed suspiciously. "No? *Bueno.* Elena, give him some hot coffee and let me know in an hour how he is."

But in her room Doña Faustina began to worry.

6

They got out just in time. Carlota was not sure they ought to leave. "Where shall we go?" she said plaintively.

"Don't think about that," said Doña Faustina. "Think about the police. We must go. I know. What good does it do me to have the power of thirty-seven if I pay no attention to what they tell me? They say we must leave. Today."

As they sat in the train, ready to pull out of the station, surrounded by baskets, Doña Faustina held Jesus Maria up to the window and made his tiny arm wave good-by to the town. "The capital is a better place for him in any case," she whispered.

They went to a small *fonda* in the capital, where the second day Doña Faustina conceived the idea of applying at the nearest *comisaría* for employment as police matron. Her physical build, plus the fact that, as she told the lieutenant, she was afraid of no human being, impressed those who interviewed her, and after various examinations, she was accepted into the force.

"You'll see," she said to Carlota when she returned that evening in high spirits. "From now on we have nothing to worry about. Nothing can harm us. We have new names. We are new people. Nothing matters but Jesus Maria."

At that very moment the inn was swarming with police. The news of the *caimán*, which José in his obstinacy insisted was really there, first to Elena and then to others in the market, had reached them and awakened their curiosity once again. When it was found that there was not one, but a pair of the beasts, in the hidden tank, the police began to look more closely. No one really believed even now that it was Doña Faustina and her sister who were responsible for the disappearance of the dozens of infants who had vanished during the past two or three years, but it was felt that it would do no harm to investigate.

In a dark corner of the laundry, under one of the washtubs, they found a bundle of bloodstained rags which on closer inspection proved beyond a doubt to be the garments of an infant. Then they discovered other such rags stuffed in the windows to fill the spaces left by broken panes. "They must be Jesus Maria's," said the loyal Elena. "The señora will be back in a day or so, and she will tell you." The police leered.

The *jefe* came and looked around the laundry. "She was not stupid," he said admiringly. "She did the work here, and *they*"—he pointed out toward the orchard—"took care of the rest."

Little by little all the stories from roundabout concurred to make one unified mass of evidence; there was no longer much doubt as to Doña Faustina's guilt, but finding her was another matter. For a while the papers were full of the affair. Indignant articles were spread across the pages, and always there was the demand that the readers be on the lookout for the two monstrous women. But it turned out that no picture was available of either of them.

Doña Faustina saw the newspapers, read the articles, and shrugged her shoulders. "All that happened long ago," she said. "It has no importance now. And even if it had, they could not catch me. I have too much power for them." Soon the papers spoke of other things.

Fifteen years passed quietly. Jesus Maria, who was unusually bright and strong for his age, was offered a position as servant in the home of the Chief of Police. He had seen the boy about with his mother for several years, and liked him. This was a great triumph for Doña Faustina.

"I know you will be a great man," she told Jesus Maria, "and will never bring dishonor upon us."

But eventually he did, and Doña Faustina was inconsolable.

After three years he grew bored with his menial work, and went into the army, carrying with him a recommendation from his employer to a close friend, a certain colonel who saw to it that Jesus Maria was pleasantly treated in the barracks. Everything went well for him; he was constantly promoted, so that by the time he was twenty-five he had become a colonel himself. It may be observed that to be a colonel in the Mexican army is not so great an attainment, nor is it necessarily a sign of exceptional merit. However, there is little doubt that Jesus Maria's military career would have continued its upward course, had he not happened to be in Zacatecas at the time of the raids on the villages thereabout by Fermín Figueroa and his band. As one more privilege in the endless chain of favors granted him by his superiors he was put in charge of the punitive expedition that was sent

out in pursuit of Figueroa. Jesus Maria could not have been completely
without ability, nonetheless, since on the third day out he succeeded in
taking the leader prisoner along with thirty-six of his men.

No one ever really knew what happened in the small mountain village
where the capture took place, save that Figueroa and the bandits had all
been tied up in a sheep corral, ready to be shot, and when a few hours later a
corporal had arrived with six soldiers to carry out the execution, the corral
was empty. And it was even said, after Jesus Maria had been stripped of his
rank, that a sheepherder had seen him enter the corral in the bright
afternoon sunlight when everyone else was asleep, loosen the ropes that
bound Figueroa, and then hand him his knife, whereupon he turned his
back and walked away. Few believed the sheepherder's story: colonels do
not do such things. Still, it was agreed that he had been inexcusably
careless, and that it was entirely his fault that the thirty-seven bandits had
escaped and thus lived to continue their depredations.

The evening Jesus Maria arrived back at his barracks in the capital, he
stood alone in the latrine looking at himself in the fly-specked mirror.
Slowly he began to smile, watching the movements of his facial muscles.
"No," he said, and tried again. He opoened his eyes wider and smiled with
all his might. The man's face had looked something like that; he would
never be able to get it exactly, but he would go on trying because it made
him happy to recall that moment—the only time he had ever known how it
feels to have power.

Tangier
1949

The Hours After Noon

> "If one could awaken all the echoes of one's memory simultaneously, they would make a music, delightful or sad as the case might be, but logical and without dissonances. No matter how incoherent the existence, the human unity is not affected."
>
> —*Baudelaire*

1

"Oh, you're a *man!* What does a man know about such things? I can tell you how much: absolutely nothing!" When she argued with her husband at mealtimes, Mrs. Callender often sought the support of the other diners in the room. In this instance, however, her appeal was purely formal, since at the moment she was the only woman present, and thus assumed she had their attention anyway. Her bright eyes flashed indignantly from one male diner to the next, and she even turned around in her chair to include old Mr. Richmond, the teller in the Bank of British West Africa. He looked up from his food and said: "Eh? Oh, yes. I dare say."

The Pension Callender was surprisingly empty these days—empty even for the hot season. Besides old Mr. Richmond, who had been with them since they had started eleven years ago, there was Mr. Burton down from London to write a book; he had come last autumn and as yet had given no indication of being ready to leave. Mr. Richmond and Mr. Burton were the only true residents of the pension. The others either came and went irregularly, like Mr. Van Siclen the archeologist and Clyde Brown who was in business in Casablanca, or were merely there for a few days waiting for money or visas before they continued southward or northward, like the two young Belgians who had left that morning.

"A young girl—any young girl—is unbelievably sensitive. Like a thermometer or a barometer. She catches hold of whatever's in the air. It's true, I tell you." Mrs. Callender looked around at each one defiantly; her black eyes flashed.

Mr. Callender was in a good humor. "That may be," he said indulgently. "But I wouldn't worry about Charlotte. And anyway, we don't even know for sure whether Monsieur Royer's coming or not. You know how he is, always changing his mind. He's probably on his way to Marrakesh right now."

"Oh, he *will* come. You know he will! You simply don't want to face facts." (Sometimes this was true of Mr. Callender. When it was obvious that one of the Moslem servants was systematically stealing foodstuffs from his

217

pantry, he would make no effort to discover who the culprit was, preferring to wait until he might possibly catch him red-handed.) "You hope
that somehow he won't get here. But he will, and he's a filthy, horrible
man, and he's going to be sitting opposite your own daughter at every
meal. I should think that might mean something to you."

Her husband looked around at the other diners, an expression of amusement on his face. "I don't think sitting opposite to him at mealtimes'll bring
about her downfall, do you?"

"Abdallah! *Otra taza de café!*" The boy who had been standing by the
fireplace trying to follow the conversation stepped forward and filled her
cup. "Silly boy!" she cried, sipping the coffee. "It's quite cold." He understood, and lifted the cup to carry it out. "No, no," she said sighing,
reaching out for it. *"Déjalo, déjalo."* And without pausing: "He has a sinister personality. It has an effect on one. Women *feel* those things. I've felt it
myself."

Her husband raised his eyebrows. "Aha! So now we come to the meat
of the conversation. Gentlemen! Wouldn't you say that my wife is the one
to watch? Don't you think *she* should be kept from Monsieur Royer?"

Mrs. Callender simpered. "Bob! You're positively appalling!" At the
same time Mr. Richmond raised his head in a startled fashion and said:
"Monsieur Royer? Oh?"

Clyde Brown was the only one of the four guests who had been following the conversation from the beginning. His watery blue eyes stared with
interest. "Who is this Monsieur Royer? A Latin Quarter Don Juan?"

There was a slight silence. The wind was blowing a blind outside the
dining-room window back and forth; the distant sound of heavy waves
pounding against the cliffs came up from below. "Don Juan?" echoed Mrs.
Callender, laughing thinly. "My dear, I wish you could see him! He looks
like a furious lobster, one that's just been cooked. Absolutely hideous!
And he's at least fifty."

"You're treading on delicate ground," said Mr. Callender into his plate.

"I know, darling, but you don't go about annoying girls and getting into
messes. He gets into the most frightful messes. You haven't forgotten
Señora Coelho's niece last year, when he . . ."

Mr. Callender pushed back his chair; the scraping sound it made on the
tile floor was very loud in the room. "Probably does, and probably richly
deserves whatever trouble he gets into," he announced. Then impatiently,
quickly, to his wife: "I know all about him. What do you want me to
do—wire him we're full up?" He knew she would say no, and she did.
There was always something in one of the stores in town which she
coveted at the time: a silk scarf, a pair of shoes or gloves, and the only
money which came in was that paid by the guests who stayed at the
pension. "But I should think you'd show more interest where your own
daughter is concerned," she added.

Mr. Burton, who had just become aware that a discussion was in progress, raised his head from the book he had been reading and smiled affably at Mrs. Callender. Old Mr. Richmond folded his napkin, stuffed it into its aluminum ring, and said: "I expect it's time to be getting back into town." Mr. Callender announced that he was going to his cottage to take his afternoon siesta. Soon only Mr. Van Siclen remained at his table by the window, sipping his coffee and looking distractedly out at the windblown landscape. He was a young man who had let his beard grow during the war when he had been stationed on some distant island in the Pacific; now finding that he looked more impressive with it (he was very young to be an archeologist, people told him), he still wore it. Mrs. Callender found herself watching him, wondering whether or not he would be better-looking without its black decoration: he would be less romantic, she decided, perhaps even a little frail of face. As he turned to look at her she felt a tiny thrill of excitement, but his expression swiftly effaced it. He always seemed pleasantly preoccupied; the cynical smile that flickered about his lips made him more remote than if there had been no smile at all. His way of being friendly was to look up from his book and say: "Good morning. How are you today?" in a very firm voice; then by the time you had replied he would be buried again in the book. She considered his behavior insufferably rude, but then, she never had met an American who did not impress her as wanting in courtesy. It was more their attitude than it was anything they did or failed to do. She herself had been born in Gibraltar of an English father and a Spanish mother, her school days had been passed in Kent, and, although Mr. Callender was an American, she considered herself English through and through. And Charlotte was going to be a typical English girl, a wholesome, simple lass without the ridiculous attitudes and featherbrained preoccupations of most American girls. Nor would she be granted the freedom so many American mothers allowed their daughters. Mrs. Callender had enough of the Mediterranean in her to believe that while a boy should have complete liberty, a girl should have none at all. The wind continued to bang the shutter.

"I see. Trying to get rid of old Royer," said Mr. Van Siclen lazily, shaking his head with mock disapproval. "Poor old Royer who never did any harm except ruin a girl's life here and there."

"Oh, I'm so glad!" she cried; the force of her emotion startled him. He glanced at her suspiciously.

"Glad about what?"

"Glad that you agree with me about Monsieur Royer."

"That he's a useless old rake who'll be up to no good until the day he dies? Sure I agree."

"Of course you do," she assured him; she did not see that he was baiting her.

"But I don't agree with you about keeping him away from anybody. Why? *Sauve qui peut*, I always say. And the devil take the hindmost."

She was genuinely indignant. "How can you talk that way? I'm being perfectly serious, even if you're not."

"I'm perfectly serious, too. After all, a girl's education has to start somewhere, some time."

"I think you're quite revolting. Education, indeed!" Her eyes looked beyond his face, through the window, to the stunted cypresses below, at the top of the cliff. She could remember some experiences she would have liked to avoid, or at least have put off until later, when she might have been ready for them. Her aunt in Málaga had been far too lenient, otherwise it never would have been possible for her to meet the sailor from the *Jaime II*, much less to have made an appointment with him in the Alameda for the following day. And the two students she had gone on the picnic with to Antequera, who had thought they could take advantage of her because she was not Spanish. "I must still have had a slight accent," she thought. She was sure it was because of such memories as these that she now had "sad days," when she felt that life would never be right again. There were many things a girl should not know until she was married, and they were the very things it seemed every man was determined to impart to her. Once she was married and it all mattered so much less, precisely then the opportunities for learning were cut down to a minimum. But of course it was better that way.

Slowly her expression was changing from indignation to wistfulness. Voluptuous memories burned in the mind like fire in the tree stump: they were impossible to put out, and they consumed from within, until suddenly nothing was left. If she had a great many memories instead of only a few, she reflected, she would surely be lost.

"You wouldn't talk that way, so playfully, if you knew the hazards of bringing up a girl in this place," she said wearily. "With these Moors all about, and strange new people coming to the pension every day. Of course, we try to get the good Moors, but you know how they are— utterly undependable and mad as hatters, every one of them. One never knows what any of them will take it into his head to do next. Thank God we can afford to send Charlotte to school in England."

"I'm chilly," said Mr. Van Siclen. He rose from the table rubbing his hands together.

"Yes, it's cool. It's the wind. Mind, I have absolutely nothing personal against Monsieur Royer. He's always been a model of fine behavior with me. It isn't that at all. If he were a young man" (she almost added: "like you"), "I'd think it was amusing. I don't object to a young man who's sowing his wild oats. That's to be expected. But Monsieur Royer is at least fifty. And he goes after such mere children. A young man is more likely to be interested in older women, don't you think? That isn't nearly so dangerous." She followed him with her gaze, turning her head as he went toward the door. "Not nearly."

He paused in the doorway, the same inexpressive smile on his lips. "Send him out to El Menar." He had a little native house at El Menar, where he was digging through the Roman and Carthaginian layers of rubble, trying to get at the earlier material. "If he chases the girls around out there they'll find him in a couple of days behind a rock with a coil of wire around his neck."

"Such brutes!" she cried. "How can you stay out there all alone with those wild men?"

"They're fine people," he said, going out.

She looked around the empty room, shivered, and went out onto the terrace, feeling unpleasantly nervous. The wind was near to being a gale, but the clouds, which until now had covered the sky, were breaking up, letting the hard blue backdrop of the sky show through in places. In the cypresses the wind whistled and hissed, and when it hit her face it took her breath away. The air was sharp with the odor of eucalyptus, and damp from the fine spray of the breaking waves below. Then, when the landscape was least prepared for such a change, the sun came out. In all these years of living in Morocco she never had ceased wondering at the astonishing difference made by the sun. Immediately she felt the heat seeping in through her pores, the wind was warm, no longer hostile; the countryside became greener, smiled, and slowly the water down there turned to a brilliant blue. She breathed deeply and said tentatively to herself that she was happy. She was not sure it was true, for it seldom happened, but sometimes she could bring it about in this way. It seemed to her that long ago she had known happiness, and that the brief moments of it she found now were only faint memories of the original state. Now, she always felt surrounded by the ugliness of humanity; the scheming little human mind was always present. A certain unawareness of what went on around her was essential if she were to find even normal contentment.

She saw a Moroccan coming toward her from the driveway. Vaguely she knew that his arrival would entail something unpleasant, but for the moment she refused to think about it. She ran her hand through her hair which the wind had blown awry, and tried to bring her mind back to the pension. There was Mr. Richmond's mirror which was broken, Brahim needed a new electric bulb in the pantry, she had to look in the laundry for an undershirt of Bob's that was missing, she must catch Pedro before he drove the station wagon into town, to remind him to stop at the Consulate and pick up Miss Peters whom she had invited for tea.

The Moroccan, his ragged *djellaba* whipping in the wind, emerged from the shadows of the nearest eucalyptus. She exclaimed with annoyance and turned to face him. He was old and he carried a basket. Suddenly she remembered him from last year: she had bought mushrooms from him. And as she remembered, she glanced involuntarily at the withered hand holding the basket and saw the six dark fingers that she knew would be there. "Go away!" she cried passionately. "*Cir f'halak!*" She wheeled about and began to run down the path to her cottage in the garden below. Without looking behind she went in and slammed the door behind her. The room smelled of damp plaster and insecticide. She stood a moment at the window looking apprehensively up the path through the bushes. Then, feeling slightly absurd, she drew the curtains across and began to remove her make-up. As a rule the mornings took care of themselves; it was the hours after noon that she had to beware of, when the day had begun to go toward the night, and she no longer trusted herself to be absolutely certain of what she would do next, or of what unlikely idea would come into her head. Once again she peered between the curtains up the sunlit path, but there was nobody.

2

The months in Spain had been not at all relaxing; he was fed up with the coy promises of eyes seen above fans, furious with mantillas, crucifixes and titters. Here in Morocco, if love lacked finesse, at least it was frank. The veils over the faces did not disturb him; he had learned long ago to decipher the features beneath. Only the teeth remained a hazard. And the eyes he could read as easily as words. When they showed any interest at all, they expressed it clearly, with no hint of the prudishness he so hated.

Above a bank of thick clouds the twilight sky burned with a fierce blueness. He turned into the crowded native quarter. He had sent his luggage to the Pension Callender by taxi and had arranged to take Mr. Callender's station wagon when it started up from the market just before dinner. That left him free to wander a half-hour or so in the Medina, nothing on his mind, nothing in his hands. He turned into the Rue Abdessadek. The hooded figures in the street moved from stall to stall, their hands making the decorative oriental gestures, their voices strident with disagreement over prices. It was all familiar to Monsieur Royer, and very comforting. He felt he could again breathe easily. Slowly he ascended the hill, trying to recall a passage of something he once had read and loved: "*Le temps qui coule ici n'a plus d'heures, mais–*" He could not get beyond this point into the other thought. Turning into a smaller street, he was suddenly met by an overpowering odor of jasmine; it came from behind the wall beside him. He stood still a moment beneath the overhanging branch of a fig tree on the other side of the wall, and inhaled slowly, deliberately, still hoping to get beyond that part of the thought which had to do with time. The jasmine would help. It was coming to him: *"mais, tant le loisir–"* No.

A child brushed against him, and he had the impression that it had done so purposely. He glanced down: sure enough, it was begging. In a cajoling, unnatural little voice that set his nerves on edge it was asking alms, raising a tiny cupped hand toward him. He began to walk quickly, still sniffing the jasmine, feeling the elusive phrase he sought moving a little further away from him. The child hurried along beside him, continuing its odious chant. "No!" he cried explosively, without looking down at it again, and forcing his legs to take enormous strides in the hope of escaping its singsong voice.

"Le temps qui coule ici n'a plus d'heures, mais tant–" he murmured aloud, to cover the sound beside him. It was impossible. Now his mood was irrevocably shattered. The child, growing bolder, touched his leg with a tentative finger. *"Dame una gorda,"* it whined. With a suddenness and ferocity which astonished him even as he acted, he dealt it a savage blow in the face, and a fraction of a second later heard it moan. Then he watched it duck and run to the side of the street where it stood against the wall holding its hand to its face and staring at him with an expression of reproach and shocked disbelief.

Already he was feeling a sharp pang of regret for his behavior. He stepped toward the cowering child, not aware of what he was about to say or do. The child looked up; its pinched face was pale in the light of the arc-lamp that swung above. He heard himself say in a tremulous voice: *"Porqué me molestas así?"* It did not answer, and he felt its silence making an unbridgeable abyss between them. He took hold of its thin arm. Again, without stirring, it made its absurd, animal moan. In a new access of rage he struck it again, much harder. This time it made no sound; it merely stood. Completely unnerved and miserable, Monsieur Royer turned and walked off in the direction from which he had just come, colliding with a shrouded woman who was emptying garbage from a pan into the middle of the street. She called after him angrily, but he paid no attention. The idea that the Moroccan urchin must consider him with the same dread and contempt it felt for any other Christian interloper was intolerable to him, for he considered himself a particularly understanding friend of the Moslems. He hurried back through the town to the market, found the station wagon, and got into it. By the light of the many flares in the vegetable stands opposite, he recognized old Mr. Richmond of the Bank of British West Africa sitting on the seat facing him.

"Good evening," said Monsieur Royer, feeling that any kind of conversation at all would help him to recover from the ill-humor induced by his walk.

Mr. Richmond grunted a reply, and after a pause said: "You're Royer, I believe?"

"Aha, you remember me," smiled Monsieur Royer. But Mr. Richmond said no more.

Presently Pedro arrived, his arms full of bundles which he piled on the floor between them. He greeted Monsieur Royer ceremoniously, and explained that they would not be going directly to the pension because they had to stop by the airport to call for Miss Charlotte, who was coming down from London. As they drove slowly through the crowded market, several times Monsieur Royer saw Mr. Richmond glance across at him with a surreptitiousness which bordered on the theatrical. "*Pauvre vieux*," he thought. "He's losing his grip."

3

It had been a nerve-racking flight down, through clouds most of the way, with sudden terrifying exits into regions of pitiless burning sunlight against which the softness of the clouds seemed a protection. She was not afraid of flying; the uneasiness had begun long before she had left school. Each morning on waking she had smelled the freshly-cut grass, heard the birds' familiar chirping in the bushes, and said to herself that she did not want to leave.

Of course there was no question of her not going home to visit her family; although her mother had come to England the year before to spend the vacation months with her, she had not seen her father for two years, and she really cared more for him than she did for her mother. He was quiet, he looked at her in a strange, appraising manner that enormously flattered her and, above all, he let her alone, refrained from making suggestions for the betterment of her appearance or character, which ostensibly meant that he considered her a fully formed individual. And while she had to admit that her mother was sweet, at the same time she could not help thinking her silly and something of a nuisance: she was so laden with advice and so eternally ready to bestow it. And the more one took, the more of it she attempted to unload upon one. There was no end to the chain of suggestions and admonitions. She told herself that this constant watching was a very common misapplication of maternal love, but that did not make it any easier to bear.

Her last two days at school she had spent packing slowly, automatically;

they had been filled with a particular anguish which she finally brought herself to diagnose. It was sheer apprehensiveness at the prospect of being again with her mother. Other years she had prepared to go home without feeling this tremulous dread. It was as they left London Airport and she was bracing herself against the plane's banking that the reason came to her; without realizing it she already had determined to resist. The discovery was a shock. For a moment she felt like a monster. "I can't go home feeling like this," she thought. But as the plane righted itself, and, soaring higher, broke through the pall of fog into the clarity above, she sighed and sat back to read, reflecting that after all the decision was purely private and could scarcely be read in her face. However, throughout the flight, as the plane moved onward from sunlight into shadow and out again, she continued from time to time to be plagued by the feeling that she had become disloyal; and with this suspicion went the fear that in some way she might hurt her mother.

It was a small airport. Before the plane had landed Charlotte had sighted the station wagon, standing in the glare of the floodlights near the shack which served as waiting-room and customs office. She was not surprised to find that her father had not come to meet her; he left the pension only when he was forced to. Pedro piled her luggage on top and helped her into the back of the car.

"Pleasant journey?" Mr. Richmond asked when they had greeted each other and she was seated beside him.

"Yes, thank you," she said, waiting to be presented to the other gentleman sitting opposite them. He was obviously from the Continent and of a rather distinguished appearance, she thought. But Mr. Richmond looked unconcernedly out at the lights of the airport, and so she spoke with the gentleman anyway.

They chatted about the weather and the natives. The car climbed the steep road; at each turn its headlights swept the white walls along the sides, crowned with masses of trailing flowers and vines. High in the dark trees a few cicadas continued to rasp their daytime song. She and the gentleman were still talking when the station wagon pulled into the garage. Mr. Richmond, however, had not said another word.

4

At the pension nothing had changed since her last visit. Her mother looked younger and prettier than ever, and seemed, if possible, still more scatterbrained and distraught—so much so that she too forgot to introduce her to the French gentleman. However, since he was seated in the farthest corner of the dining-room by the window, and was already finishing when the family sat down to eat, it did not matter much.

Her father looked at her across the table and smiled.

"So there you are," he said with satisfaction. He paused and turned to his wife: "Better get Señorita Marchena busy on a dress." And to Charlotte: "There's a big shindig Saturday night at the Country Club."

"Oh, but I have plenty of things to wear!" she objected.

"Yes, but this is very special. And calls for something very special. Señorita Marchena'll be equal to the occasion." He looked at her carefully. "And all I can say is, the Ramirez girls had better look to their laurels."

She felt herself blushing. The Ramirez girls were three sisters who held the reputation of having a local monopoly on beauty.

"The Ramirez girls!" cried Mrs. Callender, a note of scorn in her voice.

"What's the matter with them?" demanded her husband. "They're nice girls."

"Oh, they're pretty, yes, Bob, but they're scarcely what one would call nice girls." (For Mrs. Callender all Spaniards by definition were inclined to dubious morality.)

"Mother! How can you say that!" Charlotte exclaimed.

Mrs. Callender looked about uneasily; it seemed to her that Monsieur Royer was listening to their conversation. She had purposely delayed sitting down to dinner until she thought he would be finished eating, but he was still toying with his fruit. "I'll tell you about them later," she said *sotto voce* to Charlotte, and changed the subject, fervently hoping that in a moment he would leave and go down to his cottage.

In the middle of the meal the door from the terrace opened and Mr. Van Siclen burst in, fresh from El Menar, dressed in earth-stained overalls. He had a way of appearing unannounced at any hour of the day or night. Sometimes it was inconvenient for the servants, but since he paid full pension and ate few meals there, the Callenders never remarked upon his impromptu arrivals. He shut the door carefully so the wind sweeping through the room from the kitchen would not slam it. "Hello, everybody!" he said, running his hand through his hair. Mrs. Callender glanced toward the window where Monsieur Royer was slicing an apple into paper-thin sections. "Oh, how terrible! Monsieur Royer has your table! Do sit here with us. Abdallah! *Trae otra silla!*" She moved her own chair up a bit and indicated the space beside her. "Before you sit down, this is my daughter Charlotte." He acknowledged the introduction dryly, with a minimum of civility, and seated himself, sighing mightily.

"What a night!" he exclaimed as his soup was placed before him. "An ocean breeze, a full moon, and big clouds. I just came in from El Menar in my jeep," he told Charlotte. (She had decided he was pretentious, with that beard.)

"How enchanting!" cried Mrs. Callender. "Now, do tell us. Have you stumbled on something fantastic out there? Gold coins? Lapis lazuli cups?"

As he spoke, Charlotte watched his face, complacent and slightly mocking. It summed up all the things she disliked most in men: conceit, brashness, insensitivity. Still, he could not be as bad as he looked, she thought; some of it must be the beard. No one his age had a right to such a decoration.

From time to time she stole a glance at her mother, who was following his dull discourse as if it were of the greatest interest, punctuating it with little cooing sounds and exclamations of rapture. Somehow she had expected to find her less silly this time (perhaps because of her determination to resist) and instead, here she was, worse than ever. "It must be her age," she decided. At some point she would probably change suddenly, overnight. And now, becoming aware that it was precisely this quality of superficiality to which she most objected, she no longer felt even a twinge of guilt at her own rebelliousness. Trying to manage other people's lives was a definite thing. It had its limits. But the kind of irresponsibility she saw in her mother amounted to a denial of all values. There was no beginning and no end; anything was equal to anything else.

Two nurses on leave from the hospital in Gibraltar pushed back their chairs and walked across the room to the door. "Good nayt," they said. Both wore glasses; both were dressed in execrable taste. Charlotte watched them and thought: "To have reached thirty and to look like that—!"

Someone laid a hand lightly on her shoulder. She twisted her head around. The French gentleman was standing behind her chair, smiling at her mother.

"I wish to compliment you, madam. A lovely girl like this could only be the daughter of so charming a mother as you."

He bowed low, from behind her, so that for a second his head was level with hers; his hand remained on her shoulder. A short silence fell upon the table. To Mr. Van Siclen Monsieur Royer said: "Good evening, my dear fellow! How are you? Have you made any remarkable discoveries recently?"

"Hello, Royer. I was just telling the Callenders a little about the new wall I came to yesterday."

"But it's splendid! Only yesterday! I want to hear about it."

"Sit down," said Mr. Van Siclen. Mrs. Callender flashed him a furious glance.

"I'm afraid it'll be rather crowded," she said, scraping her chair back and forth on the tiles as noisily as possible, and failing to move it an inch.

"Oh, no. There's room," objected Charlotte. "Here beside me."

But Monsieur Royer laughed.

"No, no! You are very kind and I want very much to hear about the latest developments of this prodigious excavating. Perhaps tomorrow, Mr. Van Siclen?" Ceremoniously he kissed the hands of Mrs. Callender and Charlotte and went out.

Mrs. Callender rolled her eyes at her husband. "One needs the patience of Job," she said. "What an insufferable fool!"

Charlotte hesitated an instant before saying: "Why? I think he's rather sweet."

Her mother gave a little shriek, part giggle, and looked at Mr. Callender as if seeking support. Then she said very seriously: "I'm sorry to hear it, darling, because it only shows what faulty judgment you have. The man's an utter cad, a complete bounder. They don't come lower."

Charlotte in turn looked at her father. "Is that really true?" she asked.

"He's a bad egg, all right," he said.

They sat a while over coffee exchanging news. The dining-room was empty now save for their table. Abdallah leaned by the fireplace more asleep than awake. Mr. Van Siclen had ceased taking part in the talk, and tilted his chair back, puffing on a pipe. From time to time the wind shook the house. Slowly the conversation had centered itself upon Charlotte. She was telling her parents about school, about her classes and friends; she had almost forgotten Mr. Van Siclen was present. Suddenly she stopped short.

"This must all be the most frightful bore for Mr. Van Siclen," she said apologetically.

"Nonsense; go on," said her father. "If he doesn't like it he can leave."

Mr. Van Siclen smiled sleepily through the smoke. "I'm not bored at all." he assured her. "It's very instructive."

She was convinced he was making fun of her, and she grew hot with anger.

"I'm dreadfully tired. I think I should go to sleep." It was the only way to avoid going on with it; now that she was conscious of his amused eyes she could not possibly continue talking.

Her mother jumped up. "Of course she's tired, poor baby. Come along. You must get to bed immediately." She tried to take her arm, to pull her toward the door, but Charlotte could not allow that. Gently she disengaged herself and went over to kiss her father good night; she took leave of Mr. Van Siclen with more civility than she felt; then, back at the door, she seized her mother's arm and led her down the steps through the garden to the cottages below. Mrs. Callender went in and sat on the bed while she unpacked, gossiping about the servants. Hassan's eleven-year-old brother had been put in prison for reaching in through the open window into Mr. Burton's room and taking a hundred-peseta note which lay on the table.

"But, mother! that's terribly young to be in prison."

"Darling, I've said for years that the child was a thief. I've told Hassan to watch him, or we should have trouble. Isn't that the bathrobe Mrs. Grey gave you? It's rather pretty, but it seems a bit long." Eventually she went out, leaving Charlotte wide awake in the dark, listening to the rhythmical roar of the waves. They were not very loud tonight; she could remember many nights when they had seemed right in the room. But tonight the wind was from the west.

5

It was not long before she realized how foolish of her it had been to drink coffee after dinner; she would not be sleepy for hours. And since her mother generally read for an hour or so before going to sleep, and could see across to her cottage, she could not very well get up. Directly she turned on her light, her mother would be over to see what was wrong. She wanted to take a walk—perhaps down on the beach. But it would mean getting dressed in the dark and stealing out quietly at the risk of meeting her father. She had not yet heard him go into his own cottage. If she waited, it would be safer, but she did not feel like waiting. As she groped about cautiously for her skirt she heard him shut his door. She sighed with relief. Now that everyone was in, it would be much easier.

It all went very smoothly; she did not make a sound. Under the grape-arbor, through the vegetable garden, down across the open field towards the promontory where the cypresses and rocks overlooked the water beneath. The low clouds scudding overhead made waves of shadow that moved slowly across the moonlit country. She hummed happily as she walked along. To the right, under the big bent cypress, through the little ravine, up again; she knew the way perfectly. What she had not counted on was meeting Mr. Van Siclen sitting on a rock directly in the path, as she reached the edge of the cliff. He sat there looking out to sea; at her involuntary "Oh!" he turned and smiled at her in the moonlight.

The sight of him there had so thoroughly disrupted her state of mind that she merely stood still and looked at him.

"I *thought* you'd be out," he said with satisfaction.

She could only say, stupidly: "Why?"

"I didn't think you were sleepy."

She said nothing. Her impulse was to be unfriendly, but she decided it would be childish. "I thought I'd go for a walk down on the beach for a bit."

He laughed. "I saw you come sneaking out." (Why did he have to be so objectionable?) "Care to go for a little ride?"

"Oh, I don't think so, thank you," she said politely, conscious at the same time that her voice lacked forcefulness.

"Sure you would. Come on!"

He sprang up, seized her hand, and began to pull her along, back up the path. "No, really! No! Listen to me!" She wanted to resist physically, but she was afraid of seeming a whining creature—a poor sport. Presently she was obliged to stop for a moment. "Please!" she gasped. "Not so fast!" This he appeared to construe as a tacit acceptance of his suggestion; he laughed, loosened his grip, and said: "The jeep's in the upper driveway."

And once she was in the car, going up the mountain with the night wind in her face, she thought that perhaps she had meant to accept from the moment he had invited her. There was a sharp, spicy odor in the air: they were in the eucalyptus forest. It was like going through a high dark tunnel. The sound of the motor reverberated overhead. A minute later the walls of Sultan Moulay Hafid's palace loomed, growing higher as they approached the entrance. In another moment there were no walls at all; the car was on the high, flat section of road leading through the olive-grove to Bou Amar. The rolling hills stretched away to the south in a vast misty panorama whitened by the moonlight. Here and there the uncertain shadow of a cloud moved up a slope, assuming a new form as it reached the summit and spread over the valley beyond. The clouds were low and moved swiftly. She wanted to say: "It's lovely." But he had turned the windshield horizontal, and her breath was cut by the onrushing blast of air. The little white native houses of Bou Amar flitted past, and again they were in the country, among the pines now. The road did not deviate from its straight line, but it rose and dipped like a roller-coaster over the hills. He closed the windshield.

"Shall I open her up?" he called.

"Don't go any faster, if that's what you mean."

"That's what I mean."

"No!"

"This thing can't go, anyway!" he yelled.

But it seemed to her he had increased the speed.

Now there were no more trees; it was a high, open, rocky region dotted with clumps of holly and heather that glistened under the moon. Far ahead the lighthouse on the cape sent out its recurrent message. All at once he brought the jeep to a stop. It was absolutely silent up here save for the wind: there were no insects and the sea was too far away to be heard. He lit a cigarette without offering her one, and looked at her sideways.

"Are you what's laughingly called a virtuous young lady?" Her heart sank.

"What?" (And it was so idiotic, in any case.) She waited, then said: "I expect so. Why?"

"*Very* virtuous?"

"Did you bring me out here to inquire after my morals?"

"They don't mean a damn thing to me, if you want to know. I'm just

asking to be polite. You know—how's your lumbago? How's your ab-
scessed tooth?"

In spite of herself she said: "You know, I think you're quite disgusting."

He blew some smoke in her face. "All disgust, my dear young lady, is
nothing but lack of appetite—desire not to touch with the mouth."

"What?"

"Eating an object. Kissing somebody. Same thing."

"I don't know what you are talking about." She began to be alarmed: it
was like conversing with a madman.

"I'm just trying to tell you that I don't really disgust you."

The lighthouse was flashing. "How can I get him to go back?" she
thought.

"I should think I'd be the best judge of that," she said a bit shakily.

"And yet you want me to kiss you."

"What?" she cried shrilly. After a moment she said in a low voice: "Why
should I want you to kiss me?"

"I'm damned if I know. But you do."

"It's not true. I don't."

He tossed his cigarette away. "I think we've argued enough about this
little thing," he said, turning toward her.

She had never been treated this way before. When he seized her, she
could do nothing. When with all her might she tried to pull her head away,
he caught hold of her lip with his teeth, so that she cried out with pain. After
a prolonged struggle he let go and sat grinning at her. She tried to speak, but
sobbed and choked.

"Have a handkerchief," he said. Automatically she accepted it and blew
her nose. Then she dabbed at her lip and saw the dark blood on the white
linen. For some reason this gave her the courage to raise her head and look at
him.

"I—"

"Don't try to talk," he said shortly.

She stared at him, overcome by her hatred of him, opened her mouth to
speak, and choked afresh. When she had calmed herself sufficiently to be
able to think: "That was beastly," rather than "This is beastly," she handed
him his handkerchief and said quietly: "My mother was wrong. She said
they don't come lower than Monsieur Royer."

He laughed delightedly. "Oh, he's much worse! *Mu-u-uch* worse!"

"If you don't mind, I'd prefer not to talk about it any more."

"Ah, it wasn't as bad as all that," he said.

She did not answer.

"As a matter of fact," he pursued, "this ride was good for you."

"I don't think my father would agree," she said somewhat primly.

"Probably not. But he'll never be asked his opinion, will he?"

Remembering her sigh of relief when she had heard her father shut the door to his cottage, she was silent. He started up the engine, turned the jeep around, and they went back over the road as quickly as they had come. When they arrived at the garage, she jumped out without speaking again, and hurried to her cottage. All the lights in the other cottages were out. She undressed in the dark, turning on the light over the wash-basin just long enough to put a drop of iodine on her lip. As she got into bed she noticed that she was trembling. Even so, it was not long before the sound of the waves had lulled her to sleep.

6

In the morning she awoke in rather a bad humor. Perhaps the trip was just having its effect, or perhaps the unpleasantness of last night had upset her nerves. Halima, the younger of Mustapha the cook's two wives, brought her breakfast. When she had finished eating, she got out of bed and looked in the mirror. Her lower lip was still swollen. "Maybe by lunchtime it will be gone," she thought hopefully, and she put on her bathing suit and rushed down to the beach where she spent the whole morning swimming and sunbathing. About noon she caught sight of Monsieur Royer coming around the point at the base of the cliffs. He was in white flannels and flourished a cane. She watched him approach, glad he was not Mr. Van Siclen.

"Aha! A mermaid today!" he cried. "Is the sea comfortable?"

"Oh, yes. It's lovely."

He stood above her, making designs in the sand with the tip of his cane, and they talked. Finally he said: "May I be seated?"

"Oh, please! Of course!" She felt rude for not having suggested it.

When he was beside her he continued to chat and plough up the sand with his cane. After a few minutes he turned and looked into her face, smiling in such a way that his eyes seemed to shine more brightly, and said: "It is not too many times in his life that a man has the privilege of sitting with a real mermaid, you know. So you must forgive me if I enjoy this privilege."

She did not know what she ought to say, but his manner amused her, and so she laughed and said: "Thank you."

He did not seem entirely satisfied. "I don't want to embarrass you, my dear. You must realize that what I say is said quite sincerely. It is not meant to be flattery. If it seems comic, that is merely my English vocabulary."

"But it's not comic at all," she protested. "It's very charming, really. And you speak English beautifully."

His conversation consisted of very little else besides these elaborate compliments, but she found them inoffensive, a little touching, and on the whole enjoyable. As they talked, her sympathy for him increased, and she found herself wishing she could confide in him—not about anything in particular or anything serious, she thought—just about whatever came into her head at the moment. He was friendly, detached, sincere, and, she was sure, very wise. As a little fishing-boat rounded the point, bobbing up and down in the rough water, she suddenly said: "Monsieur Royer, tell me your honest opinion. Do you think it's despicable for a man to kiss a girl against her will?" She was shocked to hear the words coming out; she had not known they would be exactly those words, but apparently she needed to say them, and there was no one else to say them to.

A cloud seemed to spread across Monsieur Royer's sunburned face. Slowly he said: "Ah. I see that people have been talking to you about me."

"No! No!" she cried, startled and then horrified.

"Naturally they have," he said calmly. "We have never even been presented one to the other. Do you realize that? Yes. Of course they have. Why not? They are quite right." He paused. "Luncheon will be ready soon, and I must first prepare. But I want to answer your question. Yes. I think such a thing is despicable. You used the words: 'against her will.' But there are a great many girls who have no will, like the natives here, or even the Spanish girls of the lower class. It is all the same to them, as long as they receive a gift. They have no wish one way or the other. And if they have no will, one can scarcely go against it, can one?"

She was silent. "I wasn't talking about you," she finally said.

He looked at her very seriously; he seemed not to have heard her. "Do you see what I mean to say?"

"I'm not sure," she said, letting the sand run between her fingers. "But I really didn't mean—"

He had risen.

"Good morning, madame."

She looked around: her mother stood there. She greeted Monsieur Royer crisply. Then she looked down.

"Charlotte, it's lunchtime. Come up and dress." There was an edge of fury in her voice that recalled long-forgotten days of childhood misbehavior and recrimination.

The upward climb was steep. Charlotte went first, with her mother panting behind her. "Charlotte, I'm extremely angry with you. You're not a child any more, you know—" Between each sentence she ceased speaking and took a breath. "Your father and I as much as told you to have nothing to do with Monsieur Royer. How explicit must one be? I was going to tell you all about him this morning. But of course you disappeared. I don't know why—I couldn't be more annoyed with you. You're thoroughly thought-less and egotistical—"

Charlotte listened with apathy to the diatribe, walking quickly so that her mother, in attempting to keep up with her, would have the maximum difficulty in delivering it. At one point she had been about to protest that Monsieur Royer had only happened by a short while ago, and that she had been sitting with him only a few minutes, but she felt that this would seem to put her in the wrong; it would sound like an excuse, and she was determined to admit to no fault. Since she did not answer at all, her mother's voice softened tentatively as she continued: "Don't you think it's time you changed, and thought of others?"

"I expect so," she said vaguely, adding in a louder voice, "But I can't see what you have against poor Monsieur Royer to say such horrid things about him."

Mrs. Callender snorted impatiently.

"Oh, good heavens, Charlotte! I know all about the man. Please believe me, he has a most unsavory reputation. If only for that, he's no one for you to see. But I happen to know as well that his reputation is completely justified. He's a confirmed roué and a scoundrel. In any case, I don't intend to argue the point with you. It's an established fact. But what I do intend to have is your promise—your promise that you won't speak to him again unless either your father or I, one of us is present."

They were at the top of the cliff. Mrs. Callender would have liked to stop a moment and catch her breath, but Charlotte hurried on. The path was less steep here, and her mother quickly caught up with her, breathing heavily. She sounded angrier now.

"I refuse to stand by and watch an old libertine like that try to ruin your life—I won't *have* you seeing him. Do you understand me?"

Charlotte spoke without looking around. "Yes, of course I understand. But I don't agree."

"It's of no interest to me whether you agree or not!" cried Mrs. Callender shrilly. "I expect you think it's brilliant and becoming to show spirit—"

They had reached the vegetable garden. One of the nurses from Gibraltar was sitting on the porch of her cottage sunning herself. Mrs. Callender lowered her voice and became cajoling. "Darling, please don't ruin my pleasure in your stay by being stubborn and belligerent about this."

"Do you want me to be rude to him?"

"It's not necessary. But if you disobey me I shall be the one to be rude. I shall simply ask him to leave. And I've never done that to anyone."

"Then the only thing for me to do is to tell him in front of you that you've forbidden me to speak to him."

They stood in the garden between their respective cottages.

"If that's the pleasantest way you can devise, do so by all means," said her mother acidly. "I'm sure I don't mind." She went into her room and shut the door. Charlotte stood a moment looking after her.

In her mirror she examined her lip; the salt water had brought the swelling down. She dressed quickly and went up to the dining-room, noting to her immense relief that Mr. Van Siclen was not there. During lunch she glanced out of the window and saw Monsieur Royer being served on the terrace in the sun; she wondered if he were eating outside because he liked it, or out of consideration for her. While her parents were still finishing their dessert she excused herself and went out. She paused an instant on the steps, and then walked casually toward the table where Monsieur Royer sat sipping his coffee. He rose and seized a chair from the next table for her. Knowing she was being watched through the window, she sat down with him. Hassan brought her a cup of coffee and they talked brightly for a quarter of an hour or so. She fully expected her mother to appear and precipitate a scene, but nothing happened. When she got up and went down to her cottage she thought, "Now she'll come," but she lay awake a long time listening for her mother's footsteps, and they did not arrive. At last she sank into a heavy slumber.

7

In the rose garden behind the bar Mr. and Mrs. Callender walked back and forth, conversing in low tones.

"You saw it!" exclaimed Mrs. Callender in an intense whisper. "Pure infatuation, nothing else. It's not like Charlotte to behave this way. She'd never defy me like this. I admit it was only a provocation, the whole little act, yes. But she's never been this way before. The man has bewitched her, it's perfectly clear. We must do something. Immediately."

Back and forth along the short, bordered path they walked. "We've got to send him away," she said.

"Impossible," said Mr. Callender.

"Then I shall take Charlotte and go to a hotel until he leaves," she declared.

Mr. Callender grunted.

"All she needs," he said at length, "is to meet some boys her own age. The ones she used to know here are mostly gone. Too bad the dance at the Club isn't tonight or tomorrow night. She'd forget about Royer in short order."

Mrs. Callender sighed. "If he could only be put on ice until the dance," she mused. Then she straightened and tried once more. "Oh, Bob, we *must* get rid of him."

Her husband stood still. "The time to get rid of Monsieur Royer was before he came. You had your chance. I asked you if you wanted me to wire him there was no room, and you said no. It's one thing to tell someone the place is full up. And another to send a man away for no reason at all. You can't do it."

"No reason at all, indeed!" she snorted.

Now she sat in her room on the edge of the bed and fidgeted. The long windswept afternoon depressed her. There was too intimate and mysterious a connection between what she felt, and the aspect of the countryside, now brilliant under the ardent sun, now somber in shadow as the endless procession of separate clouds raced past. It was easy to say, "This is a sad day," and attribute it to the unfortunate coincidence which had brought Charlotte and Monsieur Royer here at the same time. But that did not really explain anything. The aching nostalgia for her own youth remained—the bright Andalusian days when each hour was filled to bursting with the promise of magic, when her life lay ahead of her, inexhaustible, as yet untouched. It was true that she had not always been happy then, but there had been the imminent possibility of it, at every moment. And the people around her had not had the faculty they now had of becoming suddenly sinister. Even her husband, when she looked at him quickly, sometimes seemed to be coming hurriedly back from somewhere not in the light. It disconcerted her, and if she ever had dwelt on it for very long at a time, it would have terrified her.

A *rhaïta* was being played fairly far away on the mountain, announcing a wedding. It would probably go on for several days and nights. She put her hands over her ears. As if that could help! Whenever she took them away, the slippery little sound would be there, twisting thinly around itself like a tree-snake. She pressed her palms more tightly against her head, until the vacuum hurt her eardrums. But the images had been awakened: the donkeys laden with blankets and painted wooden chests, the procession of lanterns, the native women in white with their drums . . . . She jumped up, looked at her watch, stepped to the mirror and powdered her face. Then she went down to Mr. Van Siclen's cottage. He had had lunch in town with the American Vice-Consul, saying that he would be back early as he was returning to El Menar before dark. She knocked; there was no answer. She went up to the bar where he often sat thumping out old tunes with one finger on the piano. He was talking with the barman.

"Mr. Van Siclen, I must speak with you."

"Sure." He followed her outside.

"I know all this won't interest you in the least, but it's the only favor I shall ever ask of you. Monsieur Royer has his eye on Charlotte. No, don't laugh. It's most serious. I'm counting on you. You *must* help me."

"Well, well!" he said. And after a bit: "O.K. What do you want me to do?"

"I thought if you could invite him out to El Menar . . . Just for a few days . . ." she hastily added as he frowned. ". . . Just for two or three days. At least until I've had the opportunity of talking with her. You see, for some mad reason *she* seems quite taken with *him* as well. There's no explaining these things. But one must act. I shall be eternally grateful to you."

"Well," he said slowly, smoothing his hair," "I'm willing to extend the invitation, but how do I know he'll accept?"

"I think you can make it attractive to him if you really try," she said, smiling significantly. "Playing up the native life a bit . . . You know him, after all. You know what amuses him."

"Damn it!" he cried, suddenly annoyed. "I don't want him out there trailing me around all day while I work."

And seeing her face, he added resignedly: "But I'll ask him, I'll ask him."

"You *are* a darling," she said.

It was done. For some reason she felt no doubt that Monsieur Royer would accept. Fittingly, the sun was shining as she went through the garden to her cottage. It was almost an anticlimax when at tea-time Monsieur Royer came to announce his departure.

"We shall miss you," she smiled. "I expect you'll want to keep your cottage." And when he said that he did, she generously suggested: "We'll put you on demi-pension for those days. That way you'll only be paying a little more than the price of the room."

"No, no," he protested politely but she saw that he was pleased.

A little while later she watched her two guests drive off in the open jeep into the twilight.

At dinner Mr. Callender looked around the room. "Where's everybody?" he said.

"Oh, Mr. Van Siclen's gone back to El Menar and taken Monsieur Royer along with him."

"*What?*" He was incredulous.

Charlotte said nothing. Several times during the meal Mrs. Callender glanced across at her, but if she was feeling any emotion she did not betray it.

"She's rather a little sneak," said Mrs. Callender to herself, disappointed; she had expected a little more reaction than this.

Charlotte was thinking: "He's gone, thank Heavens." But she meant Mr. Van Siclen. She went to bed immediately after dinner, slept soundly, and awoke early with a desire to see Gloria Gallegos, a friend from her *lycée* days. She breakfasted, dressed, and in the fresh of the morning set out on foot for town. It was not a great walk; she could make it in an hour. The moving air was a tonic. The sun had not yet begun to weigh it down with its heat, nor the flowers with their noonday scent, nor the insects with their droning. When she arrived in the market she was startled to see Mr. Van Siclen's jeep parked by the Ciné Régis. She kept her face averted as she passed, lest he should be in it. But she came face to face with him at the corner.

"Hi, there!" he said, grasping her arm, quite, she thought, as if nothing had ever occurred between them.

She was not effusive in her greeting. The crowd of Berbers passing pushed them this way and that.

"Where are you off to so early?" he demanded.

"Just up to the Boulevard," she said coldly.

"It's quite a walk. Let me take you up."

"I enjoy walking."

"Come on, be a good sport. Don't go on having hard feelings. You'll get old before your time."

He did not let go of her arm; the easiest way out was to accept. She let him lead her back to the jeep and help her in. As they went around the north end of the market they met the pension's station wagon which had just deposited Mr. Richmond at the bank. She waved to Pedro, who waved back.

"Am I forgiven?" asked Mr. Van Siclen.

"Only if you don't go on talking about it," she replied.

"That's the spirit," he said approvingly. "I had to come in for kerosene. There wasn't even enough for the lamps last night. Poor old Royer had to go to bed by moonlight, I guess. I didn't hear him come in."

He let her out at the Boulevard. At lunchtime she tried to telephone her mother to tell her that she was eating at the Gallegos', but the line was having one of its frequent bad days, and she was unable to reach the pension.

"Bob, I *am* worried about Charlotte," Mrs. Callendar was saying at lunch. (If the telephone had not been out of order it would have rung at that instant.) "She was already gone at eight when I went in to see her. It's not like her to go out so early. Where can she be?"

"Don't get so wrought up," said Mr. Callender gently. "Quit thinking she's a kid. She's in town somewhere and she can't get through on the phone, that's all."

Mrs. Callender pouted. "She's been intolerable since the moment she arrived. Inconsiderate and perverse. I've done nothing all morning but worry about her."

"I know."

"And I've a fearful migraine as a result. It's that *beastly* Monsieur Royer," she added with vehemence.

At the next table Mr. Burton laid aside his book and feebly inquired: "I expect your daughter is pleased to be back home?"

Mrs. Callender turned to face him. "Oh, yes! She adores it here. Of course it's ideal for young people."

"Oh, quite! Yes, indeed."

After lunch she took more aspirin. Now she felt a slight nausea as well. She lay on her bed, the curtains drawn, reflecting with a dim satisfaction that at least Charlotte would know she had made her mother ill. The wind still blew, the trees still swayed and roared, and through their sound from time to time crept the shrill, tiny notes of the distant *rhaïta*. She dozed, woke, dozed. At tea-time Halima knocked to ask if she wanted tea in her room. She inquired if Señorita Charlotte had returned. Halima had not seen her.

Although she wanted Charlotte to find her ill in bed when she returned, she disliked having tea in her cottage alone and, deciding to run the risk of rising, went up to the salon in the main house for her tea. Only the nurses were there, but she sat down anyway. Soon she heard Pedro's voice in the hall and excused herself.

"*Oiga*, Pedro," she called, running out. "You haven't seen Señorita Charlotte this afternoon, have you?"

"*Esta tarde? No, señora*. Not since this morning in the market, riding with Señor Van Siclen in his car."

"*Cómo!*" she cried; the word was like an explosion. Her eyes had become very large. Pedro looked at her and thought that perhaps Señora Callender was about to faint.

"Get the *camioneta*," she said weakly. "*Vamos a El Menar*."

"Now?" he asked, surprised.

"Immediately."

8

She sat in front with Pedro, her head pounding so hard that it was merely an enormous and imprecise pain she carried with her. The familiar landmarks as they passed made no sense. She could not have identified one. Nor did she know which of the three enraged her most: Charlotte, for her effrontery and disobedience, Mr. Van Siclen for his perfidy, or Monseiur Royer, for existing at all.

As long as she was sitting in the moving car her anger remained at fever pitch. But when Pedro stopped in the wilderness, pointing to a road strewn with large stones, and remarking that they would have to walk up to get to the village, her annoyance at this unexpected obstacle somewhat calmed her. It was quite dark by this time, and the faint light from Pedro's torch wavered uncertainly. Out here the wind came directly off the Atlantic; it was violent and damp.

The road led upward, zigzagging among huge boulders. Each minute the sound of the sea became more audible. She had never been here before; the idea of this absurd village perched on the crags above the ocean filled her with terror. They met a Berber on his way down, and by the flashlight's feeble glimmer she saw him, stocky and dark-skinned, and carrying a shepherd's crook. "*Msalkheir,*" he said as he passed. He was in the darkness back of them before they could ask him how far the village was. Suddenly they came to a hut. There was a flickering light inside, and the sound of many goats and sheep. A little farther on Pedro spied the jeep. She caught herself thinking, "How does he ever drive up that trail?" and quickly remembered the seriousness of her errand.

"*Pregúnteles,*" she whispered to Pedro, indicating a group of dark figures at the right. The barnyard odors were overwhelming. As Pedro left her side to approach the men, she glanced up and saw the sky, uniformly black. Not a star showed through the huge curtain of cloud. Yes, far out over the invisible sea she thought she saw one shining, but it could have been a boat. She had neglected to bring a wrap, and she was shivering.

The house was up ahead, at the top of the village. She could see the lamp through the open door, the brightest light in the landscape. Several dogs went slinking away into the dark as they approached the house. Pedro called out, "*Señor!*" and Mr. Van Siclen appeared.

"Good God!" he cried when he saw them standing in the doorway. "What are you doing here?"

She pushed past him into the tiny room. There was a chair, a table littered with papers, and a mattress on the floor in the corner. And there were large native baskets everywhere, full of pieces of stone. The light hurt her eyes.

"Where's my daughter?" she said, going to the door of the adjoining room and peering in.

"What?"

She looked at him; for the first time since she had known him he seemed really perturbed—even frightened.

"Charlotte. Where is she?"

The expression on his face did not change. Her question seemed not to have reached it. "I have no idea. I let her off early this morning on the Boulevard by the French Consulate."

Mrs. Callender hesitated, not completely sure he was telling the truth. He took the initiative. "It'd be more to the point to ask where Monsieur

Royer is. You haven't seen *him* by any chance? I don't mind telling you I'm worried."

"Monsieur Royer? Certainly not! Isn't he here with you?"

He shrugged his shoulders helplessly. "I'm afraid not. I don't know what's up. But it doesn't look good to me."

She sat down sideways on the straight-backed chair. For a second she heard the sea much closer than it should have been.

"He went out last night right after supper. There were some drums beating."

She had her hand to her head. And as so often happens in moments of great fatigue, she felt that the scene was one whose outcome she knew by heart, that although she was in it, it would go on and play itself through to the end without her participation. Mr. Van Siclen would reach into his hip-pocket, pull out a packet of cigarettes, extract one, light it, and hold the match a moment before blowing it out, just as he did do each of these things a fraction of a second after she had known he would. And he would go on speaking.

"—but I don't quite know what the hell to do. The worst thing about it is that the natives all claim not to have seen him, ever. They don't know there is such a person. I know damned well they're lying. It's too unanimous. I don't think he ever came back at all. The blankets on his mattress in there"—he indicated the next room—"haven't been touched. I didn't notice that until I got back from town this morning. I thought he was asleep."

She said nothing because she felt she was getting much too far ahead of him now. At the moment this bare room with the wind outside was the less strong of two realities. The other was a spoken sentence, a dreadful image, but she could recall neither the sentence nor the image it had evoked—only the brief horror she had felt at the time.

She was standing up, walking toward the door.

"I feel a bit ill." To say the words demanded a monstrous effort.

Outside, the sea-wind battered her face. She breathed deeply several times. Mr. Van Siclen's voice came from the door, solicitous. "Are you all right?"

"Yes," she said.

"Be careful out there. There's barbed wire strung along the edge where you are."

Now it was complete. Everything had been said. All she had to do was go on breathing deeply, facing the sea. Of course. A coil of wire around his neck. Behind a rock. A minute or two later she went back in.

"Better?"

"If I could have a drink," she said wanly. (She could not say to him: "It's not my fault. You yourself put the idea into my head," because to admit that much would establish her guilt firmly, for all time.)

"Whisky, you mean? Or water?"

"I think whisky."

As she drank it he said: "We'll have a searching party out looking for him the first thing in the morning. That is, if he doesn't turn up tonight. I'll drive you back now so you won't have to walk down the hill. And I think it might be a good idea to call the *comisaría* tonight, anyway."

She smiled ruefully. "The police won't be of much use, will they?"

"Never know," he said, slipping into his jacket. "He may be lying only a half mile from here with a broken leg."

Again she smiled: she was so sure it was not that. And so was he, she thought, but now that she was upset too he could afford to pretend.

"Well, shall we get going?" he asked her.

The wind blew, the great black cloud from the sea had covered everything. He put his arm about her waist as they stumbled downward. She thought of nothing, let herself bump against him as they avoided rocks.

They were in the jeep. At the foot of the hill Pedro got out. "Do you want to go in your own car?" said Mr. Van Siclen. "It'd be more comfortable, I guess."

"No. This air is just what I need."

Swiftly they left El Menar behind in the darkness.

From the spot where he lay, he could have heard the two motors grow fainter and be drowned by the vaster sound of the sea; he could have seen the two little red tail-lights moving away across the empty countryside. Could have, if all that had not been decided for him twenty-one hours earlier. In the bright moonlight he had sat with the child on his knee (for she was really no more than a child) letting her examine his watch. For some reason—probably the sight of this innocent animal holding the thin gold toy in her tattooed hands—he was put in mind of the phrase he had not been able to recall the evening of his arrival. He began to murmur it to himself, even at the moment her expression changed to one of terror as, looking up over his shoulder, she saw what was about to happen.

"*Le temps qui coule ici n'a plus d'heures, mais, tant l'inoccupation de chacun est parfaite—*"

This time he might have completed it.

Paris-Tangier
1950

The Successor

In the middle of the afternoon, lying on his mat, Ali sneezed. A hen that had been drowsing near him screeched and rushed out of the room to a circle of bare dusty ground under the fig tree, where she settled. He listened a while to the distant intermittent thunder in the mountains to the south of the town; then, deciding that he would be able to sleep no more until night, he sat up.

Beyond the partition of upright reeds his brother was talking to El Mehdi, one of the drivers of the carriages that brought people up from the town. From the terrace of the café the eye could wander over the tortured red earth with its old olive trees to the dark caves that lay just below the walls of the town.

The view was something visitors usually considered worth seeing. They would take one of the ancient carriages that waited down in the town and be driven up along the winding road that baked all day in the sunlight; it took less than an hour to reach the café. There they would sit under the trellis in the shade of the vines and drink their tea or their beer. The driver would give the horses water and before twilight they would start back.

On Sundays many carriages and cars came; the café was full all day. His brother, who owned the café and kept the accounts and the money, claimed that he made more on a Sunday than during all the rest of the week. Ali was skeptical of that, not because the statement seemed incredible, but simply because his brother had made it. There was the overwhelming fact that his brother was older than he and therefore had inherited the café from their father. In the face of such crushing injustice there was nothing to be done. Nor was anything his brother had to say of interest to him. His brother was like the weather: one watched it and was a victim of its whims. It was written, but that did not mean it could not change.

He leaned against the wall matting and stretched. His brother and El Mehdi were drinking beer; he was certain of it by the way their voices died down when there was any sound outside the room. They wanted to be able to hide the glasses swiftly if someone should come near the door, so they were listening as they talked. The idea of this childish secrecy disgusted him; he spat on the floor by his feet, and began to rub his bare toe back and forth in the little white mass of saliva.

The thunder rolled in the south mountains, no louder but longer than before. It was a little early in the season for rain, but the rain might come.

He reached for the water jug and drank lengthily. Then he sat quite still for a while, his eyes fixed on the framed portrait of the Sultan that hung on the opposite wall.

The thunder came again, still scarcely any louder, but this time unmistakably nearer, the sound more intimate in its movements. It was like a person taking pains to conceal his approach. There was a clapping of hands on the terrace, and a man's voice called: "*Garçon!*" His brother went out, and he heard El Mehdi gulp the rest of his beer and follow him. Presently a woman's voice remarked that it was going to rain. Then El Mehdi shouted, "*Eeeeee!*" to his horses, and the carriage began to creak as it started down the road.

After the customers had left, his brother remained outside. Ali went silently to the door, saw him standing by the parapet, his hands behind him, looking out over the town. At the other end of the terrace squatted the boy who washed the glasses and swept the floor. His eyes were closed. There was very little sound from the town below. Occasionally a bird flew out from the hill behind and let itself drop down toward the lower land. The sky was dark. His brother turned and saw him standing in the doorway.

"You slept?"

"Yes."

"It's going to rain."

"*Incha' Allah.*"

"Listen." His brother's hand went up and he turned his face sideways. Very faintly from the town came the sound of the small boys' voices as they ran through the streets chanting the song to Sidi Bou Chta, the song they always sang just before the rain.

"Yes."

Now the thunder was over the nearest mountains. His brother came toward the door and Ali stepped aside to let him pass.

"We'll close up," said his brother. He called to the boy, who began to carry the chairs and tables into the room where they were kept piled. Ali and his brother sat on the mattress and yawned. When the boy had finished he closed the door, snapped the padlock and came into the front part of the room, where he set to fanning the fire with the bellows. Presently he brought them each a glass of tea.

"Go to the house. We'll eat early," said his brother. The boy went out.

A crash of thunder directly above them made them look at each other. Ali said: "I'll close the house. The boy is an idiot."

The little house was behind the café, built against the low cliff, just beneath the road. When he got to the fig tree he heard his brother talking to someone. Surprised, he stopped and listened. Great drops of rain began to fall here and there onto the dust. It was hard to hear what his brother was saying. He went on to the house.

No one lived there but the two of them and the boy, who slept outside. It was never very clean. If only his brother had been willing to get married, Ali would have had an excuse for going away. Until then, it would be impossible, because his father had told him to stay and help his brother with the café. All he got for staying was a dirty room and the bad food the boy cooked for them.

On the other hand, when his brother walked through the Moulay Abdallah *quartier* he was greeted by the women of every house. The money went on bracelets for them, and on wine and beer for his friends. Besides these women, with whom he spent most of his nights, there was always a young girl of good reputation whom he had hopes of seducing; usually he failed in these endeavors, but his setbacks only increased his interest.

At the moment it was Kinza, the daughter of a shopkeeper from Taza, whose favors he sought. She had granted him short conversations in unfrequented alleys, with a maidservant standing a few feet away; he had met her one twilight outside Bab Segma and put his arm around her (after persuading the servant to stand facing in the other direction), and he even had had a *tête-à-tête* alone with her in a room behind a café, when he had lifted her veil and kissed her. But she had refused any further intimacies, threatening, if he used force, to call the servant who was outside the door. After accepting a good many gifts she had promised him another such rendezvous, so he still had hopes.

Ali knew all about his brother's life and about Kinza, since, in spite of the fact that such subjects cannot be discussed between brothers, it is perfectly proper to talk about them with anyone and everyone else. He knew all about Kinza and he hoped his brother would have no luck with her.

The rain was falling more heavily now. He closed the windows so it would not come in. Then, out of boredom and because he was curious to know who had arrived at the café, he went across the open space between the two establishments, taking long strides, and re-entered the back room. Behind the partition the fire was being fanned again, this time by his brother.

"I'm very fond of your tea here in Morocco," a man's voice was saying; they were speaking French.

His brother said: "Me, I like beer best."

"Have another bottle," said the stranger magnanimously. "Drink to the end of this damned rain. If it keeps up I won't get back to town before dark."

Ali tried to look through the cracks to see what sort of person it was who would walk all the way up to the café, but the man was seated in the doorway looking out at the rain and he could see nothing but his back.

"We are glad to have the rain," said his brother. "Each drop is money. The *fellahin* give thanks."

"*Oui, bien sûr*," said the stranger without interest.

The thunder had passed over, but the rain was roaring; soon a stream of water burst through the ceiling in a corner of the room and spattered onto the earthen floor. The added noise made it more difficult to hear their talk. He put his ear close to the reeds.

"Isn't Belgium near France?" his brother asked.

"Next door."

"It's a good country?"

"Oh, yes."

His brother handed the stranger a glass of tea.

"Have another bottle of beer," the stranger suggested.

Ali heard the bottle being opened and the cap fall on to the stone door-sill.

"What's that?" said his brother, his voice bright with interest.

"Just a pill. If I'm nervous I take one. It makes me feel better. If I can't sleep I take two."

"And then you sleep?"

"Like a child."

There was a pause. Then his brother asked: "And would they do that to anyone?"

The stranger laughed. "Of course," he said. "Some people might have to take three, some only one."

"And how long does it make you sleep?"

"All night."

"If someone touched you, you'd wake up?"

"Why, yes,"

"But if you took four or five?"

"*Oh, là, là!* You could ride a horse over me then, and I wouldn't know it. That's too many."

This time there was a long silence, and Ali heard only the noise of the rain all around. The water leaking through the roof had made a channel in the mud to the back door. Now and then a distant growl of thunder came from the hills on the north. The air that moved in through the door was cold and smelled of earth.

Presently his brother said: "It's getting dark."

"I suppose you want to close."

"*Oh, ne t'en fais pas!*" said his brother cordially. "Stay until it stops raining."

The stranger laughed. "It's very kind of you, but I'm afraid I'm going to get wet anyway, because it's not going to stop."

"No, no!" his brother cried, an anxious note creeping into his voice.

"Wait a few minutes. Soon it will stop. Besides, I enjoy talking with you. You aren't like a Frenchman."

The man laughed again; he sounded pleased and flattered.

Then Ali heard his brother saying timidly: "Those pills. Where could I buy a bottle?"

"My doctor in Belgium gave them to me, but I imagine you could get a doctor here to prescribe some."

"No," said his brother hopelessly.

"Why do you want them? You don't look as though you had trouble sleeping."

His brother squatted down beside the stranger. "It's not that," he said, almost whispering.

Ali peered intently between the reeds, making an effort to follow the movements of his brother's lips. "*C'est une fille.* I give her everything. She always says no. I was thinking, if just once I could—"

The man interrupted him. "You give her enough of these and she won't be able to say anything." He chuckled maliciously. "Here. Hold out your hand."

With a few inarticulate phrases of thanks, his brother rose to his feet, probably to get a box or an envelope for the pills.

Quickly Ali went out of the door through the rain to the house, where he changed his shirt and spread the wet one over the pillows, and lighted the lamp. Then he sat reading, with some difficulty, a newspaper that a customer had left behind the day before. A few minutes later his brother came in, looking pleased and a little mysterious.

It rained most of the night. At dawn, however, when they got up, the sky was clear. His brother drank his coffee hurriedly and went out, saying he would be back about noon.

Two couples came to the café during the morning, but since they took beer the boy did not have to light the fire.

Somewhat later than twelve his brother returned. Ali looked up at his face as he came in the door, and said to himself: "Something has happened." But he pretended to have noticed nothing and turned away unconcernedly after greeting him. Whatever it might be, he knew his brother would never tell him anything.

The afternoon was exceptionally fine. A good many visitors came, as they always did when the weather was clear and the view good. His brother's face did not change. He carried the trays of tea glasses out to the tables like a man walking in his sleep, and he kept his eyes averted from the customers' faces. Each time someone arrived and walked under the arbor onto the terrace, Ali's brother looked as though he were about to run and jump off the edge of the parapet. Once when Ali saw him smoking, he noticed his hand trembling so violently that he had difficulty in getting the cigarette to his lips, and he looked away quickly so his brother would not see him watching.

When the evening call to prayer was over and the last carriage had rattled away down the road, the boy brought the tables and chairs in and swept the floor of the terrace. Ali stood in the doorway. His brother sat on the parapet, looking down over the olive trees in the dimming light, while the town below sank deeper into the gulf of shadow between the hills. An automobile came along the road, stopped. Against the sky Ali saw his brother's head jerk upward. There were the two sounds of a car's doors being shut. His brother rose, took two hesitant steps, and sat down again.

Ali moved backward into the room, away from the door. It was not yet too dark for him to see that the two men walking across the terrace were policemen. Without slipping into his babouches he ran barefoot through the inner room of the café, across the open space to the house. He lay down on his mattress, breathing rapidly. The boy was in the kitchen preparing the evening meal.

For a long time Ali lay there, thinking of nothing, watching the cobwebs that dangled from the ceiling move slowly in the breeze. It seemed so long to him that he thought the two men must have gone away without his having heard them. He tiptoed to the door. The boy was still in the kitchen. Ali stepped outside. The crickets were singing all around and the moonlight looked blue. He heard voices on the terrace. Without making a sound he crept into the café's back room and lay down on the mat.

The policemen were making fun of his brother, but not pleasantly. Their voices were harsh and they laughed too loud.

"A Belgian, no less!" cried one with mock surprise. "He fell out of the sky like an angel, *bien sûr*, with the Veronal in one hand. But nobody saw him. Only you."

Ali caught his breath, sprang up. Then very slowly he lay down again, scarcely breathing now, still listening. "Nobody," said his brother, his voice very low. It sounded as though he had his hands over his face. "He said she'd just go to sleep."

They thought this very funny. "She did that, all right," said one at length. Then their speech became abrupt, the tone brutal: "*Allez, assez! On se débine!*" They rose, yanking him up with them.

As they pushed him into the car, his brother was still saying: "I didn't know. He didn't tell me."

The motor started up; they turned the car around and drove down the road. Soon the distant sound of its motor was covered by the song of the crickets.

For a while Ali lay very still. Then, being hungry, he went to the house and had his dinner.

Kandy, Sri Lanka
1950

If I Should Open My Mouth

Monday 26th–

At last succeeded in finding the correct mixture of gum-arabic, sugar and essence of peppermint. Had the most complicated time getting Mrs. Crawford out of the house and keeping her out for a sufficiently long time so that I could clean up the kitchen properly before she returned. I find this plan most exhilarating, however, and I intend to carry it through to its conclusion in the face of all obstacles. The subway station details are clear in my mind, and I have worked out the entire plan of action. In fact, the project is so extremely simple that it seems at times almost suspect. It is as if I were constantly being reassured by an invisible person whose face, if only I could see it, might easily prove to be wearing a falsely benign expression. However, it is only in the evenings that I begin to think of such things. A Seconal or two ought to arrange matters, at least for tonight, so that I can knit up some of that raveled sleeve of care. Curious how disturbing the sound of a motorcycle can be out here in the still night air. There has been one idling somewhere up the road for the past ten minutes, popping and sputtering in a way calculated to drive a listener crazy. When it finally purred off into the distance it was like a relief from a constant pain. Why were machines ever invented? And what is this strange calm confidence that mankind has placed in these senseless toys it has managed to put together? That question I don't expect ever to be able to answer. I can only say that I know it is wrong.

Wednesday 28th—

More complications, getting rid of Mrs. C. while I dipped the tablets. The rest, gluing the ends of the boxes and so on, can be done up here in my room. A ridiculous facet of my feeling about all this is that while I am quite aware of the reprehensible aspects of my silly little project, for some unfathomable reason I feel hugely righteous about it all—more satisfyingly virtuous than I have in years. A quirk of human nature, I suppose.

Saturday 1st—

I don't know why it is that ideas never occur to me except when I lack the time to put them down or when it is literally impossible to do so, as for

251

instance when I am seated in a dentist's chair or surrounded by talking people at a dinner party, or even sound asleep, when often the best things come to light and are recognized as such by a critical part of my mind which is there watching, quite capable of judging but utterly unable to command an awakening and a recording. Sick-bed and fever often bring up astonishing things, but again, to what avail? A less ingenuous man than I might ask just why it should be of any importance to me that what goes on inside my mind should be put down. I am not a literary person and I never expect to be one, nor have I any intention of showing my notebooks to my friends. But that is a point not even to be discussed; long ago I determined to extract from my mind whatever by-products it could furnish. I have done it, I am still doing it, and I expect to continue to do it. The only difficulty is that whatever I am able to catch hold of is captured only after engaging in the most elaborate intrigues with my mind, playing hide-and-seek with various parts of it, exhausting myself in inventing disguises with which to surprise it, and in general having a most unpleasant time. Such as this very moment, this very page. A typical example of an occasion when there is not a single idea in view on the vast inner horizon. I am using up pages of my notebook, minutes when I might be strolling on the beach smelling the sea, in scribbling these absurd excuses, inventing alibis for not living, trying to find one more reason why I should feel justified in keeping these nonsensical journals year after year. Year after year, and life does not last forever, not even an unsatisfactory one like mine. Perhaps this is the very thing which is keeping my life so unsatisfactory. If I could argue myself into stopping it all, even into destroying the notebooks, would it be better? Yes. Each minute would be complete in itself, like a room with four walls in which one can stand, sit, move about. Each day would be like a complete city shining in the sun, with its streets, parks and crowds. And the years would be whole countries to roam in. That much is certain. But the whole? That is to say, the interstices in time, the tiny chinks in consciousness when the total is there, enveloping one, and one knows that life is not made of time any more than the world is made of space. They would still occur, and they would be illicit because there would have been no arrangements made for them. What a man can distil and excrete will necessarily have some value for him (if only for him, as in my case) because its essence is of the interstices in time. One more justification, as idiotic as all the others, of the need for living an unsatisfactory life.

It seems to me that if one could accept existence as it is, partake of it fully, the world could be magical. The cricket on my balcony at the moment piercing the night repeatedly with its hurried needle of sound, would be welcome merely because it is there, rather than an annoyance because it distracts me from what I am trying to do. Here I am, a man of fifty-five, who enjoys a certain respect on the part of his friends, cursing a small black insect outside the window. But I dare say all this is merely procrastination. I am probably trying to put off writing down what is really on my mind. It must go down, of course, because everything must go down, and truthfully. (I thought the cricket had stopped just then, but it has started again, quite the same as before.) I delivered the first twenty boxes today.

Sunday 2nd—

The cricket got to be too much for me last night. It seemed to keep increasing its tempo, although I don't know how it could have managed to chirp any faster than it had been doing at the beginning. In any case, when I put down the great fact, I waited a while trying to decide how to go about describing the distribution. Nothing untoward happened, it is quite true, while I was making the deliveries, but still, it seemed to me last night in my overwrought condition that a special effort was required for me to be able to go into the details. And while I waited, the cricket went on and on and on; faster and faster, or so it seemed to me, until it would have been impossible to set down another word. This morning, however, I am in fine shape.

It was raining a little when I started out, a warm, fine summer drizzle. One of the things I have noticed about myself since Anna and I split up is the fact that I have a sneaking fondness for walking in the rain without rubbers or a hat. Doubtless this is a predilection I have always had without realizing it, since first it was Mother and then Anna who always seemed somehow to prevent me from indulging in it. Quite rightly, too; I should probably have caught pneumonia and died long before this if it had not been for them. But since Anna left me and I have been here in Manor Heights alone, I occasionally slip out bareheaded and without rubbers, if the rain is not too heavy. Mrs. Crawford, like a good housekeeper, has sometimes caught me at it, and brought it to my attention, hurrying to supply the needed accessories and thus obliging me to wear them. Yesterday morning, however, I managed to get out of the front door while she was in the kitchen talking to the delivery man from Macy's. I knew he would be coming, and I had everything ready, the twenty little boxes in the left-hand pocket of my jacket, the pennies in the right-hand trouser-pocket. The only way to do anything is to have it so well rehearsed in one's imagination that when the moment comes one does it automatically, as though for the hundredth time. Then it is all natural, and there is little likelihood of a slip-up. And there was no slip-up anywhere along the way. It was a heavy day, but not too hot because of the rain, which fell quietly as I walked down the road to the station. On the train I was not in the slightest degree perturbed: I knew there was no chance of any trouble. I kept marveling at the peculiar pleasure afforded by the knowledge that one has planned a thing so perfectly there can be no room for the possibility of failure, all the while being conscious that both the pleasure and the idea itself were completely childish, and that my conviction of success was, at the very least, ill-founded. But certain situations call forth certain emotions, and the mind is a thing entirely apart. I have cakes of soap that I bought twenty-five years ago, still in their wrappers, and I am saving them in the perfect confidence that the right day will come to unwrap each one and use it. And there are probably a hundred books downstairs in the library that I am eager to read, have been eager to read for years, yet refuse to read until the day comes, the day that says to me: This is the morning to start Villiers de l'Ile Adam, or George Borrow, or Psichari, or someone else. Now, in my logical mind, I know quite well that these promised days are not likely ever to arrive: I shall never use those old cakes of soap that are stored in the linen closet, and I am reasonably sure of never reading *Romany Rye*, because it doesn't interest *me*. But there is that other person, the ideal one that I ought to be, whom it does interest, and it comforts me to think that those things are there waiting for him. Certainly, the mind is a thing absolutely apart.

From Grand Central I took the shuttle across to Times Square, then walked underground to the Eighth Avenue Subway. I chose the Independent as my territory, because of the great length of the stations. The air in that tunnel was almost steamy, and smelled of wet cement, hot metal and sewage. I took an express all the way up to Fort Tryon, worked slowly down through Harlem and then all the way to Canal Street. There was no hitch, no real difficulty, anywhere. The only place where there was even a meeting of any sort was at Twenty-third Street, where a colored woman who was standing near the machine came up behind me as I was reaching in to take out the real package, which of course made it impossible for me to put in the one I held in my left hand. I did not hesitate for a fraction of a second. It was my determination that everything be carried off perfectly. I turned aside, put my left hand back into my coat pocket, and proceeded to open the little box, shake out its two white candy-coated pellets into my hand and pop them into my mouth. If I were to suggest to anyone that this was an excellent piece of strategy, it would sound laughable, and yet it required quick thinking and a certain courage. In the first place, I have never chewed gum, and the idea of it disgusts me. (It occurs to me now that this distaste may easily have had some bearing on my choice of method for carrying out my project.) But much more than that secondary consideration was the fact that my co-ordination is not always of the best. On occasion it takes terrific concentration for me to distinguish right from left. And a second before, I had held in my left hand the *other* box, one of *my* boxes. What if, I said to myself, through some dark perversity of the subconscious, I should somehow have opened the wrong box? And as I crunched through the enamel walls of mint-sugar I found myself wondering if what I was tasting was the normal flavor, or whether it might be my flavor, my special mixture. I did not wait to get at that machine again, but continued downtown, skipping the West Fourth Street station because of the central platforms and the undesirable placing of the machines.

At Canal Street I had the pleasure of actually seeing the bait snapped up. I had no sooner put the penny in, retrieved the untouched box, and placed one of mine at the back of the shelf, when a young girl (Italian, I think) pushed past me and worked the machine. There was an expression of amusement on her face as she rejoined her friends at the edge of the platform. "Gee, I'm gettin' good," she said. "I got two."

I delivered the three final boxes in Brooklyn, returned to Manhattan, had a light meal at a Longchamps on Madison Avenue, and came home, feeling that the day had certainly not been wasted. I venture to say that I am embarked on the biggest comedy to be played in the subways of New York until the day Russia's super-bombs lay them all bare to the sun. This is an infantile pastime I have devised, but at the same time it carries its own weight, and thus must have a meaning. However, I paid for my jaunt with a feeling of considerable fatigue, mostly of nervous origin, I suppose. Naturally, it was something of a strain. On an ordinary evening a cricket would not have been able to disturb me. Mrs. Crawford was indignant about the rubbers and the hat and the fact that my clothes were quite damp, of course. She is a good old soul. Today I have done nothing but sit in the garden reading the Sunday *Times.* The sun was out and in, all day, but it was not too hot.

This morning the Stewarts very kindly invited me on a picnic to Rye Beach. I could not entertain the thought of going, certainly. It's bad enough to have them living next door, to have to hear their abominable radio at all hours of the day and night, and put up with the depredations wrought in the garden by that untrained brat of theirs, without going out of my way to accompany them on an outing. It was a kind thought, however, and I have decided to go downtown the first thing tomorrow morning and buy a toy of some sort for little Dorothy. Maybe a tricycle, or something that will keep her on the sidewalk. Anywhere, anywhere, out of my garden!

Monday 3rd—

I scarcely dared open the paper this morning, for fear of what I should find. Still, reading of the consequences is most assuredly a part of the procedure, and so I went ahead. But for some reason the police are keeping it quiet. There was nothing, anywhere. This silence managed to make me feel uncomfortable; in a way I feel as though I were being watched.

The Stewarts were most pleased with the velocipede, or whatever the chromium-plated contraption is called. Little Dorothy seemed quite over-whelmed by its splendor. As yet I have not seen her use it. I dare say she is too small to pull it by herself, up and down the two flights of steps between the front door and the sidewalk. I imagine for a while her parents will have to take it up and down for her.

Thursday 6th—

The newspapers continue to maintain a stubborn silence, being filled instead with asinine stories about the electoral campaign. As if it could possibly change the course of history which of the two scarecrows gets into the seat of power. It was already too late to do that a hundred and seventy-five years ago. Too late to avert the sheer, obscene horror that has been on its way ever since, and is nearly here now. Voltaire, Marx, Roosevelt, Stalin, what were they but buds along the branch, like sores that have a way of bursting through the skin where it is thinnest? Who planted the tree of poison, who infected the blood? I am not qualified to say; the complexities of the question are endless. But I believe that one of the culprits was our friend Rousseau. That unpardonable mechanism, the intellect, has several detestable aspects. Perhaps the worst is the interpenetration of minds; the influence, unconscious, even, that one mind can have over millions, is unforeseeable, immeasurable. You never know what form it will take, when it will make itself manifest.

Saturday 8th—

The police assuredly are playing some sort of game. There must have been at least fifteen deaths, and not a word about one of them has appeared. That of course is their business, but I am amused and a little mystified to see how they are conducting it. Mrs. C. has a heavy summer cold. I tried hard to make her stay in bed, but she is the soul of conscientiousness, and insists on continuing with her regular work.

Sunday 9th—

It is an odd thing, that part of the mind which invents dreams and retains them, sometimes making a certain dream a colored lens, as it were, which comes between one's consciousness and one's vision of what passes for reality. That is, the feeling of the dream can remain when every detail has been lost. For several days now a particular atmosphere, taste, sensation, or whatever it may be called, has been haunting me. It can only be a dream-vestige, yet in spite of the fact that I have forgotten the dream it is very strong. And since it is gone it is unlocatable in time. It may have been this week or many years ago that the dream itself took place. The feeling, if it can be put into words at all, is one connected with languor, forgetfulness, lostness, emptiness, endlessness—one thing which would be all those things. Living my life and thinking my thoughts through that lens makes for a certain melancholy. I have tried desperately to find a door into the dream; perhaps if I could recall it, get back there, I could destroy its power. It is often a way. But it is almost as if it were an entity in itself, aware of my efforts to find it, and determined to remain hidden. As I feel I am approaching it I seem to sense a springing away, a definite recoil into some airless, unreachable region within. I don't like it; it worries me.

Monday 10th—

When things become wholly unbelievable, all one can do is laugh. There is nothing to fall back upon but the bare fact of one's existence; one must forsake logic for magic. Because it was raining this morning (a morning rather like the day of my excursion to the city) and I wanted to take a short stroll, I went to the clothes closet and took out my gray flannel suit. I was entirely dressed when I suddenly recalled that there was a large hole in the right trouser-pocket. A strange feeling of confusion came over me, even before I started to think. But then the mental process commenced. How had the pennies stayed in my pocket that day? It was quite simple. I had changed my suit; now I remembered clearly taking off the gray flannel and putting on the herring-bone tweed. Perhaps if I had been able to live completely in the mind at that moment, I should have given it no further thought, and the unacceptable discovery would not have been made—at least, not then. But evidently I could not be satisfied with anything so simple. Another reflex sent my left hand to the pocket of the jacket, and that was the instant of my undoing. Later I took them all out and counted them sitting on the bed, but then I merely stood still, my hand inside the pocket feeling the jumble of small cardboard boxes, my mouth hanging open like an idiot's. It was inescapable—they were there. A second later I said aloud: "Oh." And I rushed over to the bureau drawer and opened it, because I wanted to be sure that these were not the untouched boxes I had collected. But they too were there, scattered among the piles of clean handkerchiefs. Then the others—? There is nothing to think. I *know* I delivered them.

At least, I believe I know. If I am to doubt my own eyes and ears, then it is time I gave up entirely. But in connection with that idea a ghastly little thought occurs to me: am I doubting my eyes and ears? Obviously not; only my memory. Memory is a cleverer trickster by far. In that case, however, I am stark, raving mad, because I remember every detail of those hours spent in the subway. But here are the boxes piled in front of me on the desk, all twenty. I know them intimately. I glued down each little flap with the maximum of care. There is no mistaking them. It is a shattering experience, and I feel ill, ill in every part of my being. A voice in me says: "Accept the impossible. Leave off trying to make this fit in with your preconceived ideas of logic and probability. Life would be a sad affair if it reserved no surprises at all." "But not this sort!" I reply. "Nothing quite so basically destructive of my understanding of the world!" I am going to bed. Everything is all wrong.

3:15 AM—

The dream has emerged from its wrappings of fog. Not all of it, but that does not matter. I recognized it immediately when only a piece of it appeared, as I was lying here in the dark, half asleep. I relaxed and let more of it come. A senseless dream, it would seem, and yet powerful enough to have colored all these past few days with its sadness. It is almost impossible to put down, since nothing *happens* in it: I am left only with vague impressions of being solitary in the park of some vast city. Solitary in the sense that although life is going on all around me, the cords that could connect me in any way with the life have been severed, so that I am as alone as if I were a spirit returned from the dead. Traffic moves past at some distance from where I am reclining on the ground under the trees. The time—timeless. I know there are streets full of people behind the trees, but I will never be able to touch them. If I should open my mouth to cry out, no sound would come forth. Or if I should stretch my arms toward one of the figures that occasionally wanders along the path nearby, that would have no effect, because I am invisible. It is the terrible contradiction that is unbearable: being there and yet knowing that I am not there, for in order to *be*, one must not only be to one's self: it is absolutely imperative that one be for others. One must have a way of basing one's being on the certainly that others know one is there. I am telling myself that somewhere in this city Mrs. Crawford is thinking of me. If I could find her, she would be able to see me, and could give me a sign that would mean everything was all right. But she will never come by this place. I am hidden. I cannot move, I was born here, have always been here under these trees on this wet grass. And if I was born, perhaps I can die, and the city making its roar out beyond this park will stop being. That is my only hope. But it will take almost forever. That is about all there is to the dream. Just the static picture of sadness and lostness.

The boxes are still there on my desk. They at least are no dream!

That little Dorothy is a horror. This evening at dusk I was returning from a short walk. It was nearly dark, and for some reason the street lights had not yet been put on. I turned into the front walk, climbed up the steps, and had almost reached the house, when I banged full-force into her damned tricycle. I am afraid my anger ran away with me, for I deliberately gave it such a push that it bumped all the way down both flights of steps and ran out into the middle of the street. A truck coming down the hill finished it off in a somewhat spectacular fashion. When I got inside I found the child in the kitchen talking with Mrs. C. I did not mention the incident, but came directly upstairs.

It is a lovely evening. After dinner I am going to take all forty boxes to the woods behind the school and throw them on to the rubbish heap there. It's too childish a game to go on playing at my age. Let the kids have them.

Tangier
1952

The Frozen Fields

The train was late because the hot-box under one of the coaches had caught fire in the middle of a great flat field covered with snow. They had stayed there about an hour. After the noise and rushing of the train, the sudden silence and the embarrassed stirring of people in their seats induced a general restlessness. At one point another train had shot by on the next track with a roar worse than thunder; in the wake of that, the nervousness of the passengers increased, and they began to talk fretfully in low voices.

Donald had started to scratch pictures with his fingernail in the ice that covered the lower part of the windowpane by his seat. His father had said: "Stop that." He knew better than to ask "Why?" but he thought it; he could not see what harm it would do, and he felt a little resentful toward his mother for not intervening. He could have arranged for her to object to the senseless prohibition, but experience had taught him that she could be counted on to come to his defense only a limited number of times during any given day, and it was imprudent to squander her reserve of good will.

The snow had been cleared from the station platform when they got out. It was bitter cold; a fat plume of steam trailed downward from the locomotive, partially enveloping the first coach. Donald's feet ached with the cold.

"There's Uncle Greg and Uncle Willis!" he cried, and he jumped up and down several times.

"You don't have to shout," said his father. "We see them. And stand still. Pick up your bag."

Uncle Willis wore a black bearskin coat that almost touched the ground. He put his hands under Donald's arms and lifted him up so that his head was at a level with his own, and kissed him hard on the mouth. Then he swung him over into Uncle Greg's arms, and Uncle Greg did the same thing. "How's the man, hey?" cried Uncle Greg, as he set him down.

"Fine," said Donald, conscious of a feeling of triumph, because his father did not like to see boys being kissed. "Men shake hands," he had told him. "They don't kiss each other."

The sky was crystal clear, and although it was already turning lavender with the passing of afternoon, it still shone with an intense light, like the sky in one scene at the Russian Ballet. His mother had taken him a few weeks

261

earlier because she wanted to see Pavlova; it was not the dancing that had excited him, but the sudden direct contact with the world of magic. This was a magic sky above him now, nothing like the one he was used to seeing above the streets of New York. Everything connected with the farm was imbued with magic. The house was the nucleus of an enchanted world more real than the world that other people knew about. During the long green summers he had spent there with his mother and the members of her family he had discovered that world and explored it, and none of them had ever noticed that he was living in it. But his father's presence here would constitute a grave danger, because it was next to impossible to conceal anything from him, and once aware of the existence of the other world he would spare no pains to destroy it. Donald was not yet sure whether all the entrances were safely guarded or effectively camouflaged.

They sat in the back of the sleigh with a brown buffalo robe tucked around them. The two big gray horses were breathing out steam through their wide nostrils. Silently the white countryside moved past, its frozen trees pink in the late light. Uncle Greg held the reins, and Uncle Willis, sitting beside him, was turned sideways in his seat, talking to Donald's mother.

"My feet hurt," said Donald.

"Well, God Almighty, boy!" cried Uncle Willis. "Haven't you got 'em on the bricks? There are five hot bricks down there. That's what they're there for." He bent over and lifted up part of the heavy lap-robe. The bricks were wrapped in newspaper.

"*My* feet are like blocks of ice, too," said Donald's mother. "Here, take your shoes off and put your feet on these." She pushed two of the bricks toward Donald.

"He just wants attention," said Donald's father. But he did not forbid him to have the bricks.

"Is that better?" Uncle Willis asked a moment later.

"It feels good. How many miles is it to the farm?"

"Seven miles to The Corner, and a mile and a half from there."

"Oh, I know it's a mile and a half from The Corner," said Donald. He had walked it many times in the summer, and he knew the names of the farms along the road. "First you come to the Elders, then the Landons, then the Madisons—"

His father pushed him hard in the ribs with his elbow. "Just keep quiet for a while."

Uncle Willis pretended not to have heard this. "Well, well. You certainly have a good memory. How old are you now?"

Donald's throat had constricted; it was a familiar occurrence which did not at all mean that he was going to cry—merely that he felt like crying. He coughed and said in a stifled voice: "Six." Then he coughed again; ashamed, and fearful that Uncle Willis might have noticed something amiss, he added: "But I'll be seven the day after New Year's."

They were all silent after that; there were only the muffled rhythm of the horses' trot and the soft, sliding sound of the runners on the packed snow. The sky was now a little darker than the white meadows, and the woods on the hillside beyond, with their millions of bare branches, began to look frightening. Donald was glad to be sitting in the middle. He knew there were no wolves out there, and yet, could anybody be really certain? There had been wolves at one time—and bears as well—and simply because nobody had seen one in many years, they now said there weren't any. But that was no proof.

They came to The Corner, where the road to the farm turned off from the main road. Seven rusty mail-boxes stood there in a crooked row, one for each house on the road.

"R.F.D. Number One," said Uncle Willis facetiously. This had always been a kind of joke among them, ever since they had bought the farm, because they were townspeople and thought the real farmers were very funny.

Now Donald felt he was on home ground, and it gave him the confidence to say: "Rural Free Delivery." He said the words carefully, since the first one sometimes gave him difficulty. But he pronounced it all right, and Uncle Greg, without turning round, shouted: "That's right! You go to school now?"

"Yes." He did not feel like saying more, because he was following the curves in the road, which he knew by heart. But everything looked so different from the way he remembered it that he found it hard to believe it was the same place. The land had lost its intimacy, become bare and unprotected. Even in the oncoming night he could see right through the leafless bushes that should have hidden the empty fields beyond. His feet were all right now, but his hands in their woolen mittens under the buffalo skin were numb with cold.

The farm came into view; in each downstairs window there was a lighted candle and a holly wreath. He bent over and put his shoes on. It was hard because his fingers ached. When he sat up again the sleigh had stopped. The kitchen door had opened; someone was coming out. Everyone was shouting "Hello!" and "Merry Christmas!" Between the sleigh and the kitchen he was aware only of being kissed and patted, lifted up and set down, and told that he had grown. His grandfather helped him take off his shoes again and removed a lid from the top of the stove so he could warm his hands over the flames. The kitchen smelled, as in summer, of woodsmoke, sour milk and kerosene.

It was always very exciting to be in the midst of many people. Each one was an added protection against the constant watchfulness of his mother and father. At home there were only he and they, so that mealtimes were periods of torture. Tonight there were eight at the supper table. They put an enormous old leather-bound dictionary in a chair so he would be high enough, and he sat between his grandmother and Aunt Emilie. She had dark brown eyes and was very pretty. Uncle Greg had married her a year ago, and Donald knew from many overheard conversations that none of the others really liked her.

Gramma was saying: "Louisa and Ivor couldn't get down till tomorrow. Mr. Gordon's driving them down as far as Portersville in his car. They'll all stay in the hotel tonight, and we've got to go in first thing in the morning and bring them out."

"Mr. Gordon, too, I suppose," said his mother.

"Oh, probably," Uncle Greg said. "He won't want to stay alone Christmas Day."

His mother looked annoyed. "It seems sort of unnecessary," she said. "Christmas is a *family* day, after all."

"Well, he's part of the family now," said Uncle Willis with a crooked smile.

His mother replied with great feeling: "I think it's terrible."

"He's pretty bad these days," put in Grampa, shaking his head.

"Still on the old fire-water?" asked his father.

Uncle Greg raised his eyebrows. "That and worse. You know. . . . And Ivor too."

Donald knew they were being mysterious because of him. He pretended not to be listening, and busied himself making marks on the tablecloth with his napkin ring.

His father's mouth had fallen open with astonishment. "Where do they get it?" he demanded.

"Prescription," said Uncle Willis lightly. "Some crooked Polack doctor up there."

"Oh, honestly," cried his mother. "I don't see how Louisa *stands* it."

Aunt Emilie, who had been quiet until now, suddenly spoke. "Oh, I don't know," she said speculatively. "They're both very good to her. I think Mr. Gordon's very generous. *He* pays the rent on her apartment, you know, and gives her the use of the car and chauffeur most afternoons."

"You don't know anything about it," said Uncle Greg in a gruff, unpleasant voice which was meant to stop her from talking. But she went on, a bit shrilly, and even Donald could hear that they were in the habit of arguing.

"I *do* happen to know that Ivor's perfectly willing to give her a divorce any time she wants it, because she told me so herself."

There was silence at the table; Donald was certain that if he had not been there they would all have begun to talk at that point. Aunt Emilie had said something he was not supposed to hear.

"Well," said Uncle Willis heartily, "how about another piece of cake, Donald, old man?"

"How about bed, you mean," said his father. "It's time he went to bed."

His mother said nothing, helped him from his chair and took him upstairs.

The little panes of his bedroom window were completely covered with ice. Opening his mouth, he breathed on one pane until a round hole had been melted through and he could see blackness outside. "Don't do that, dear," said his mother. "Gramma'll have to clean the window. Now come on; into bed with you. There's a nice hot brick under the covers so your feet won't get cold." She tucked the blankets around him, kissed him, and took the lamp from the table. His father's voice, annoyed, came up from the foot of the stairs. "Hey, Laura! What's going on up there? Come on."

"Won't there be any light in my room at all?" Donald asked her.

"I'm coming," she called. She looked down at Donald. "You never have a light at home."

"I know, but home I can turn it on if I need it."

"Well, you're not going to need it tonight. Your father would have a fit if I left the lamp. You know that. Now just go to sleep."

"But I won't be able to sleep," he said miserably.

"Laura!" shouted his father.

"Just a *minute!*" she cried, vexed.

"Please, Mother . . . ?"

Her voice was adamant. "This cold air will put you to sleep in two shakes of a lamb's tail. Now go to sleep." She went to the doorway, the lamp in her hand, and disappeared through it, closing the door behind her.

There was a little china clock on the table that ticked very loud and fast. At infrequent intervals from below came a muffled burst of laughter which immediately subsided. His mother had said: "I'll open this window about an inch; that'll be enough." The room was growing colder by the minute. He pushed the sole of one foot against the heated brick in the middle of the bed, and heard the crackle of the newspaper that enfolded it. There was nothing left to do but go to sleep. On his way through the borderlands of consciousness he had a fantasy. From the mountain behind the farm, running silently over the icy crust of the snow, leaping over the rocks and bushes, came a wolf. He was running toward the farm. When he got there he would look through the windows until he found the dining-room where the grownups were sitting around the big table. Donald shuddered when he saw his eyes in the dark through the glass. And now, calculating every movement perfectly, the wolf sprang, smashing the panes, and seized Donald's father by the throat. In an instant, before anyone could move or cry out, he was gone again with his prey still between his jaws, his head turned sideways as he dragged the limp form swiftly over the surface of the snow.

The white light of dawn was in the room when he opened his eyes. Already there were bumpings in the bowels of the house: people were stirring. He heard a window slammed shut, and then the regular sound of someone splitting wood with a hatchet. Presently there were nearer noises, and he knew that his parents in the next room had gotten up. Then his door was flung open and his mother came in, wearing a thick brown flannel bathrobe, and with her hair falling loose down her back. "Merry Christmas!" she cried, holding up a gigantic red mesh stocking crammed with fruit and small packages. "Look what I found hanging by the fireplace!" He was disappointed because he had hoped to go and get his stocking himself. "I brought it up to you because the house is as cold as a barn," she told him. "You stay put right here in bed till it's warmed up a little."

"When'll we have the tree?" The important ritual was the tree: the most interesting presents were piled under it.

"You just hold your horses," she told him. "You've got your stocking. We can't have the tree till Aunt Louisa gets here. You wouldn't want her to miss it, would you?"

"Where's my present for Aunt Louisa and Uncle Ivor? Uncle Ivor's coming, too, isn't he?"

"Of course he's coming," she replied, with that faintly different way of speaking she used when she mentioned Uncle Ivor. "I've already put it under the tree with the other things. Now you just stay where you are, all covered up, and look at your stocking. I'm going to get dressed." She shivered and hurried back into her room.

The only person he had to thank at breakfast was his grandfather, for a box of colored pencils which had been jammed into the foot of the stocking. The other gifts had been tagged: "For Donald from Santa." Uncle Willis and Uncle Greg had eaten an early breakfast and gone in the sleigh to the hotel in Portersville to fetch Aunt Louisa and Uncle Ivor. When they got back, Donald ran to the window and saw that Mr. Gordon had come. Everyone had talked so mysteriously about Mr. Gordon that he was very eager to see him. But at that moment his mother called him upstairs to help her make the beds. "We all have to do as much as we can for Gramma," she told him. "Lord knows she's got all she can manage with the kitchen work."

But eventually he heard Aunt Louisa calling up the staircase. They went down: he was smothered in kisses, and Aunt Louisa asked him: "How's my boy? You're *my* boy, aren't you? Then Uncle Ivor kissed him, and he shook hands with Mr. Gordon, who was already sitting in Grampa's armchair, where nobody else ever sat. He was plump and pale, and he wore two big diamond rings on one hand and an even bigger sapphire on the other. As he breathed he wheezed slightly; now and then he pulled an enormous yellow silk handkerchief out of his breast pocket and wiped his forehead with it. Donald sat down on the other side of the room and turned the pages of a magazine, from time to time looking up to observe him. He had called Donald "my lad," which sounded very strange, like someone talking in a book. At one point he noticed Donald's attention, and beckoned to him. Donald went and stood beside the armchair while Mr. Gordon reached into his pocket and pulled out a fat watch with a little button, and tiny chimes struck inside the watch. A few minutes later he signaled to him afresh; Donald bounded over to him and pressed the button again. The next time, his mother told him to stop bothering Mr. Gordon.

"But he *asked* me to," objected Donald.

"Sit down right there. We're all going in and have our tree in a little while. Uncle Ivor's going to be Santa Claus."

Presently Uncle Willis came into the room. "Well, everybody, he said, rubbing his hands together, "I think the parlor's warm enough now. How about our tree?"

"It's about time," said Aunt Emilie. She was wearing a red taffeta dress which Donald had heard his mother discussing with his father earlier. "*Most* inappropriate," she had said. "The girl doesn't seem to realize she's living on a farm." Aunt Emilie reached down and took Donald's hand. "Would you care to accompany me, sir?" she said. They walked into the parlor holding hands. The fire in the fireplace roared and crackled.

"Where's Ivor?" said Uncle Greg. "Has everybody got a seat?"

"Here he is," said Uncle Ivor, coming in from the hallway. He had put on an old red knitted skull-cap and a red dressing gown, and he had a wreath of green fluted paper around his neck. "This is all Santa Claus could find," he announced.

Aunt Louisa began to laugh. "Look at your Uncle Ivor," she told Donald. "I am," said Donald. But he was really looking at the tree. It was a tall hemlock that reached to the ceiling, and underneath it was piled the most enormous assortment of packages he had ever seen. "Look at that!" they all cried.

"What *do* you suppose is in them all?" said Aunt Louisa.

"I don't know," he replied.

Uncle Ivor sat down on the floor as near the tree as he could get, and lifting up a large crate he passed it to Uncle Greg, who stood in the middle of the room. "Let's get this out of the way first," he said. Then Uncle Greg intoned: "To Donald from the Folks at Rutland."

While Uncle Ivor went on passing out packages, Donald struggled with his box. He was vaguely aware of the little cries that were being uttered around him: "How lovely! But it's too much!" "Oh, you shouldn't have!" "Why did you do it?" as the others opened their gifts, but he was too preoccupied to notice that most of the exclamations were being addressed to Mr. Gordon, who sat in the window looking very pleased.

It was too good to believe: a fire engine three feet long, with rubber tires and a bell and a siren and three ladders that shot upward automatically when it stopped. Donald looked at it, and for a moment was almost frightened by the power he knew it had to change his world.

"Oh . . . isn't . . . that . . . lovely!" said his mother, her annoyance giving a sharp edge to each word. "Louisa, why did you do it?" Donald glanced up quickly and saw Aunt Louisa indicate Mr. Gordon with a jerk of her head, as if she were saying: "Everything is his fault."

His mother moved along the floor toward the crate and fished out the greeting card. "I want you to keep each card in with the present it came with," she told Donald, "because you'll have a lot of thank-you notes to write tomorrow, and you don't want to get them mixed up. But you can thank Aunt Louisa and Uncle Ivor right now."

He hated to be told to thank a person in that person's presence, as though he were a baby. But he said the words bravely, facing Mr. Gordon: "Thank you so much for the beautiful fire engine."

"There's more there, my lad," beamed Mr. Gordon; the diamonds flashed in the sunlight.

Aunt Emilie was holding out her arm in front of her, looking at her new wrist-watch. Grampa had put on a black silk dressing gown and was smoking a cigar. He looked perfectly content as he turned to Mr. Gordon and said: "Well, you've spoiled us all." But Donald's mother interpreted his phrase as a reproach, and added in explanation: "We're not used to getting such *elaborate* gifts, Mr. Gordon."

Mr. Gordon laughed, and turning to Donald, told him: "You've barely started, my lad. Tell your Uncle Ivor to get on with it."

Now it seemed as though nearly every package was for Donald. He opened them as fast as he could, and was freshly bewildered by the apparition of each new marvel. There were, of course, the handkerchiefs and books and mufflers from the family, but there was also a Swiss music box with little metal records that could be changed; there were roller skates, a large set of lead soldiers, a real accordion, and a toy village with a streetcar system that ran on a battery. As Donald opened each package, the little cries of admiration made by his parents came closer to sounding like groans. Finally his father said, in a voice loud enough for Mr. Gordon to hear him above the general conversation: "It's bad business for one kid to get so much."

Mr. Gordon had heard him. "You were young once yourself," he said airily.

Aunt Emilie was trying on a fur jacket that Uncle Greg had given her. Her face was flushed with excitement; she had just planted a big kiss on Uncle Greg's cheek.

"The little Astor baby got five thousand dollars' worth of toys on its last birthday," she said to Donald's father, running her hand back and forth along the fur.

Donald's father looked at her with narrowed eyes. "That," he said, enunciating very clearly, "is what might be called an *asinine* remark."

Save for the crackling of the fire there was silence for a moment in the room. Those who had not heard knew that something had happened. Uncle Greg looked quickly at Donald's father, and then at Aunt Emilie. Maybe there would be a quarrel, thought Donald, with everyone against his father. The idea delighted him; at the same time he felt guilty, as though it were his doing.

Uncle Ivor was handing him a package. Automatically he untied the ribbon, and pulled out a tan cashmere sweater. "That's Mother's and Daddy's present to you," his mother said quietly. "It's a little big for you now, but I got it big purposely so you could grow into it." The small crisis had passed; they all began to talk again. Donald was relieved and disappointed. "How about christening that bottle of brandy?" cried Uncle Willis.

"You menfolk sit here," Gramma told them. "We've got to get out into the kitchen."

"I'll bring yours out to you," said Uncle Ivor to Aunt Louisa as she got up.

On her way out of the room Donald's mother bent over and touched his shoulder. "I want you to put every present back into its box just the way it was. After that you carry them all up into our room and stack them carefully in the corner under the window. You hear me?"

She went out. Donald sat a moment; then he jumped up and ran after her to ask if he might save out just one thing—the fire engine, perhaps. She was saying to Gramma: ". . . quite uncalled for. Besides, I don't know how we're *ever* going to get it all back to New York. Owen can take the big things at least with him tomorrow, I suppose."

He stopped running, and felt peace descend upon him. His father was leaving the farm. Then let him take everything with him, fire engine and all; it would not matter. He turned and went back into the parlor, where he meticulously packed the toys into their boxes, put the covers on, and tied them up with lengths of ribbon and string.

"What's all this?" exclaimed Mr. Gordon suddenly, noticing him. "What are you doing?"

"I have to take everything upstairs," said Donald.

His father joined the conversation. "I don't want to find those boxes lying all over the place up there, either. See that you pile 'em neatly. Understand?"

Donald continued to work without looking up.

After a moment Mr. Gordon said under his breath: "Well, I'll be damned." Then to Donald's father: "I've seen some well-behaved kids in my time, but I don't mind telling you I never saw one like *that*. Never."

"Discipline begins in the cradle," said his father shortly.

"It's sinister," murmured Mr. Gordon to himself.

Donald glanced up and saw his father looking at Mr. Gordon with hatred.

In the kitchen his grandmother, his aunts and his mother were busy preparing dinner. Donald sat by the window mashing potatoes. The blue of the sky had disappeared behind one curtain of cloud, uniformly white. "We'll have more snow before night," said Gramma, looking out of the window above the sink.

"Want to smell something good?" Donald's mother asked him. He ran across to the stove and she opened the oven door: the aroma of onions mingled with that of the roasting turkey. "He's coming along beautifully," she announced. She shut the oven door with a bang and hung the potholders on their hooks. Then she went into the pantry. Donald followed her. It was very cold in here, and it smelled of pickles and spices. His mother was searching for something along the shelves, among the jars and tin boxes.

"Mother," he said.

"Hmm?" she replied distraughtly, without looking down at him.

"Why does Mr. Gordon live at Uncle Ivor's?"

Now she did look at him, and with an intensity that startled him. "What was that?" she demanded sharply. Then, before he could repeat his question, she went on in a suddenly matter-of-fact voice: "Dear, don't you know that Uncle Ivor's what they call a male nurse? Like Miss Oliver, you remember, who took care of you when you had influenza? Only a man. A man nurse."

"Is Mr. Gordon sick?"

"Yes, he is," she said, lowering her voice to little more than a whisper. "He's a very sick man, but we don't talk about it."

"What's he got?" He was conscious of being purposely childish at the moment, in the hope of learning more. But his mother was already saying: "I don't know, dear. You go back into the kitchen now. It's too cold for you in here. Scoot! Out with you!" He giggled, ran back into the kitchen, satisfied for having definitely established the existence of a mystery.

During dinner his father looked across at him with the particular kind of sternness he reserved for remarks which he knew were unwelcome, said: "You haven't been outside yet today, young man. We'll take a walk down the road later."

Aunt Louisa had brought a large glass of brandy to the table with her, and was sipping it along with her food. "It's too cold, Owen," she objected. "He'll catch his death o' cold." Donald knew she was trying to help him, but he wished she had kept quiet. If it became an issue, his father would certainly not forget about the walk.

"Too cold!" scoffed his father. "We have a few basic rules in *our* little family, and one of them is that he has to get some fresh air every day."

"Couldn't you make an exception for Christmas? Just for one day?" demanded Aunt Louisa.

Donald did not dare look up, for fear of seeing the expression on his father's face.

"Listen, Louisa," he said acidly. "I suggest you just stay on your side of the fence, and I'll stay on mine. We'll get along a lot better." Then as an afterthought he snapped: "That all right with you?"

Aunt Louisa leaned across Grampa's plate toward Donald's father and spoke very loud, so that everyone stopped eating. "No, it's not all right with me!" she cried. "All you do is pick on the child from morning till night. It's shameful! I won't sit by and watch my own flesh and blood plagued that way!"

Both Gramma and Donald's father began to speak at once. Gramma was saying, "Louisa," trying to soothe her. Donald's father shouted: "You've never *had* a kid. You don't know the first thing *about* raising kids."

"I know when a man's selfish and plain cussed," Aunt Louisa declared.

"Louisa!" cried Gramma in a tone of surprise and mild reproof. Donald continued to look at his plate.

"Have I ever come up to Rutland and stuck my nose in your affairs and criticized? Have I?" demanded Donald's father.

"Now come on," said Uncle Willis quickly. "Let's not spoil a beautiful Christmas."

"That's right," Grampa said. "We're all happy. Let's not say anything we'll be sorry for later."

But Aunt Louisa would not retreat. She took a fast gulp of brandy and almost choked on it. Then, still leaning toward Donald's father, she went on: "What do you mean, come to Rutland and criticize? What've you got to criticize in Rutland? Something wrong there?"

For an instant Donald's father did not reply. During that instant it was as though everyone felt the need to say something without being able to say it. The one who broke the short silence was Donald's father, using a peculiar, soft voice which Donald recognized immediately as a vicious imitation of Uncle Ivor. "Oh, *no!* There's nothing wrong in *Rut*land!"

Suddenly, with two simultaneous motions, Donald's mother slapped her napkin into her place and pushed her chair back violently. She rose and ran out of the room, slamming the door. No one said anything. Donald sat frozen, unable to look up, unable even to breathe. Then he realized that his father had got up, too, and was on his way out.

"Leave her alone, Owen," said Gramma.

"You keep out of this," his father said. His footsteps made the stairs creak as he went up. No one said anything until Gramma made as if to rise. "I'm going up," she declared.

"For God's sake, Abbie, sit still," Grampa told her. Gramma cleared her throat, but did not get up.

Aunt Louisa looked very red, and the muscles of her face were twitching. "Hateful," she said in a choked voice. "Just hateful."

"I felt like slapping his face," confided Aunt Emilie. "Did you hear what he said to me when we were having our presents?"

At a glance from Uncle Greg, Aunt Emilie stopped. "Why, Donald!" she exclaimed brightly, "you've scarcely touched your dinner! Aren't you hungry?"

In his mind's eye he was seeing the bedroom upstairs, where his father was twisting his mother's arm and shaking her to make her look at him. When she wouldn't, he punched her, knocking her down, and kicked her as hard as he could, all over her body. Donald looked up. "Not very," he said.

Without warning Mr. Gordon began to talk, holding his glass in front of him and examining it as he turned it this way and that. "Family quarrels," he sighed. "Same old thing. Reminds me of my boyhood. When I look back on it, it seems to me we never got through a meal without a fight, but I suppose we must have once in a while." He set the glass down. "Well, they're all dead now, thank God."

Donald looked quickly across at Mr. Gordon as if he were seeing him for the first time.

"It's snowing!" cried Gramma triumphantly. "Look, it's snowing again. I knew we'd have more snow before dark." She did not want Mr. Gordon to go on talking.

Aunt Louisa sobbed once, got up, and went out into the kitchen. Uncle Ivor followed her.

"Why, Donald! You've got the wishbone!" cried Aunt Emilie. "Eat the meat off it and we'll hang it up over the stove to dry, and tomorrow we'll wish on it. Wouldn't that be fun?"

He picked it up in his fingers and began to chew on the strips of white meat that clung to it. When he had carefully cleaned it, he got down and went out into the kitchen with it.

The room was very quiet; the tea-kettle simmered on the stove. Outside the window the falling snowflakes looked dark against the whiteness beyond. Aunt Louisa was sitting on the high stool, doubled over, with a crumpled handkerchief in her hand, and Uncle Ivor was bending over her talking in a very low voice. Donald laid the wishbone on the sink shelf and started to tiptoe out, but Uncle Ivor saw him. "How'd you like to go up to the henhouse with me, Donald?" he said. "I've got to find us a dozen eggs to take back to Rutland."

"I'll get my coat," Donald told him, eager to go out before his father came back downstairs.

The path up the hill to the henhouse had been made not by clearing the snow away, but by tramping it down. The new snow was drifting over the track; in some places it already had covered it. When Uncle Ivor went into the henhouse Donald stood still, bending his head back to catch some snowflakes in his mouth. "Come on in and shut the door. You'll let all the heat out," Uncle Ivor told him.

"I'm coming," said Donald. He stepped through the doorway and closed the door. The smell inside was very strong. As Uncle Ivor approached the hens, they set up a low, distrustful murmur.

"Tell me, Donald," said Uncle Ivor as he explored the straw with his hands.

"What?" said Donald.

"Does your mother often run to her room and shut the door, the way she did just now?"

"Sometimes."

"Why? Is your father mean to her?"

"Oh," said Donald vaguely, "they have fights." He felt uncomfortable.

"Yes. Well, it's a great pity your father ever got married. It would have been better for everybody if he'd stayed single."

"But then I wouldn't have been born at all," cried Donald, uncertain whether Uncle Ivor was serious or not.

"At least, we *hope* not!" said Uncle Ivor, rolling his eyes and looking silly. Now Donald knew it was a kind of joke, and he laughed. The door was flung open. "Donald!" roared his father.

"What is it?" he said, his voice very feeble.

"Come out here!"

He stumbled toward the door; his father was peering inside uncertainly. "What are you doing in there?" he demanded.

"Helping Uncle Ivor look for eggs."

"Hmmph!" Donald stepped out and his father shut the door.

They started to walk along the road in the direction of the Smithson farm. Presently his father fell in behind him and prodded him in the back, saying: "Keep your head up. Chest out! D'you want to get round-shouldered? Before you know it you'll have curvature of the spine."

When they had got out of sight of the house, in a place where the tangle of small trees came to the edge of the road on both sides, his father stopped walking. He looked around, reached down, picked up a handful of the new snow, and rolled it into a hard ball. Then he threw it at a fairly large tree, some distance from the road. It broke, leaving a white mark on the dark trunk. "Let's see you hit it," he told Donald.

A wolf could be waiting here, somewhere back in the still gloom of the woods. It was very important not to make him angry. If his father wanted to take a chance and throw snowballs into the woods, he could, but Donald would not. Then perhaps the wolf would understand that he, at least, was his friend.

"Go on," said his father.

"No. I don't want to."

With mock astonishment his father said: "Oh, you don't?" Then his face became dangerous and his voice cracked like a whip. "Are you going to do what I told you?"

"No." It was the first time he had openly defied him. His father turned very red.

"Listen here, you young whippersnapper!" he cried, his voice tight with anger. "You think you're going to get away with this?" Before Donald knew what was happening, his father had seized him with one hand while he bent over and with the other scooped up as much snow as he could. "We'll settle this little matter right now," he said through his teeth. Suddenly he was rubbing the snow violently over Donald's face, and at the same time that Donald gasped and squirmed, he pushed what was left of it down his neck. As he felt the wet, icy mass sliding down his back, he doubled over. His eyes were squeezed shut; he was certain his father was trying to kill him. With a desperate lunge he bounded free and fell face-downward into the snow.

"Get up," his father said disgustedly. He did not move. If he held his breath long enough he might die.

His father yanked him to his feet. "I've had just about enough of your monkeyshines," he said. Clutching him tightly with both hands, he forced him to hobble ahead of him, back through the twilight to the house.

Donald moved forward, looking at the white road in front of him, his mind empty of thoughts. An unfamiliar feeling had come to him: he was not sorry for himself for being wet and cold, or even resentful at having been mistreated. He felt detached; it was an agreeable, almost voluptuous sensation which he accepted without understanding or questioning it.

As they advanced down the long alley of maple trees in the dusk his father said: "Now you can go and cry in your mother's lap."

"I'm not crying," said Donald loudly, without expression. His father did not answer.

Fortunately the kitchen was empty. He could tell from the sound of the voices in the parlor that Aunt Louisa, Uncle Ivor and Mr. Gordon were getting ready to leave. He ran upstairs to his room and changed his clothes completely. The hole he had breathed in the ice on the windowpane had frozen over thickly again, but the round mark was still visible. As he finished dressing his mother called him. It was completely dark outside. He went downstairs. She was standing in the hallway.

"Oh, you've changed your clothes," she said. "Come out and say good-by to Aunt Louisa and Uncle Ivor. They're in the kitchen." He looked quickly at her face to see if there were signs of her recent tears: her eyes were slightly bloodshot.

Together they went into the kitchen. "Donald wants to say good-by to you" she told Mr. Gordon, steering Donald to Aunt Louisa. "You've given him a wonderful Christmas"—her voice became reproachful—"but it was *much* too much."

The thick beaver collar of Mr. Gordon's overcoat was turned up over his ears, and he had on enormous fur gloves. He smiled and clapped his hands together expectantly; it made a cushioned sound. "Oh, it was a lot of fun," he said. "He reminds me a little of myself, you know, when I was his age. I was a sort of shy and quiet lad, too." Donald felt his mother's hand tighten on his shoulder as she pushed him toward Aunt Louisa. "Mm," she said. "Well, Auntie Louisa, here's somebody who wants to say good-by to you."

Even in the excitement of watching Uncle Willis and Uncle Greg drive the others off in the sleigh, Donald did not miss the fact that his father had not appeared in the kitchen at all. When the sleigh had moved out of sight down the dark road, everyone went into the parlor and Grampa put another log on the fire.

"Where's Owen?" Gramma said in a low voice to Donald's mother.

"He must be upstairs. To tell the truth, I don't care very much where he is."

"Poor child," said Gramma. "Headache a little better?"

"A little." She sighed. "He certainly managed to take all the pleasure out of *my* Christmas."

"A mean shame," said Gramma.

"It was all I could do to look Ivor in the face just now. I meant it."

"I'm sure they all understood," said Gramma soothingly. "Just don't you fret about it. Anyway, Owen'll be gone tomorrow, and you can rest up."

Shortly after Uncle Willis and Uncle Greg got back, Donald's father came downstairs. Supper was eaten in almost complete silence; at no time did his father speak to him or pay him any attention. As soon as the meal was over his mother took him upstairs to bed.

When she had left him, he lay in the dark listening to the sound of the fine snow as the wind drove it against the panes. The wolf was out there in the night, running along paths that no one had ever seen, down the hill and across the meadow, stopping to drink at a deep place in the brook where the ice had not formed. The stiff hairs of his coat had caught the snow; he shook himself and climbed up the bank to where Donald sat waiting for him. Then he lay down beside him, putting his heavy head in Donald's lap. Donald leaned over and buried his face in the shaggy fur of his scruff. After a while they both got up and began to run together, faster and faster, across the fields.

MS Chakdara
(London-Colombo)
January, 1957

Tapiama

Just behind the hotel was the river. If it had come from very far inland it would have been wide and silent, but because it was really only a creek swollen by the rains, and its bed was full of boulders, it made a roaring noise which the photographer briefly mistook for more rain. The heat and the trip had tired him out; he had eaten the cold fried fish and the leathery omelet that oozed grease, the brown bean paste with rice and burned bananas, and had been overtaken suddenly by a sleepiness powerful as the effect of a drug. Staggering to his bed, he had ripped off his shirt and trousers, lifted the stiff mosquito-net that reeked of dust, and dropped like a stone onto the mattress, only distantly noticing its hardness before he lost himself in sleep.

But in the night when he awoke he realized he had been in the false sleep of indigestion; staring into the blackness over his head he told himself that it was going to be hard to find the way back into oblivion. It was then that he had become aware of the night's changeless backdrop of sound, and had taken it for rain. Now and then, far above his head (how could the ceiling be that high?) a firefly's nervous little light flashed its indecipherable code for an instant or two. He was lying on his back; something small was crawling down his chest. He put his hand there; it was a slowly moving drop of sweat. The rough sheet under him was wet. He wanted to move, but if he did there would be no end to the shifting, and each new position would be more uncomfortable than the last. In the anonymous darkness of a nearby room someone coughed from time to time; he could not tell whether it was a man or a woman. The meal he had eaten lay like ten meals in his stomach. Slowly the memory of it was suffused with a nebulous horror—particularly the heavy cold omelet shining with grease.

Lying there smelling the dust from the netting was like being tied up inside a burlap bag. To get out into the street and walk—that was what he wanted, but there were difficulties. The electricity went off at midnight; the old man who ran the hotel had told him that. Instead of putting the matches under his pillow he had left them in his trouser-pocket, and the idea of stepping out on to the floor barefoot without a light did not appeal to him. Besides, he reminded himself, listening again to the wide, strangely distant

277

clamor out there, it was raining. But to move along the dead streets even
under the invisible rain would be a pleasure . . . . If he lay quite still, sleep
might return. Finally, in desperation he yanked the net aside and sprang out
of bed, across the room in the direction of the chair over which he had thrown
his clothes.

He managed to get into his shirt and trousers in the space of three matches;
his shoes he pounded on the concrete floor in the dark, to tumble out a possible
centipede or scorpion. Then he struck a fourth match and opened the door
into the *patio*. Here it was no longer pitch-black. The huge potted plants were
visible in the night's lead-colored light, but the sky, stifled by a cloud that no
starlight could pierce, seemed not to be there at all. It was not raining. "The
river must be very close," he thought.

He walked along the covered *corredor,* grazing the tentacles of orchids that
hung in baskets and jars from the eaves, bumping into the pieces of wicker
furniture, and found the entrance door, closed and doubly bolted. Carefully
he slid back the metal bars and opened the door, pulling it shut after him. The
gloom of the street was as profound as that of the *patio* and the air as still as it
had been under the mosquito-net. But it had an indefinite vegetable scent—a
sweet odor of both fulfillment and exhaustion.

He turned to the left: the long empty main street, lined with one-story
buildings, led straight down to the *paseo* along the sea. As he walked, the
unmoving hot-house air became veined with the fresher smell of seaweed on
the beach. At each intersecting street he had to go down six steps to the road
level, cross, and climb up again to the sidewalk. In the rainy season, the
propietario of the hotel had told him, there was a rowboat at each corner to
ferry the pedestrians across. Like the intermingling of the land and sea odors
that he breathed, two opposing but entwined sensations took possession of
him: a relief amounting almost to delight, and a faint feeling of nausea which
he decided to combat because he felt that not to have been able to leave all
suggestion of illness behind showed a lack of strength. He tried to put more
springiness into his walk, but discovered almost immediately that it was too
hot to make any more than a minimum of effort. He was sweating even more
now than he had been in his bed. He lighted an Ovalado. The taste of the
sweet tobacco was a part of the night.

The *paseo* bordering the sea-front was about half a mile long. He had
imagined there would be some slight stirring of the air here, but he could
detect no difference. Still, now and then there was the soft intimate sound of a
small wave breaking gently on the sand just below. He sat down on the
balustrade and rested, in the hope of cooling off a little. The sea was invisible.
He could have been sitting on the peak of a cloud-covered mountain—the
gloom in front of him would have been that formless and all-embracing.
Yet the sea's casual noises had no element of distance in them, as

sea sounds have. It was as though they were taking place in a vast, closed courtyard. The concrete slabs on which he sat were damp, and a little cooler than his flesh. He smoked two cigarettes and strained his ears to hear some sound, made even indirectly, by human agency. But there was nothing more than the desultory slipping and sucking of the lazy water on the beach below. He glanced up and down the empty *paseo*. Far out along the shore to the west there was a light. It was orange, it flickered: a bonfire? He resumed walking, more slowly than before, ahead of him the distant blaze, the one point of light in the landscape.

A wide flight of steps led down onto the beach. Just beyond, he could see the flimsy structure of a pier that had been built out over the water. He stood still and listened. The fitful licking of small waves around the piles sounded as though it were happening in an echo-chamber.

He ran lightly down the steps and passed underneath the pier. It was definitely cooler walking along on the sand than it had been up on the *paseo*. He felt wide-awake now, and decided to see how much nearer to the light down the shore fifteen minutes would put him. Night-colored crabs hurried along the sand just ahead of his moving feet, completely soundless and almost invisible. A little beyond the end of the *paseo* the sand gave place to a hard coral surface which was easier to walk on. Out of prudence he kept as near to the water's edge as possible.

There was a difference between this walk and innumerable other mid-night jaunts he had made, and he was inclined to wonder what made it so pleasant. Perhaps he was enjoying it simply because the fabric here was of pure freedom. He was not looking for anything; all the cameras were back in the hotel room.

Occasionally he lifted his eyes from the dim brainlike configurations of coral beneath his feet and looked inland, to see whether he could make out any signs of habitation. It seemed to him that there might be sand dunes a few hundred feet back, but in the absence of light it was impossible to be certain of even that much. The sweat trickled down his spine and over his coccyx, sliding in between his buttocks. Maybe the best idea would be to undress completely. But then there would be the bother of carrying his clothing, and he wanted his hands free, even at the risk of chafing.

The question of freedom was governed by the law of diminishing re-turns, he said to himself, walking faster. If you went beyond a certain point of intensity in your consciousness of desiring it, you furnished yourself with a guarantee of not achieving it. In any case, he thought, what is freedom in the last analysis, other than the state of being totally, instead of only partially, subject to the tyranny of chance?

There was no doubt that this walk was dispelling the miasma of indiges-tion that had lain within him. Three minutes to go, said the bright minute-hand of his watch; the orange light ahead seemed smaller than it had from the town. Why an arbitrary fifteen minutes? He smiled at the precise urban pattern in which his mind had automatically moved. If he lifted his arm he could touch the sky, and it would be moist, tepid and voluptuously soft.

And now in the distance ahead, on the landward side, he heard sounds which he quickly identified as the voices of hundreds of young frogs. The light, now that he studied it, was moving in a strange fashion: slightly up and down, and sideways as well, but without appearing to alter its position. All at once it became a huge flame belching upward, an instant later scattering cascades of red sparks, and he understood that he had arrived. The bonfire burned on the floor of a gently swaying craft not a hundred feet ahead of him. A naked man stood above it, tossing it palm branches. The photographer stopped walking and listened for the sound of human voices, but the happy chorus of frogs filled the air.

He stepped ahead several paces and decided to call out. "*Hola!*" The man wheeled about, jumped over the nearer side of the boat (the water was extremely shallow) and came running up to him.

Without greeting him, taking him perhaps for someone else, the man said: "*Tapiama? Vas a Tapiama?*" The photographer, never having heard of Tapiama, stuttered a bit and finally said, "*Sí,*" whereupon the other seized his arm and pulled him along to the edge of the water. "The tide's all the way out. We'll start in a minute."

He could see two other people in the craft, lying flat on the floor, one on each side of the fire, as far from its heat as possible. The photographer squatted down and removed his shoes and socks, then waded to the boat. When he stood in the center of it (the fire was still crackling brightly) he turned and watched the naked man loosening the rope that held the craft in place.

"The whole thing is absurd." He could only distrust the very naturalness with which all this was coming about—the indifference to his unexpected arrival on the part of the two passengers, and perhaps even more, the highly suspect readiness of the boatmen to take off the moment he had appeared. He told himself, "Things don't happen this way," but since beyond a doubt they were doing so, any questioning of the process could lead only in the direction of paranoia. He dropped to the floor of the boat and pulled out his packet of Ovalados. The naked boatman, the coil of dripping rope around his black forearm like a bracelet, sprang aboard, and with his big toe nudged one of the supine passengers who stirred, rose to his knees, and glanced about with annoyance. "Where is it?" he demanded. Without replying, the boatman handed him the shorter of two poles that had lain along the gunwale. Together they began to propel the punt along the invisible surface of the water. The frogs' canticle and the fire's flare filled the night.

Having answered "*Sí*," to the Tapiama question, the photographer felt he could scarcely take the retrogressive step of asking "What is Tapiama?" or "Where is Tapiama?" And so, much as he would have liked to know, he decided to wait. This shallow body of water beneath them—estuary, lagoon? River more likely, since the boatman had said the tide was out. But not the stream whose troubled passage among the boulders he had heard from his bed.

They pushed on, now and then passing beneath clumps of high vegetation where the frogs' song was briefly covered by another sound, inexplicable and brutal, like the sudden tearing of a vast sheet of strong linen. From time to time something solid and heavy splashed nearby, as if a man had fallen into the water. And occasionally the other passenger raised himself on one elbow and without too much effort managed to revive the dying fire with another dry palm-leaf.

Probably it was less than an hour before they came to a landing in the mud. The two passengers leapt out and hurried away into the darkness. The boatman, after carefully donning a pair of short underpants, tapped the photographer on the arm and asked him for sixty centavos. He gave him seventy-five and clambered out into the soft mud, his shoes in his hand.

"Wait a minute," said the man. "I'll go with you." The photographer was pleased. When the boatman, looking blacker now in his white shorts, had secured the punt to an upright log driven into the mud, he led the way upward through a tangle of undergrowth, saying casually at one point: "Are you going across tomorrow?"

"Across? No."

"Aren't you here for the company?" The voice implied that to be here otherwise than for the company laid one open to unnameable suspicion.

The time had come to be truthful, he feared, although he did not relish the position he knew it would put him in. "I never heard of the company," he said. "I just arrived in Rio Martillo tonight. What sort of company?"

"Sugar," said the other. Then he stood still in the dark and spoke slowly: "*Entonces*—why have you come to Tapiama? They don't like *millonarios* here, you know." Understanding that this was the contemptuous coastal term for Americans, the photographer quickly lied. "I'm Danish," he said, but feeling that his voice lacked conviction he immediately added: "Do we go through any more mud, or can I put my shoes on?"

The man had started up again. "Wash your feet at the *cantina*, if you like," he told him over his shoulder. In another minute they were there: all in the dimness an open space, a dozen or so palm-leaf huts at one end of it, at the other a platform which must be a loading dock, the empty night and openness of water behind it; and half-way between the dock and the cluster of dwellings, the *cantina*, itself only a very large hut without a front wall.

A faint light came from within; there was no sound but the frogs on all sides, and the occasional tearing rasp in the branches high overhead. "Why is the place open at this hour?" demanded the photographer. The boatman stopped in the middle of the clearing and adjusted his shorts briefly. "Don Octavio runs it from six in the morning until six at night. His brother runs it from six at night until six in the morning. The company lets the men off from work at different hours. They come here with their *pago* and spend it. They like it better here than at home. Not so many mosquitoes." It could have been the photographer's imagination that made the man's voice sound bitter as he spoke the last words. They continued across the clearing and stepped into the *cantina*.

There was no floor; the ground was covered with white sand. A counter of boards had been built diagonally across a far corner. Here an oil lamp smoldered and two men stood drinking. Wooden packing-cases were scattered here and there, some standing on end with empty beer bottles on them, and others on their sides, to be used as seats. "*Muy triste,*" commented the boatman, glancing around. Then he went behind the bar and disappeared through a small door in the wall there. Apart from the two at the bar, who had ceased their conversation and now stood staring at the photographer, there was no one else in the place. "When in doubt, speak," he told himself, advancing toward them, although it occurred to him that he might just as well have made it, "When in doubt, keep quiet," even as he opened his mouth to say, "*Buenas noches,*" for their expressions did not alter in any manner that he could detect. For a full three seconds they continued to gaze at him before they replied, which they then did more or less simultaneously. These two had nothing in common, he noted: one was a soldier in uniform, an Indian boy of perhaps eighteen, the other a tired-looking mulatto civilian of indeterminate age. Or perhaps—the idea came to him as he put his elbow on the bar with a show of casualness—they did have at least a common antagonism, now that he had entered the *cantina*. "Oh, well, I'm barefoot and my shoes are covered with mud," he thought.

"*Hay alguien?*" he said aloud to the palm-leaf wall behind the bar. The two neither resumed their conversation nor spoke further with him, and he did not turn his head again toward them. Presently the small door opened and a fat man pushed through. He stood with his hands outspread on the bar, his eyebrows raised in anticipation. "I'll have a *cumbiamba,*" said the photographer, remembering the name of the coastal region's favorite drink, a herbal concoction famous for its treacherous effects.

It was foul-tasting but strong. The second one seemed less objectionable. He walked across to the open side of the *cantina* and sat down on a packing-case, looking out at the formless night. The two at the bar were talking again in low tones. It was not long before five men appeared from the platform end of the clearing; they straggled in and stood at the bar, laughing as they waited for their drinks. All of them were black, and wore only underpants, like the boatman. Now a mulatto girl with gold teeth came through the little door behind the bar and joined them. Almost immediately, however, she became aware of the photographer sitting by himself, and with her hands on her hips, half dancing, she made her way across the open space toward him. When she arrived, she squatted down beside him grinning and with one thin yellow hand reached out to unfasten his fly. His reaction was instantaneous and automatic: he drew back his leg and kicked her full in the breast, so that she toppled over backward in silence onto the sand. The noise of the resulting laughter at the bar was not sufficient to cover her thin voice, made sharp by rage: "*Qué bruto, tú! Pendejo!*" Hands on hips again, she retreated to the bar and was given a beer by one of the workmen. Although the photographer had not meant to kick her, he felt no regret at the turn the incident had taken. The *cumbiambas* seemed to be having their effect; he was beginning to feel very well. He sat still a while, tapping rhythms on the side of his empty glass. Soon more Negro workmen came in and joined the others at the bar. One carried a guitar on which he set to work strumming a syncopated chordal accompaniment for a melody which failed to appear. However, it was music of a sort, and everyone was pleased with it. Perhaps awakened by the sound, the dogs of the village had now started an angry chorus of barking; this was particularly audible to the photographer who sat at the entrance, and it bothered him. He rose and moved over to an empty crate alongside the opposite wall, resting his head against a rough-hewn pole that was one of the supports of the roof. A foot or so above his head there was a strange object dangling from a nail. Now and then he rolled his eyes upward and studied it.

All at once he jumped up and began violently to brush the back of his neck and head. The pole behind him was swarming with tiny ants, thousands upon thousands of them: someone had hung a small crushed coral snake over the nail, and they had come to eat the flesh. It took him a good while not to feel any more of the insects running over his back; during that time two other individuals had come into the *cantina* (whether from the outside or through the door behind the counter, he had not noticed), and now sat between him and the bar in such a fashion that both of them faced him. The old man looked Nordic, the innocent-looking one-legged boy with him could be Spanish; the old man was telling the boy a humorous story, leaning toward him with great interest, occasionally poking his arm with a forefinger to drive home a point, but the boy was distraughtly making designs in the sand with the tip of his crutch.

The photographer stood up; he had never before had such an effect from two drinks. "A very peculiar sensation," he said to himself. "Very peculiar," he repeated aloud under his breath as he started toward the bar to order another. It was not that he felt drunk so much as that he had become someone who was not he, someone for whom the act of living was a thing so different from what he had imagined it could be, that he was left stranded in a region of sensation far from any he had heretofore known. It was not unpleasant: it was merely indefinable. *"Dispénseme,"* he said to a tall Negro in pink and white striped BVD's and he handed his empty glass to the fat man. He wanted to see what went into a *cumbiamba*, but the barman did everything quickly beneath the counter and handed him back the glass, brimming with the slightly frothy mixture. He took a good swallow of it and set it down, turning a little to his right as he did so. Standing beside him was the Indian soldier, his cap at an angle atop a pre-Colombian face. "Why does the army put such big visors on them?" he wondered.

He saw that the soldier was about to speak. "Whatever he says is going to turn out to be an insult," he warned himself, in the hope that this would help him to avoid possible anger later.

"Do you like this place?" the soldier said; his voice was silken.

"Es simpático. Yes, I like it."

"Why?" The dogs outside had come nearer; he could hear their yapping now above the laughter.

"Can you tell me why they hung that dead snake on the wall there?" he found himself asking, and supposed it was to change the subject. But the soldier was going to be even more boring than he had feared. "I asked you why you like this *cantina*," he insisted.

"And I told you it was *simpático.* Isn't that enough?"

The soldier tilted his head back and looked down his nose.

"Far from being enough," he replied, his manner pedantic, his expression infuriating.

The photographer returned to his drink, picked it up, slowly finished it off. Then he pulled out his cigarettes and offered one to the other. With exaggerated deliberateness the soldier reached for the cigarette, took it, and began to tap it on the counter. The man playing the guitar at last had started to sing in a small falsetto voice along with it, but most of the words were in a dialect the photographer could not understand. When the cigarettes were lighted, he found himself wondering who had lighted them—he or the soldier.

"Just where did you come from?" asked the soldier.

He was not bothering to answer, but the soldier misunderstood even this. "I can see you're inventing something," he said, "and I don't want to hear it."

The photographer, disgusted, exclaimed, "Aaah!" and ordered another *cumbiamba*. This most recent one had done something extraordinary to him:

he felt that he had become very precise, thin and hard, an object made of enamel or some similar material, something other than a living being, but intensely conscious all the same. "Four ought to do the trick," he thought.

The empty glass was in his hand, the fat barman was staring at him, and at that point he had not the slightest idea whether he had already drunk the fourth one or whether it was still the moment just after he had ordered it. He felt himself laughing, but he could not hear whether any sound was coming out or not. The mangled snake, seething with ants, had upset him a little; recognizing it, he had then been made aware of its smell, which he was not sure he had escaped even now. Here at the bar the kerosene lamp smoked heavily; its strong fumes choked him. "*Gracias a Dios*," he confided to the barman, handing him the glass.

The old man who had been sitting on the crate behind them rose and came vaguely toward the bar. "Where did this come from?" said the photographer, laughing apologetically, looking at the full glass in his hand. The frenzied dogs out in the clearing yapped and howled, an exasperating sound. "*Qué tienen esos perros?*" he demanded of the soldier.

The old man had stopped beside them. "Say, Jack, I don't mean to butt in or anything," he began. He was bald, sunburned; he wore a fishnet shirt. The furrows between his ribs showed as parallel shadows, and irregular tufts of gray hair waved out from his chest between the meshes of the shirt. He stretched his lips in a smile, showing naked white gums. The soldier's stance became over-nonchalant; he stared at the newcomer, open hatred suddenly in his eyes, and gently blew the smoke from his cigarette into the old man's face.

"You from Milwaukee? Siddown."

"In a little while, thanks," said the photographer.

"A little while?" the old man echoed incredulously, running his hand over the top of his head. Then he called out in Spanish to the one-legged boy. The photographer was thinking: "This is not going to work out right, at all. It's just not going to work out." He wished the Negro would stop singing and the dogs would stop barking. He looked at the glass in his hand, full of what looked like soapsuds. Someone tapped him on the shoulder. "Say, bud, lemme give you a little advice." The old man again. "There's money in this country if you know where to look. But the guy that finds it is the guy that sticks to his own kind, if you know what I mean." He put his face nearer and lowered his voice. Three skeletal fingers touched the photographer's arm. "You take it from me, from one white man to another. I'm tellin' you!" The three fingers, dark with tobacco stain, lifted themselves, trembled, and dropped back. "These guys all mean trouble from the word go."

The boy having both gathered up his crutch and managed to rise from where he had been sitting, had now arrived at the bar. "Take a look at this, Jack," the old man said. "Show him," he told the boy in Spanish, and the boy, leaning on his crutch, bent over and rolled up the right leg of his ragged khaki shorts until he had exposed the stump of his amputated leg. It was not far below the groin; the scar tissue had puckered and wrinkled curiously in countless tiny convolutions. "See?" cried the old man. "Two hundred and sixty tons of bananas went over that. Feel it."

"You feel it," said the photographer, wondering how it was possible for him to go on standing and talking exactly as if he were a person like the rest of them. (Could it be that what had happened to him did not show?) He turned his head and looked towards the entrance. The mulatto girl was vomiting just outside. With a cry the barman rushed across and furiously pushed her farther away, out into the clearing. When he came back in he was theatrically holding his nose. "That prostitute ape!" he yelled. "In another minute we'd have had the dogs inside here."

The boy was still looking expectantly at the old man, to see if it was time to lower his trouser leg. "You think he got a centavo from them?" said the old man sadly. "Hah!"

The photographer had begun to suspect that something had gone very wrong inside him. He felt sick, but since he was no longer a living creature he could not conceive it in those terms. He had shut his eyes and put his hand over his face. "It's going around backward," he said. The undrunk *cumbiamba* was in his other hand.

Saying the sentence had made it more true. It was definitely going around backward. The important thing was to remember that he was alone here and that this was a real place with real people in it. He could feel how dangerously easy it would be to go along with the messages given him by his senses, and dismiss the whole thing as a nightmare in the secret belief that when the breaking-point came he could somehow manage to escape by waking himself up. A little unsteadily he set his drink down on the counter. An argument which had arisen a while ago between the Indian soldier and his sad companion had now reached its noisy stage, with the companion attempting to drag the soldier away from the bar against his will, and the soldier, his two booted legs firmly apart, breathing rapidly, noisily in his resistance. Suddenly there was a small, shining knife in his right hand, and his face assumed the look of a little boy about to burst into tears. The old man quickly moved around to the photographer's other side. "That guy's bad news in any language," he muttered, gesturing nervously to the boy with the crutch as he bade him move out of the way.

The photographer was saying to himself: "If I can hold out. If I can only hold out." The whole place was slipping away from him, downward and outward; the guitar strummed and the dogs barked, the soldier flashed his knife and pouted, the old American talked about caves with buried emeralds only six days up the Tupurú, the lamp grew redder and more smoke came out of it. He understood nothing except that he must stay there and suffer; to try to escape would be fatal. The soldier's face was very near his own now, breathing black tobacco smoke at him. Languorously, with an insane natural coquetry, he made his long lashes tremble as he asked: "Why have you not offered me a *copita?* All night I have been waiting for you to invite me." The hand holding the knife hung listlessly at his side; the photographer thought of a sleeping baby still clutching its rattle.

"*Sí quieres . . . . Qué tomas?*" he murmured, reflecting that his shoes should be in his hand and were not; then where were they? Someone had brought a large spider monkey into the *cantina* and was forcing it to dance to the guitar's syncopations, making it stand upright by holding its two front paws. With an air of distraught gravity it stepped about, peering this way and that, grimacing nervously at the loud peals of laughter that came from those at the bar watching its antics. The dogs, having noticed its arrival, had rushed to the very entrance of the *cantina,* where they braced themselves to shriek and snap with determined fury.

The soldier's drink had been bought and paid for, but he was not drinking it. He was leaning far back against the bar, reclining on his elbow almost as though he were in bed, his eyes simple black slits, whispering: "You don't like it here. You want to go, *verdad?* But you are afraid to go."

In spite of the constant sliding away, everything had remained just as it was. It would have been better if he could have sat down. "Oh, God," he asked himself. "Am I going to be able to stand this?"

"Why are you afraid to go?" pursued the other tenderly, smiling so that the photographer could admire his small, perfect teeth. The photographer laughed silently, did not reply.

The face of the soldier, ovoid, honey-colored, so near to his, moved now with consummate smoothness into another face, that of a general. ("*Sí, mi general,*" with stiff *bigotes* sprouting from beneath the nostrils, almond eyes, black, deadly with a delicate lust, the uniform svelte, plaited steel riding crop in hand, sharpened spurs shining by the anklebone. "*Bien, mi general.*" Lying on the hot barrack mattress, *tarde tras tarde,* the soldier had dreamed of being the general. Which mountain village had he said he was from? How long had he been talking?)

". . . and that day alone they killed forty-one pigs before my eyes. There in the corral. *Me hizo algo; no sé . . . .*" His smile was apologetic, intimate; he lowered his eyes imperceptibly, made the effort and raised them again to look at the photographer in such a way that, since they were wider than before, they glistened. "I never forgot it; I don't know why."

Between them the gold-toothed girl came sliding, her hands wriggling over her head, her hips circling, her thin voice shouting: *"Ahii! Ahii! El fandango de la Guajira."* The soldier must have pushed her, for all at once she slapped him. But it was happening very slowly. How could it take the soldier so long to bring up his knife, and as he raised his hand, how could the stupid girl wait that way before screaming and ducking aside? Even so, the blade caught her only on the arm; she was in the middle of the floor, kneeling on the sand, moaning: "He cut me! Oh God! He cut me!" And because the man who had been dancing with the spider monkey let go of it to get as quickly as all the others to the bar, the beast toddled over to the girl and distractedly wrapped one long hairy arm around her neck. But then the photographer was being roughly jostled, his bare feet were being stepped on as everyone tried to get at the soldier and disarm him. (A demon mask shiny with venom, a voice of barbed wire that rasped: *"Os mato a todos! A todos!"*)

It was exactly nineteen steps from the place where he had stood to the trunk of a small papaya tree in front of the entrance. The tree was not very strong; it swayed slightly as he leaned against it. The dogs were yelping now from inside the *cantina*. Here the air was sweet and almost cool; the faintest glimmer of morning was in the sky and water behind the landing. "I must start to walk," he told himself; it seemed important to believe it. The shouts and screams inside the *cantina* were growing in volume, and people were beginning to call to one another from the doors of their huts. The landing platform was empty—just boards and no railing. Shuffling along with great care because he was not used to going barefoot, he followed what he thought was the path he had taken earlier, through the undergrowth back down to the river's edge, and there was the punt, mud-beached in the mangroves.

It was easy to get in, easy to untie the rope, and easy (for the level of the water had risen considerably since the craft had been left) to pry it loose from the shelf of mud where it rested. But once he was floating among the now nearly visible trunks and branches, bumping against them and being spun to face first the dark chaotic riverbank and then the wide whitening emptiness of open sky and water, he understood dimly that it was not going to be possible to pole his way back to the beach whence he had come, since the tide was still coming in. It was a comforting thought, he decided, because it meant that everything was going ahead instead of backward. A minute later he was floating quietly by the base of the landing: people were running around the clearing. Quickly he lay down flat on the bottom of the punt, and there he stayed, looking straight up at the gray sky, hoping in this way to remain invisible until he had been carried out of sight, beyond Tapiama.

It was going to be one of those stillborn tropical days, when there would be no sun, no wind, no clouds—because the entire sky was enfolded in one vast suffocating blanket of cloud—when nothing at all would happen save that hourly it would grow hotter until an approximate dusk came along. Already the eastern side of the sky was the hot side, arching above the flatness of the swampland. The punt scarcely moved now, the channel having broadened into this wide marshy lake. The photographer lay still and groaned. Little by little the fear that someone might see him gave way to the hope that what current there was would propel the craft in the direction of the shore rather than out toward the wilderness of water and tiny islands; sometimes, even though suffering be implicit in it, contact with others is preferable to the terror of solitude and the unknown. He laid an arm over his eyes to shield them from the corrosive gray light that beat down upon him from the spaces above. The other hand lay in the ashes of last night's fire. And he floated in utter silence on the calm bosom of the lagoon, not stirring as the morning hours moved along, but growing increasingly conscious of the infernal seething of the *cumbiambas* in his brain, a seething which expressed itself as a senseless nightmare imposed from without, in the face of which he could only be totally passive. It was an invisible spectacle whose painful logic he followed with the entire fiber of his being, without, however, once being given a clear vision of what agonizing destinies were at stake.

Some time toward mid-morning the punt grazed a submerged root and was swung into an eddyless pool in the shelter of the vegetation near the shore. Here fierce flies stung him, and from among the leaves high above, a talking bird remarked casually, over and over again: *"Idigaraga. Idigaraga. Idigaraga."*

It was no particular consolation to him, so intent was he on the obscure drama being enacted within him, to hear human voices presently, or to feel the craft seized by the hands of someone splashing in the water alongside. Only when several people had climbed in and crouched chattering around him did he move his arm and squint up at them. Five young men, all of whom looked remarkably alike, surrounded him. Water dripped down upon him from their naked bodies. He shut his eyes again: it was too unlikely a scene. During this time one of them dived overboard, was gone a short while, and returned with a green coconut whose top he had sliced off. He began to let the water dribble into the photographer's face, whereupon the photographer partially sat up and drank the rest of it. In minute he looked around at them again, and said: "Are you brothers?"

"Si si" they chorused. This was for some reason a consolation. *"Hermanos,"* he sighed, sliding down into the ashes again. Then he added desperately, hoping they could still hear him: "Please take me to Rio Martillo."

It had been a brief interlude of clarity. Now they poled the punt back out under the hot sky, letting him lie there and moan as he liked. At one point he felt he must try to explain that he would give them each seventy-five centavos for their trouble, but they giggled and pushed him back down.

"My shoes!" he cried. "There are no shoes," they told him. "Lie still."

"And when we get to the beach," he panted, seizing a brown ankle beside his face, "how will you get me to Rio Martillo?" "We are not going to any beach," they replied. "We go through the swamp and the canal."

He lay still a while, trying to disassociate himself from the irrational ideas boiling up in his head. "Is this the way to Rio Martillo?" he demanded, thrusting himself up a little and gasping, trying to see beyond the enclosing thicket of brown legs and arms, and feeling a deep unreasoned shame at having once again accepted defeat. They laughed, pushed him gently down to the floor, and went on rhythmically poling the craft eastward. "The factory chimney," they said to one another, pointing into the distance. His mind took him back to the quiet region by the riverbank where the small bird had spoken, high up in the trees, and he heard again the conversational tone. "*Idigaraga*," he said aloud, imitating perfectly its voice and intonation. There was an explosion of mirth around him. One of the youths took his arm, shook it lightly. "You know that bird?" he said. "It is a very comic bird. It goes to the nests of other birds and wants to sit there, and when the other birds fight with it and drive it away, it sits down in the same tree there and says: '*Idigaraga*.' That means: '*Iri garagua, nadie me quiere*, nobody likes me.' And it says it over and over, until they make it go farther away so they can't hear it any more. You said it just right. Say it again." "*Sí, sí*" the others agreed, "*otra vez!*"

The photographer had no intention of saying it again. His shame at having accepted defeat already troubled him less. It was hard in his present condition to fit the bird correctly into the pattern, but he knew it had to be done.

When the Compañia Azucarera Riomartillense blew a long blast on its whistle to announce the advent of noon, the sound hovered for an instant over the empty swampland like an invisible trail of smoke. "*Las doce*," said one of the brothers. A great black and gold dragonfly came skimming across the water and lighted on the photographer's bare foot. After raising and lowering its wings twice, it was again on its crooked course, curving and swooping over the lagoon toward Tapiama. "Say it again," the brothers begged him.

London
October, 1957

The Hyena

A stork was passing over desert country on his way north. He was thirsty, and he began to look for water. When he came to the mountains of Khang el Ghar, he saw a pool at the bottom of a ravine. He flew down between the rocks and lighted at the edge of the water. Then he walked in and drank.

At that moment a hyena limped up and, seeing the stork standing in the water, said: "Have you come a long way?" The stork had never seen a hyena before. "So this is what a hyena is like," he thought. And he stood looking at the hyena because he had been told that if the hyena can put a little of his urine on someone, that one will have to walk after the hyena to whatever place the hyena wants him to go.

"It will be summer soon," said the stork. "I am on my way north." At the same time, he walked further out into the pool, so as not to be so near the hyena. The water here was deeper, and he almost lost his balance and had to flap his wings to keep upright. The hyena walked to the other side of the pool and looked at him from there.

"I know what is in your head," said the hyena. "You believe the story about me. You think I have that power? Perhaps long ago hyenas were like that. But now they are the same as everyone else. I could wet you from here with my urine if I wanted to. But what for? If you want to be unfriendly, go to the middle of the pool and stay there."

The stork looked around at the pool and saw that there was no spot in it where he could stand and be out of reach of the hyena.

"I have finished drinking," said the stork. He spread his wings and flapped out of the pool. At the edge he ran quickly ahead and rose into the air. He circled above the pool, looking down at the hyena.

"So you are the one they call the ogre," he said. "The world is full of strange things."

The hyena looked up. His eyes were narrow and crooked. "Allah brought us all here," he said. "You know that. You are the one who knows about Allah."

The stork flew a little lower. "That is true," he said. "But I am surprised to hear you say it. You have a very bad name, as you yourself just said.

Magic is against the will of Allah."

The hyena tilted his head. "So you still believe the lies!" he cried.

"I have not seen the inside of your bladder," said the stork. "But why does everyone say you can make magic with it?"

"Why did Allah give you a head, I wonder? You have not learned how to use it." But the hyena spoke in so low a voice that the stork could not hear him.

"Your words got lost," said the stork, and he let himself drop lower.

The hyena looked up again. "I said: 'Don't come too near me. I might lift my leg and cover you with magic!'" He laughed, and the stork was near enough to see that his teeth were brown.

"Still, there must be some reason," the stork began. Then he looked for a rock high above the hyena, and settled himself on it. The hyena sat and stared up at him. "Why do they call you an ogre? What have you done?"

The hyena squinted. "You are lucky," he told the stork. "Men never try to kill you, because they think you are holy. They call you a saint and a sage. And yet you seem like neither a saint nor a sage."

"What do you mean?" said the stork quickly.

"If you really understood, you would know that magic is a grain of dust in the wind, and that Allah has power over everything. You would not be afraid."

The stork stood for a long time, thinking. He lifted one leg and held it bent in front of him. The ravine grew red as the sun went lower. And the hyena sat quietly looking up at the stork, waiting for him to speak.

Finally the stork put his leg down, opened his bill, and said: "You mean that if there is no magic, the one who sins is the one who believes there is."

The hyena laughed. "I said nothing about sin. But you did, and you are the sage. I am not in the world to tell anyone what is right or wrong. Living from night to night is enough. Everyone hopes to see me dead."

The stork lifted his leg again and stood thinking. The last daylight rose into the sky and was gone. The cliffs at the sides of the ravine were lost in the darkness.

At length the stork said: "You have given me something to think about. That is good. But now night has come. I must go on my way." He raised his wings and started to fly straight out from the boulder where he had stood. The hyena listened. He heard the stork's wings beating the air slowly, and then he heard the sound of the stork's body as it hit the cliff on the other side of the ravine. He climbed up over the rocks and found the stork. "Your wing is broken," he said. "It would have been better for you to go while there was still daylight."

"Yes," said the stork. He was unhappy and afraid.

"Come home with me," the hyena told him. "Can you walk?"

"Yes," said the stork. Together they made their way down the valley. Soon they came to a cave in the side of the mountain. The hyena went in first and called out: "Bend your head." When they were well inside, he said: "Now you can put your head up. The cave is high here."

There was only darkness inside. The stork stood still. "Where are you?" he said.

"I am here," the hyena answered, and he laughed.

"Why are you laughing?" asked the stork.

"I was thinking that the world is strange," the hyena told him. "The saint has come into my cave because he believed in magic."

"I don't understand," said the stork.

"You are confused. But at least now you can believe that I have no magic. I am like anyone else in the world."

The stork did not answer right away. He smelled the stench of the hyena very near him. Then he said, with a sigh: "You are right, of course. There is no power beyond the power of Allah."

"I am happy," said the hyena, breathing into his face. "At last you understand." Quickly he seized the stork's neck and tore it open. The stork flapped and fell on his side.

"Allah gave me something better than magic," the hyena said under his breath. "He gave me a brain."

The stork lay still. He tried to say once more: "There is no power beyond the power of Allah." But his bill merely opened very wide in the dark.

The hyena turned away. "You will be dead in a minute," he said over his shoulder. "In ten days I shall come back. By then you will be ready."

Ten days later the hyena went to cave and found the stork where he had left him. The ants had not been there. "Good," he said. He devoured what he wanted and went outside to a large flat rock above the entrance to the cave. There in the moonlight he stood a while, vomiting.

He ate some of his vomit and rolled for a long time in the rest of it, rubbing it deep into his coat. Then he thanked Allah for eyes that could see the valley in the moonlight, and for a nose that could smell carrion on the wind. He rolled some more and licked the rock under him. For a while he lay there panting. Soon he got up and limped on his way.

Tangier
1960

A Friend of the World

Salam rented two rooms and a kitchen on the second floor of a Jewish house at the edge of the town. He had decided to live with the Jews because he had already lived with Christians and found them all right. He trusted them a little more than he did other Moslems, who were like him and said: "No Moslem can be trusted." Moslems are the only true people, the only people you can understand. But because you do understand them, you do not trust them. Salam did not trust the Jews completely, either, but he liked living with them because they paid no attention to him. It had no importance if they talked about him among themselves, and they never would talk about him to Moslems. If he had a sister who lived here and there, getting what money she could from whatever man she found, because she had to eat, that was all right, and the Jews did not point at her when she came to visit him. If he did not get married, but lived instead with his brother and spent his time smoking kif and laughing, if he got his money by going to Tangier once a month and sleeping for a week with old English and American ladies who drank too much whisky, they did not care. He was a Moslem. Had he been rich he would have lived in the Spanish end of the town in a villa with concrete benches in the garden and a big round light in the ceiling of the *sala*, with many pieces of glass hanging down from it. He was poor and he lived with the Jews. To get to his house he had to go to the end of the Medina, cross an open space where the trees had all been cut down, go along the street where the warehouses had been abandoned by the Spanish when they left, and into a newer, dirtier street that led to the main highway. Halfway down was the entrance to the alley where he and his brother and fourteen Jewish families lived. There were the remains of narrow sidewalks along the edges of the wide gutter, full of mounds of rotten watermelon-rind and piles of broken bricks. The small children played here all day. When he was in a hurry he had to be careful not to step on them as they waded in the little puddles of dishwater and urine that were in front of all the doors. If they had been Moslem children he would have spoken to them, but since they were Jews he did not see them as children at all, but merely as nuisances in his way, like cactuses that had to be stepped over carefully because there was no way of going around them. Although he

295

had lived here for almost two years, he did not know the names of any of the Jews. For him they had no names. When he came home and found his door locked, because his brother had gone out and taken both keys with him, he went into any house where the door was open and dropped his bundles on the floor, saying: "I'll be back in a little while." He knew they would not touch his property. The Jews were neither friendly nor unfriendly. They too, if they had had money, would have been living in the Spanish end of town. It made the alley seem less like a Mellah, where only Jews live, to have the two Moslems staying among them.

Salam had the best house in the alley. It was at the end, and its windows gave onto a wilderness of fig trees and canebrake where squatters had built huts out of thatch and hammered pieces of tin. On the hot nights (for the town was in a plain and the heat stayed in the streets long after the sun had gone) his rooms had a breeze from the south that blew through and out onto the terrace. He was happy with his house and with the life that he and his brother had in it. "I'm a friend of the world," he would say. "A clean heart is better than everything."

One day he came home and found a small kitten sitting on the terrace. When it saw him it ran to him and purred. He unlocked the door into the kitchen and it went inside. After he had washed his hands and feet in the kitchen he went into his room. The kitten was lying on the mattress, still purring. "Mimí," he said to it. He gave it some bread. While it ate the bread it did not stop purring. Bou Ralem came home. He had been drinking beer with some friends in the Café Granada. At first he did not understand why Salam had let the kitten stay. "It's too young to be worth anything," he said. "If it saw a rat it would run and hide." But when the kitten lay in his lap and played with him he liked it. "Its name is Mimí," Salam told him. Nights it slept on the mattress with Salam near his feet. It learned to go down into the alley to relieve itself in the dirt there. The children sometimes tried to catch it, but it ran faster than they did and got to the steps before them, and they did not dare follow it upstairs.

During Ramadan, when they stayed up all night, they moved the mats and cushions and mattresses out onto the terrace and lived out there, talking and laughing until the daylight came. They smoked more kif than usual, and invited their friends home at two in the morning for dinner. Because they were living outside and the kitten could hear them from the alley, it grew bolder and began to visit the canebrake behind the house. It could run very fast, and even if a dog chased it, it could get to the stairs in time. When Salam missed it he would stand up and call to it over the railing, on one side down the alley and on the other over the trees and the roofs of the shacks. Sometimes when he was calling into the alley a Jewish woman would run out of one of the doors and look at him. He noticed that it was always the

same woman. She would put one hand above her eyes and stare up at him, and then she would put both hands on her hips and frown. "A crazy woman," he thought, and he paid no attention to her. One day while he was calling the kitten, the woman shouted up to him in Spanish. Her voice sounded very angry. "*Oyé!*" she cried, shaking her arm in the air, "why are you calling the name of my daughter?"

Salam kept calling: *Mimí! Agi! Agiagi, Mimí!*

The woman moved closer to the steps. She put both hands above her eyes, but the sun was behind Salam, so that she could not see him very well. "You want to insult people?" she screamed. "I understand your game. You make fun of me and my daughter."

Salam laughed. He put the end of his forefinger to the side of his head and made circles with it. "I'm calling my cat. Who's your daughter?"

"And your cat is called Mimí because you knew my little girl's name was Mimí. Why don't you behave like civilized people?"

Salam laughed again and went inside. He did not think of the woman again. Not many days after that the kitten disappeared, and no matter how much he called, it did not come back. He and Bou Ralem went out that night and searched for it in the canebrake. The moon was bright, and they found it lying dead, and carried it back to the house to look at it. Someone had given it a pellet of bread with a needle inside. Salam sat slowly on the mattress. "The *Yehoudía*," he said.

"You don't know who did it," Bou Ralem told him.

"It was the *Yehoudía*. Throw me the *mottoui*." And he began to smoke kif, one pipe after another. Bou Ralem understood that Salam was looking for an answer, and he did not talk. After a while he saw that the time had come to turn off the electricity and light the candle. When he had done this, Salam lay back quietly on the mattress and listened to the dogs barking outside. Now and then he sat up and filled his *sebsi*. Once he passed it to Bou Ralem, and lay back down on the cushions smiling. He had an idea of what he would do. When they went to bed he said to Bou Ralem: "She's one mother who's going to wet her pants."

The next day he got up early and went to the market. In a little stall there he bought several things: a crow's wing, a hundred grams of *jduq jmel* seeds, powdered porcupine quills, some honey, a pressed lizard, and a quarter kilo of *fasoukh*. When he had finished paying for all this he turned away as if he were going to leave the stall, then he said: "*Khaï*, give me another fifty grams of *jduq jmel*." When the man had weighed the seeds out and put them into a paper and folded it up, he paid him and carried the paper in his left hand as he went on his way home. In the alley the children were throwing clots of mud at one another. They stopped while he went by. The women sat in the doorways with their shawls over their heads. As he passed before the house

of the woman who had killed Mimí he let go of the package of *jduq jmel* seeds. Then he went upstairs onto his terrace, walked to the door, and pounded on it. No one answered. He stood in the middle of the terrace where everyone could see him, rubbing his hand over his chin. A minute later he climbed to the terrace next to his and knocked on that door. He handed his parcel to the woman who came to open. "I left my keys in the market," he told her. "I'll be right back." He ran downstairs, through the alley, and up the street.

Behind the Gailan Garage Bou Ralem was standing. When Salam passed him, he nodded his head once and went along without stopping. Bou Ralem began to walk in the other direction, back to the house. As he opened the gate onto the terrace, the woman from next door called to him. "Haven't you seen your brother? He left his keys in the market." "No," Bou Ralem said, and went in, leaving the door open. He sat down and smoked a cigarette while he waited. In a little while the talking in the alley below sounded louder. He stood up and went to the door to listen. A woman was crying: "It's *jduq jmel!* Mimí had it in her hand!" Soon there were many more voices, and the woman from the next terrace ran downstairs in her bathrobe, carrying a parcel. "That's it," Bou Ralem said to himself. When she arrived the shouting grew louder. He listened for a time, smiling. He went out and ran downstairs. They were all in the alley outside the woman's door, and the little girl was inside the house, screaming. Without looking toward them he ran by on the far side of the alley.

Salam was inside the café, drinking a glass of tea. "Sit down," he told Bou Ralem. "I'm not going to get Fatma Daifa before eleven." He ordered his brother a tea. "Were they making a lot of noise?" he asked him. Bou Ralem nodded his head. Salam smiled. "I'd like to hear them," he said. "You'll hear them," Bou Ralem told him. "They're not going to stop."

At eleven o'clock they left the café and went through the back passages of the Medina to Fatma Daifa's house. She was the sister of their mother's mother, and thus not of their family, so that they did not feel it was shameful to use her in the game. She was waiting for them at the door, and together they went back to Salam's house.

The old woman went into the alley ahead of Salam and Bou Ralem, and walked straight to the door where all the women were gathered. She held her *haïk* tightly around her head so that no part of her face showed, except one eye. She pushed against the Jewish women and held out one hand. 'Give me my things,' she told them. She did not bother to speak Spanish with them because she knew they understood Arabic. "You have my things." They did have them and they were still looking at them, but then they turned to look at her. She seized all the packages and put them into her *kouffa* quickly. "No shame!" she shouted at the women. "Go and look after your children." She pushed the other way and went back into the alley

where Salam and Bou Ralem stood waiting. The three went upstairs and into Salam's house, and they shut the door. They had lunch there and stayed all day, talking and laughing. When everyone had gone to bed, Salam took Fatma Daifa home.

The next day the Jews all stared at them when they went out, but no one said anything to them. The woman Salam had wanted to frighten did not come to her door at all, and the little girl was not in the alley playing with the other children. It was clear that the Jews thought Fatma Daifa had put a spell on the child. They would not have believed Salam and Bou Ralem alone could do such a thing, but they knew a Moslem woman had the power. The two brothers were very much pleased with the joke. It is forbidden to practice magic, but the old woman was their witness that they had not done such a thing. She had taken home all the packages just as they had been when she had snatched them away from the Jewish women, and she had promised to keep them that way, so that in case of trouble she could prove that nothing had been used.

The Jewish woman went to the *comisaría* to complain. She found a young policeman sitting at his desk listening to a small radio he had in his hand, and she began to tell him that the Moslems in her *haouma* had bought charms to use against her daughter. The policeman did not like her, partly because she was Jewish and spoke Spanish instead of Arabic, and partly because he did not approve of people who believed in magic, but he listened politely until she said: "That Moslem is a *sinvergüenza.*" She tried to go on to say that there were many very good Moslems, but he did not like her words. He frowned at the woman and said: "Why do you say all this? What makes you think they put a spell on your little girl?" She told him how the three had shut themselves in all day with the packages of bad things from the market. The policeman looked at her in surprise. "And for a dead lizard you came all the way here?" he laughed. He sent her away and went on listening to his radio.

The people in the alley still did not speak to Salam and Bou Ralem, and the little girl did not come out to play with the others. When the woman went to the market she took her with her. "Hold on to my skirt," she would tell her. But one day in front of the service station the child let go of the woman's skirt for a minute. When she ran to catch up with her mother, she fell and her knee hit a broken bottle. The woman saw the blood and began to scream. People stopped walking. In a few minutes a Jew came by and helped the woman carry the child to a pharmacy. They bandaged the little girl's knee and the woman took her home. Then she went back to the pharmacy to get her baskets, but on the way she stopped at the police station. She found the same policeman sitting at his desk.

"If you want to see the proof of what I told you, come and look at my little girl now," she told him. "Again?" said the policeman. He was not friendly with her, but he took her name and address, and later that day on his way home he called at her house. He looked at the little girl's knee and tickled her ribs so that she laughed. "All children fall down," he said. "But who is this Moslem? Where does he live?" The mother showed him the stairs at the end of the alley. He did not intend to speak with Salam, but he wanted to finish with the woman once and for all. He went out into the alley, and saw that the woman was watching him from the door, so he walked slowly to the foot of the stairs. When he had decided she was no longer looking, he started to go. At that moment he heard a voice behind him. He turned and saw Salam standing above him on the terrace. He did not much like his face, and he told himself that if he ever saw him in the street he would have a few words with him.

One morning Salam went early to the market to get fresh kif. When he found it he bought three hundred francs' worth. As he went out through the gates into the street the policeman, who was waiting for him, stopped him. "I want to speak with you," he told him. Salam stretched his fingers tightly around the kif in his pocket. "Is everything all right?" said the policeman. "Everything is fine," Salam replied. "No trouble?" the policeman insisted, looking at him as if he knew what Salam had just bought. Salam answered: "No trouble." The policeman said: "See that it stays like that." Salam was angry at being spoken to in this way for no reason, but with the kif in his pocket he could only be thankful that he was not being searched. "I'm a friend of the world," he said, trying to smile. The policeman did not answer, and turned away.

"A very bad thing," thought Salam as he hurried home with the kif. No policeman had bothered him before this. When he reached his room he wondered if he should hide the package under a tile in the floor, but he decided that if he did that, he himself would be living like a Jew, who each time there is a knock at the door ducks his head and trembles. He spread the kif out on the table defiantly and left it there. During the afternoon he and Bou Ralem cut it. He did not mention the policeman, but he was thinking of him all the time they were working. When the sun had gone down behind the plain and the soft breeze began to come in through the windows he took off his shirt and lay back on the pillows to smoke. Bou Ralem filled his *mottoui* with the fresh kif and went out to a café. "I'm staying here," said Salam.

He smoked for an hour or more. It was a hot night. The dogs had begun to bark in the canebrake. A woman and a man in one of the huts below were cursing one another. Sometimes the woman stopped shouting and merely screamed. The sound bothered Salam. He could not be happy. He got up and dressed, took his *sebsi* and his *mottoui*, and went out. Instead of turning toward the town when he left the alley, he walked toward the highway. He wanted to sit in a quiet place in order to find out what to do. If the policeman had not suspected him, he would not have stopped him. Since he had stopped him once, he might do it again, and the next time he might search him. "That's not freedom," he said to himself. A few cars went by. Their headlights made the tree-trunks yellow as they passed. After each car had gone, there was only the blue light of the moon and the sky. When he got to the bridge over the river, he climbed down the bank under the girders, and went along a path to a rock that hung out high above the water. There he sat and looked over the edge at the deep muddy river that was moving below in the moonlight. He felt the kif in his head, and he knew he was going to make it work for him.

He put the plan together slowly. It was going to cost a thousand francs, but he had that, and he was willing to spend it. After six pipes, when he had everything arranged in his mind, he stuffed his *sebsi* into his pocket, jumped up, and climbed the path to the highway. He walked back to the town quickly, going into the Medina by a dirt road where the houses had gardens, and where behind the walls all along the way there were dogs barking at the moon. Not many people walked at night in this part of town. He went to the house of his cousin Abdallah, who was married to a woman from Sidi Kacem. The house was never empty. Two or three of her brothers were always there with their families. Salam spoke privately with Abdallah in the street outside the door, asking for one of the brothers whose face was not known in the town. Abdallah went in and quickly came out again with someone. The man had a beard, wore a country *djellaba*, and carried his shoes in his hand. They spoke together for a few minutes. "Go with him," said Abdallah, when they had finished talking. Salam and the bearded man said goodnight and went away.

At Salam's house that night the man slept on a mat in the kitchen. When morning came, they washed and had coffee and pastries. While they were eating Salam took out his thousand-franc note and put it into an envelope. On the outside of it Bou Ralem had printed the word GRACIAS in pencil. Soon Salam and the man from the country got up and went out through the town until they came to a side street opposite the back entrance of the police station. There they stood against the wall and talked. "You don't know his name," said the man. "We don't have to," Salam told him. "When he comes out and gets into one of the cars and drives away, you run over to the officer and give them the envelope, and say you tried to catch him before he left." He waved the envelope in his hand. "Ask them to give this to him when he comes back. They'll take it."

"He may walk," said the man. "Then what will I do?"

"The police never walk," Salam said. "You'll see. Then you run out again. This street is the best one. Keep going, that's all. I won't be here. I'll see you at Abdallah's."

They waited a long time. The sun grew hotter and they moved into the shade of a fig tree, always watching the door of the *comisaría* from where they stood. Several policemen came out, and for each one the man from the country was ready to run, but Salam held onto him and said: "No, no, no!" When the policeman they were waiting for finally did stand in the doorway, Salam drew in his breath and whispered: "There he is. Wait till he drives off, then run." He turned away and walked very fast down the street into the Medina.

When the man from the country had explained clearly who the envelope was for, he handed it to the policeman at the desk, said, "Thank you," and ran out quickly. The policeman looked at the envelope, then tried to call him back, but he had gone. Since all messages which came for any of the policemen had to be put on the captain's desk first he sent the envelope in to his office. The captain held it up to the light. When the policeman came back he called him in and made him open it in front of him. "Who is it from?" said the captain. The policeman scratched his head. He could not answer. "I see," said the captain. The next week he had the man transferred. Word came from the capital that he was to be sent to Rissani. "See how many friends you can make in the desert," the captain told him. He would not listen to anything the policeman tried to say.

Salam went to Tangier. When he returned he heard that the policeman had been sent to the Sahara. This made him laugh a great deal. He went to the market and bought a half-grown goat. Then he invited Fatma Daifa and Abdallah and his wife and two of the brothers with their wives and children, and they killed the goat and ate it. It was nearly dawn by the time they all went home. Fatma Daifa did not want to go through the streets alone, and since Salam and Bou Ralem were too drunk to take her, she slept in the kitchen on the floor. When she woke up it was late, but Salam and Bou Ralem were still asleep. She got her things together, put her *haïk* on and went out. As she came to the house of the woman with the little girl, she stood still and looked in. The woman saw her and was frightened. "What do you want?" she cried. Fatma Daifa knew she was meddling, but she thought this was the right thing to do for Salam. She pretended not to see the woman's frightened face, and she shook her fist back at the terrace, crying into the air: "Now I see what sort of man you are! You think you can cheat me? Listen to me! None of it's going to work, do you hear?" She walked on down the alley shouting: "None of it!" The other Jewish women came and stood around the door and sat on the curb in front of it. They agreed that if the old woman had fought with the two men there was no more danger from the magic, because only the old woman had the power to make it work. The mother of the little girl was happy, and the next day the child was playing in the mud with the others.

Salam went in and out of the alley as always, not noticing the children or the people. It was half a month before he said one day to Bou Ralem: "I think the Jews are feeling better. I saw the wrong Mimí out loose this morning." He was free again now that the policeman was gone, and he could carry his kif in his pocket without worrying when he went out through the streets to the café. The next time he saw Fatma Daifa she asked him about the Jews in his alley. "It's finished. They've forgotten," he said. "Good," she replied. Then she went to her house and got out the porcupine quill powder and the crow's wing and the seeds and all the rest of the packages. She put them into her basket, carried them to the market, and sold them there, and with the money she bought bread, oil, and eggs. She went home and cooked her dinner.

Tangier
1960

The Story of Lahcen and Idir

Two friends, Lahcen and Idir, were walking on the beach at Merkala. By the rocks stood a girl, and her *djellaba* blew in the wind. Lahcen and Idir stopped walking when they saw her. They stood still, looking at her. Lahcen said: "Do you know that one?" "No. I never saw her." "Let's go over," said Lahcen. They looked up and down the beach for a man who might be with the girl, but there was no one. "A whore," said Lahcen. When they got closer to the girl, they saw that she was very young. Lahcen laughed. "This is easy." "How much have you got?" Idir asked him. "You think I'm going to pay her?" cried Lahcen.

Idir understood that Lahcen meant to beat her. ("If you don't pay a whore you have to beat her.") And he did not like the idea, because they had done it before together, and it nearly always meant trouble later. Her sister or someone in her family went to the police and complained, and in the end everybody was in jail. Being shut into prison made Idir nervous. He tried to keep out of it, and he was usually able to. The difference between Lahcen and Idir was that Lahcen liked to drink and Idir smoked kif. Kif smokers want to stay quiet in their heads, and drinkers are not like that. They want to break things.

Lahcen rubbed his groin and spat onto the sand. Idir knew he was going over the moves in the game he was going to play with the girl, planning when and where he would knock her down. He was worried. The girl looked the other way. She held down the skirt of her *djellaba* so the wind would not blow it. Lahcen said: "Wait here." He went on to her and Idir saw her lips moving as she spoke to him, for she wore no veil. All her teeth were gold. Idir hated women with gold teeth because at fourteen he had been in love with a gold-toothed whore named Zohra, who never had paid him any attention. He said to himself: "He can have her." Besides, he did not want to be with them when the trouble began. He stood still until Lahcen whistled to him. Then he went over to where they stood. "Ready?" Lahcen asked. He took the girl's arm and started to walk along beside the rocks. "It's late. I've got to go," Idir told him. Lahcen looked surprised, but he said nothing. "Some other day," Idir told Lahcen, looking at him and trying to warn him. The girl laughed spitefully, as if she thought that might shame him into coming along.

305

He was glad he had decided to go home. When he went by the Mendoub's fig orchard a dog barked at him. He threw a rock at it and hit it.

The next morning Lahcen came to Idir's room. His eyes were red from the wine he had been drinking. He sat down on the floor and pulled out a handkerchief that had a knot tied in one corner. He untied the knot and let a gold ring fall out into his lap. Picking up the ring, he handed it to Idir. "For you. I got it cheap." Idir saw that Lahcen wanted him to take the ring, and he put it on his finger, saying: "May Allah give you health." Lahcen rubbed his hand across his chin and yawned. Then he said: "I saw you look at me, and afterward when we got to the quarry I thought that would be the best place. And then I remembered the night the police took us at Bou Khach Khach, and I remembered you looking at me. I turned around and left her there. Garbage!"

"So you're not in jail and you're drunk," said Idir, and he laughed.

"That's true," said Lahcen. "And that's why I give you the ring."

Idir knew the ring was worth at least fifty dirhams, and he could sell it if he needed money badly. That would end his friendship with Lahcen, but there would be no help for it.

Sometimes Lahcen came by in the evening with a bottle of wine. He would drink the whole bottle while Idir smoked his kif pipe, and they would listen to the radio until the end of the program at twelve o'clock. Afterward, very late, they would walk through the streets of Dradeb to a garage where a friend of Lahcen was night watchman. When the moon was full, it was brighter than the street lights. With no moon, there was nobody in the streets, and in a few late cafés the men told one another about what thieves had done, and how there were more of them than ever before. This was because there was almost no work to be had anywhere, and the country people were selling their cows and sheep to be able to pay their taxes, and then coming to the city. Lahcen and Idir worked now and then, whenever they found something to do. They had a little money, they always ate, and Lahcen sometimes was able to afford his bottle of Spanish wine. Idir's kif was more of a problem, because each time the police decided to enforce the law they had made against it, it grew very scarce and the price went up. Then when there was plenty to be had, because the police were busy looking for guns and rebels instead, the price stayed high. He did not smoke any less, but he smoked by himself in his room. If you smoke in a café, there is always someone who has left his kif at home and wants to use yours. He told his friends at the Café Nadjah that he had given up kif, and he never accepted a pipe when it was offered to him.

Back in his room in the early evening, with the window open and the sleepy sounds of the town coming up, for it was summer and the voices of people filled the streets, Idir sat in the chair he had bought and put his feet on the windowsill. That way he could see the sky as he smoked. Lahcen would come in and talk. Now and then they went together to Emsallah to a *barraca* there near the slaughter house where two sisters lived with their feeble-minded mother. They would get the mother drunk and put her to bed in the inner room. Then they would get the girls drunk and spend the night with them, without paying. The cognac was expensive, but it did not cost as much as whores would have.

In midsummer, at the time of Sidi Kacem, it suddenly grew very hot. People set up tents made of sheets on the roofs of their houses and cooked and slept there. At night in the moonlight Idir could see all the roofs, each one with its box of sheets flapping in the wind, and inside the sheets the red light made by the fire in the pot. Daytimes, the sun shining on the sea of white sheets hurt his eyes, and he remembered not to look out when he passed the window as he moved about his room. He would have liked to live in a more expensive room, one with a blind to keep out the light. There was no way of being protected from the bright summer day that filled the sky outside, and he waited with longing for dusk. His custom was not to smoke kif before the sun went down. He did not like it in the daytime, above all in summer when the air is hot and the light is powerful. When each day came up hotter than the one before it, he decided to buy enough food and kif to last several days, and to shut himself into his room until it got cooler. He had worked two days at the port that week and had some money. He put the food on the table and locked the door. Then he took the key out of the lock and threw it into the drawer of the table. Lying with the packages and cans in his market basket was a large bundle of kif wrapped in a newspaper. He unfolded it, took out a sheaf and sniffed of it. For the next two hours he sat on the floor picking off the leaves and cutting them on a breadboard, sifting, and cutting, again and again. Once, as the sun reached him, he had to move to get out of its heat. By the time the sun went down he had enough ready for three or four days. He got up off the floor and sat in his chair with his pouch and his pipe in his lap, and smoked, while the radio played the Chleuh music that was always broadcast at this hour for the Soussi shop-keepers. In cafés men often got up and turned it off. Idir enjoyed it. Kif smokers usually like it, because of the *naqous* that always pounds the same design.

The music played a long time, and Idir thought of the market at Tiznit and the mosque with the tree trunks sticking out of its mud walls. He looked down at the floor. The room still had daylight in it. He opened his eyes wide. A small bird was walking slowly along the floor. He jumped up. The kif pipe fell, but its bowl did not break. Before the bird had time to move, he had put his hand over it. Even when he held it between his two hands it did not struggle. He looked at it, and thought it was the smallest bird he had ever seen. Its head was gray, and its wings were black and white. It looked at him, and it did not seem afraid. He sat down in the chair with the bird in his lap. When he lifted his hand it stayed still. "It's a young bird and can't fly," he thought. He smoked several pipes of kif. The bird did not move. The sun had gone down and the houses were growing blue in the evening light. He stroked the bird's head with his thumb. Then he took the ring from his little finger and slipped it over the smooth feathers of its head. The bird paid no attention. "A gold collar for the sultan of birds," he said. He smoked some more kif and looked at the sky. Then he began to be hungry, and he thought the bird might like some breadcrumbs. He put his pipe down on the table and tried to take the ring from the bird's head. It would not come off over the feathers. He pulled at it, and the bird fluttered its wings and struggled. For a second he let go of it, and in that instant it flew straight from his lap into the sky. Idir jumped up and stood watching it. When it was gone, he began to smile. "The son of a whore!" he whispered.

He prepared his food and ate it. After that he sat in the chair smoking and thinking about the bird. When Lahcen came he told him the story. "He was waiting all the time for a chance to steal something," he said. Lahcen was a little drunk, and he was angry. "So he stole my ring!" he cried. "Ah," said Idir. "Yours? I thought you gave it to me."

"I'm not crazy yet," Lahcen told him. He went away still angry, and did not return for more than a week. The morning he came into the room Idir was certain that he was going to begin to talk again about the ring, and he quickly handed him a pair of shoes he had bought from a friend the day before. "Do these fit you?" he asked him. Lahcen sat down in the chair, put them on, and found they did fit. "They need new bottoms, but the tops are like new," Idir told him. "The tops are good," said Lahcen. He felt of the leather and squeezed it between his thumb and fingers. "Take them," said Idir. Lahcen was pleased, and he said nothing about the ring that day. When he got the shoes to his room he looked carefully at them and decided to spend the money that it would cost to have new soles made.

The next day he went to a Spanish cobbler, who agreed to repair the shoes for fifteen dirhams. "Ten," said Lahcen. After a long discussion the cobbler lowered his price to thirteen, and he left the shoes there, saying that he would call for them in a week. The same afternoon he was walking through Sidi Bouknadel, and he saw a girl. They talked together for two hours or more, standing not very near to each other beside the wall, and looking down at the ground so that no one could see they were talking. The girl was from Meknes, and that was why he had never seen her before. She was visiting her aunt, who lived there in the quarter, and soon her sister was coming from Meknes. She looked to him the best thing he had seen that year, but of course he could not be sure of her nose and mouth because her veil hid them. He got her to agree to meet him at the same place the next day. This time they took a walk along the Hafa, and he could see that she would be willing. But she would not tell him where her aunt's house was.

Only two days later he got her to his room. As he had expected, she was beautiful. That night he was very happy, but in the morning when she had gone, he understood that he wanted to be with her all the time. He wanted to know what her aunt's house was like and how she was going to pass her day. In this way a bad time began for Lahcen. He was happy only when she was with him and he could get into bed and see her lying on one side of him and a bottle of cognac on the other, upright on the floor beside his pillow, where he could reach it easily. Each day when she had gone he lay thinking about all the men she might be going to see before she came back to him. When he talked about it to her she laughed and said she spent all her time with her aunt and sister, who now had arrived from Meknes. But he could not stop worrying about it.

Two weeks went by before he remembered to go and get his shoes. On his way to the cobbler's he thought about how he would solve his problem. He had an idea that Idir could help him. If he brought Idir and the girl together and left them alone, Idir would tell him afterward everything that had happened. If she let Idir take her to bed, then she was a whore and could be treated like a whore. He would give her a good beating and then make it up with her, because she was too good to throw away. But he had to know whether she was really his, or whether she would go with others.

When the cobbler handed him his shoes, he saw that they looked almost like new, and he was pleased. He paid the thirteen dirhams and took the shoes home. That night when he was going to put them on to wear to the café, he found that his feet would not go into them. They were much too small. The cobbler had cut down the last in order to stitch on the new soles. He put his old shoes back on, went out, and slammed the door. That night he had a quarrel with the girl. It took him until almost dawn to stop her crying. When the sun came up and she was asleep, he lay with his arms folded behind his head looking at the ceiling, thinking that the shoes had cost him thirteen dirhams and now he was going to have to spend the day trying to sell them. He got rid of the girl early and went in to Bou Araqia with the shoes. No one would give him more than eight dirhams for them. In the afternoon he went to the Joteya and sat in the shade of a grapevine, waiting for the buyers and sellers to arrive. A man from the mountains finally offered him ten dirhams, and he sold the shoes. "Three dirhams gone for nothing," he thought when he put the money into his pocket. He was angry, but instead of blaming the cobbler, he felt that the fault was Idir's.

That afternoon he saw Idir, and he told him he would bring a friend with him to Idir's room after the evening meal. Then he went home and drank cognac. When the girl arrived he had finished the bottle, and he was drunk and more unhappy than ever. "Don't take it off," he told her when she began to unfasten her veil. "We're going out." She said nothing. They took the back streets to Idir's room.

Idir sat in his chair listening to the radio. He had not expected a girl, and when he saw her take off her veil the beating of his heart made his head ache. He told her to sit in the chair, and then he paid no more attention to her and sat on the bed talking only with Lahcen, who did not look at her either. Soon Lahcen got up. "I'm going out to get some cigarettes," he said. "I'll be right back." He shut the door after him, and Idir quickly went and locked it. He smiled at the girl and sat on the table beside her, looking down at her. Now and then he smoked a pipe of kif. He wondered why Lahcen was taking so long. Finally he said: "He's not coming back, you know." The girl laughed and shrugged. He jumped up, took her hand, and led her to the bed.

In the morning when they were getting dressed, she told him she lived at the Hotel Sevilla. It was a small Moslem hotel in the center of the Medina. He took her there and left her. "Will you come tonight?" she asked him. Idir frowned. He was thinking of Lahcen. "Don't wait for me after midnight," he said. On his way home he stopped at the Café Nadjah. Lahcen was there. His eyes were red and he looked as though he had not slept at all. Idir had the feeling that he had been waiting for him to appear, for when he came into the café Lahcen quickly got up and paid the *qahouaji*. They walked down the main street of Dradeb without saying anything, and when they got to the road that leads to the Merkala beach, they turned down it, still without speaking.

It was low tide. They walked on the wet sand while the small waves broke at their feet. Lahcen smoked a cigarette and threw stones into the water. Finally he spoke. "How was it?"

Idir shrugged, tried to keep his voice flat. "All right for one night," he said. Lahcen was ready to say carelessly: "Or even two." But then he realized that Idir did not want to talk about the night, which meant that it had been a great event for him. And when he looked at his face he was certain that Idir wanted the girl for himself. He was sure he had already lost her to him, but he did not know why he had not thought of that in the beginning. Now he forgot the true reason why he had wanted to take her to Idir.

"You thought I brought her just to be good to you!" he cried. "No, sidi! I left her there to see if you were a friend. And I see what kind of friend you are! A scorpion!" He seized the front of Idir's garments and struck him in the face. Idir moved backward a few steps, and got ready to fight. He understood that Lahcen had seen the truth, and that now there was nothing at all to say, and nothing to do but fight. When they were both bloody and panting, he looked for a flash at Lahcen's face, and saw that he was dizzy and could not see very well. He drew back, put his head down, and with all his force ran into Lahcen, who lost his balance and fell onto the sand. Then quickly he kicked him in the head with the heel of his shoe. He left him lying there and went home.

In a little while Lahcen began to hear the waves breaking on the sand near him. "I must kill him," he thought. "He sold my ring. Now I must go and kill him." Instead, he took off his clothes and bathed in the sea, and when he had finished, he lay in the sun on the sand all day and slept. In the evening he went and got very drunk.

At eleven o'clock Idir went to the Hotel Sevilla. The girl was sitting in a wicker chair by the front door, waiting for him. She looked carefully at the cuts on his face. Under her veil he saw her smile.

"You fought?" Idir nodded his head. "How is he?" He shrugged. This made her laugh. "He was always drunk, anyway," she said. Idir took her arm, and they went out into the street.

Tangier
1961

He of the Assembly

He salutes all parts of the sky and the earth where it is
bright. He thinks the color of the amethysts of Aguelmous
will be dark if it has rained in the valley of Zerekten. The
eye wants to sleep, he says, but the head is no mattress.
When it rained for three days and water covered the
flatlands outside the ramparts, he slept by the bamboo
fence at the Café of the Two Bridges.

It seems there was a man named Ben Tajah who went to Fez to
visit his cousin. The day he came back he was walking in the Djemaa el Fna,
and he saw a letter lying on the pavement. He picked it up and found that
his name was written on the envelope. He went to the Café of the Two
Bridges with the letter in his hand, sat down on a mat and opened the
envelope. Inside was a paper which read: "The sky trembles and the earth is
afraid, and the two eyes are not brothers." Ben Tajah did not understand,
and he was very unhappy because his name was on the envelope. It made
him think that Satan was nearby. He of the Assembly was sitting in the
same part of the café. He was listening to the wind in the telephone wires.
The sky was almost empty of daytime light. "The eye wants to sleep," he
thought, "but the head is no mattress. I know what that is, but I have
forgotten it." Three days is a long time for rain to keep falling on flat bare
ground. "If I got up and ran down the street," he thought, "a policeman
would follow me and call to me to stop. I would run faster, and he would
run after me. When he shot at me, I'd duck around the corners of houses."
He felt the rough dried mud of the wall under his fingertips. "And I'd be
running through the streets looking for a place to hide, but no door would be
open, until finally I came to one door that was open, and I'd go in through
the rooms and courtyards until finally I came to the kitchen. The old
woman would be there." He stopped and wondered for a moment why an
old woman should be there alone in the kitchen at that hour. She was
stirring a big kettle of soup on the stove. "And I'd look for a place to hide
there in the kitchen, and there'd be no place. And I'd be waiting to hear the
policeman's footsteps, because he wouldn't miss the open door. And I'd
look in the dark corner of the room where she kept the charcoal, but it
wouldn't be dark enough. And the old woman would turn and look at me

313

and say: 'If you're trying to get away, my boy, I can help you. Jump into the soup-kettle.'" The wind sighed in the telephone wires. Men came into the Café of the Two Bridges with their garments flapping. Ben Tajah sat on his mat. He had put the letter away, but first he had stared at it a long time. He of the Assembly leaned back and looked at the sky. "The old woman," he said to himself. "What is she trying to do? The soup is hot. It may be a trap. I may find there's no way out, once I get down there." He wanted a pipe of kif, but he was afraid the policeman would run into the kitchen before he was able to smoke it. He said to the old woman: "How can I get in? Tell me." And it seemed to him that he heard footsteps in the street, or perhaps even in one of the rooms of the house. He leaned over the stove and looked down into the kettle. It was dark and very hot down in there. Steam was coming up in clouds, and there was a thick smell in the air that made it hard to breathe. "Quick!" said the old woman, and she unrolled a rope ladder and hung it over the edge of the kettle. He began to climb down, and she leaned over and looked after him. "Until the other world!" he shouted. And he climbed all the way down. There was a rowboat below. When he was in it he tugged on the ladder and the old woman began to pull it up. And at that instant the policeman ran in, and two more were with him, and the old woman had just the time to throw the ladder down into the soup. "Now they are going to take her to the commissariat," he thought, "and the poor woman only did me a favor." He rowed around in the dark for a few minutes, and it was very hot. Soon he took off his clothes. For a while he could see the round top of the kettle up above, like a porthole in the side of a ship, with the heads of the policemen looking down in, but then it grew smaller as he rowed, until it was only a light. Sometimes he could find it and sometimes he lost it, and finally it was gone. He was worried about the old woman, and he thought he must find a way to help her. No policeman can go into the Café of the Two Bridges because it belongs to the Sultan's sister. This is why there is so much kif smoke inside that a *berrada* can't fall over even if it is pushed, and why most customers like to sit outside, and even there keep one hand on their money. As long as the thieves stay inside and their friends bring them food and kif, they are all right. One day police headquarters will forget to send a man to watch the café, or one man will leave five minutes before the other gets there to take his place. Outside everyone smokes kif too, but only for an hour or two—not all day and night like the ones inside. He of the Assembly had forgotten to light his *sebsi*. He was in a café where no policeman could come, and he wanted to go away to a kif world where the police were chasing him. "This is the way we are now," he thought. "We work backwards. If we have something good, we look for something bad instead." He lighted the *sebsi* and smoked it. Then he blew the hard ash out of the *chqaf*. It landed in the brook beside the second bridge.

"The world is too good. We can only work forward if we make it bad again first." This made him sad, so he stopped thinking, and filled his *sebsi*. While he was smoking it, Ben Tajah looked in his direction, and although they were facing each other, He of the Assembly did not notice Ben Tajah until he got up and paid for his tea. Then he looked at him because he took such a long time getting up off the floor. He saw his face and he thought: "That man has no one in the world." The idea made him feel cold. He filled his *sebsi* again and lighted it. He saw the man as he was going to go out of the café and walk alone down the long road outside the ramparts. In a little while he himself would have to go out to the *souks* to try to borrow money for dinner. When he smoked a lot of kif he did not like his aunt to see him, and he did not want to see her. "Soup and bread. No one can want more than that. Will thirty francs be enough the fourth time? The *qahouaji* wasn't satisfied last night. But he took it. And he went away and let me sleep. A Moslem, even in the city, can't refuse his brother shelter." He was not convinced, because he had been born in the mountains, and so he kept thinking back and forth in this way. He smoked many *chqofa*, and when he got up to go out into the street he found that the world had changed.

Ben Tajah was not a rich man. He lived alone in a room near Bab Doukkala, and he had a stall in the bazaars where he sold coathangers and chests. Often he did not open the shop because he was in bed with a liver attack. At such times he pounded on the floor from his bed, using a brass pestle, and the postman who lived downstairs brought him up some food. Sometimes he stayed in bed for a week at a time. Each morning and night the postman came in with a tray. The food was not very good because the postman's wife did not understand much about cooking. But he was glad to have it. Twice he had brought the postman a new chest to keep clothes and blankets in. One of the postman's wives a few years before had taken a chest with her when she had left him and gone back to her family in Kasba Tadla. Ben Tajah himself had tried having a wife for a while because he needed someone to get him regular meals and to wash his clothes, but the girl was from the mountains, and was wild. No matter how much he beat her she would not be tamed. Everything in the room got broken, and finally he had to put her out into the street. "No more women will get into my house," he told his friends in the bazaars, and they laughed. He took home many women, and one day he found that he had *en noua*. He knew that was a bad disease, because it stays in the blood and eats the nose from inside. "A man loses his nose only long after he has already lost his head." He asked a doctor for medicine. The doctor gave him a paper and told him to take it to the Pharmacie de l'Etoile. There he bought six vials of penicillin in a box. He took them home and tied each little bottle with a silk thread, stringing them so that they made a necklace. He wore this always around his neck, taking care that the glass vials touched his skin. He thought it likely that by now he was cured, but his cousin in Fez had just told him that he must go on wearing the medicine for another three months, or at least until the beginning of the moon of Chouwal. He had thought about this now and then on the way home, sitting in the bus for two days, and he had decided that his cousin was too cautious. He stood in the Djemaa el Fna a minute watching the trained monkeys, but the crowd pushed too much, so he walked on. When he got home he shut the door and put his hand in his pocket to pull out the envelope, because he wanted to look at it again inside his own room, and be sure that the name written on it was beyond a doubt his. But the letter was gone. He remembered the jostling in the Djemaa el Fna. Someone had reached into his pocket and imagined his hand was feeling money, and taken it. Yet Ben Tajah did not truly believe this. He was convinced that he would have known such a theft was happening. There had been a letter in his pocket. He was not even sure of that. He sat down on the cushions. "Two days in the bus," he thought. "Probably I'm tired. I found no letter." He searched in his pocket again, and it seemed to him he could still remember how the fold of the envelope had felt. "Why would it have my name on it? I never found any letter at all." Then he wondered if anyone had seen him in the café with the envelope in one hand and the sheet of paper in the other, looking at them both for such a long time. He stood up. He wanted to go back to the Café of the Two Bridges and ask the *qahouaji:* "Did you see me an hour ago? Was I looking at a letter?" If the *qahouaji* said, "Yes," then the letter was real. He repeated the words aloud: "The sky trembles and the earth is afraid, and the two eyes are not brothers." In the silence afterwards the memory of the sound of the words frightened him. "If there was no letter, where are these words from?" And he shivered because the answer to that was: "From Satan." He was about to open the door when a new fear stopped him. The *qahouaji* might say, "No," and this would be still worse, because it would mean that the words had been put directly into his head by Satan, that Satan had chosen him to reveal Himself to. In that case He might appear at any moment. "*Ach haddou laillaha ill' Allah . . .* ," he prayed, holding his two forefingers up, one on each side of him. He sat down again and did not move. In the street the children were crying. He did not want to hear the *qahouaji* say: "No. You had no letter." If he knew that Satan was coming to tempt him, he would have that much less power to keep Him away with his prayers, because he would be more afraid. ⸱

He of the Assembly stood. Behind him was a wall. In his hand was the *sebsi.* Over his head was the sky, which he felt was about to burst into light. He was leaning back looking at it. It was dark on the earth, but there was still light up there behind the stars. Ahead of him was the pissoir of the

Carpenters' Souk which the French had put there. People said only Jews used it. It was made of tin, and there was a puddle in front of it that reflected the sky and the top of the pissoir. It looked like a boat in the water. Or like a pier where boats land. Without moving from where he stood, He of the Assembly saw it approaching slowly. He was going toward it. And he remembered he was naked, and put his hand over his sex. In a minute the rowboat would be bumping against the pier. He steadied himself on his legs and waited. But at that moment a large cat ran out of the shadow of the wall and stopped in the middle of the street to turn and look at him with an evil face. He saw its two eyes and for a while could not take his own eyes away. Then the cat ran across the street and was gone. He was not sure what had happened, and he stood very still looking at the ground. He looked back at the pissoir reflected in the puddle and thought: "It was a cat on the shore, nothing else." But the cat's eyes had frightened him. Instead of being like cats' eyes, they had looked like the eyes of a person who was interested in him. He made himself forget he had had this thought. He was still waiting for the rowboat to touch the landing pier, but nothing had happened. It was going to stay where it was, that near the shore but not near enough to touch. He stood still a long time, waiting for something to happen. Then he began to walk very fast down the street toward the bazaars. He had just remembered that the old woman was in the police station. He wanted to help her, but first he had to find out where they had taken her. "I'll have to go to every police station in the Medina," he thought, and he was not hungry any more. It was one thing to promise himself he would help her when he was far from land, and another when he was a few doors from a commissariat. He walked by the entrance. Two policemen stood in the doorway. He kept walking. The street curved and he was alone. "This night is going to be a jewel in my crown," he said, and he turned quickly to the left and went along a dark passageway. At the end he saw flames, and he knew that Mustapha would be there tending the fire of the bakery. He crawled into the mud hut where the oven was. "Ah, the jackal has come back from the forest!" said Mustapha. He of the Assembly shook his head. "This is a bad world," he told Mustapha. "I've got no money," Mustapha said. He of the Assembly did not understand. "Everything goes backwards," he said. "It's bad now, and we have to make it still worse if we want to go forwards." Mustapha saw that He of the Assembly was *mkiyif ma rassou* and was not interested in money. He looked at him in a more friendly way and said: "Secrets are not between friends. Talk." He of the Assembly told him that an old woman had done him a great favor, and because of that three policemen had arrested her and taken her to the police station. "You must go for me to the commissariat and ask them if they have an old woman there." He pulled out his *sebsi* and took a very long time filling it. When he finished it he smoked it himself and did not offer any to Mustapha, because Mustapha never offered him any of his. "You see how full of kif my head is," he said laughing. "I can't go." Mustapha laughed too and said it would not be a good idea, and that he would go for him.

"I was there, and I heard him going away for a long time, so long that he had to be gone, and yet he was still there, and his footsteps were still going away. He went away and there was nobody. There was the fire and I moved away from it. I wanted to hear a sound like a muezzin crying *Allah akbar!* or a French plane from the Pilot Base flying over the Medina, or news on the radio. It wasn't there. And when the wind came in the door it was made of dust high as a man. A night to be chased by dogs in the Mellah. I looked in the fire and I saw an eye in there, like the eye that's left when you burn *chibb* and you know there was a *djinn* in the house. I got up and stood. The fire was making a noise like a voice. I think it was talking. I went out and walked along the street. I walked a long time and I came to Bab el Khemiss. It was dark there and the wind was cold. I went to the wall where the camels were lying and stood there. Sometimes the men have fires and play songs on their *aouadas*. But they were asleep. All snoring. I walked again and went to the gate and looked out. The big trucks went by full of vegetables and I thought I would like to be on a truck and ride all night. Then in another city I would be a soldier and go to Algeria. Everything would be good if we had a war. I thought a long time. Then I was so cold I turned around and walked again. It was as cold as the belly of the oldest goat of Ijoukak. I thought I heard a muezzin and I stopped and listened. The only thing I heard was the water running in the *seguia* that carries the water out to the gardens. It was near the *mçid* of Moulay Boujemaa. I heard the water running by and I felt cold. Then I knew I was cold because I was afraid. In my head I was thinking: 'If something should happen that never happened before, what would I do?' You want to laugh? Hashish in your heart and wind in your head. You think it's like your grandmother's prayer-mat. This is the truth. This isn't a dream brought back from another world past the customs like a teapot from Mecca. I heard the water and I was afraid. There were some trees by the path ahead of me. You know at night sometimes it's good to pull out the *sebsi* and smoke. I smoked and I started to walk. And then I heard something. Not a muezzin. Something that sounded like my name. But it came up from below, from the *seguia*, *Allah istir!* And I walked with my head down. I heard it again saying my name, a voice like water, like the wind moving the leaves in the trees, a woman. It was a woman calling me. The wind was in the trees and the water was running, but there was a woman too. You think it's kif. No, she was calling my name. Now and then, not very loud. When I was under the trees it was louder, and I heard that the voice was my mother's. I heard that the way I can hear you. Then I knew the cat was not a cat, and I knew that Aïcha Qandicha wanted me. I thought of other nights when perhaps she had been watching me from the eyes of a cat or a donkey. I knew she was not going to catch me. Nothing in the seven skies could make me turn around. But I was cold and afraid and when I licked my lips my tongue had no spit on it. I was under the *safsaf* trees and I thought: 'She's going to reach down and try to touch me. But she can't touch me from the front and I won't turn around, not even if I hear a pistol.' I remembered how the policeman had fired at me and how I'd found only one door open. I began to yell: 'You threw me the ladder and told me to climb down. You brought me here! The filthiest whore in the Mellah, with the pus coming out of her, is a thousand times cleaner than you, daughter of all the padronas and dogs in seven worlds.' I got past the trees and I began to run. I called up to the sky so she could hear my voice behind: 'I hope the police put a hose in your mouth and pump you full of salt water until you crack open!' I thought: 'Tomorrow I'm going to buy *fasoukh* and *tib* and *nidd* and *hasalouba* and *mska* and all the *bakhour* in the Djemaa, and put them in the *mijmah* and burn them, and walk back and forth over the *mijmah* ten times slowly, so the smoke can clean out all my clothes. Then I'll see if there's an eye in the ashes afterwards. If there is, I'll do it all over again right away. And every Thursday I'll buy the *bakhour* and every Friday I'll burn it. That will be strong enough to keep her away.' If I could find a window and look through and see what they're doing to the old woman! If only they could kill her! I kept running. There were a few people in the streets. I didn't look to see where I was going, but I went to the street near Mustapha's oven where the commissariat was. I stopped running before I got to the door. The one standing there saw me before that. He stepped out and raised his arm. He said to me: 'Come here.'"

He of the Assembly ran. He felt as though he were on horseback. He did not feel his legs moving. He saw the road coming toward him and the doors going by. The policeman had not shot at him yet, but it was worse than the other time because he was very close behind and he was blowing his whistle. "The policeman is old. At least thirty-five. I can run faster." But from any street others could come. It was dangerous and he did not want to think about danger. He of the Assembly let songs come into his head. When it rains in the valley of Zerekten the amethysts are darker in Aguelmous. The eye wants to sleep but the head is no mattress. It was a song. Ah, my brother, the ink on the paper is like smoke in the air. What words are there to tell how long a night can be? Drunk with love, I wander in the dark. He was running through the dye-souk, and he splashed into a puddle. The whistle blew again behind him, like a crazy bird screaming. The sound made him feel like laughing, but that did not mean he was not afraid. He thought: "If I'm seventeen I can run faster. That has to be true." It was very dark ahead. He had to slow his running. There was no time for his eyes to get used to the dark. He nearly ran into the wall of the shop at the end of the street. He turned to the right and saw the narrow alley ahead of him. The police had tied the old woman naked to a table with her thin legs wide apart and were sliding electrodes up inside her. He ran ahead. He could see the course of the alley now even in the dark. Then he stopped dead, moved to the wall, and stood still. He heard the footsteps slowing down. "He's going to turn to the left." And he whispered aloud: "It ends that way." The footsteps stopped and there was silence. The policeman was looking into the silence and listening into the dark to the left and to the right. He of the Assembly could not see him or hear him, but he knew that was what he was doing. He did not move. When its rains in the valley of Zerekten. A hand seized his shoulder. He opened his mouth and swiftly turned, but the man had moved and was pushing him from the side. He felt the wool of the man's *djellaba* against the back of his hand. He had gone through a door and the man had shut it without making any noise. Now they both stood still in the dark, listening to the policeman walking quickly by outside the door. Then the man struck a match. He was facing the other way, and there was a flight of stairs ahead. The man did not turn around, but he said, "Come up," and they both climbed the stairs. At the top the man took out a key and opened a door. He of the Assembly stood in the doorway while the man lit a candle. He liked the room because it had many mattresses and cushions and a white sheepskin under the tea-tray in the corner of the floor. The man turned around and said: "Sit down." His face looked serious and kind and unhappy. He of the Assembly had never seen it before, but he knew it was not the face of a policeman. He of the Assembly pulled out his *sebsi*.

Ben Tajah looked at the boy and asked him: "What did you mean when you said down there: 'It ends that way?' I heard you say it." The boy was embarrassed. He smiled and looked at the floor. Ben Tajah felt happy to have him there. He had been standing outside the door downstairs in the dark for a long time, trying to make himself go to the Café of the Two Bridges and talk to the *qahouaji*. In his mind it was almost as though he had already been there and spoken with him. He had heard the *qahouaji* telling him that he had seen no letter, and he had felt his own dismay. He had not wanted to believe that, but he would be willing to say yes, I made a mistake and there was no letter, if only he could find out where the words had come from. For the words were certainly in his head: ". . . and the two eyes are not brothers." That was like a footprint found in the garden the morning after a bad dream, the proof that there had been a reason for the dream, that something had been there after all. Ben Tajah had not been able to go or to stay. He had started and stopped so many times that now, although he did not know it, he was very tired. When a man is tired he mistakes the hopes of children for the knowledge of men. It seemed to him that He of the Assembly's words had a meaning all for him. Even though the boy might not know it, he could have been sent by Allah to help him at that minute. In a nearby street a police whistle blew. The boy looked at him. Ben Tajah did not care very much what the answer would be, but he said: "Why are they looking for you?" The boy held out his lighted *sebsi* and his *mottoui* fat with kif. He did not want to talk because he was listening. Ben Tajah smoked kif only when a friend offered it to him, but he understood that the police had begun once more to try to enforce their law against kif. Each year they arrested people for a few weeks, and then stopped arresting them. He looked at the boy, and decided that probably he smoked too much. With the *sebsi* in his hand he was sitting very still listening to the voices of some passers-by in the street below. "I know who he is," one said. "I've got his name from Mustapha." "The baker?" "That's the one." They walked on. The boy's expression was so intense that Ben Tajah said to him: "It's nobody. Just people." He was feeling happy because he was certain that Satan would not appear before him as long as the boy was with him. He said quietly: "Still you haven't told me why you said: 'It ends that way.'" The boy filled his *sebsi* slowly and smoked all the kif in it. "I meant," he said, "thanks to Allah. Praise the sky and the earth where it is bright. What else can you mean when something ends?" Ben Tajah nodded his head. Pious thoughts can be of as much use for keeping Satan at a distance as camphor or *bakhour* dropped onto hot coals. Each holy word is worth a high column of smoke, and the eyelids do not smart afterward. "He has a good heart," thought Ben Tajah, "even though he is probably a guide for the Nazarenes." And he asked himself why it would not be possible for the boy to have been sent to protect him from Satan. "Probably not. But it could be." The boy offered him the *sebsi*. He took it and smoked it. After that Ben Tajah began to think that he would like to go to the Café of the Two Bridges and speak to the *qahouaji* about the letter. He felt that if the boy went with him the *qahouaji* might say there had been a letter, and that even if the man could not remember, he would not mind so much because he would be less afraid. He waited until he thought the boy was not nervous about going into the street, and then he said: "Let's go out and get some tea." "Good," said the boy. He was not afraid of the police if he was with Ben Tajah. They went through the empty streets, crossed the Djemaa el Fna and the garden beyond. When they were near the café, Ben Tajah said to the boy: "Do you know the Café of the Two Bridges?" The boy said he always sat there, and Ben Tajah was not surprised. It seemed to him that perhaps he had even seen him there. He seized the boy's arm. "Were you there today?" he asked him. The boy said, "Yes," and turned to look at him. He let go of the arm. "Nothing," he said. "Did you ever see me there?" They came to the gate of the café and Ben Tajah stopped walking. "No," the boy said. They went across the first bridge and then the second bridge, and sat down in a corner.

Not many people were left outside. Those inside were making a great noise. The *qahouaji* brought the tea and went away again. Ben Tajah did not say anything to him about the letter. He wanted to drink the tea quietly and leave trouble until later.

When the muezzin called from the minaret of the Koutoubia, He of the Assembly thought of being in the Agdal. The great mountains were ahead of him and the olive trees stood in rows on each side of him. Then he heard the trickle of water and he remembered the *seguia* that is there in the Agdal, and he swiftly came back to the Café of the Two Bridges. Aïcha Qandicha can be only where there are trees by running water. "She comes only for single men by trees and fresh moving water. Her arms are gold and she calls in the voice of the most cherished one." Ben Tajah gave him the *sebsi*. He filled it and smoked it. "When a man sees her face he will never see another woman's face. He will make love with her all the night, and every night, and in the sunlight by the walls, before the eyes of children. Soon he will be an empty pod and he will leave this world for his home in Jehennem." The last carriage went by, taking the last tourists down the road beside the ramparts to their rooms in the Mamounia. He of the Assembly thought: "The eye wants to sleep. But this man is alone in the world. He wants to talk all night. He wants to tell me about his wife and how he beat her and how she broke everything. Why do I want to know all those things? He is a good man but he has no head." Ben Tajah was sad. He said: "What have I done? Why does Satan choose me?" Then at last he told the boy about the letter, about how he wondered if it had had his name on the envelope and how he was not even sure there had been a letter. When he finished he looked sadly at the boy. "And you didn't see me." He of the Assembly shut his eyes and kept them shut for a while. When he opened them again he said: "Are you alone in the world?" Ben Tajah stared at him and did not speak. The boy laughed. "I did see you," he said, "but you had no letter. I saw you when you were getting up and I thought you were old. Then I saw you were not old. That's all I saw." "No, it isn't," Ben Tajah said. "You saw I was alone." He of the Assembly shrugged. "Who knows?" He filled the *sebsi* and handed it to Ben Tajah. The kif was in Ben Tajah's head. His eyes were small. He of the Assembly listened to the wind in the telephone wires, took back the *sebsi* and filled it again. Then he said: "You think Satan is coming to make trouble for you because you're alone in the world. I see that. Get a wife or somebody to be with you always, and you won't think about it any more. That's true. Because Satan doesn't come to men like you." He of the Assembly did not believe this himself. He knew that Father Satan can come for anyone in the world, but he hoped to live with Ben Tajah, so he would not have to borrow money in the *souks* to buy food. Ben Tajah drank some tea. He did not want the boy to see that his face was happy. He felt that the boy was right, and that there never had been a letter. "Two days on a bus is a long time. A man can get very tired," he said. Then he called the *qahouaji* and told him to bring two more glasses of tea. He of the Assembly gave him the *sebsi*. He knew that Ben Tajah wanted to stay as long as possible in the Café of the Two Bridges. He put his finger into the *mottoui*. The kif was almost gone. "We can talk," he said. "Not much kif is in the *mottoui*." The *qahouaji* brought the tea. They talked for an hour or more. The *qahouaji* slept and snored. They talked about Satan and the bad thing it is to live alone, to wake up in the dark and know that there is no one else nearby. Many times He of the Assembly told Ben Tajah that he must not worry. The kif was all gone. He held his empty *mottoui* in his hand. He did not understand how he had got back to the town without climbing up out of the soup kettle. Once he said to Ben Tajah: "I never climbed back up." Ben Tajah looked at him and said he did not understand. He of the Assembly told him the story. Ben Tajah laughed. He said: "You smoke too much kif, brother." He of the Assembly put his *sebsi* into his pocket. "And you don't smoke and you're afraid of Satan," he told Ben Tajah. "No!" Ben Tajah shouted. "By Allah! No more! But one thing is in my head, and I can't put it out. The sky trembles and the earth is afraid, and the two eyes are not brothers. Did you ever hear those words? Where did they come from?" Ben Tajah looked hard at the boy. He of the Assembly understood that these had been the words on the paper, and he felt cold in the middle of his back because he had never heard them before and they sounded evil. He knew, too, that he must not let Ben Tajah know this. He began to laugh. Ben Tajah took hold of his knee and shook it. His face was troubled. "Did you ever hear them?" He of the Assembly went on laughing. Ben Tajah shook his leg so hard that he stopped and said: "Yes!" When Ben Tajah waited and he said nothing more, he saw the man's face growing angry, and so he said: "Yes, I've heard them. But will you tell me what happened to me and how I got out of the soup-kettle if I tell you about those words?" Ben Tajah understood that the kif was going away from the boy's head. But he saw that it had not all gone, or he would not have been asking that question. And he said: "Wait a while for the answer to that question." He of the Assembly woke the *qahouaji* and Ben Tajah paid him, and they went out of the café. They did not talk while they walked. When they got to the Mouassine mosque, Ben Tajah held out his hand to say goodnight, but He of the Assembly said: "I'm looking in my head for the place I heard your words. I'll walk to your door with you. Maybe I'll remember." Ben Tajah said: "May Allah help you find it." And he took his arm and they walked to Ben Tajah's door while He of the Assembly said nothing. They stood outside the door in the dark. "Have you found it?" said Ben Tajah. "Almost," said He of the Assembly. Ben Tajah thought that perhaps when the kif had gone out of the boy's head he might be able to tell him about the words. He wanted to know how the boy's head was, and so he said: "Do you still want to know how you got out of the soup-kettle?" He of the Assembly laughed. "You said you would tell me later," he told Ben Tajah. "I will," said Ben Tajah. "Come upstairs. Since we have to wait, we can sit down." Ben Tajah opened the door and they went upstairs. This time He of the Assembly sat down on Ben Tajah's bed. He yawned and stretched. It was a good bed. He was glad it was not the mat by the bamboo fence at the Café of the Two Bridges. "And so, tell me how I got out of the soup-kettle," he said laughing. Ben Tajah said: "You're still asking me that? Have you thought of the words?" "I know the words," the boy said. "The sky trembles . . . ." Ben Tajah did not want him to say them again. "Where did you hear them? What are they? That's what I want to know." The boy shook his head. Then he sat up very straight and looked beyond Ben Tajah, beyond the wall of the room, beyond the streets of the Medina, beyond the gardens, toward the mountains where the people speak Tachelhait. He remembered being a little boy. "This night is a jewel in my crown," he thought. "It went this way." And he began to sing, making up a melody for the words Ben Tajah had told him. When he had finished ". . . and the two eyes are not brothers," he added a few more words of his own and stopped singing. "That's all I remember of the song," he said. Ben Tajah clapped his hands together hard. "A song!" he cried. "I must have heard it on the radio." He of the Assembly shrugged. "They play it sometimes," he said. "I've made him happy," he thought. "But I won't ever tell him another lie. That's the only one. What I'm going to do now is not the same as lying." He got up off the bed and went to the window. The muezzins were calling the *fjer*. "It's almost morning," he said to Ben Tajah. "I still have kif in my head." "Sit down," said Ben Tajah. He was sure now there had been no letter. He of the Assembly took off his *djellaba* and got into bed. Ben Tajah looked at him in surprise. Then he undressed and got into bed beside him. He left the candle burning on the floor beside the bed. He meant to stay awake, but he went to sleep because he was not used to smoking kif and the kif was in his head. He of the Assembly did not believe he was asleep. He lay for a long time without moving. He listened to the voices of the muezzins, and he thought that the man beside him would speak or move. When he saw that Ben Tajah was surely asleep, he was angry. "This is how he treats a friend who has made him happy. He forgets his trouble and his friend too." He thought about it more and he was angrier. The muezzins were still calling the *fjer*. "Before they stop, or he will hear." Very slowly he got out of the bed. He put on his *djellaba* and opened the door. Then he went back and took all the money out of Ben Tajah's pockets. In with the banknotes was an envelope that was folded. It had Ben Tajah's name written across it. He pulled out the piece of paper inside and held it near the candle, and then he looked at it as he would have looked at a snake. The words were written there. Ben Tajah's face was turned toward the wall and he was snoring. He of the Assembly held the paper above the flame and burned it, and then he burned the envelope. He blew the black paper-ashes across the floor. Without making any noise he ran downstairs and let himself out into the street. He shut the door. The money was in his pocket and he walked fast to his aunt's house. His aunt awoke and was angry for a while. Finally he said: "It was raining. How could I come home? Let me sleep." He had a little kif hidden under his pillow. He smoked a pipe. Then he looked across his sleep to the morning and thought: "A pipe of kif before breakfast gives a man the strength of a hundred camels in the courtyard."

Tangier
1961

The Wind at Beni Midar

At Beni Midar there is a barracks. It has many rows of small buildings, whitewashed, and everything is in the middle of big rocks, on the side of the mountain behind the town. A quiet place when the wind is not blowing. A few Spanish still live in the houses along the road. They run the shops. But now the people in the streets are Moslems, mountain men with goats and sheep, or soldiers from the *cuartel* looking for wine. The Spanish sell wine to men they know. One Jew sells it to almost anybody. But there never is enough wine in the town for everybody who wants it. Beni Midar has only one street, that comes down out of the mountains, curves back and forth like a snake between the houses for a while, and goes on, back into the mountains. Sunday is a bad day, the one free time the soldiers have, when they can walk back and forth all day between the shops and houses. A few Spaniards in black clothes go into the church at the hour when the Rhmara ride their donkeys out of the *souk*. Later the Spaniards come out of the church and go home. Nothing else happens because all the shops are shut. There is nothing the soldiers can buy.

Driss had been stationed for eight months in Beni Midar. Because the cabran in charge of his unit had been a neighbor of his in Tetuan, he was not unhappy. The cabran had a friend with a motorcycle. Together they went each month to Tetuan. There the cabran always saw Driss's sister, who made a big bundle of food to send back to the barracks for him. She sent him chickens and cakes, cigarettes and figs, and always many hard-boiled eggs. He shared the eggs with two or three friends, and did not complain about being in Beni Midar.

Not even the brothels were open on Sunday. It was the day when everyone walked from one end of the town to the other, back and forth, many times. Sometimes Driss walked like this with his friends. Usually he took his gun and went down into the valley to hunt for hares. When he came back at twilight he stopped in a small café at the edge of town and had a glass of tea and a few pipes of kif. If it had not been the only café he would never have gone into it. Shameful things happened there. Several times he had seen men from the mountains get up from the mat and do dances that left blood on the floor. These men were Jilala, and no one thought of stopping

327

them, not even Driss. They did not dance because they wanted to dance, and it was this that made him angry and ashamed. It seemed to him that the world should be made in such a way that a man is free to dance or not as he feels. A Jilali can do only what the music tells him to do. When the musicians, who are Jilala too, play the music that has the power, his eyes shut and he falls on the floor. And until the man has shown the proof and drunk his own blood, the musicians do not begin the music that will bring him back to the world. They should do something about it, Driss said to the other soldiers who went with him to the café, and they agreed.

He had talked about it with his cabran in the public garden. The cabran said that when all the children in the land were going to school every day there would be no more *djenoun*. Women would no longer be able to put spells on their husbands. And the Jilala and the Hamatcha and all the others would stop cutting their legs and arms and chests. Driss thought about this for a long time. He was glad to hear that the government knew about these bad things. "But if they know," he thought, "why don't they do something now? The day they get every one of the children in school I'll be lying beside Sidi Ali el Mandri." He was thinking of the cemetery at Bab Sebta in Tetuan. When he saw the cabran again he said: "If they can do something about it, they ought to do it now." The cabran did not seem interested. "Yes," he said.

When Driss got his permission and went home he told his father what the cabran had said. "You mean the government thinks it can kill all evil spirits?" his father cried.

"That's right. It can," said Driss. "It's going to."

His father was old and had no confidence in the young men who now ran the government. "It's impossible," he said. "They should let them alone. Leave them under their stones. Children have gone to school before, and how many were hurt by *djenoun*? But if the government begins to make trouble for them, you'll see what will happen. They'll go after the children first."

Driss had expected his father to speak this way, but when he heard the words he was ashamed. He did not answer. Some of his friends were without respect for God. They ate during Ramadan and argued with their fathers. He was glad not to be like them. But he felt his father was wrong.

One hot summer Sunday when the sky was very blue Driss lay in bed late. The men who slept in his room at the barracks had gone out. He listened to the radio. "It would be good down in the valley on a day like this," he thought. He saw himself swimming in one of the big pools, and he thought of the hot sun on his back afterward. He got up and unlocked the cupboard to look for his gun. Even before he took it out he said, "*Yah latif!*" because he remembered that he had only one cartridge left, and it was

Sunday. He slammed the cupboard door shut and got back into bed. The radio began to give the news. He sat up, spat as far out as he could from the bed, and turned it off. In the silence he heard many birds singing in the *safsaf* tree outside the window. He scratched his head. Then he got up and dressed. In the courtyard he saw Mehdi going toward the stairs. Mehdi was on his way to do sentry duty in the box outside the main gate.

"*Khaï!* Does four rials sound good to you?"

Medhi looked at him. "Is this number sixty, three, fifty-one?" This was the name of an Egyptian song that came over the radio nearly every day. The song ended with the word nothing. Nothing, nothing, sung over and over again.

Why not? As they walked along together, Driss moved closer, so that his thigh rubbed against Mehdi's.

"The price is ten, *khoya.*"

"With all its cartridges?"

"You want me to open it up and show you here?" Mehdi's voice was angry. The words came out of the side of his mouth.

Driss said nothing. They came to the top of the stairs. Mehdi was walking fast. "You'll have to have it back here by seven," he said. "Do you want it?"

In his head Driss saw the long day in the empty town. "Yes," he said. "Stay there." He hurried back to the room, unlocked his cupboard, and took out his gun. From the shelf he pulled down his pipe, his kif, and a loaf of bread. He put his head outside the door. There was no one in the courtyard but Mehdi sitting on the wall at the other end. Then with the old gun in his hands he ran all the way to Mehdi. Mehdi took it and went down the stairs, leaving his own gun lying on the wall. Driss took up the gun, waited a moment, and followed him. When he went past the sentry box he heard Mehdi's voice say softly: "I need the ten at seven, *khoya.*"

Driss grunted. He knew how dark it was in there. No officer ever stuck his head inside the door on Sundays. Ten rials, he thought, and he's running no risk. He looked around at the goats among the rocks. The sun was hot, but the air smelled sweet, and he was happy to be walking down the side of the mountain. He pulled the visor of his cap further down over his eyes and began to whistle. Soon he came out in front of the town, below it on the other side of the valley. He could see the people on the benches in the park at the top of the cliff, small but clear and black. They were Spaniards and they were waiting for the bell of their church to begin to ring.

He got to the highest pool about the time the sun was overhead. When he lay on the rocks afterward eating his bread, the sun burned him. No animals will move before three, he thought. He put his trousers on and crawled into the shade of the oleander bushes to sleep. When he awoke the air was cooler. He smoked all the kif he had, and went walking through the valley. Sometimes he sang. He found no hares, and so he put small stones on the tops of the rocks and fired at them. Then he climbed back up the other side of the valley and followed the highway into the town.

He came to the café and went in. The musicians were playing and singing. The tea drinkers clapped their hands with the music. A soldier cried: "Driss! Sit down!" He sat with his friends and smoked some of their kif. Then he bought four rials' worth from the cutter who sat on the platform with the musicians, and went on smoking. "Nothing was moving in the valley today," he told them. "It was dead down there."

A man with a yellow turban on his head who sat nearby closed his eyes and fell against the man next to him. The others around him moved to a further part of the mat. The man toppled over and lay on the floor.

"Another one?" cried Driss. "They should stay in Djebel Habib. I can't look at him."

The man took a long time to get to his feet. His arms and legs had been captured by the drums, but his body was fighting, and he groaned. Driss tried to pay no attention to him. He smoked his pipe and looked at his friends, pretending that no Jilali was in front of him. When the man pulled out his knife he could not pretend any longer. He watched the blood running into the man's eyes. It made a blank red curtain over each hole. The man opened his eyes wider, as if he wanted to see through the blood. The drums were loud.

Driss got up and paid the *qahouaji* for his tea. He said good-by to the others and went out. The sun would soon go below the top of the mountains. Its light made him want to shut his eyes, because he had a lot of kif in his head. He walked through the town to the higher end and turned into a lane that led up into another valley. In this place there was no one. Cactuses grew high on each side of the lane, and the spiders had built a world of webs between their thorns. Because he walked fast, the kif began to boil in his head. Soon he was very hungry, but all the fruit had been picked from the cactuses along the lane. He came to a small farmhouse with a thatched roof. Behind it on the empty mountainside there were more cactuses still pink with hundreds of *hindiyats*. A dog in a shed beside the house began to bark. There was no sign of people. He stood still for a while and listened to the dog. Then he walked toward the cactus patch. He was sure no one was in the house. Many years ago his sister had shown him how to pick *hindiyats* without letting the needles get into the flesh of his hands. He laid his gun on the ground behind a low stone wall and began to gather the fruit. As he picked he saw in his head the two blind red holes of the Jilali's eyes, and under his breath he cursed all Jilala. When he had a great pile of fruit on the ground he sat down and began to eat, throwing the peels over his shoulder. As he ate he grew hungrier, and so he picked more. The picture he had in his head of the man's face shiny with blood slowly faded. He thought only of the *hindiyats* he was eating. It was almost dark there on the mountainside. He looked at his watch and jumped up, because he remembered that Mehdi had to have his gun at seven o'clock. In the dim light he could not see the gun anywhere. He searched behind the wall, where he thought he had laid it, but he saw only stones and bushes.

"It's gone, *Allah istir*," he said. His heart pounded. He ran back to the lane and stood there a while. The dog barked without stopping.

It was dark before he reached the gate of the barracks. Another man was in the sentry box. The cabran was waiting for him in the room. The old gun Driss's father had given him lay on his bed.

"Do you know where Mehdi is?" the cabran asked him.

"No," said Driss.

"He's in the dark house, the son of a whore. And do you know why?"

Driss sat down on the bed. The cabran is my friend, he was thinking. "It's gone," he said, and told him how he had laid the gun on the ground, and a dog had been barking, and no one had come by, and still it had disappeared. "Maybe the dog was a *djinn*," he said when he had finished. He did not really believe the dog had anything to do with it, but he could not think of anything else to say then.

The cabran looked at him a long time and said nothing. He shook his head. "I thought you had some brains," he said at last. Then his face grew very angry, and he pulled Driss out into the courtyard and told a soldier to lock him up.

At ten o'clock that night he went to see Driss. He found him smoking his *sebsi* in the dark. The cell was full of kif smoke. "Garbage!" cried the cabran, and he took the pipe and the kif away from him. "Tell the truth," he said to Driss. "You sold the gun, didn't you?"

"On my mother's head, it's just as I told you! There was only the dog."

The cabran could not make him say anything different. He slammed the door and went to the café in the town to have a glass of tea. He sat listening to the music, and he began to smoke the kif he had taken from Driss. If Driss was telling the truth, then it was only the kif in Driss's head that had made him lose the gun, and in that case there was a chance that it could be found.

The cabran had not smoked in a long time. As the kif filled his head he began to be hungry, and he remembered the times when he had been a boy smoking kif with his friends. Always they had gone to look for *hindiyats* afterward, because they tasted better than anything else and cost nothing. They always knew where there were some growing. "A *kouffa* full of good *hindiyats*," he thought. He shut his eyes and went on thinking.

The next morning early the cabran went out and stood on a high rock behind the barracks, looking carefully all around the valley and the bare mountainside. Not far away he saw a lane with cactuses along it, and farther up there was a whole forest of cactus. "There," he said to himself.

He walked among the rocks until he came to the lane, and he followed the lane to the farmhouse. The dog began to bark. A woman came to the doorway and looked at him. He paid no attention to her, but went straight to the high cactuses on the hillside behind the house. There were many *hindiyats* still to be eaten, but the cabran did not eat any of them. He had no kif in his head and he was thinking only of the gun. Beside a stone wall there was a big pile of *hindiya* peelings. Someone had eaten a great many. Then he saw the sun shining on part of the gun's barrel under the peelings. "Hah!" he shouted, and he seized the gun and wiped it all over with his handkerchief. On his way back to the barracks he felt so happy that he decided to play a joke on Driss.

He hid the gun under his bed. With a glass of tea and a piece of bread in his hand he went to see Driss. He found him asleep on the floor in the dark.

"Daylight is here!" he shouted. He laughed and kicked Driss's foot to wake him up. Driss sat on the floor drinking the tea and the cabran stood in the doorway scratching his chin. He looked down at the floor, but not at Driss. After a time he said: "Last night you told me a dog was barking?"

Driss was certain the cabran was going to make fun of him. He was sorry he had mentioned the dog. "Yes," he said, not sounding sure.

"If it was the dog," the cabran went on, "I know how to get it back. You have to help me."

Driss looked up at him. He could not believe the cabran was being serious. Finally he said in a low voice: "I was joking when I said that. I had kif in my head."

The cabran was angry. "You think it's a joke to lose a gun that belongs to the Sultan? You did sell it! You haven't got kif in your head now. Maybe you can tell the truth." He stepped toward Driss, and Driss thought he was going to hit him. He stood up quickly. "I told you the truth," he said. "It was gone."

The cabran rubbed his chin and looked down at the floor again for a minute. "The next time a Jilali begins to dance in the café, we'll do it," he told him. He shut the door and left Driss alone.

Two days later the cabran came again to the dark house. He had another soldier with him. "Quick!" he told Driss. "There's one dancing now."

They went out into the courtyard and Driss blinked his eyes. "Listen," said the cabran. "When the Jilali is drinking his own blood he has power. What you have to do is ask him to make the *djinn* bring me the gun. I'm going to sit in my room and burn *djaoui*. That may help."

"I'll do it," said Driss. "But it won't do any good."

The other soldier took Driss to the café. The Jilali was a tall man from the mountains. He had already taken out his knife, and he was waving it in the air. The soldier made Driss sit down near the musicians, and then he waited until the man began to lick the blood from his arms. Then, because he thought he might be sick if he watched any longer, Driss raised his right arm toward the Jilali and said in a low voice: "In the name of Allah, *khoya*, make the *djinn* that stole Mehdi's gun take it now to Aziz the cabran." The Jilali seemed to be staring at him, but Driss could not be sure whether he had heard his words or not.

The soldier took him back to the barracks. The cabran was sitting under a plum tree beside the kitchen door. He told the soldier to go away and jumped up. "Come," he said, and he led Driss to the room. The air was blue with the smoke of the *djaoui* he had been burning. He pointed to the middle of the floor. "Look!" he cried. A gun was lying there. Driss ran and picked it up. After he had looked at it carefully, he said: "It's the gun." And his voice was full of fear. The cabran could see that Driss had not been sure the thing was possible, but that now he no longer had any doubt.

The cabran was happy to have fooled him so easily. He laughed. "You see, it worked," he said. "It's lucky for you Mehdi's going to be in the dark house for another week."

Driss did not answer. He felt even worse than when he had been watching the Jilali slicing the flesh of his arms.

That night he lay in bed worrying. It was the first time he had had anything to do with a *djinn* or an *affrit*. Now he had entered into their world. It was a dangerous world and he did not trust the cabran any longer. "What am I going to do?" he thought. The men all around him were sleeping, but he could not close his eyes. Soon he got up and stepped outside. The leaves of the *safsaf* tree were hissing in the wind. On the other side of the courtyard there was light in one of the windows. Some of the officers were talking there. He walked slowly around the garden in the middle and looked up at the sky, thinking of how different his life was going to be now. As he came near the lighted window he heard a great burst of laughter. The cabran was telling a story. Driss stopped walking and listened.

"And he said to the Jilali: 'Please, sidi, would you ask the dog that stole my gun—' "

The men laughed again, and the sound covered the cabran's voice.

He went quickly back and got into bed. If they knew he had heard the cabran's story they would laugh even more. He lay in the bed thinking, and he felt poison come into his heart. It was the cabran's fault that the *djinn* had been called, and now in front of his superior officers he was pretending that he had had nothing to do with it. Later the cabran came in and went to bed, and it was quiet in the courtyard, but Driss lay thinking for a long time before he went to sleep.

In the days that came after that, the cabran was friendly again, but Driss did not want to see him smile. He thought with hatred: "In his head I'm afraid of him now because he knows how to call a *djinn*. He jokes with me now because he has power."

He could not laugh or be happy when the cabran was nearby. Each night he lay awake for a long time after the others had gone to sleep. He listened to the wind moving the hard leaves of the *safsaf* tree, and he thought only of how he could break the cabran's power.

When Mehdi came out of the dark house he spoke against the cabran. Driss paid him his ten rials. "A lot of money for ten days in the dark house," Mehdi grumbled, and he looked at the bill in his hand. Driss pretended not to understand. "He's a son of a whore," he said.

Mehdi snorted. "And you have the head of a needle," he said. "It all came from you. The wind blows the kif out your ears!"

"You think I wasn't in the dark house too?" cried Driss. But he could not tell Mehdi about the Jilali and the dog. "He's a son of a whore," he said again.

Mehdi's eyes grew narrow and stiff. "I'll do his work for him. He'll think he's in the dark house himself when I finish."

Mehdi went on his way. Driss stood watching him go.

The next Sunday Driss got up early and walked into Beni Midar. The *souk* was full of rows of mountain people in white clothes. He walked in among the donkeys and climbed the steps to the stalls. There he went to see an old man who sold incense and herbs. People called him El Fqih. He sat down in front of El Fqih and said: "I want something for a son of a whore."

El Fqih looked at him angrily. "A sin!" He raised his forefinger and shook it back and forth. "Sins are not my work." Driss did not say anything. El Fqih spoke more quietly now. "To balance that, it is said that each trouble in the world has its remedy. There are cheap remedies and remedies that cost a lot of money." He stopped.

Driss waited. "How much is this one?" he asked him. The old man was not pleased because he wanted to talk longer. But he said: "I'll give you a name for five rials." He looked sternly at Driss, leaned forward and whispered a name in his ear. "In the alley behind the sawmill," he said aloud. "The blue tin shack with the canebrake in back of it." Driss paid him and ran down the steps.

He found the house. The old woman stood in the doorway with a checkered tablecloth over her head. Her eyes had turned white like milk. They looked to Driss like the eyes of an old dog. He said: "You're Anisa?"

"Come into the house," she told him. It was almost dark inside. He told her he wanted something to break the power of a son of a whore. "Give me ten rials now," she said. "Come back at sunset with another ten. It will be ready."

After the midday meal he went out into the courtyard. He met Mehdi and asked him to go with him to the café in Beni Midar. They walked through the town in the hot afternoon sun. It was still early when they got to the café, and there was plenty of space on the mats. They sat in a dark corner. Driss took out his kif and his *sebsi* and they smoked. When the musicians began to play, Mehdi said: "The circus is back!" But Driss did not want to talk about the Jilala. He talked about the cabran. He gave the pipe many times to Mehdi, and he watched Mehdi growing more angry with the cabran as he smoked. He was not surprised when Mehdi cried: "I'll finish it tonight!"

"No, *khoya*," said Driss. "You don't know. He's gone way up. He's a friend of all the officers now. They bring him bottles of wine."

"He'll come down," Mehdi said. "Before dinner tonight. In the court-yard. You be there and watch it."

Driss handed him the pipe and paid for the tea. He left Mehdi there and went into the street to walk up and down because he did not want to sit still any longer. When the sky was red behind the mountain he went to the alley by the sawmill. The old woman was in the doorway.

"Come in," she said as before. When they were inside the room she handed him a paper packet. "He has to take all of it," she said. She took the money and pulled at his sleeve. "I never saw you," she said. "Good-by."

Driss went to his room and listened to the radio. When dinner time came he stood inside the doorway looking out into the courtyard. In the shadows at the other end he thought he could see Mehdi, but he was not sure. There were many soldiers walking around in the courtyard, waiting for dinner. Soon there was shouting near the top of the steps. The soldiers began to run toward the other end of the courtyard. Driss looked from the doorway and saw only the running soldiers. He called to the men in the room. "Some-thing's happening!" They all ran out. Then with the paper of powder in his hand he went back into the room to the cabran's bed and lifted up the bottle of wine one of the officers had given the cabran the day before. It was almost full. He pulled out the cork and let the powder slide into the bottle. He shook the bottle and put the cork back. There was still shouting in the courtyard. He ran out. When he got near the crowd, he saw Mehdi being dragged along the ground by three soldiers. He was kicking. The cabran sat on the wall with his head down, holding his arm. There was blood all over his face and shirt.

It was almost a half hour before the cabran came to eat his dinner. His face was covered with bruises and his arm was bandaged and hung in a sling. Mehdi had cut it with his knife at the last minute when the soldiers had begun to pull them apart. The cabran did not speak much, and the men did not try to talk with him. He sat on his bed and ate. While he was eating he drank all the wine in the bottle.

That night the cabran moaned in his sleep. A dry wind blew between the mountains. It made a great noise in the *safsaf* tree outside the window. The air roared and the leaves rattled, but Driss still heard the cabran's voice crying. In the morning the doctor came to look at him. The cabran's eyes were open but he could not see. And his mouth was open but he could not speak. They carried him out of the room where the soldiers lived and put him somewhere else. "Maybe the power is broken now," thought Driss.

A few days later a truck came to the barracks, and he saw two men carrying the cabran on a stretcher to the truck. Then he was sure that the cabran's soul had been torn out of his body and that the power was truly broken. In his head he made a prayer of thanks to Allah. He stood with some other soldiers on a rock above the barracks watching the truck grow smaller as it moved down the mountain.

"It's bad for me," he told a man who stood nearby. "He always brought me food from home." The soldier shook his head.

Tangier
1962

The Time of Friendship

The trouble had been growing bigger each year, ever since the end of the war. From the beginning, although aware of its existence, Fräulein Windling had determined to pay it no attention. At first there were only whispered reports of mass arrests. People said: "Many thousands of Moslems have been sent to prison in France." Soon some of her own friends had begun to disappear, like young Bachir and Omar ben Lakhdar, the postmaster of Timimoun, who suddenly one morning were gone, or so she was told, for when she returned the following winter they were not there, and she never had seen them since. The people simply made their faces blank when she tried to talk about it. After the hostilities had begun in earnest, even though the nationalists had derailed the trains and disrupted the trans-Saharan truck service on several occasions, still it was possible to get beyond the disturbed region to her oasis. There in the south the fighting was far away, and the long hours of empty desert that lay between made it seem much farther, almost as though it had been across the sea. If the men of her oasis should ever be infected by the virus of discontent from the far-off north—and this seemed to her almost inconceivable—then in spite of the fact that she was certain that war could bring them nothing but unhappiness, she would have no recourse but to hope for their victory. It was their own land they would be fighting for, their own lives they would be losing in order to win the fight. In the meantime people did not talk; life was hard but peaceful. Each one was aware of the war that was going on in the north, and each one was glad it was far away.

Summers, Fräulein Windling taught in the Freiluftschüle in Bern, where she entertained her pupils with tales of the life led by the people in the great desert in Africa. In the village where she lived, she told them, everything was made by the people themselves out of what the desert had to offer. They lived in a world of objects fashioned out of baked earth, woven grass, palmwood and animal skins. There was no metal. Although she did not admit it to the children, this was no longer wholly true, since recently the women had taken to using empty oil tins for carrying water, instead of the goathide bags of a few years before. She had tried to discourage her friends among the village women from this innovation, telling them that the tins

337

could poison the water; they had agreed, and gone on using them. "They are lazy," she decided. "The oil tins are easier to carry."

When the sun went down and the cool air from the oasis below with its sting of woodsmoke rose to the level of the hotel, she would smell it inside her room and stop whatever she was doing. Then she would put on her burnoose and climb the stairs to the roof. The blanket she lay on while she sunbathed each morning would be there, and she would stretch out on it facing the western sky, and feel the departed sun's heat still strong underneath her body. It was one of the pleasures of the day, to watch the light changing in the oasis below, when dusk and the smoke from the evening fires slowly blotted out the valley. There always came a moment when all that was left was the faint outline, geometric and precise, of the mass of mud prisms that was the village, and a certain clump of high date palms that stood outside its entrance. The houses themselves were no longer there, and eventually the highest palm disappeared; and unless there was a moon all that remained to be seen was the dying sky, the sharp edges of the rocks on the hammada, and a blank expanse of mist that lay over the valley but did not reach as far up the cliffs as the hotel.

Perhaps twice each winter a group of the village women would invite Fräulein Windling to go with them up into the vast land of the dunes to look for firewood. The glare here was cruel. There was not even the trace of a twig or a stem anywhere on the sand, yet as they wandered along the crests barefoot the women could spot the places where roots lay buried beneath the surface, and then they would stoop, uncover them, and dig them up. "The wind leaves a sign," they told her, but she was never certain of being able to identify the sign, nor could she understand how there might be a connection between the invisible roots in the sand and the wind in the air above. "What we have lost, they still possess," she thought.

Her first sight of the desert and its people had been a transfiguring experience; indeed, it seemed to her now that before coming here she had never been in touch with life at all. She believed firmly that each day she spent here increased the aggregate of her resistance. She coveted the rugged health of the natives, when her own was equally strong, but because she was white and educated, she was convinced that her body was intrinsically inferior.

All the work in the hotel was done by one quiet, sad-faced man named Boufelja. He had been there when she had first arrived many years ago; for Fräulein Windling he had come to be as much a part of the place as the cliffs across the valley. She often sat on her table by the fireplace after lunch, playing cards by herself, until the logs no longer gave out heat. There were two very young French soldiers from the fort opposite, who ate in the hotel dining-room. They drank a great amount of wine, and it annoyed her to see their faces slowly turning red as they sat there. At first the soldiers had tipped their caps to her as they went out, and they had stopped their laughing long enough to say, *"Bonjour, madame,"* to her, but now they no longer did. She was happy when they had left, and savored the moment before the fire burned out, while it still glowed under the gusts of wind that wandered down the wide chimney.

Almost always the wind sprang up early in the afternoon, a steady, powerful blowing that roared through the thousands of palms in the oasis below and howled under each door in the hotel, covering the more distant village sounds. This was the hour when she played solitaire, or merely sat, watching the burnt-out logs as they fell to pieces before her eyes. Later she would go along the terrace, a high, bright place like the deck of a great ship sailing through the desert afternoon, hurrying into her room for an instant to get her sweater and cane, and start out on a walk. Sometimes she went southward following the river valley, along the foot of the silent cliffs and through the crooked gorges, to an abandoned village built in a very hot place at a turn in the canyon. The sheer walls of rock behind it sent back the heat, so that the air burned her throat as she breathed it in. Or she went farther, to where the cliff dwellings were, with their animals and symbols incised in the rock.

Returning along the road that led to the village, deep in the green shade of the thickest part of the palm forest, she was regularly aware of the same group of boys sitting at the turn of the road, at a place just before it led up the hill to the shops and the village. They squatted on the sand behind the feathery branches of a giant tamarisk, quietly talking. When she came up to them she greeted them, and they always replied, remained silent a moment until she had passed by, and then resumed their conversation. As far as she could tell, there was never any reference to her by word, and yet this year it sometimes seemed to her that once she had gone by, their inflection had subtly altered, as though there had been a modulation into another key. Did their attitude border on derision? She did not know, but since this was the first time during all her years in the desert that the idea had ever suggested itself to her, she put it resolutely out of her mind. "A new generation requires a new technique if one is to establish contact," she thought. "It is for me to find it." Nevertheless she was sorry that there was no other way of getting into the village save along this main road where they invariably gathered. Even the slight tension caused by having to go past them marred the pleasure of her walks.

One day she realized with a slight shock of shame that she did not even know what the boys looked like. She had seen them only as a group from a distance; when she drew near enough to say good-day to them, she always had her head down, watching the road. The fact that she had been afraid to look at them was unacceptable; now, as she came up to them, she stared into the eyes of one after the other, carefully. Nodding gravely, she went on. Yes, they were insolent faces, she thought—not at all like the faces of their elders. The respectful attitudes into which they had been startled were the crudest sort of shamming. But the important thing to her was that she had won: she was no longer preoccupied with having to pass by them every day. Slowly she even grew to recognize each boy.

There was one, she noted, younger than the others, who always sat a little apart from them, and it was this shy one who stood talking to Boufelja in the hotel kitchen early one morning when she went in. She pretended not to notice him. "I am going to my room to work on the machine for about an hour," she told Boufelja. "You can come then to make up the room," and she turned to go out. As she went through the doorway she glanced at the boy's face. He was looking at her, and he did not turn away when his eyes met hers. "How are you?" she said. Perhaps half an hour later, when she was typing her second letter, she raised her head. The boy was standing on the terrace looking at her through the open door. He squinted, for the wind was strong; behind his head she saw the tops of the palms bending.

"If he wants to watch, let him watch," she said to herself, deciding to pay him no attention. After a while he went away. While Boufelja served her lunch, she questioned him about the boy. "Like an old man," said Boufelja. "Twelve years old but very serious. Like some old, old man." He smiled, then shrugged. "It's the way God wanted him to be."

"Of course," she said, remembering the boy's alert, unhappy face. "A young dog that everyone has kicked," she thought, "but he hasn't given up."

In the days that followed, he came often to the terrace and stood watching her while she typed. Sometimes she waved to him, or said: "Good morning." Without answering he would take a step backward, so that he was out of her range. Then he would continue to stand where he was. His behavior irked her, and one day when he had done this, she quickly got up and went to the door. "What is it?" she asked him, trying to smile as she spoke.

"I didn't do anything," he said, his eyes reproachful.

"I know," she answered. "Why don't you come in?"

The boy looked swiftly around the terrace as if for help; then he bowed his head and stepped inside the door. Here he stood waiting, his head down, looking miserable. From her luggage she brought out a bag of hard candy, and handed him a piece. Then she put a few simple questions to him, and found that his French was much better than she had expected. "Do the other boys know French as well as you?" she asked him.

"*Non, madame,*" he said, shaking his head slowly. "My father used to be a soldier. Soldiers speak good French."

She tried to keep her face from expressing the disapproval she felt, for she despised everything military. "I see," she said with some asperity, turning back to her table and shuffling the papers. "Now I must work," she told him, immediately adding in a warmer voice, "but you come back tomorrow, if you like." He waited an instant, looking at her with unchanged wistfulness. Then slowly he smiled, and laid the candy wrapper, folded into a tiny square, on the corner of her table. "*Au revoir, madame,*" he said, and went out of the door. In the silence she heard the scarcely audible thud of his bare heels on the earth floor of the terrace. "In this cold," she thought. "Poor child! If I ever buy anything for him it will be a pair of sandals."

Each day thereafter, when the sun was high enough to give substance to the still morning air, the boy would come stealthily along the terrace to her door, stand a few seconds, and then say in a lost voice that was all the smaller and more hushed for the great silence outside: "*Bonjour, madame.*" She would tell him to come in, and they would shake hands gravely, he afterward raising the backs of his fingers to his lips, always with the same slow ceremoniousness. She sometimes tried to fathom his countenance as he went through this ritual, to see if by any chance she could detect a shade of mockery there; instead she saw an expression of devotion so convincing that it startled her, and she looked away quickly. She always kept a bit of bread or some biscuits in a drawer of the wardrobe; when she had brought the food out and he was eating it, she would ask him for news about the families in his quarter of the village. For discipline's sake she offered him a piece of candy only every other day. He sat on the floor by the doorway, on a torn old camel blanket, and he watched her constantly, never turning his head away from her.

She wanted to know what he was called, but she was aware of how secretive the inhabitants of the region were about names, seldom giving their true ones to strangers; this was a peculiarity she respected because she knew it had its roots in their own prehistoric religion. So she forbore asking him, sure that the time would come when he trusted her enough to give it of his own volition. And the moment happened one morning unexpectedly, when he had just recounted several legends involving the great Moslem king of long ago, whose name was Solomon. Suddenly he stopped, and forcing himself to gaze steadily at her without blinking, he said: "And my name too is Slimane, the same as the king."

She tried to teach him to read, but he did not seem able to learn. Often just as she felt he was about to connect two loose ends of ideas and perhaps at last make a contact which would enable him to understand the principle, a look of resignation and passivity would appear in his face, and he would willfully cut off the stream of effort from its source, and remain sitting, merely looking at her, shaking his head from side to side to show that it was useless. It was hard not to lose patience with him at such moments.

The following year she decided not to go on with the lessons, and to use Slimane instead as a guide, bearer and companion, a role which she immediately saw was more suited to his nature than that of pupil. He did not mind how far they went or how much equipment he had to carry; on the contrary, to him a long excursion was that much more of an event, and whatever she loaded onto him he bore with the air of one upon whom an honor is conferred. It was probably her happiest season in the desert, that winter of comradeship when together they made the countless pilgrimages down the valley. As the weeks passed the trips grew in scope, and the hour of departure was brought forward until it came directly after she had finished her breakfast. All day long, trudging in the open sun and in the occasional shade of the broken fringe of palms that skirted the river-bed, she conversed passionately with him. Sometimes she could see that he felt like telling her what was in his head, and she let him speak for as long as his enthusiasm lasted, often reviving it at the end with carefully chosen questions. But usually it was she who did the speaking as she walked behind him. Pounding the stony ground with her steel-tipped stick each time her right foot went down, she told him in great detail the story of the life of Hitler, showing why he was hated by the Christians. This she thought necessary since Slimane had been under a different impression, and indeed had imagined that the Europeans thought as highly of the vanished leader as did he and the rest of the people in the village. She talked a good deal about Switzerland, casually stressing the cleanliness, honesty and good health of her countrymen in short parables of daily life. She told him about Jesus, Martin Luther and Garibaldi, taking care to keep Jesus distinct from the Moslem prophet Sidna Aissa, since even for the sake of argument she could not agree for an instant with the Islamic doctrine according to which the Savior was a Moslem. Slimane's attitude of respect bordering on adoration with regard to her never altered unless she inadvertently tangled with the subject of Islam; then, no matter what she said (for at that point it seemed that automatically he was no longer within hearing) he would shake his head interminably and cry: "No, no, no, no! Nazarenes know nothing about Islam. Don't talk, madame, I beg you, because you don't know what you're saying. No, no, no!"

Long ago she had kept the initial promise to herself that she would buy him sandals; this purchase had been followed by others. At fairly regular intervals she had taken him to Benaissa's store to buy a shirt, a pair of baggy black cotton trousers of the kind worn by the Chaamba camel-drivers, and ultimately a new white burnoose, despite the fact that she knew the entire village would discuss the giving of so valuable an object. She also knew that it was only the frequent bestowing of such gifts that kept Slimane's father from forbidding him to spend his time with her. Even so, according to reports brought by Slimane, he sometimes objected. But Slimane himself, she was sure, wanted nothing, expected nothing.

It was each year when March was drawing to a close that the days began to be painfully hot and even the nights grew breathless; then, although it always required a strenuous effort of the will to make herself take the step which would bring about renewed contact with the outside world, she would devote two or three days to washing her clothing and preparing for the journey. When the week set for her departure had come, she went over to the fort and put in a call to the café at Kerzaz, asking the proprietor to tell the driver of the next northbound truck to take the detour that would enable her to catch him at a point only about three kilometers from the village.

She and Slimane had come back to the hotel on the afternoon of their last excursion down the valley; Fräulein Windling stood on the terrace looking out at the orange mountains of sand behind the fort. Slimane had taken the packs into the room and put them down. She turned and said: "Bring the big tin box." When he had pulled it out from under the bed he carried it to her, dusting it off with the sleeve of his shirt, and she led the way up the stairs to the roof. They sat down on the blanket; the glow of the vanished sun's furnace heated their faces. A few flies still hovered, now and then attacking their necks. Slimane handed her the biscuit tin and she gave him a fistful of chocolate-covered cakes. "So many all at once?"

"Yes," she said. "You know I'm going home in four days."

He looked down at the blanket a moment before replying. "I know," he murmured. He was silent again. Then he cried out aggrievedly: "Boufelja says it's hot here in the summer. It's not hot! In our house it's cool. It's like the oasis where the big pool is. You would never be hot there."

"I have to earn money. You know that. I want to come back next year."

He said sadly: "Next year, madame! Only Moulana knows how next year will be."

Some camels growled as they rolled in the sand at the foot of the fort; the light was receding swiftly. "Eat your biscuits," she told him, and she ate one herself. "Next year we'll go to Abadla with the caid, *incha'Allah.*"

He sighed deeply. "Ah, madame!" he said. She noted, at first with a pang of sympathy and then, reconsidering, with disapproval, the anguish that lent his voice its unaccustomed intensity. It was the quality she least liked in him, this faintly theatrical self-pity. "Next year you'll be a man," she told him firmly. Her voice grew less sure, assumed a hopeful tone. "You'll remember all the things we talked about?"

She sent him a postcard from Marseille, and showed her classes photographs they had taken of one another, and of the caid. The children were impressed by the caid's voluminous turban. "Is he a Bedouin?" asked one.

When she left the embassy office she knew that this was the last year she would be returning to the desert. There was not only the official's clearly expressed unfriendliness and suspicion: for the first time he had made her answer a list of questions which she found alarming. He wanted to know what subjects she taught in the Freiluftschüle, whether she had ever been a journalist, and exactly where she proposed to be each day after arriving in the Sahara. She had almost retorted: I go where I feel like going. I don't make plans. But she had merely named the oasis. She knew that Frenchmen had no respect for elderly Swiss ladies who wore woolen stockings; this simply made them more contemptible in her eyes. However, it was they who controlled the Sahara.

The day the ship put into the African port it was raining. She knew the gray terraced ramps of the city were there in the gloom ahead, but they were invisible. The ragged European garments of the dock workers were soaked with rain. Later, the whole rain-sodden city struck her as grim, and the people passing along the streets looked unhappy. The change, even from the preceding year, was enormous; it made her sad to sit in the big, cold café where she went for coffee after dinner, and so she returned to her hotel and slept. The next day she got on the train for Perrégaux. The rain fell most of the day. In Perrégaux she took a room in a hotel near the station, and stayed in it, listening to the rain rattle down the gutter by her window. "This place would be a convenient model for Hell," she wrote to a friend in Basel before going to sleep that night. "A full-blown example of the social degeneracy achieved by forced cultural hybridism. Populace debased and made hostile by generations of merciless exploitation. I take the southbound narrow-gauge train tomorrow morning for a happier land, and trust that my friend the sun will appear at some point during the day. *Seien Sie herzlich gegrüsst von Ihrer Maria.*"

As the train crawled southward, up over the high plateau land, the clouds were left behind and the sun took charge of the countryside. Fräulein Windling sat attentively by the smeared window, enveloped in an increasing sadness. As long as it had been raining, she had imagined the rain as the cause of her depression: the gray cloud light gave an unaccustomed meaning to the landscape by altering forms and distances. Now she understood that the more familiar and recognizable the contours of the desert were to become, the more conscious she would be of having no reason to be in it, because it was her last visit.

Two days later, when the truck stopped to let her out, Boufelja stood in the sun beside the boulders waving; one of the men of the village was with him to help carry the luggage. Once the truck had gone and its cloud of yellow dust had fled across the hammada, the silence was there; it seemed that no sound could be louder than the crunch of their shoes on the ground.

"How is Slimane?" she asked. Boufelja was noncommittal. "He's all

right," he said. "They say he tried to run away. But he didn't get very far."
The report might be true, or it might be false; in any case she determined
not to allude to it unless Slimane himself mentioned it first.

She felt an absurd relief when they came to the edge of the cliffs and she
saw the village across the valley. Not until she had made the rounds of the
houses where her friends lived, discussed their troubles with them and left
some pills here and some candy there, was she convinced that no important
change had come to the oasis during her absence. She went to the house of
Slimane's parents: he was not there. "Tell him to come and see me," she said
to his father as she left the house.

On the third morning after her arrival Slimane appeared, and stood there
in the doorway smiling. Once she had greeted him and made him sit down
and have coffee with her, she plied him with questions about life in the
village while she had been in Europe. Some of his friends had gone to
become patriots, he said, and they were killing the French like flies. Her
heart sank, but she said nothing. As she watched him smiling she was able
to exult in the reflection that Slimane had been reachable, after all; she had
proved that it was possible to make true friends of the younger people. But
even while she was saying, "How happy I am to see you, Slimane," she
remembered that their time together was now limited, and an expression of
pain passed over her face as she finished the phrase. "I shall not say a word to
him about it," she decided. If he, at least, still had the illusion of unbounded
time lying ahead, he would somehow retain his aura of purity and innocence, and she would feel less anguish during the time they spent together.

One day they went down the valley to see the caid, and discussed the
long-planned trip to Abadla. Another day they started out at dawn to visit
the tomb of Moulay Ali ben Said, where there was a spring of hot water. It
was a tiny spot of oasis at the edge of a ridge of high dunes; perhaps fifty
palms were there around the decayed shrine. In the shade of the rocks below
the walls there was a ruined cistern into which the steaming water dribbled.
They spread blankets on the sand nearby, at the foot of a small tamarisk,
and took out their lunch. Before starting to eat, they drank handfuls of the
water, which Slimane said was famed for its holiness. The palms rattled and
hissed in the wind overhead.

"Allah has sent us the wind to make us cool while we eat," Slimane said
when he had finished his bread and dates.

"The wind has always been here," she answered carelessly, "and it
always will be here."

He sat up straight. "No, no!" he cried. "When Sidna Aissa has returned
for forty days there will be no more Moslems and the world will end.
Everything, the sky and the sun and the moon. And the wind too. Everything." He looked at her with an expression of such satisfaction that she felt

one of her occasional surges of anger against him.

"I see," she said. "Stand over by the spring a minute. I want to take your picture." She had never understood why it was that the Moslems had conceded Jesus even this Pyrrhic victory, the coda to all creation: its inconsistency embarrassed her. Across the decayed tank she watched Slimane assume the traditional stiff attitude of a person about to be photographed, and an idea came into her head. For Christmas Eve, which would come within two weeks, she would make a crèche. She would invite Slimane to eat with her by the fireplace, and when midnight came she would take him in to see it.

She finished photographing Slimane; they gathered up the equipment and set out against the hot afternoon wind for the village. The sand sometimes swept by, stinging their faces with its invisible fringe. Fräulein Windling led the way this time, and they walked fast. The image of the crèche, illumined by candles, occurred to her several times on the way back over the rocky erg; it made her feel inexpressibly sad, for she could not help connecting it with the fact that everything was ending. They came to the point north of the village where the empty erg was cut across by the wandering river valley. As they climbed slowly upward over the fine sand, she found herself whispering: "It's the right thing to do." "*Right* is not the word," she thought, without being able to find a better one. She was going to make a crèche because she loved Christmas and wanted to share it with Slimane. They reached the hotel shortly after sunset, and she sent Slimane home in order to sit and plan her project on paper.

It was only when she began actually to put the crèche together that she realized how much work it was going to be. Early the next morning she asked Boufelja to find her an old wooden crate. Before she had been busy even a half-hour, she heard Slimane talking in the kitchen. Quickly she pushed everything under the bed and went out onto the terrace.

"Slimane," she said. "I'm very busy. Come in the afternoon." And that afternoon she told him that since she was going to be working every morning until after the day of the Christ Child, they would not be making any more long trips during that time. He received the information glumly. "I know," he said. "You are getting ready for the holy day. I understand."

"When the holy day comes, we will have a feast," she assured him.

"If Allah wills."

"I'm sorry," she said, smiling.

He shrugged. "Good-by," he told her.

Afternoons they still walked in the oasis or had tea on the roof, but her mornings she spent in her room sewing, hammering and sculpting. Once she had the platform constructed, she had to model the figures. She carried up a great mass of wet clay from the river to her room. It was two days before she managed to make a Virgin whose form pleased her. From an old strip of muslin she fashioned a convincing tent to house the Mother and the Child in its nest of tiny white chicken feathers. Shredded tamarisk needles made a fine carpet for the interior of the tent. Outside she poured sand, and then pushed the clay camels' long legs deep into it; one animal walked behind the other over the dune, and a Wise Man sat straight on top of each, his white *djellaba* falling in long pointed folds to either side of the camel's flanks. The Wise Men would come carrying sacks of almonds and very small liqueur chocolates wrapped in colored tinfoil. When she had the crèche finished, she put it on the floor in the middle of the room and piled tangerines and dates in front of it. With a row of candles burning behind it, and one candle on each side in front, it would look like a Moslem religious chromolithograph. She hoped the scene would be recognizable to Slimane; he might then be more easily persuaded of its poetic truth. She wanted only to suggest to him that the god with whom he was on such intimate terms was the god worshipped by the Nazarenes. It was not an idea she would ever try to express in words.

An additional surprise for the evening would be the new flash-bulb attachment to her camera, which Slimane had not yet seen. She intended to take a good many pictures of the crèche and of Slimane looking at it; these she would enlarge to show her pupils. She went and bought a new turban for Slimane; he had been wearing none for more than a year now. This was a man's turban, and very fine: ten meters of the softest Egyptian cotton.

The day before Christmas she overslept, duped by the heavy sky. Each winter the oasis had a few dark days; they were rare, but this was one of them. While she still lay there in bed, she heard the roar of the wind, and when she got up to look out the window she found no world outside—only a dim rose-gray fog that hid everything. The swirling sand sprayed ceaselessly against the glass; it had formed in long drifts on the floor of the terrace. When she went for breakfast, she wore her burnoose with the hood up around her face. The blast of the wind as she stepped out onto the terrace struck her with the impact of a solid object, and the sand gritted on the concrete floor under her shoes. In the dining-room Boufelja had bolted the shutters; he greeted her enthusiastically from the gloom inside, glad of her presence.

"A very bad day for your festival, alas, mademoiselle!" he observed as he set her coffee pot on the table.

"Tomorrow's the festival," she said. "It begins tonight."

"I know. I know." He was impatient with Nazarene feasts because the hours of their beginnings and ends were observed in so slipshod a manner. Moslem feasts began precisely, either at sundown or an hour before sunup, or when the new moon was first visible in the western sky at twilight. But the Nazarenes began their feasts whenever they felt like it.

She spent the morning in her room writing letters. By noon the air outside was darker with still more sand; the wind shook the hotel atop its rock as if it would hurl it over the tips of the palms below into the river-bed. Several times she rose and went to the window to stare out at the pink emptiness beyond the terrace. Storms made her happy, although she wished this one could have come after Christmas. She had imagined a pure desert night—cold, alive with stars, and the dogs yapping from the oasis. It might yet be that; there was still time, she thought, as she slipped her burnoose over her head to go in to lunch.

With the wind, the fireplace was an unsure blessing: besides the heat it gave, it provided the only light in the dining-room, but the smoke that belched from it burned her eyes and throat. The shutters at the windows rattled and pounded, covering the noise of the wind itself.

She got out of the dining-room as soon as she had finished eating, and hurried back to her room to sit through the slowly darkening afternoon, as she continued with her letter-writing and waited for the total extinction of daylight, Slimane was coming at eight. There would be enough time to carry everything into the dining-room before that, and to set the crèche up in the dark unused wing into which Boufelja was unlikely to go. But when she came to do it, she found that the wind's force was even greater than she had imagined. Again and again she made the trip between her room and the dining-room, carrying each object carefully wrapped in her burnoose. Each time she passed in front of the kitchen door she expected Boufelja to open it and discover her. She did not want him there when she showed the crèche to Slimane; he could see it tomorrow at breakfast.

Protected by the noise of the gale she succeeded in transporting all the parts to the far dark corner of the dining-room without alerting Boufelja. Long before dinner time the crèche was in readiness, awaiting only the lighting of the candles to be brought alive. She left a box of matches on the table beside it, and hurried back to her room to arrange her hair and change her clothing. The sand had sifted through her garments and was now everywhere; it showered from her underwear and stuck like sugar to her skin. Her watch showed a few minutes after eight when she went out.

Only one place had been laid at table. She waited, while the blinds chattered and banged, until Boufelja appeared carrying the soup tureen. "What a bad night," he said.

"You forgot to prepare for Slimane," she told him. But he was not paying attention. "He's stupid!" he exclaimed, beginning to ladle out the soup.

"Wait!" she cried. "Slimane's coming. I mustn't eat until he comes."

Still Boufelja misunderstood. "He wanted to come into the dining-room," he said. "And he knows it's forbidden at dinner time."

"But I invited him!" She looked at the lone soup plate on the table. "Tell him to come in, and set another place."

Boufelja was silent. He put the ladle back into the tureen. "Where is he?" she demanded, and without waiting for him to reply she went on. "Didn't I tell you he was going to have dinner with me tonight?" For suddenly she suspected that in her desire for secrecy she might indeed have neglected to mention the invitation to Boufelja.

"You didn't say anything," he told her. "I didn't know. I sent him home. But he'll be back after dinner."

"Oh, Boufelja!" she cried. "You know Slimane never lies."

He looked down at her with reproach on his face. "I didn't know anything about mademoiselle's plans," he said aggrievedly. This made her think for a swift instant that he had discovered the crèche, but she decided that if he had he would have spoken of it.

"Yes, yes, I know. I should have told you. It's my fault."

"That's true, mademoiselle," he said. And he served the remaining courses observing a dignified silence which she, still feeling some displeasure with him, did not urge him to break. Only at the end of the meal, when she had pushed back her chair from the table and sat studying the pattern of the flames in the fireplace, did he decide to speak. "Mademoiselle will take coffee?"

"I do want some," she said, trying to bring a note of enthusiasm into her voice. "*Bien*," murmured Boufelja, and he left her alone in the room. When he returned carrying the coffee, Slimane was with him, and they were laughing, she noted, quite as though there had been no misunderstanding about dinner. Slimane stood by the door an instant, stamping his feet and shaking the sand from his burnoose. As he came forward to take her hand, she cried: "Oh, Slimane, it's my fault! I forgot to tell Boufelja. It's terrible!"

"There is no fault, madame," he said gravely. "This is a festival."

"Yes, this is a festival," she echoed. "And the wind's still blowing. Listen!"

Slimane would not take coffee, but Boufelja, ceding to her pressure, let her pour him out a cup, which he drank standing by the fireplace. She suspected him of being secretly pleased that Slimane had not managed to eat with her. When he had finished his coffee, he wished them good-night and went off to bed in his little room next to the kitchen.

They sat a while watching the fire, without talking. The wind rushed past in the emptiness outside, the blinds hammered. Fräulein Windling was content. Even if the first part of the celebration had gone wrong, the rest of the evening could still be pleasant.

She waited until she was sure that Boufelja had really gone to bed, and then she reached into her bag and brought out a small plastic sack full of chocolate creams, which she placed on the table.

"Eat," she said carelessly, and she took a piece of candy herself. With some hesitation Slimane put out his hand to take the sack. When he had a chocolate in his mouth, she began to speak. She intended to tell him the story of the Nativity, a subject she already had touched upon many times during their excursions, but only in passing. This time she felt she should tell him the entire tale. She expected him to interrupt when he discovered that it was a religious story, but he merely kept his noncommittal eyes on her and chewed mechanically, showing that he followed her by occasionally nodding his head. She became engrossed in what she was saying, and began to use her arms in wide gestures. Slimane reached for another chocolate and went on listening.

She talked for an hour or more, aware as from a distance of her own eloquence. When she told him about Bethlehem she was really describing Slimane's own village, and the house of Joseph and Mary was the house down in the *ksar* where Slimane had been born. The night sky arched above the Oued Zousfana and its stars glared down upon the cold hammada. Across the erg on their camels came the Wise Men in their burnooses and turbans, pausing at the crest of the last great dune to look ahead at the valley where the dark village lay. When she had finished, she blew her nose.

Slimane appeared to be in a state bordering on trance. She glanced at him, expected him to speak, but as he did not, she looked more closely at him. His eyes had an obsessed, vacant expression, and although they were still fixed on her face, she would have said that he was seeing something much farther away than she. She sighed, not wanting to make the decision to rouse him. The possibility she would have liked to entertain, had she not been so conscious of its unlikelihood, was that the boy somehow had been captivated by the poetic truth of the story, and was reviewing it in his imagination. "Certainly it could not be the case," she decided; it was more likely that he had ceased some time back to listen to her words, and was merely sitting there, only vaguely aware that she had come to the end of her story.

Then he spoke. "You're right. He was the King of Men."

Fräulein Windling caught her breath and leaned forward, but he went on. "And later Satan sent a snake with two heads. And Jesus killed it. Satan was angry with Him. He said: 'Why did you kill my friend? Did it hurt you, perhaps?' And Jesus said: 'I knew where it came from.' And Satan put on a black burnoose. That's true," he added, as he saw the expression of what he took to be simple disbelief on her face.

She sat up very straight and said: "Slimane, what are you talking about? There are no such stories about Jesus. Nor about Sidna Aissa either." She was not sure of the accuracy of this last statement; it was possible, she supposed, that such legends did exist among these people. "You know those are just stories that have nothing to do with the truth."

He did not hear her because he had already begun to talk. "I'm not speaking of Sidna Aissa," he said firmly. "He was a Moslem prophet. I'm talking about Jesus, the prophet of the Nazarenes. Everyone knows that Satan sent Him a snake with two heads."

She listened to the wind for an instant. "Ah," she said, and took another chocolate; she did not intend to carry the argument further. Soon she dug into her bag again and pulled out the turban, wrapped in red and white tissue paper.

"A present for you," she said, holding it out to him. He seized it mechanically, placed it on his lap and remained staring down at it. "Aren't you going to open it?" she demanded.

He nodded his head twice and tore open the paper. When he saw the pile of white cotton he smiled. Seeing his face at last come to life, she jumped up. "Let's put it on you!" she exclaimed. He gave her one end, which she pulled taut by walking all the way to the door. Then with his hand holding the other end to his forehead, he turned slowly round and round, going toward her all the time, arranging the form of the turban as it wound itself about his head. "Magnificent!" she cried. He went over to the row of black windows to look at himself.

"Can you see?" she asked.

"Yes, I can see the sides of it," he told her. "It's very beautiful."

She walked back toward the center of the room. "I'd like to take your picture, Slimane," she said, seeing an immediate look of puzzlement appear in his face. "Would you do me a favor? Go to my room and get the camera."

"At night? You can take a picture at night?"

She nodded, smiling mysteriously. "And bring me the yellow box on the bed."

Keeping the turban on his head, he got into his burnoose, took her flashlight and went out, letting the wind slam the door. She hoped the sound had not wakened Boufelja; for an instant she listened while there was no sound but the roar of air rushing through the corridor outside. Then she ran to the dark wing of the room and struck a match. Quickly she lighted all the candles around the crèche, straightened a camel in the sand, and walked back around the corner to the fireplace. She would not have thought the candles could give so much light. The other end of the room was now brighter than the end where she stood. In a moment the door burst open and Slimane came back in, carrying the camera slung over his shoulder. He put it down carefully on the table. "There was no yellow box on the bed," he told her. Then his glance caught the further walls flickering with the unfamiliar light, and he began to walk toward the center of the room. She saw that this was the moment. "Come," she said, taking his arm and pulling him gently around the corner to where the crèche was finally visible, bright with its multiple shuddering points of light. Slimane said nothing; he stopped walking and stood completely still. After a moment of silence, she plucked tentatively at his arm. "Come and see," she urged him. They continued to walk toward the crèche; as they came up to it she had the impression that if she had not been there he would have reached out his hand and touched it, perhaps would have lifted the tiny gold-clad infant Jesus out of His bed of feathers. But he stood quietly, looking at it. Finally he said: "You brought all that from Switzerland?"

"Of course not!" It was a little disappointing that he should not have recognized the presence of the desert in the picture, should not have sensed that the thing was of his place, and not an importation. "I made it all here," she said. She waited an instant. "Do you like it?"

"Ah, yes," he said with feeling. "It's beautiful. I thought it came from Switzerland."

To be certain that he understood the subject-matter, she began to identify the figures one by one, her voice taking on such an unaccustomed inflection of respect that he glanced up at her once in surprise. It was almost as if she too were seeing it for the first time. "And the Wise Men are coming down out of the erg to see the child."

"Why did you put all those almonds there?" asked Slimane, touching some with his forefinger.

"They're gifts for the little Jesus."

"But what are you going to do with them?" he pursued.

"Eat them, probably, later," she said shortly. "Take one if you like. You say there was no yellow box on the bed?" She wanted to take the photographs while the candles were still of equal height.

"There was nothing but a sweater and some papers, madame."

She left him there by the crèche, crossed the room and put on her burnoose. The darkness in the corridor was complete; there was no sign that Boufelja had awakened. She knew her room was in great disorder, and she played the beam of the flashlight around the floor before entering. In the welter of displaced things that strewed the little room there seemed small chance of finding anything. The feeble ray illumined one by one the meaningless forms made by the piling of disparate objects one on the other; the light moved over the floor, along the bed, behind the flimsy curtain of the armoire. Suddenly she stopped and turned the beam under the bed. The box was in front of her face; she had put it with the crèche.

"I mustn't fall," she thought, running along the corridor. She forced herself to slow her pace to a walk, entered the dining-room and shut the door after her carefully. Slimane was on his knees in the middle of the room, a small object of some sort in his hand. She noted with relief that he was amusing himself. "I'm sorry it took me so long," she exclaimed. "I'd forgotten where I'd put it." She was pulling her burnoose off over her head; now she hung it on a nail by the fireplace, and taking up the camera and the yellow box, she walked over to join him.

Perhaps a faint glimmer of guilt in his expression as he glanced up made her eyes stray along the floor toward another object lying nearby, similar to the one he held in his hand. It was one of the Wise Men, severed at the hips from his mount. The Wise Man in Slimane's hand was intact, but the camel had lost its head and most of its neck.

"Slimane! What are you doing?" she cried with undisguised anger. "What have you done to the crèche?" She advanced around the corner and looked in its direction. There was not really much more than a row of candles and a pile of sand that had been strewn with tangerine peel and date stones; here and there a carefully folded square of lavender or pink tinfoil had been planted in the sand. All three of the Wise Men had been enlisted in Slimane's battle on the floor, the tent ravaged in the campaign to extricate the almonds piled inside, and the treasure sacks looted of their chocolate liqueurs. There was no sign anywhere of the infant Jesus or his gold-lamé garment. She felt tears come into her eyes. Then she laughed shortly, and said: "Well, it's finished. Yes?"

"Yes, madame," he said calmly. "Are you going to make the photograph now?" He got to his feet and laid the broken camel on the platform in the sand with the other debris.

Fräulein Windling spoke evenly. "I wanted to take a picture of the crèche."

He waited an instant, as if he were listening to a distant sound. Then he said: "Should I put on my burnoose?"

"No." She began to take out the flash-bulb attachment. When she had it ready, she took the picture before he had time to strike a pose. She saw his astonishment at the sudden bright light prolong itself into surprise that the thing was already done, and then become resentment at having been caught off his guard; but pretending to have seen nothing, she went on snapping covers shut. He watched her as she gathered up her things. "Is it finished?" he said, disappointed. "Yes," she replied. "It will be a very good picture."

"*Incha' Allah.*"

She did not echo his piety. "I hope you've enjoyed the festival," she told him.

Slimane smiled widely. "Ah yes, madame. Very much. Thank you."

She let him out into the camel-square and turned the lock in the door. Quickly she went back into her room, wishing it were a clear night like other nights, when she could stand out on the terrace and look at the dunes and stars, or sit on the roof and hear the dogs, for in spite of the hour she was not sleepy. She cleared her bed of all the things that lay on top of it, and got in, certain that she was going to lie awake for a long time. For it had shaken her, the chaos Slimane had made in those few minutes of her absence. Across the seasons of their friendship she had come to think of him as being very nearly like herself, even though she knew he had not been that way when she first had met him. Now she saw the dangerous vanity at the core of that fantasy: she had assumed that somehow his association with her had automatically been for his ultimate good, that inevitably he had been undergoing a process of improvement as a result of knowing her. In her desire to see him change, she had begun to forget what Slimane was really like. "I shall never understand him," she thought helplessly, sure that just because she felt so close to him she would never be able to observe him dispassionately.

"This is the desert," she told herself. Here food is not an adornment; it is meant to be eaten. She had spread out food and he had eaten it. Any argument which attached blame to that could only be false. And so she lay there accusing herself. "It has been too much head and high ideals," she reflected, "and not enought heart." Finally she traveled on the sound of the wind into sleep.

At dawn when she awoke she saw that the day was going to be another dark one. The wind had dropped. She got up and shut the window. The early morning sky was heavy with clouds. She sank back into bed and fell asleep. It was later than usual when she rose, dressed, and went into the dining-room. Boufelja's face was strangely expressionless as he wished her good morning. She supposed it was the memory of last night's misunderstanding, still with him—or possibly he was annoyed at having had to clean up the remains of the crèche. Once she had sat down and spread her napkin across her lap, he unbent sufficiently to say to her: "Happy festival."

"Thank you. Tell me, Boufelja," she went on, changing her inflection. "When you brought Slimane back in after dinner last night, do you know where he had been? Did he tell you?"

"He's a stupid boy," said Boufelja. "I told him to go home and eat and come back later. You think he did that? Never. He walked the whole time up and down in the courtyard here, outside the kitchen door, in the dark."

"I understand!" exclaimed Fräulein Windling triumphantly. "So he had no dinner at all."

"I had nothing to give him," he began, on the defensive.

"Of course not," she said sternly. "He should have gone home and eaten."

"Ah, you see?" grinned Boufleja. "That's what I told him to do."

In her mind she watched the whole story being enacted: Slimane aloofly informing his father that he would be eating at the hotel with the Swiss lady, the old man doubtless making some scornful reference to her, and Slimane going out. Unthinkable, once he had been refused admittance to the dining-room, for him to go back and face the family's ridicule. "Poor boy," she murmured.

"The commandant wants to see you," said Boufelja, making one of his abrupt conversational changes. She was surprised, since from one year to the next the captain never gave any sign of being aware of her existence; the hotel and the fort were like two separate countries. "Perhaps for the festival," Boufelja suggested, his face a mask. "Perhaps," she said uneasily.

When she had finished her breakfast, she walked across to the gates of the fort. The sentry seemed to be expecting her. One of the two young French soldiers was in the compound painting a chair. He greeted her, saying that the captain was in his office. She went up the long flight of stairs and paused an instant at the top, looking down at the valley in the unaccustomed gray light, noting how totally different it looked from its usual self, on this dim day.

A voice from inside called out: *"Entrez, s'il vous plait!"* She opened the door and stepped in. The captain sat behind his desk; she had the unwelcome sensation of having played this same scene on another occasion, in another place. And she was suddenly convinced that she knew what he was going to say. She seized the back of the empty chair facing his desk. "Sit down, Mademoiselle Windling," he said, rising halfway out of his seat, waving his arm, and sitting again quickly.

There were several topographical maps on the wall behind him, marked with lavender and green chalk. The captain looked at his desk and then at her, and said in a clear voice: "It is an unfortunate stroke of chance that I should have to call you here on this holiday." Fräulein Windling sat down in the chair; leaning forward, she seemed about to rest her elbow on his desk, but instead crossed her legs and folded her arms tight. "Yes?" she said, tense, waiting for the message. It came immediately, for which she was conscious, even then, of being grateful to him. He told her simply that the entire area had been closed to civilians; this order applied to French nationals as well as to foreigners, so she must not feel discriminated against. The last was said with a wry attempt at a smile. "This means that you will have to take tomorrow morning's truck," he continued. "The driver has already been advised of your journey. Perhaps another year, when the disturbances are over . . . ." ("Why does he say that?" she thought, "when he knows it's the end, and the time of friendship is finished?") He rose and extended his hand.

She could not remember going out of the room and down the long stairway into the compound, but now she was standing outside the sentry gate beside the wall of the fort, with her hand on her forehead. "Already," she thought. "It came so soon." And it occurred to her that she was not going to be given the time to make amends to Slimane, so that it was really true she was never going to understand him. She walked up to the parapet to look down at the edge of the oasis for a moment, and then went back to her room to start packing. All day long she worked in her room, pulling out boxes, forcing herself to be aware only of the decisions she was making as to what was to be taken and what was to be left behind once and for all.

At lunchtime Boufelja hovered near her chair. "Ah, mademoiselle, how many years we have been together, and now it is finished!" "Yes," she thought, but there was nothing to do about it. His lamentations made her nervous and she was short with him. Then she felt guilt-stricken and said slowly, looking directly at him: "I am very sad, Boufelja." He sighed "Ay, mademoiselle, I know!"

By nightfall the pall of clouds had been blown away across the desert, and the western sky was partly clear. Fräulein Windling had finished all her packing. She went out onto the terrace, saw the dunes pink and glowing, and climbed the steps to the roof to look at the sunset. Great skeins of fiery storm-cloud streaked the sky. Mechanically she let her gaze follow the meanders of the river valley as it lost itself in the darkening hammada to the south. "It is in the past," she reminded herself; this was already the new era. The desert out there looked the same as it always had looked. But the sky, ragged, red and black, was like a handbill that had just been posted above it, announcing the arrival of war.

It was a betrayal, she was thinking, going back down the steep stairs, running her hand along the familiar rough mud wall to steady herself, and the French of course were the culprits. But beyond that she had the irrational and disagreeable conviction that the countryside itself had connived in the betrayal, that it was waiting to be transformed by the struggle. She went into her room and lit the small oil lamp; sitting down, she held her hands over it to warm them. At some point there had been a change: the people no longer wanted to go on living in the world they knew. The pressure of the past had become too great, and its shell had broken.

In the afternoon she had sent Boufelja to tell Slimane the news, and to ask him to be at the hotel at daybreak. During dinner she discussed only the details of departure and travel; when Boufelja tried to pull the talk in emotional directions, she did not reply. His commiseration was intolerable; she was not used to giving voice to her despair. When she got to her room she went directly to bed. The dogs barked half the night.

It was cold in the morning. Her hands ached as she gathered up the wet objects from around the washbowl on the table, and somehow she drove a sliver deep under the nail of her thumb. She picked some of it out with a needle, but the greater part remained. Before breakfast she stepped outside.

Standing in the waste-land between the hotel and the fort, she looked down at the countryside's innocent face. The padlocked gasoline pump, triumphant in fresh red and orange paint, caught the pure early sunlight. For a moment it seemed the only living thing in the landscape. She turned around. Above the dark irregular mass of palm trees rose the terraced village, calm under its morning veil of woodsmoke. She shut her eyes for an instant, and then went into the hotel.

She could feel herself sitting stiffly in her chair while she drank her coffee, and she knew she was being distant and formal with Boufelja, but it was the only way she could be certain of being able to keep going. Once he came to tell her that Slimane had arrived bringing the donkey and its master for her luggage. She thanked him and set down her coffee cup. "More?" said Boufelja. "No," she answered. "Drink another, mademoiselle," he urged her. "It's good on a cold morning." He poured it out and she drank part of it. There was a knocking at the gate. One of the young soldiers had been sent with a jeep to carry her out to the truck-stop on the trail.

"I can't!" she cried, thinking of Slimane and the donkey. The young soldier made it clear that he was not making an offer, but giving an order. Slimane stood beside the donkey outside the gate. While she began to speak with him the soldier shouted: "Does he want to come, the *gosse*? He can come too, if he likes." Slimane ran to get the luggage and Fräulein Windling rushed inside to settle her bill. "Don't hurry," the soldier called after her. "There's plenty of time."

Boufelja stood in the kitchen doorway. Now for the first time it occurred to her to wonder what was going to become of him. With the hotel shut he would have no work. When she had settled her account and given him a tip which was much larger than she could afford, she took both his hands in hers and said: "*Mon cher* Boufelja, we shall see one another very soon."

"Ah, yes," he cried, trying to smile. "Very soon, mademoiselle."

She gave the donkey-driver some money, and got into the jeep beside the soldier. Slimane had finished bringing out the luggage and stood behind the jeep, kicking the tires. "Have you got everything?" she called to him. "Everything?" She would have liked to see for herself, but she was loath to go back into the room. Boufelja had disappeared; now he came hurrying out, breathless, carrying a pile of old magazines. "It's all right," she said. "No, no! I don't want them." The jeep was already moving ahead down the hill. In what seemed to her an unreasonably short time they had reached the boulders. When Fräulein Windling tried to lift out her briefcase the pain of the sliver under her nail made the tears start to her eyes, and she let go with a cry. Slimane glanced at her, surprised. "I hurt my hand," she explained. "It's nothing."

The bags had been piled in the shade. Sitting on a rock near the jeep, the soldier faced Fräulein Windling; from time to time he scanned the horizon behind her for a sign of the truck. Slimane examined the jeep from all sides; eventually he came to sit nearby. They did not say very much to one another. She was not sure whether it was because of the soldier with them, or because her thumb ached so constantly, but she sat quietly waiting, not wanting to talk.

It was a long time before the far-off motor made itself heard. When the truck was still no more than a puff of dust between sky and earth, the soldier was on his feet watching; an instant later Slimane jumped up. "It is coming, madame," he said. Then he bent over, putting his face very close to hers. "I want to go with you to Colomb-Bechar," he whispered. When she did not respond, because she was seeing the whole story of their friendship unrolled before her, from the its end back to its beginning, he said louder, with great urgency: "Please, madame."

Fräulein Windling hesitated only an instant. She raised her head and looked carefully at the smooth brown face that was so near. "Of course, Slimane," she said. It was clear that he had not expected to hear this; his delight was infectious, and she smiled as she watched him run to the pile of bags and begin carrying them out into the sunlight to align them in the dust beside the edge of the trail.

Later, when they were rattling along the hammada, she in front beside the driver and Slimane squatting in the back with a dozen men and a sheep, she considered her irresponsible action in allowing him to make this absurd trip with her all the way to Colomb-Bechar. Still, she knew she wanted to give this ending to their story. A few times she turned partially around in her seat to glance at him through the dirty glass. He sat there in the smoke and dust, laughing like the others, with the hood of his burnoose hiding most of his face.

It had been raining in Colomb-Bechar; the streets were great puddles to reflect the clouded sky. At the garage they found a surly Negro boy to help them carry the luggage to the railway station. Her thumb hurt a little less.

"It's a cold town," Slimane said to her as they went down the main street. At the station they checked the bags and then went outside to stand and watch a car being unloaded from an open freight train: the roof of the automobile was still white with snow from the high steppes. The day was dark, and the wind rippled the surface of the water in the flooded empty lots. Fräulein Windling's train would not be leaving until late in the afternoon. They went to a restaurant and ate a long lunch.

"You really will go back home tomorrow?" she asked him anxiously at one point, while they were having fruit. "You know we have done a very wicked thing to your father and mother. They will never forgive me." A curtain seemed to draw across Slimane's face. "It doesn't matter," he said shortly.

After lunch they walked in the public garden and looked at the eagles in their cages. A fine rain had begun to be carried on the wind. The mud of the paths grew deeper. They went back to the center of the town and sat down on the terrace of a large, shabby modern café. The table at the end was partly sheltered from the wet wind; they faced an empty lot strewn with refuse. Nearby, spread out like the bones of a camel fallen on the trail, were the rusted remains of an ancient bus. A long, newly-felled date palm lay diagonally across the greater part of the lot. Fräulein Windling turned to look at the wet orange fiber of the stump, and felt an idle pity for the tree. "I'm going to have a Coca-Cola," she declared. Slimane said he, too, would like one.

They sat there a long time. The fine rain slanted through the air outside the arcades and hit the ground silently. She had expected to be approached by beggars, but none arrived, and now that the time had come to leave the café and go to the station she was thankful to see that the day had passed so easily. She opened her pocket-book, took out three thousand francs, and handed them to Slimane, saying: "This will be enough for everything. But you must buy your ticket back home today. When you leave the railway station. Be very careful of it."

Slimane put the money inside his garments, rearranged his burnoose, and thanked her. "You understand, Slimane," she said, detaining him with her hand, for he seemed about to rise from the table. "I'm not giving you any money now, because I need what I have for my journey. But when I get to Switzerland I shall send you a little, now and then. Not much. A little."

His face was swept by panic; she was perplexed.

"You haven't got my address," he told her.

"No, but I shall send it to Boufelja's house," she said, thinking that would satisfy him. He leaned toward her, his eyes intense. "No, madame," he said with finality. "No. I have your address, and I shall send you mine. Then you will have it, and you can write to me."

It did not seem worth arguing about. For most of the afternoon her thumb had not hurt too much; now, as the day waned, it had begun to ache again. She wanted to get up, find the waiter, and pay him. The fine rain still blew; the station was fairly far. But she saw Slimane had something more to say. He leaned forward in his chair and looked down at the floor. "Madame," he began.

"Yes?" she said.

"When you are in your country and you think of me you will not be happy. It's true, no?"

"I shall be very sad," she answered, rising.

Slimane got slowly to his feet and was quiet for an instant before going on. "Sad because I ate the food out of the picture. That was very bad. Forgive me."

The shrill sound of her own voice exclaiming, "No!" startled her. "No!" she cried. "That was good!" She felt the muscles of her cheeks and lips twisting themselves into grimaces of weeping; fiercely she seized his arm and looked down into his face. "*Oh, mon pauvre petit!*" she sobbed, and then covered her face with both hands. She felt him gently touching her sleeve. A truck went by in the main street, shaking the floor.

With an effort she turned away and scratched in her bag for a handkerchief. "Come," she said, clearing her throat. "Call the waiter."

They arrived at the station cold and wet. The train was being assembled; passengers were not allowed to go out onto the platform and were sitting on the floor inside. While Fräulein Windling bought her ticket Slimane went to get the bags from the checkroom. He was gone for a long time. When he arrived he came with his burnoose thrown back over his shoulders, grinning triumphantly, with three valises piled on his head. A man in ragged European jacket and trousers followed behind carrying the rest. As he came nearer she saw that the man held a slip of paper between his teeth.

The ancient compartment smelled of varnish. Through the window she could see, above some remote western reach of waste-land, a few strips of watery white sky. Slimane wanted to cover the seats with the luggage, so that no one would come into the compartment. "No," she said. "Put them in the racks." There were very few passengers in the coach. When everything was in place, the porter stood outside in the corridor and she noticed that he still held the slip of paper between his teeth. He counted the coins she gave him and pocketed them. Then quickly he handed the paper to Slimane, and was gone.

Fräulein Windling bent down a bit, to try and see her face in the narrow mirror that ran along the back of the seat. There was not enough light; the oil lantern above illumined only the ceiling, its base casting a leaden shadow over everything beneath. Suddenly the train jolted and made a series of crashing sounds. She took Slimane's head between her hands and kissed the middle of his forehead. "Please get down from the train," she told him. "We can talk here." She pointed to the window and began to pull on the torn leather strap that lowered it.

Slimane looked small on the dark platform, staring up at her as she leaned out. Then the train started to move. She thought surely it would go only a few feet and then stop, but it continued ahead, slowly. Slimane walked with it, keeping abreast of her window. In his hand was the paper the porter had given him. He held it up to her, crying: "Here is my address! Send it here!"

She took it, and kept waving as the train went faster, kept calling: "Good-by!" He continued to walk quickly along beside the window, increasing his gait until he was running, until all at once there was no more platform. She leaned far out, looking backward, waving; straightway he was lost in the darkness and rain. A bonfire blazed orange by the track, and the smoke stung in her nostrils. She pulled up the window, glanced at the slip of paper she had in her hand, and sat down. The train jolted her this way and that; she went on staring at the paper, although now it was in shadow; and she remembered the first day, long ago, when the child Slimane had stood outside the door watching her, stepping back out of her range of vision each time she turned to look at him. The words hastily printed for him on the scrap of paper by the porter were indeed an address, but the address was in Colomb-Bechar. "They said he tried to run away. But he didn't get very far." Each detail of his behavior as she went back over it clarified the pattern for her. "He's too young to be a soldier," she told herself. "They won't take him." But she knew they would.

Her thumb was hot and swollen; sometimes it seemed almost that its throbbing accompanied the side-to-side jolting of the coach. She looked out at the few remaining patches of colorless light in the sky. Sooner or later, she argued, he would have done it.

"Another year, perhaps," the captain had said. She saw her own crooked, despairing smile in the dark window-glass beside her face. Maybe Slimane would be among the fortunate ones, an early casualty. "If only death were absolutely certain in wartime," she thought wryly, "the waiting would not be so painful." Listing and groaning, the train began its long climb upwards over the plateau.

Tangier
1962

The Garden

A man who lived in a distant town of the southern country was working in his garden. Because he was poor his land was at the edge of the oasis. All the afternoon he dug channels, and when the day was finished he went to the upper end of the garden and opened the gate that held back the water. And now the water ran in the channels to the beds of barley and the young pomegranate trees. The sky was red, and when the man saw the floor of his garden shining like jewels, he sat down on a stone to look at it. As he watched, it grew brighter, and he thought: "There is no finer garden in the oasis."

A great happiness filled him, and he sat there a long time, and did not get home until very late. When he went into the house, his wife looked at him and saw the joy still in his eyes.

"He has found a treasure," she thought; but she said nothing.

When they sat face to face at the evening meal, the man was still remembering his garden, and it seemed to him that now that he had known this happiness, never again would he be without it. He was silent as he ate.

His wife too was silent. "He is thinking of the treasure," she said to herself. And she was angry, believing that he did not want to share his secret with her. The next morning she went to the house of an old woman and bought many herbs and powders from her. She took them home and passed several days mixing and cooking them, until she had made the medicine she wanted. Then at each meal she began to put a little of the *tseuheur* into her husband's food.

It was not long before the man fell ill. For a time he went each day to his garden to work, but often when he got there he was so weak that he could merely sit leaning against a palm tree. He had a sharp sound in his ears, and he could not follow his thoughts as they came to him. In spite of this, each day when the sun went down and he saw his garden shining red in its light, he was happy. And when he got home at night his wife could see that there was joy in his eyes.

"He has been counting the treasure," she thought, and she began to go secretly to the garden to watch him from behind the trees. When she saw that he merely sat looking at the ground, she went back to the old woman and told her about it.

"You must hurry and make him talk, before he forgets where he has hidden the treasure," said the old woman.

That night the wife put a great amount of *tseubeur* into his food, and when they were drinking tea afterward she began to say many sweet words to him. The man only smiled. She tried for a long time to make him speak, but he merely shrugged his shoulders and made motions with his hands.

The next morning while he was still asleep, she went back to the old woman and told her that the man could no longer speak.

"You have given him too much," the old woman said. "He will never tell you his secret now. The only thing for you to do is go away quickly, before he dies."

The woman ran home. Her husband lay on the mat with his mouth open. She packed her clothing and left the town that morning.

For three days the man lay in a deep sleep. The fourth day when he awoke, it was as if he had made a voyage to the other side of the world. He was very hungry, but all he could find in the house was a piece of dry bread. When he had eaten that, he walked to his garden at the edge of the oasis and picked many figs. Then he sat down and ate them. In his mind there was no thought of his wife, because he had forgotten her. When a neighbor came by and called to him, he answered politely, as if speaking to a stranger, and the neighbor went away perplexed.

Little by little the man grew healthy once more. He worked each day in the garden. When dusk came, after watching the sunset and the red water, he would go home and cook his dinner and sleep. He had no friends, because although men spoke to him, he did not know who they were, and he only smiled and nodded to them. Then the people in the town began to notice that he no longer went to the mosque to pray. They spoke about this among themselves, and one evening the imam went to the man's house to talk with him.

As they sat there, the imam listened for sounds of the man's wife in the house. Out of courtesy he could not mention her, but he was thinking about her and asking himself where she might be. He went away from the house full of doubts.

The man went on living his life. But the people of the town now talked of little else. They whispered that he had killed his wife, and many of them wanted to go together and search the house for her remains. The imam spoke against this idea, saying that he would go and talk again with the man. And this time he went all the way to the garden at the edge of the oasis, and found him there working happily with the plants and the trees. He watched him for a while, and then he walked closer and spoke a few words with him.

It was late in the afternoon. The sun was sinking in the west, and the water on the ground began to be red. Presently the man said to the imam: "The garden is beautiful."

"Beautiful or not beautiful," said the imam, "you should be giving thanks to Allah for allowing you to have it."

"Allah?" said the man. "Who is that? I never heard of him. I made this garden myself. I dug every channel and planted every tree, and no one helped me. I have no debts to anyone."

The imam had turned pale. He flung out his arm and struck the man very hard in the face. Then he went quickly out of the garden.

The man stood with his hand to his cheek. "He has gone mad," he thought, as the imam walked away.

That night the people spoke together in the mosque. They decided that the man could no longer live in their town. Early the next morning a great crowd of men, with the imam going at the head of it, went out into the oasis, on its way to the man's garden.

The small boys ran ahead of the men, and got there long before them. They hid in the bushes, and as the man worked they began to throw stones and shout insults at him. He paid no attention to them. Then a stone hit the back of his head. He jumped up quickly. As they ran away, one of them fell, and the man caught him. He tried to hold him still so he could ask him: "Why are you throwing stones at me?" But the boy only screamed and struggled.

And the townspeople, who were on their way, heard the screaming, and they came running to the garden. They pulled the boy away from him and began to strike at the man with hoes and sickles. When they had destroyed him, they left him there with his head lying in one of the channels, and went back to the town, giving thanks to Allah that the boy was safe.

Little by little the trees died, and very soon the garden was gone. Only the desert was there.

Asilah
1963

Afternoon With Antaeus

You wanted to see me? They told you right. That's my name. Ntiuz. The African Giant's what they've called me ever since I started fighting. What can I do for you? Have you seen the town? It isn't such a bad place. You're lucky the wind's not blowing these days. We have a bad wind that comes through here. But without it the sun's too hot. Argos? Never heard of it. I've never been over to the other side.

A man named Erakli? Yes, yes, he was here. It was a long time ago. I remember him. We even put on a fight together.

Killed me! Is that what he told them back there? I see. And when you got here you heard I was still around, and so you wanted to meet me? I understand.

Why don't we sit here? There's a spring in the courtyard that has the coldest water in town. You asked about Erakli. No, he had no trouble here, except losing his fight. Why would anyone bother him? A man alone. You never saw him before. You let him go on his way. You don't bother him. Only savages attack a stranger walking alone. They kill him and fight over his loincloth. We let people go through without a word. They come in on one side and go out on the other. That's the way we like it. Peaceful and friendly with everyone. We have a saying: Never hit a man unless you know you can kill him, and then kill him fast. Up where I come from we're rougher than they are down here on the coast. We have a harder life, but we're healthier. Look at me, and I could almost be your father. If I'd lived down here on the coast all my life I wouldn't be like this now. And still I'm nothing to what I was twenty years ago. In those days I went to every festival and put on shows for people. I'd lift a bull with one hand and hit him between the horns with the other, so he'd fall dead. People like to see that. Sometimes I broke beams with my head. That was popular, too, but the bull was religious, of course, so it was the one people wanted to see most. There was nobody who didn't know about me.

Have some nuts? I eat them all day. I get them up in the forest. There are trees up there bigger than any you ever saw.

It was at least twenty years ago he came through here, but I remember him, all right. Not because he was any good as a fighter, but because he was so crazy. You can't help remembering a man as crazy as Erakli.

Have some more. I've got a whole sack full. That's true, the flavor's not quite like anything else. I don't suppose you have them over on the other side.

I'll be only too glad to take you up to the forest, if you'd like to see it. It's not far. You don't mind climbing a little?

Of course he didn't make any friends here, but a man like that can't have friends. He was so full of great ideas about himself that he didn't even see us. He thought we were all savages, ready to swallow his stories. Even before the fight everybody was laughing at him. Strong, yes, but not a good fighter. An awful boaster and a terrible liar. And ignorant.

We'll turn here and go up this path. He talked all the time. If you believed him, there was nothing he couldn't do, and do it better than anybody else.

You'll get a fine view on the way. The edge of the world. How does it feel, when you're used to being in the middle, to be out here at the end? It must be a different feeling.

Erakli came into town without anyone noticing him. He must have had a little money with him, because he began to meet two or three men I knew every day and pay for their drinks. They told me about him, and I went along one day just to see what he looked like, not to meet him. Right away I knew he was no good. No good as a fighter, no good as a man. I didn't even take him seriously enough to challenge him. How can you take a man seriously when he has a beard that looks like the wool on a sheep?

He stayed around town a while and saw me kill a few bulls. I fought a match or two, too, while he was here, and it seems he came each time to watch me. The next thing I knew, he'd challenged me. It was he who wanted the match. It was hard to believe. And what's more, they told me he held it against me that I hadn't been the one who challenged him. It just never entered my mind.

All this land you see up here is mine. This and the forest up ahead. I keep everybody out. I like to walk, and I don't want to meet people while I'm walking. It makes me nervous. I used to fight every man I met. At least, in the beginning.

When I was a small boy in my village I liked to go late in the afternoon to a big rock. I'd sit on it and look down the valley and pretend enemies were coming. I'd let them get to a certain point, and then I'd start a boulder rolling down the mountain to hit them. I killed them every time. My father caught me and I got punished. I might have hit a sheep or goats, or even men down there.

But I'm not dead, as you can see, no matter what Erakli may be saying. I want you to look at my trees. Look at the size of the trunk of that one. Follow it up, up, up, to where the first branches begin. Have you ever seen trees this big anywhere?

When I got a little older I learned how to throw a calf, and later a bull. By that time I was fighting. Never lost yet. They forgot my name was Ntiuz and began to call me The Giant. Not because of my size, of course. I'm not so big. But because nobody could beat me in a match. They came from all around, and afterwards from far away. You know how they do when they hear of a fighter who's never lost. They can't believe that somehow or other they won't manage to get him down. That was the way with your Erakli. I didn't meet him until the fight, but I'd heard all about him from my friends. He told them he'd studied me, and he knew how to beat me. He didn't say how he was going to do it. And I never even found out what he thought he was going to do until after the fight.

No, I'm not dead. I'm still the champion. Anybody here can tell you. It's too bad you never met Erakli yourself. You wouldn't be so surprised. You'd understand that whatever he said when he got back home was what he wanted to tell and nothing more. He couldn't tell the truth if he wanted to.

Are you tired? It's a steep climb if you're not used to it. The fight itself? It didn't last long. He was so busy trying to use the system he'd worked out. He'd back away, and then come up to me and just stand there with his hands on me. I couldn't understand what he was trying to do. The crowd was jeering. For a minute I thought: He's the kind that gets his pleasure this way, running his hands over a man's chest and squeezing his waist. He didn't like it because I laughed and shouted to the crowd. He was very serious the whole time. And I was wrong anyway. Are we going too fast? And you're carrying that heavy pouch at your waist. We can go as slowly as you want to. There's no hurry.

That's a good idea. Why don't we sit a minute and rest? Do you feel all right? No. Nothing. I thought you looked a little pale. It may be the light. The sun never gets down in here.

It was only after the fight that one of my friends told me what Erakli wanted to do. Instead of trying to throw me, the crazy fool was trying to lift me off the ground and hold me in the air! Not so he could throw me down better, but just to hold me up there. It's hard to believe, isn't it? But that's what he had in his mind. That was his great system. Why? Don't ask me. I'm an African. I don't know what goes on in the heads of the men of your country.

Have some more nuts. No, no, they couldn't have hurt you. It's the air. Our climate doesn't suit people from the other side. While he was trying to make up his mind how to lift me I finished him. They had to drag him out.

Shall we go on? Or would you rather wait a while? Are you still out of breath? There's no air here in the forest.

Don't you think we ought to wait a while? Of course, if you want to go.

We can walk slowly. Let me help you up. It's too bad we couldn't have gone further. The biggest trees are up that way.

Yes, they dragged him out, and he stayed three days lying on a mat before he left here. Finally he limped out of town like a dog, with everybody laughing at him along the way. Hand onto me. I won't let you fall. You're walking all right. Just keep going. He didn't look left or right on his way out of town. Must have been glad to get into the mountains.

Relax. First one foot, then the other foot. I don't know where he went. I'm afraid there's no water here. We'll get some as soon as we get to town. You'll be all right. I suppose he went back where he came from. We never saw him again here, in any case.

Does it seem like such a long time that we've been walking? It's only a few minutes. You recognize the path but you don't know where you are? Why should you know where you are? It's not your forest. Relax. Step. Step. Step.

You're right. It's the rock where we were sitting a few minutes ago. I wondered if you'd notice. Of course I know my way! I thought you'd better rest again before we started into town. That's right, you just lie back there. You'll be fine as soon as you've had a little sleep. It's very quiet here.

No, you haven't been asleep so long. How do you feel now? Good. I knew a little sleep would do it. You're not used to the air here. A pouch? I don't think you were carrying anything.

There's no need to make a face like that. You don't think I took it, do you?

I thought we were friends. I treated you like a friend. And now you pay me back.

I'm not going to take you anywhere. Get down to the town by yourself. I'm going the other way.

Go on back to your country and tell them about me. You can walk all right.

Just keep going.

And get out of the forest fast!

Tangier
1970

Mejdoub

A man who spent his nights sleeping in cafés or under the trees or wherever he happened to be at the time when he felt sleepy, wandered one morning through the streets of the town. He came to the market place, where an old mejdoub dressed in rags cavorted before the populace, screaming prophecies into the air. He stood watching until the old man had finished and gathered up the money the people offered him. It astonished him to see how much the madman had collected, and having nothing else to do, he decided to follow him.

Almost before he got out of the market he was aware that small boys were hurrying from under the arcades to run alongside the mejdoub, who merely strode forward, chanting and waving his sceptre, and from time to time threatening the children who came too close. Walking at some distance behind, he saw the old man go into several shops. He came out each time with a banknote in his hand, which he promptly gave to one of the small boys.

It occurred to him then that there was much he could learn from this mejdoub. He had only to study the old man's behavior and listen carefully to the words he uttered. Then with practice he himself could make the same gestures and shout the same words. He began to look each day for the mejdoub and to follow him wherever he went in the town. At the end of a month he decided that he was ready to put his knowledge to use.

He travelled south to another city where he had never gone before. Here he took a very cheap room by the slaughterhouse, far from the center of town. In the flea-market he bought an old and tattered djellaba. Then he went to the iron-mongers and stood watching while they made him a long sceptre like the one the mejdoub had carried.

The next day, after practicing for a while, he went into the town and sat down in the street at the foot of the largest mosque. For a while he merely looked at the people going past. Slowly he began to raise his arms to the sky, and then to gesture with them. No one paid him any attention. This reassured him, as it meant that his disguise was successful. When he began to shout words the passers-by looked toward him, but it was as if they could not see him, and were only waiting to hear what he had to say. For a time he shouted short quotations from the Koran. He moved his eyes in a circular motion and let his turban fall over his face. After crying the words *fire* and *blood* several times he lowered his arms and bent his head, and said no more. The people moved on, but not before many of them had tossed coins on the ground in front of him.

On succeeding days he tried other parts of the city. It did not seem to matter where he sat. The people were generous to him in one place the same as in another. He did not want to risk going into the shops and cafés until he was certain that the town had grown used to his presence. One day he stormed throught the streets, shaking his sceptre to the sky and screaming: Sidi Rahal is here! Sidi Rahal tells you to prepare for the fire! This was in order to give himself a name for the townspeople to remember.

He began to stand in the doorways of shops. If he heard anyone refer to him as Sidi Rahal, he would step inside, glare at the proprietor, and without saying a word, hold out his hand. The man would give him money, and he would turn and walk out.

For some reason no children followed him. He would have been happier to have a group of them with him, like the old mejdoub, but as soon as he spoke to them, they were frightened and ran away. It's quieter like this, he told himself, but secretly it bothered him. Still, he was earning more money that he ever had thought possible. By the time the first rains arrived, he had saved up a large sum. Leaving his sceptre and ragged djellaba in his room by the slaughterhouse, he paid the landlord several months' rent in advance. He waited until night. Then he locked the door behind him and took a bus back to his own city.

First he bought a great variety of clothing. When he was richly dressed he went out and looked for a house. Soon he found one that suited him. It was small and he had enough money left to pay for it. He furnished two rooms and prepared to spend the winter eating and smoking kif with all his old friends.

When they asked him where he had been all summer, he spoke of the hospitality and generosity of his wealthy brother in Taza. Already he was impatient for the rains to stop. For there was no doubt that he truly enjoyed his new work.

The winter finally came to an end. He packed his bag and told his friends that he was going on a business trip. In the other town he walked to the room. His djellaba and sceptre were there.

This year many more people recognized him. He grew bolder and entered the shops without waiting in the doorways. The shopkeepers, eager to show their piety to the customers, always gave a good deal more than the passers-by.

One day he decided to make a test. He hailed a taxi. As he got in he bellowed: I must go to Sidi Larbi's tomb! Fast! The driver, who knew he was not going to be paid, nevertheless agreed, and they rode out to a grove of olive trees on a hill far from the town.

He told the driver to wait, and jumped out of the taxi. Then he began the long climb up the hill to the tomb. The driver lost patience and drove off. On the way back to the town he missed a curve and hit a tree. When he was let out of the hospital he spread the word that Sidi Rahal had caused the car to go off the road. Men talked at length about it, recalling other holy maniacs who had put spells on motors and brakes. The name of Sidi Rahal was on everyone's lips, and people listened respectfully to his rantings.

That summer he amassed more money than the year before. He returned home and bought a larger house to live in, while he rented out the first one. Each year he bought more houses and lands, until finally it was clear that he had become a very prosperous man.

Always when the first rains fell he would announce to his friends that he was about to travel abroad. Then he would leave secretly, never allowing anyone to see him off. He was delighted with the pattern of his life, and with the good luck he had been granted in being able to continue it. He assumed that Allah did not mind if he pretended to be one of His holy maniacs. The money was merely his reward for providing men with an opportunity to exercise their charity.

One winter a new government came to power and announced that all beggars were to be taken off the streets. He talked about this with his friends, all of whom thought it an excellent thing. He agreed with them, but the news kept him from sleeping at night. To risk everything by going back, merely because that was what he wanted to do, was out of the question. Sadly he resigned himself to spending the summer at home.

It was not until the first few weeks of spring had gone by that he realized how close it had been to his heart, the starting out on a fine starry night to go in the bus to the other city, and what a relief it had been each time to be able to forget everything and live as Sidi Rahal. Now he began to understand that his life here at home had been a pleasure only because he had known that at a certain moment he was going to leave it for the other life.

As the hot weather came on he grew increasingly restless. He was bored and lost his appetite. His friends, noticing the change in him, advised him to travel, as he always had done. They said that men had been known to die as a result of breaking a habit. Again he lay awake at night worrying, and then secretly he determined to go back. As soon as he had made the decision he felt much better. It was as though until then he had been asleep, and suddenly had awakened. He announced to his friends that he was going abroad.

That very night he locked up his house and got onto a bus. The next day he strode joyously through the streets to sit in his favorite spot by the mosque. Passers-by looked at him and remarked to one another: He's back again, after all. You see?

He sat there quietly all day, collecting money. At the end of the afternoon, since the weather was very hot, he walked down to the river outside the gates of the town, in order to bathe. As he was undressing behind some oleander bushes, he glanced up and saw three policemen coming down the bank toward him. Without waiting he seized his slippers, threw his djellaba over his shoulder, and began to run.

Sometimes he splashed into the water, and sometimes he slipped in the mud and fell. He could hear the men shouting after him. They did not chase him very far, for they were laughing. Not knowing this, he kept on running, following the river, until he was breathless and had to stop. He put on the djellaba and the slippers, thinking: I can't go back to the town, or to any other town, in these clothes.

He continued at a slower gait. When evening came he was hungry, but there were no people or houses in sight. He slept under a tree, with only the ragged djellaba to cover him.

The next morning his hunger had grown. He got up, bathed in the river, and set out again. All that day he walked under the hot sun. In the late afternoon he sat down to rest. He drank a little water from the river and looked around him at the countryside. On the hill behind him stood a partially ruined shrine.

When he was rested, he climbed up to the building. There was a tomb inside, in the center of the big domed room. He sat down and listened. Cocks crowed, and he heard the occasional barking of dogs. He imagined himself running to the village, crying to the first man he met: Give me a piece of bread, for the love of Moulay Abdelqader! He shut his eyes.

It was nearly twilight when he awoke. Outside the door stood a group of small boys, watching him. Seeing him awaken, they laughed and nudged one another. Then one boy tossed in a piece of dry bread, so that it fell beside him. Soon they were all chanting: He's eating bread! He's eating bread!

They played the game for a while, throwing in clods of earth and even uprooted plants along with the scraps of bread. In their faces he could read wonder, malice and contempt, and shining through these shifting emotions the steady gleam of ownership. He thought of the old mejdoub, and a shiver ran through him. Suddenly they had gone. He heard a few shrill cries in the distance as they raced back to the village.

The bread had given him a little nourishment. He slept where he was, and before it grew light he set out again along the river, giving thanks to Allah for having allowed him to get beyond the village without being seen.

He understood that heretofore the children had run from him only because they knew that he was not ready for them, that they could not make him theirs. The more he thought about this, the more fervently he hoped never to know what it was like to be a true mejdoub.

That afternoon as he turned a bend in the river, he came suddenly upon a town. His desperate need for food led him straight to the market. Paying no heed to the people's stares, he went into a stall and ordered a bowl of soup. When he had finished it and paid, he entered another stall for a dish of stew. In a third place he ate skewered meat. Then he walked to the bread market for two loaves of bread to carry with him. While he was paying for these, a policeman tapped him on the shoulder and asked for his papers. He had none. There was nothing to say. At the police station they locked him into a small foul-smelling room in the cellar. Here in this closet he passed four days and nights of anguish. When at the end of that time they took him out and questioned him, he could not bring himself to tell them the truth. Instead he frowned, saying: I am Sidi Rahal.

They tied his hands and pushed him into the back of a truck. Later in the hospital they led him to a damp cell where the men stared and shivered and shrieked. He bore it for a week, and then he decided to give the officials his true name. But when he asked to be taken before them, the guards merely laughed. Sometimes they said: Next week, but usually they did not answer at all.

The months moved by. Through nights and days and nights he lived with the other madmen, and the time came when it scarcely mattered to him any more, getting to the officials to tell them who he was. Finally he ceased thinking about it.

Tangier
1974

The Fqih

One midsummer afternoon a dog went running through a village, stopping just long enough to bite a young man who stood on the main street. It was not a deep wound, and the young man washed it at a fountain nearby and thought no more about it. However, several people who had seen the animal bite him mentioned it to his younger brother. You must take your brother to a doctor in the city, they said.

When the boy went home and suggested this, his brother merely laughed. The next day in the village the boy decided to consult the fqih. He found the old man sitting in the shade under the figtree in the courtyard of the mosque. He kissed his hand, and told him that a dog no one had ever seen before had bitten his brother and run away.

That's very bad, said the fqih. Have you got a stable you can lock him into? Put him there, but tie his hands behind him. No one must go near him, you understand?

The boy thanked the fqih and set out for home. On the way he determined to cover a hammer with yarn and hit his brother on the back of the head. Knowing that his mother would never consent to seeing her son treated in this way, he decided that it would have to be done when she was away from the house.

That evening while the woman stood outside by the well, he crept up behind his brother and beat him with the hammer until he fell to the floor. Then he fastened his hands behind him and dragged him into a shed next to the house. There he left him lying on the ground, and went out, padlocking the door behind him.

When the brother came to his senses, he began a great outcry. The mother called to the boy: Quick! Run and see what's the matter with Mohammed. But the boy only said: I know what's the matter with him. A dog bit him, and the fqih said he has to stay in the shed.

The woman began to pull at her hair and scratch her face with her fingernails and beat her breasts. The boy tried to calm her, but she pushed him away and ran out to the shed. She put her ear to the door. All she could hear was her son's loud panting as he tried to free his hands from the cords that bound them. She pounded on the wood and screamed his name, but he

377

was struggling, his face in the dirt, and did not reply. Finally the boy led her back to the house. It was written, he told her.

The next morning the woman got astride her donkey and rode to the village to see the fqih. He, however, had left that morning to visit his sister in Rhafsai, and no one knew when he would be back. And so she bought bread and started out on the road for Rhafsai, along with a group of villagers who were on their way to a souq in the region. That night she slept at the souq and the following morning at daybreak she started out again with a different group of people.

Each day the boy threw food in to his brother through a small barred window high above one of the stalls in the shed. The third day he also threw him a knife, so he could cut the ropes and use his hands to eat with. After a while it occurred to him that he had done a foolish thing in giving him the knife, since if he worked long enough with it he might succeed in cutting his way through the door. Thus he threatened to bring no more food until his brother had tossed the knife back through the window.

The mother had no sooner arrived at Rhafsai than she fell ill with a fever. The family with whom she had been travelling took her into their house and cared for her, but it was nearly a month before she was able to rise from the pallet on the floor where she had been lying. By that time the fqih had returned to his village.

Finally she was well enough to start out again. After two days of sitting on the back of the donkey she arrived home exhausted, and was greeted by the boy.

And your brother? she said, certain that by now he was dead.

The boy pointed to the shed, and she rushed to the door and began to call out to him.

Get the key and let me out! he cried.

I must see the fqih first, aoulidi. Tomorrow.

The next morning she and the boy went to the village. When the fqih saw the woman and her son come into the courtyard he raised his eyes to heaven. It was Allah's will that your son should die as he did, he told her.

But he's not dead! she cried. And he shouldn't stay in there any longer.

The fqih was astounded. Then he said: But let him out! Let him out! Allah has been merciful.

The boy however begged the fqih to come himself and open the door. So they set out, the fqih riding the donkey and the woman and boy following on foot. When they got to the shed, the boy handed the key to the old man, and he opened the door. The young man bounded out, followed by a stench so strong that the fqih shut the door again.

They went to the house, and the woman made tea for them. While they sat drinking the fqih told the young man: Allah has spared you. You must never mistreat your brother for having shut you away. He did it on my orders.

The young man swore that never would he raise his hand against the boy. But the boy was still afraid, and could not bring himself to look at his brother. When the fqih left to return to the village, the boy went with him, in order to bring back the donkey. As they went along the road, he said to the old man: I'm afraid of Mohammed.

The fqih was displeased. Your brother is older than you, he said. You heard him swear not to touch you.

That night while they were eating, the woman went to the brazier to make the tea. For the first time the boy stole a glance at his brother, and grew cold with fear. Mohammed had swiftly bared his teeth and made a strange sound in his throat. He had done this as a kind of joke, but to the boy it meant something very different.

The fqih should never have let him out, he said to himself. Now he'll bite me, and I'll get sick like him. And the fqih will tell him to throw me into the shed.

He could not bring himself to look again at Mohammed. At night in the dark he lay thinking about it, and he could not sleep. Early in the morning he set out for the village, to catch the fqih before he began to teach the pupils at the msid.

What is it now? asked the fqih.

When the boy told him what he feared, the old man laughed. But he has no disease! He never had any disease, thanks to Allah.

But you yourself told me to lock him up, sidi.

Yes, yes. But Allah has been merciful. Now go home and forget about it. Your brother's not going to bite you.

The boy thanked the fqih and left. He walked through the village and out along the road that led finally to the highway. The next morning he got a ride in a truck that took him all the way to Casablanca. No one in the village ever heard of him again.

Tangier
1974

The Waters of Izli

No one would have guessed, from seeing the two villages spread out there, one higher up than the other on the sunny slope of the mountain, that enmity existed between them. And yet, if you looked closely, you would see certain marked differences in the respective designs they made on the landscape. Tamlat was higher, the houses were farther apart, and there were trees between them. In Izli everything was crowded together, for there was not enough space. The entire village seemed to have been built on top of boulders and at the edges of cliffs. Green fields and meadows surrounded Tamlat. It lay above, where the valley was wide, so that there was ample room for farming, and thus the people lived well. But the orchards down in Izli were little more than steep stairways of terraces. No matter how hard they worked trying to raise vegetables and fruit, the villagers never had enough.

What ought to have helped compensate for Izli's unlucky site was the large spring just outside the village, whose water was the sweetest in the region. The people of Izli claimed great curative powers for it, an idea that was dismissed by the inhabitants of Tamlat, although they themselves often went down and filled their skins and jars with it to take home with them. There was no way of fencing off the land around the spring, or the natives of Izli long ago would have seen to it that no one else had access to the water. If only the people of Tamlat had been willing to admit that the water was superior to their own, eventually they might have been persuaded to trade a few vegetables for it. However, they were careful never to mention it, and except for going casually to fetch it, behaved as if it did not exist.

The man whose land lay nearest to the spring was Ramadi, said to be the most prosperous one in Izli. By the standards of Tamlat he would not have been considered well-off. But his black mare was the only horse in Izli, and his orchard had twenty-three almond trees growing on eight different levels, and on each level he had built a channel that ran with clear water. The mare was a beautiful animal, and he kept her in perfect condition. When he dressed in his white selham and rode the mare through the street out of the village, the people of Izli remarked to each other that he looked almost like Sidi Bouhajja. This was a great compliment, since Sidi Bouhajja was the most important saint in the region. He too wore white garments and rode a black horse, although his was a stallion.

For a long time Ramadi had been on the lookout for a fitting mate for his mare. However, not one stallion among all those he had looked at in the neighboring villages could be called her equal. In fact, the only horse he would have accepted for her was the shining black stallion ridden by Sidi Bouhajja, and this was out of the question, since there was no way of asking a saint for such a favor.

It was assumed by many people that Sidi Bouhajja and his horse were able to converse together. And it was common knowledge, for he had proclaimed it in public on several occasions, that at the moment of his death it was to be the horse that would decide on his burial place. He asked that his body be fastened astride the animal, which was then to be allowed to go where it pleased. Where it stopped, at that spot Sidi Bouhajja was to be interred. This doubtless lent weight to the belief that the old man and his horse had a secret language between them.

It was a subject for much speculation around the countryside as to which region might prove fortunate enough to witness this event, but everything was cut short by Sidi Bouhajja's sudden collapse one afternoon as he sat outside the mosque at Tamlat.

The saint had ridden up through Izli earlier in the day, passing by Ramadi's house as the mare stood in front of it, shaded by an old olive tree. The stallion wanted to stop, and Sidi Bouhajja had some difficulty in getting him to continue. Ramadi watched, fingered his beard, thinking what a great thing it would be if the stallion should suddenly rise up, saint and all, and mount the mare. Then, feeling ashamed, he looked away.

Later in the day Ramadi got onto the mare and rode up to Tamlat. There in a corner of the market he caught sight of an Aissaoui snake charmer from Izli whom he knew, and he sat down to talk with him. It was then that he heard the news of Sidi Bouhajja's death.

He sat up very straight. The Aissaoui added that soon they would be tying the saint to his horse.

Where do you think it'll go? Ramadi asked him.

It'll probably come here and go into the grain market, the Aissaoui said.

Have you got your snakes with you?

The Aissaoui looked surprised. Yes, I have them, he said.

Get them out there to the turn-off and let him see them, Ramadi told him. He's got to go down the hill instead.

He rose, jumped onto his mare, and rode off.

The Aissaoui ran to the fondouq where he had left his basket of vipers and cobras. Then he hurried up to the corner where the road turned off from the main street and led down the side of the mountain.

Since everyone in Tamlat was watching the elders strap Sidi Bouhajja's body onto the back of the stallion, Ramadi on his mare passed unnoticed as he galloped down the road to Izli. When he got to his house, he left the mare standing under the olive tree and waited.

Up in Tamlat the Assaoui sat by the edge of the road with his basket. At length he saw the horse come into view, its sacred burden strapped to its back. It cantered down the street toward him, followed at some distance by the elders. He opened his basket and took out two of the larger serpents, holding one in each hand. As the horse approached him, he stood up and made the reptiles writhe in the air. Immediately the horse opened its eyes very wide and turned to the right, down the road leading out of the village.

The Aissaoui put the snakes back into the basket and sauntered out of the bushes which until then had hidden him from the approaching elders. They paid him no attention, and he set out along the road to Izli. Far ahead of him he could see the black form of the stallion racing down the mountainside, the white bundle it carried flopping in the sunlight. After he had walked along for a while, he turned to look back. The elders stood up there at the corner, shading their eyes as they peered down into the valley.

And as Ramadi sat in his doorway waiting, the stallion stormed into the village, stood quiet for an instant, and then trotted directly to Ramadi's house. The mare still stood under the olive tree, switching her tail against the flies. Before anyone arrived to watch, the stallion reared himself up to a great height, bursting the straps that had bound Sidi Bouhajja to his back. The body in the white selham dropped to the ground at the same moment the stallion seized the mare. Ramadi ran forward and pulled it out of the way. Then he returned to the doorway to look on.

A little later some neighbors arrived, and they carried Sidi Bouhajja into Ramadi's courtyard, all the while praising Allah. By the time the men of Tamlat had got down to Izli, the stallion and the mare were standing quietly under the olive tree, and the tolba of Izli chanted inside Ramadi's house.

The men from Tamlat hid their chagrin and accepted the will of Allah. The horse had come to Izli and stopped here, therefore this was where Sidi Bouhajja had to be buried. They helped the men of Izli dig the grave, and the news went out to all the villages around, so that tolba came from many places to chant at the tomb.

It was no time before crowds of pilgrims began to arrive in Izli, seeking baraka at Sidi Bouhajja's tomb. Soon it was necessary to demolish Ramadi's house and in its place to build a sanctuary where the pilgrims could sleep. At the same time they constructed a domed qoubba over the saint's resting place by the olive tree, and then built a high wall around it. Ramadi was given another house nearby.

Since the pilgrims all carried away with them water from the spring, the water's fame soon spread, and it took on great importance. Even those who did not venerate Sidi Bouhajja came to drink it and take it home with them. In exchange they left offerings of food and money in the sanctuary. Before a year was up, Izli had become more prosperous than Tamlat.

Only Ramadi and the Aissaoui knew of the part they had played in bringing about the stroke of good luck that had changed their village, and they considered it of slight importance, since everything is decided by Allah. What mattered to Ramadi was the beauty of the black colt that now followed the mare wherever he rode her, even if it was down to the plain or up to the market in Tamlat.

Tangier
1975

Reminders of Bouselham

When I was a boy, Mother's favorite spot for reading, the place where she sat when she was going to read for a long time, was an old chaise longue, kept always in the same position in a corner of the east room, far enough from the walls so that the light came in over her shoulders on both sides. The back of the chaise longue was piled with dozens of small down-stuffed cushions. It was a comfortable seat to recline in. Sometimes I would use it for a few minutes in the morning before she was up. Once she caught me there and ridiculed me.

Getting decrepit in your old age! she scoffed. You're a growing boy. That's a chair for an adult.

The garden was the place to lie on a summer afternoon. Overhead the wind hissed in the high eucalyptus and cypress trees. There were flying skeins of fog that swept by very fast, just above, sometimes catching the tops of the trees and swooping down through the branches. One summer when I was back from school in England I did all my studying out there on the ground behind bushes or hedges, or anywhere that was hidden from the sight of the house.

And I would lie face-down in the hot garden, and look beneath the cut tips of the grass spears, into the miniature forest where the ants lived. Most of them were very small, and were not troubled by the mat I spread out over their domain. If the large red ones discovered it, as now and then they did, they attacked at once, and there was nothing to do but carry the mat somewhere else.

It went without saying that the Medina was forbidden territorry. Mother would have reacted very badly had she known I had ever been in it alone. But from time to time I went on an errand and had the opportunity to slip into the old town and find my way along the alleys for a few minutes. I loved the way they suddenly changed direction and burrowed under the houses. In fact, you went under a house to get into the alley where Mama Tiemponada's brothel stood. Hers was not the only one there, but it was the biggest. All the houses in the alley were brothels. The women leaned in the doorways and made remarks to the men walking by. I found the place mysterious and sinister. It seemed natural enough that Mother should not want me to come to the Medina.

One evening as I stood outside Mama Tiemponada's in the alley watching the door, it opened and a single Moroccan boy came out. He stood still for an instant, and looking up at the full moon directly above, whistled once at it, then walked away. This struck me as very strange, and I remembered it. The whistle was casual and intimate, suggesting that the moon and he had been good friends for a long time. A year or two later, when Bouselham came to work for us, I thought I recognized him as the same boy.

Probably it would have been better for me if I'd got to know Father, but I never did. It did not occur to me to wonder what sort of man he was. His fiftieth birthday was well behind him when I was born, and by then he was interested primarily in golf. He paid no attention to me, and very little to Mother. At daybreak he would get up, eat a big breakfast, and ride his favorite horse to the country club at Boubana. We would not see him again until evening. The ladies said to Mother: Colonel Driscoll is so impressive up there on his horse! Their own husbands drove in their cars to the country club. I was convinced that they were secretly laughing at us because Father was so odd.

As a boy I sometimes played with Amy, because she lived on the property next to ours, down the road. She was five years older than I, a tomboy, and full of sadistic impulses which she often vented on me. When she was twenty her mother died, and Amy was left alone in a house far too big for her. Then she began to spend almost all her time with Mother.

I was not surprised when Mother announced casually one day: Amy has a buyer for Villa Vireval. She's coming to stay with us for a while.

Soon Amy was with us. She had changed with the years, and was now an introverted, nervous young woman with a passion for precision. She had an annoying tic: the constantly repeated clearing of her throat. In the beginning Father made an effort to converse with her, even though he was very much against having her with us. She was neurotic, he said; she was morbid and self-centered, and she sapped Mother's energy.

What's wrong with that girl? Can't she leave you alone for a minute?

Mother, who like anyone else enjoyed being admired, was grateful even for Amy's devotion.

She's a well-balanced girl. I can't think what you have against her.

As usual the gossip got the basic facts fairly straight, but the motivations wrong. Everyone was certain that Father had left home because of Bouselham, when actually it was because he could no longer bear to be in the same house with Amy. He put up with her for six months. Then, seeing that she had no intention of leaving, and that Mother was adamant in her refusal to suggest to her that she find another place to live, he suddenly went off to Italy. Mother was unperturbed. Your father needs a holiday, she said to me after he had gone. Of course she assumed he would return.

It was precisely at that point that Bouselham emerged from his obscurity. Father had engaged him a year or so earlier, when he was sixteen, as an assistant gardener. He weeded, raked, and carried water in the lower garden, and one seldom saw him anywhere near the house. But when Father left, he began to come into the kitchen, where the maids would give him tea. Before long he was eating regularly there with them, rather than sitting under a tree with whatever he had brought with him from home.

How did the relationship start between him and Mother? What was the beginning of it? There is no way of bringing up the subject with Bouselham, since it has never been mentioned and thus does not exist between us. But I know that whatever the beginning may have been, it was Mother who set it in motion.

Often Bouselham had nothing to do but sit in a café smoking kif, and it was not always certain that there would be someone who could play cards with him. Most men worked during the day and came into the café after they had finished. Bouselham did not have to work. Ever since the colonel had gone away he had been with the colonel's wife. She did not want him to work, because then he would have to get up very early every morning, whereas she liked to sleep late and have him with her. All the men in the café knew that Bouselham had a rich Nazarene woman who gave him whatever he wanted.

And this was what Amy eventually began to say to Mother in one way or another, over and over. In her view it was wrong of Mother to have Bouselham with her, not only because his culture, religion and social class were not hers, but also because he was too young for a woman of her age. Usually Mother replied blandly that she didn't agree, but now and then she said a bit more. I heard her say one day: You're trying to encroach on my private life, Amy, and you have no right to.

Not too long after that, Amy decided to go to Paris where a friend had invited her. She packed up very quickly and was suddenly gone. Mother limited her comment to saying: Amy's a very sweet girl who has everything to learn, I'm afraid. And whether she will or not, I wonder.

The day Amy left I wandered into her room and looked around. It needed a thorough cleaning. I pulled the bureau out from the wall and peered down behind it. Underneath, wedged behind a back leg, was a crumpled postcard-size glossy print of Bouselham in bathing trunks on the beach at Sidi Qanqouch. For me this put Amy's quarrel with Mother in a new light. For a moment I was even sorry she was gone; it would have been fun to see what a few leading questions might have brought out from behind those thin precise lips of hers. Had she coveted Bouselham for herself? Or did Mother interrupt something that was already going on between them when she brought Bouselham into the house to sleep in her room.

The tale had been going around Tangier for many months. I heard it first from an English woman; she had just arrived here, and so had no way of knowing that the subject of her story was my mother. The colonel's wife used to disappear every night into the dark corners of the garden to meet the gardener, who was no more than a boy, an ordinary Moroccan workman. And when the colonel had had enough of her nonsense he had left, whereupon she had calmly taken the servant into the house and lived with him. I'm told she's even given him a racing car! she added, pretending to burst into laughter.

Probably, I said.

There is no doubt that Mother changed in certain respects during the time Bouselham was living in the house. She did buy a second-hand Porsche convertible for him, and this was certainly most unlike her. Her manner became distant; she seemed uninvolved in all the things that heretofore had been her life. When I suggested that I move out of the house and take a flat in town, she merely raised her eyebrows. You'll come to dinner twice a week, was all she said.

What finally decided her against Bouselham was a long and complicated saga involving his sister. Once she had carefully checked on the details of the story, her resolve to get rid of him was instantaneous. However, the only way she could devise for accomplishing this was so drastic as to be laughable. Mother has lived in this country for many years, and should not have been so deeply disturbed by Bouselham's behavior, particularly since it had nothing whatever to do with her. To me what he did seems natural enough, but then, I was born here. I first heard about it from Bouselham himself, not long after I moved out of the house and took the apartment in town.

I had been out to dinner and had walked home afterward. A thunderstorm was approaching from the direction of the strait. Soon hail showered against the windows. There was a very bright bolt of lightning, and the electricity was gone. I got out a flashlight, started some candles burning, and stood in front of the fireplace for a while. The thunderstorm circled around and came back, and it rained harder. In the midst of this there was a banging on the door, and when I opened it found Bouselham standing there, completely wet.

He looked as wild and as pleased with himself as ever, in spite of the rivulets of rain running down his face. Immediately he took off his shoes and socks and crouched in front of the fireplace, almost inside it, while he talked. Every day, he said, he was seeing a lawyer friend of his who was helping him.

To do what? I asked.

Avoiding a direct answer, he pivoted on his heels to face me, and asked if I could let him have ten thousand francs. The lawyer had to have the money for photocopies and notarizations. His fee would be contingent upon the success of his case, later. As soon as I had agreed to let him have the money, the story began to come out.

A certain rich merchant of the Medina, intent on the pleasures of the twilight hour, used to go each day and sit in a café at the end of the city. Here he could see in three directions, and hundreds of people were visible nearby and in the distance, walking along the roads. Each day, sooner or later, a girl passed by with an older woman who carried a basket. He sat at a table on the sidewalk, facing in the direction from which they always came, so that he could see them from far away, and watch the girl as she approached. Every afternoon he saw her eyes pick him out from among the others at the café, but from that moment on she would give no sign of knowing he was there.

How many years since I've seen such a beauty? he sighed. He would notice them coming far down the road under the eucalyptus trees, long before she could see him, for they were walking into the sunset light. The instant came when she saw him, and then her head bent forward. The rich merchant would watch her as she came nearer, his eyes never leaving her. It seemed to him that she was dancing rather than walking, and as she went past, often so near that he could have touched her djellaba by stretching out his arm, he was exasperated by the impossibility of speaking with her.

Maybe one day they'll let her out by herself, he thought, and so he waited.

The day finally came when he saw her walking along carrying the basket herself, and no one was with her. Ah, he said softly, rubbing the ends of his fingers together. He called the waiter and paid him. Then he sat quietly until she had gone by. As the girl turned the corner he got up and began to walk after her.

He caught up with her only after she had gone into another street. May I drive you somewhere? he asked her.

You may drive me home if you like, she said.

This was not what the rich merchant had hoped to hear. However, he led her to his car, which was parked not far away.

I brought Bouselham a cup of coffee. He sipped it, still crouching by the fire, and said nothing for several minutes. Then abandoning his story-telling manner, he went on casually, as though recapitulating a tale I already knew.

And I was just coming out of a bacal there, and I saw this Mercedes parked up ahead. And not with Belgian license-plates, either. Moroccan ones, and that means money. And then, while I was still looking, I stopped believing what I was seeing, because the door of the car opened and my sister got out and ran up toward the corner. I knew she'd seen me and didn't think I'd seen her. The first thing I thought of was going after her and killing her. While I stood there the car drove away. I didn't see the man or get the number.

What good would that have done, if you'd killed her? I said, although I knew that for him it was one of those meaningless European remarks. Surprisingly, he laughed and said: I'm not that stupid. I felt sorry for her, though, that night when I got her alone at home and saw how frightened she was.

I saw you get out of the car, I told her. But then I said: You say he's always at the Café Dakhla. Tomorrow you're going to show me which one he is. As you walk past him you're going to cough.

And she did, and when he left the café I followed him and saw him get into his Mercedes. I watched him drive away and I thought: Maybe. Maybe. Incha'Allah!

Once he had identified the man through his license-plate, he began to ask questions, first going to the qahouaji there in the café, and then having narrowed his search, to several merchants and bazaar-keepers in the city.

I found out more about him than his mother knows, said Bouselham. He owns half the textile factory at the Plaza Mozart, and an apartment house in the Boulevard de Paris. And three bazaars. So one night when I got home I took my sister up on the roof where we could talk, and I said to her: You like this Qasri?

She began to stammer and protest. I don't even know him. How can I say if I like him?

That made me angry and I grabbed her. You don't know whether you like him. But you got into his car and sat beside him. What does that mean?

She thought I was going to hit her, and she hid her face in her hands and backed away. I had the right to beat her, of course. But I let her know I was on her side, and would never mention it to the rest of the family. I even bought her new clothes the next day, so El Qasri could get some idea of how she could look if she wanted to. And I decided to wait and see if things happened by themselves.

He kept after her and she went on putting him off. Then once my father and mother and the whole family had to go to Meknes overnight, and she and I were the only ones who stayed home. I thought: I'm going to spend the night in Tetuan and see what happens. So I told her I wasn't going to be there that night, and that she would have to sleep at our aunt's house. And I asked her please not to mention my trip to Tetuan to our parents, because of course I was supposed to be in the house taking care of her. I thought: If anything's going to happen by itself, tonight's the night when it'll happen.

And I was right. I went to Tetuan and she went with him to his house, and it wasn't a long time later when she came to me and said she thought there was a child in her belly.

Right away I took her over to Gibraltar, to the biggest hospital. We stayed there four days, and I got the papers on each test, and there was no doubt about it, they said: there was a child inside.

Having nothing more urgent to do with his time, Bouselham continued to go each day to the café at the end of the city. Here he fell into conversation and eventual companionship with the rich merchant. Even after he had brought his sister back from Gibraltar, and the lawyer was busy preparing his strategy, even after the lawyer had called on the rich merchant to advise him that the only way of avoiding a scandal was to ask for the girl in marriage, before her family discovered her pregnancy, Bouselham sat daily with him in the café listening to the story of this troubled romance.

She's got a brother, the rich merchant told him. He's the one who wants my blood. The son of a whore found out about it.

Then Bouselham said to him: But why son of a whore? He's letting you marry her. If he wanted to, he could put you in jail today. Are you crazy? She was a virgin.

The rich merchant agreed that this was so. Less than a week later he made the offer of marriage to Bouselham's father.

After he stopped talking, I looked down at him, trying to see the expression on his face, but his head was outlined against the flames, and there was only the light of two candles in the room.

He's not going to like it much when he finds out you're her brother, I said.

He only laughed. Some day, he said. Some day.

I brought a fresh log, and he finally stood up.

Bouselham did not keep silent about the dubious part he'd played in the arranging of his sister's wedding; on the contrary, he discussed it at length with his Moroccan friends. To him it was a business matter in whose success he took a healthy pride. Thus several garbled versions of the story began to travel around Tangier. Mother heard them, but discounted them as fables invented purely out of spite. It was not until months after Bouselham's visit to me at the flat that she brought herself to accepting them as fact. At that instant she became irrational.

The whole thing is vile! she said. I've got rid of him. His dismissal had been summary, with no explanation offered. She had handed him a sum of money and told him to leave the premises instantly. Two days later she had set out for Italy. It was clear to me that she half expected to be blackmailed, but was ashamed to put it into words. If only she had mentioned her fear, I could have tried to reassure her. I believe I know Bouselham better then she did.

Until the day when he called to me from inside the Café Raqassa, I had not seen him for several weeks. We sat in a back corner where it was dark and the air smelled of damp cement and charcoal smoke. Bouselham spoke briefly of Mother, shaking his head ruefully. There was no mention of anything more than that he had lost his job as gardener when Madame went away. He was aware of somehow having offended her, but her arbitrary behavior had bewildered and aggrieved him. The way he saw it, he had been turned out of the house for no reason at all. Still, as we parted, he said: When you write to Madame, tell her Bouselham sends his greetings.

I did not pass on the message, or any subsequent ones, from him to Mother. She sold the house without returning to Tangier, and it seemed to me that living over there in Italy with Father she must be miserable enough without getting reminders of Bouselham from me.

Tangier
1976

You Have Left Your
Lotus Pods on the Bus

I soon learned not to go near the windows or to draw aside the double curtains in order to look at the river below. The view was wide and lively, with factories and warehouses on the far side of the Chao Phraya, and strings of barges being towed up and down through the dirty water. The new wing of the hotel had been built in the shape of an upright slab, so that the room was high and had no trees to shade it from the poisonous onslaught of the afternoon sun. The end of the day, rather than bringing respite, intensified the heat, for then the entire river was made of sunlight. With the redness of dusk everything out there became melodramatic and forbidding, and still the oven heat from outside leaked through the windows.

Brooks, teaching at Chulalongkorn University, was required as a Fulbright Fellow to attend regular classes in Thai; as an adjunct to this he arranged to spend much of his leisure time with Thais. One day he brought along with him three young men wearing the bright orange-yellow robes of Buddhist monks. They filed into the hotel room in silence and stood in a row as they were presented to me, each one responding by joining his palms together, thumbs touching his chest.

As we talked, Yamyong, the eldest, in his late twenties, explained that he was an ordained monk, while the other two were novices. Brooks then asked Prasert and Vichai if they would be ordained soon, but the monk answered for them.

"I do not think they are expecting to be ordained," he said quietly, looking at the floor, as if it were a sore subject all too often discussed among them. He glanced up at me and went on talking. "Your room is beautiful. We are not accustomed to such luxury." His voice was flat; he was trying to conceal his disapproval. The three conferred briefly in undertones. "My friends say they have never seen such a luxurious room," he reported, watching me closely through his steel-rimmed spectacles to see my reaction. I failed to hear.

They put down their brown paper parasols and their reticules that bulged with books and fruit. Then they got themselves into position in a row along the couch among the cushions. For a while they were busy adjusting the folds of their robes around their shoulders and legs.

"They make their own clothes," volunteered Brooks. "All the monks do."

I spoke of Ceylon; there the monks bought the robes all cut and ready to sew together. Yamyong smiled appreciatively and said: "We use the same system here."

The air-conditioning roared at one end of the room and the noise of boat motors on the river seeped through the windows at the other. I looked at the three sitting in front of me. They were very calm and self-possessed, but they seemed lacking in physical health. I was aware of the facial bones beneath their skin. Was the impression of sallowness partly due to the shaved eyebrows and hair?

Yamyong was speaking. "We appreciate the opportunity to use English. For this reason we are liking to have foreign friends. English, American; it doesn't matter. We can understand." Prasert and Vichai nodded.

Time went on, and we sat there, extending but not altering the subject of conversation. Occasionally I looked around the room. Before they had come in, it had been only a hotel room whose curtains must be kept drawn. Their presence and their comments on it had managed to invest it with a vaguely disturbing quality; I felt that they considered it a great mistake on my part to have chosen such a place in which to stay.

"Look at his tattoo," said Brooks. "Show him."

Yamyong pulled back his robe a bit from the shoulder, and I saw the two indigo lines of finely written Thai characters. "That is for good health," he said, glancing up at me. His smile seemed odd, but then, his facial expression did not complement his words at any point.

"Don't the Buddhists disapprove of tattooing?" I said.

"Some people say it is backwardness." Again he smiled. "Words for good health are said to be superstition. This was done by my abbot when I was a boy studying in the *wat*. Perhaps he did not know it was a superstition."

We were about to go with them to visit the *wat* where they lived. I pulled a tie from the closet and stood before the mirror arranging it.

"Sir," Yamyong began. "Will you please explain something? What is the significance of the necktie?"

"The significance of the necktie?" I turned to face him. "You mean, why do men wear neckties?"

"No. I know that. The purpose is to look like a gentleman."

I laughed. Yamyong was not put off. "I have noticed that some men wear the two ends equal, and some wear the wide end longer than the narrow, or the narrow longer than the wide. And the neckties themselves, they are not all the same length, are they? Some even with both ends equal reach below the waist. What are the different meanings?"

"There is no meaning," I said. "Absolutely none."

He looked to Brooks for confirmation, but Brooks was trying out his Thai on Prasert and Vichai, and so he was silent and thoughtful for a moment. "I believe you, of course," he said graciously. "But we all thought each way had a different significance attached."

As we went out of the hotel, the doorman bowed respectfully. Until now he had never given a sign that he was aware of my existence. The wearers of the yellow robe carry weight in Thailand.

A few Sundays later I agreed to go with Brooks and our friends to Ayudhaya. The idea of a Sunday outing is so repellent to me that deciding to take part in this one was to a certain extent a compulsive act. Ayudhaya lies less than fifty miles up the Chao Phraya from Bangkok. For historians and art collectors it is more than just a provincial town; it is a period and a style—having been the Thai capital for more than four centuries. Very likely it still would be, had the Burmese not laid it waste in the eighteenth century.

Brooks came early to fetch me. Downstairs in the street stood the three bhikkus with their book bags and parasols. They hailed a cab, and without any previous price arrangements (the ordinary citizen tries to fix a sum beforehand) we got in and drove for twenty minutes or a half-hour, until we got to a bus terminal on the northern outskirts of the city.

It was a nice, old-fashioned, open bus. Every part of it rattled, and the air from the rice fields blew across us as we pieced together our bits of synthetic conversation. Brooks, in high spirits, kept calling across to me: "Look! Water buffaloes!" As we went further away from Bangkok there were more of the beasts, and his cries became more frequent. Yamyong, sitting next to me, whispered: "Professor Brooks is fond of buffaloes?" I laughed and said I didn't think so.

"Then?"

I said that in America there were no buffaloes in the fields, and that was why Brooks was interested in seeing them. There were no temples in the landscape, either, I told him, and added, perhaps unwisely: "He looks at buffaloes. I look at temples." This struck Yamyong as hilarious, and he made allusions to it now and then all during the day.

The road stretched ahead, straight as a line in geometry, across the verdant, level land. Paralleling it on its eastern side was a fairly wide canal, here and there choked with patches of enormous pink lotuses. In places the flowers were gone and only the pods remained, thick green disks with the circular seeds embedded in their flesh. At the first stop the bhikkus got out. They came aboard again with mangosteens and lotus pods and insisted on giving us large numbers of each. The huge seeds popped out of the fibrous lotus cakes as though from a punchboard; they tasted almost like green almonds. "Something new for you today, I think," Yamyong said with a satisfied air.

Ayudhaya was hot, dusty, spread-out, its surrounding terrain strewn with ruins that scarcely showed through the vegetation. At some distance from the town there began a wide boulevard sparingly lined with important-looking buildings. It continued for a way and then came to an end as abrupt as its beginning. Growing up out of the scrub, and built of small russet-colored bricks, the ruined temples looked still unfinished rather than damaged by time. Repairs, done in smeared cement, veined their façades.

The bus's last stop was still two or three miles from the center of Ayudhaya. We got down into the dust, and Brooks declared: "The first thing we must do is find food. They can't eat anything solid, you know, after midday."

"Not noon exactly," Yamyong said. "Maybe one o'clock or a little later."

"Even so, that doesn't leave much time," I told him. "It's quarter to twelve now."

But the bhikkus were not hungry. None of them had visited Ayudhaya before, and so they had compiled a list of things they most wanted to see. They spoke with a man who had a station wagon parked nearby, and we set off for a ruined *stupa* that lay some miles to the southwest. It had been built atop a high mound, which we climbed with some difficulty, so that Brooks could take pictures of us standing within a fissure in the decayed outer wall. The air stank of the bats that lived inside.

When we got back to the bus stop, the subject of food arose once again, but the excursion had put the bhikkus into such a state of excitement that they could not bear to allot time for anything but looking. We went to the museum. It was quiet; there were Khmer heads and documents inscribed in Pali. The day had begun to be painful. I told myself I had known beforehand that it would.

Then we went to a temple. I was impressed, not so much by the gigantic Buddha which all but filled the interior, as by the fact that not far from the entrance a man sat on the floor playing a *ranad* (pronounced *lanat*). Although I was familiar with the sound of it from listening to recordings of Siamese music, I had never before seen the instrument. There was a graduated series of wooden blocks strung together, the whole slung like a hammock over a boat-shaped resonating stand. The tones hurried after one another like drops of water falling very fast. After the painful heat outside, everything in the temple suddenly seemed a symbol of the concept of coolness—the stone floor under my bare feet, the breeze that moved through the shadowy interior, the bamboo fortune sticks being rattled in their long box by those

praying at the altar, and the succession of insubstantial, glassy sounds that
came from the *ranad*. I thought: If only I could get something to eat, I
wouldn't mind the heat so much.

We got into the center of Ayudhaya a little after three o'clock. It was hot
and noisy; the bhikkus had no idea of where to look for a restaurant, and the
prospect of asking did not appeal to them. The five of us walked aimlessly. I
had come to the conclusion that neither Prasert nor Vichai understood
spoken English, and I addressed myself earnestly to Yamyong. *"We've got to
eat."* He stared at me with severity. "We are searching," he told me.

Eventually we found a Chinese restaurant on a corner of the principal
street. There was a table full of boisterous Thais drinking *mekong*
(categorized as whiskey, but with the taste of cheap rum) and another table
occupied by an entire Chinese family. These people were doing some
serious eating, their faces buried in their rice bowls. It cheered me to see
them: I was faint, and had half expected to be told that there was no hot food
available.

The large menu in English which was brought us must have been typed
several decades ago and wiped with a damp rag once a week ever since.
Under the heading SPECIALITIES were some dishes that caught my eye, and
as I went through the list I began to laugh. Then I read it aloud to Brooks.

> *"Fried Sharks Fins and Bean Sprout*
> *Chicken Chins Stuffed with Shrimp*
> *Fried Rice Birds*
> *Shrimps Balls and Green Marrow*
> *Pigs Lights with Pickles*
> *Braked Rice Bird in Port Wine*
> *Fish Head and Bean Curd"*

Although it was natural for our friends not to join in the laughter, I felt that
their silence was not merely failure to respond; it was heavy, positive.

A moment later three Pepsi-Cola bottles were brought and placed on the
table. "What are you going to have?" Brooks asked Yamyong.

"Nothing, thank you," he said lightly. "This will be enough for us
today."

"But this is terrible! You mean no one is going to eat *anything?*"

"You and your friend will eat your food," said Yamyong. (He might as
well have said "fodder.") Then he, Prasert, and Vichai stood up, and
carrying their Pepsi-Cola bottles with them, went to sit at a table on the
other side of the room. Now and then Yamyong smiled sternly across at us.

"I wish they'd stop watching us," Brooks said under his breath.

"They were the ones who kept putting it off," I reminded him. But I felt guilty, and I was annoyed at finding myself placed in the position of the self-indulgent unbeliever. It was almost as bad as eating in front of Moslems during Ramadan.

We finished our meal and set out immediately, following Yamyong's decision to visit a certain temple he wanted to see. The taxi drive led us through a region of thorny scrub. Here and there, in the shade of spreading flat-topped trees, were great round pits, full of dark water and crowded with buffaloes; only their wet snouts and horns were visible. Brooks was already crying: "Buffaloes! Hundreds of them!" He asked the taxi driver to stop so that he could photograph the animals.

"You will have buffaloes at the temple," said Yamyong. He was right; there was a muddy pit filled with them only a few hundred feet from the building. Brooks went and took his pictures while the bhikkus paid their routine visit to the shrine. I wandered into a courtyard where there was a long row of stone Buddhas. It is the custom of temple-goers to plaster little squares of gold leaf onto the religious statues in the *wats*. When thousands of them have been stuck onto the same surface, tiny scraps of the gold come unstuck. Then they tremble in the breeze, and the figure shimmers with a small, vibrant life of its own. I stood in the courtyard watching this quivering along the arms and torsos of the Buddhas, and I was reminded of the motion of the bô-tree's leaves. When I mentioned it to Yamyong in the taxi, I think he failed to understand, for he replied: "The bô-tree is a very great tree for Buddhists."

Brooks sat beside me on the bus going back to Bangkok. We spoke only now and then. After so many hours of resisting the heat, it was relaxing to sit and feel the relatively cool air that blew in from the rice fields. The driver of the bus was not a believer in cause and effect. He passed trucks with oncoming traffic in full view. I felt better with my eyes shut, and I might even have dozed off, had there not been in the back of the bus a man, obviously not in control, who was intent on making as much noise as possible. He began to shout, scream, and howl almost as soon as we had left Ayudhaya, and he did this consistently throughout the journey. Brooks and I laughed about it, conjecturing whether he was crazy or only drunk. The aisle was too crowded for me to be able to see him from where I sat. Occasionally I glanced at the other passengers. It was as though they were entirely unaware of the commotion behind them. As we drew closer to the city, the screams became louder and almost constant.

"God, why don't they throw him off?" Brooks was beginning to be annoyed.

"They don't even hear him," I said bitterly. People who can tolerate noise inspire me with envy and rage. Finally I leaned over and said to Yamyong: "That poor man back there! It's incredible!"

"Yes," he said over his shoulder. "He's very busy." This set me thinking what a civilized and tolerant people they were, and I marvelled at the sophistication of the word "busy" to describe what was going on in the back of the bus.

Finally we were in a taxi driving across Bangkok. I would be dropped at my hotel and Brooks would take the three bhikkus on to their *wat*. In my head I was still hearing the heartrending cries. What had the repeated word patterns meant?

I had not been able to give an acceptable answer to Yamyong in his bewilderment about the significance of the necktie, but perhaps he could satisfy my curiosity here.

"That man in the back of the bus, you know?"

Yamyong nodded. "He was working very hard, poor fellow. Sunday is a bad day."

I disregarded the nonsense. "What was he saying?"

"Oh, he was saying: 'Go into second gear,' or 'We are coming to a bridge,' or 'Be careful, people in the road.' Whatever he saw."

Since neither Brooks nor I appeared to have understood, he went on. "All the buses must have a driver's assistant. He watches the road and tells the driver how to drive. It is hard work because he must shout loud enough for the driver to hear him."

"But why doesn't he sit up in front with the driver?"

"No, no. There must be one in front and one in the back. That way two men are responsible for the bus."

It was an unconvincing explanation for the grueling sounds we had heard, but to show him that I believed him I said: "Aha! I see."

The taxi drew up in front of the hotel and I got out. When I said good-by to Yamyong, he replied, I think with an shade of aggrievement: "Good-by. You have left your lotus pods on the bus."

Tangier
1971

Istikhara, Anaya, Medagan
and the Medaganat

In the Sahara, where the air, the light, even the sky suggest some as yet unvisited planet, it is not surprising to find certain patterns of human comportment equally unfamiliar. Behavior is strictly formulated, with little margin allowed for individual variations. If circumstances offer the opportunity for attack and pillage, the action is expected; indeed, custom demands it.

This is common knowledge. What may be less well-known are the two institutions of *istikhara* and *anaya*. The first is an invocation, offered up just before going to sleep, in which the supplicant implores Allah to send a dream which will make it possible for him to solve his difficulties. The prayer must be uttered in full four times over before the request is made for the specific revelatory details that will determine the sleeper's course of action when he awakens. The orison may or may not be answered. It is up to the supplicant to decide whether his dream is a result of *istikhara* or not, and, if it seems to him that it is, to interpret its material correctly. The practice seems a sound one: not only does it assume that dreams can be therapeutic, but it offers Moslems a practical technique for producing them.

Anaya, on the other hand, is a custom devoid of meaning save in a feudal society. It is the last feeble hope left to a soldier defeated in battle. If he can manage to crawl to one of the enemy and get his head totally under the folds of the other's burnous, he is automatically saved from death. His pardon, however, involves him with the wearer of the burnous for the rest of his life, or until the wearer dies. He becomes his enemy's permanent possession and responsibility. At the time when the events cited here took place, which is to say roughly a hundred years ago, *anaya* still functioned as an integral part of Saharan military etiquette.

A man named Medagan appeared one day in Ouargla, accompanied by seven of his sons. They sat with the Chaamba and told them of how for some misdemeanor or other their own tribe of Kelkhela Tuareg had driven them out of their homeland in the Hoggar, and how they had wandered and suffered ever since. The Chaamba listened and took them in to live with

401

them. First they lent them some of their camels, and later let them have large quantities of dates and wheat on credit. This gave the Tuareg the mobility they seemed to require. For several months they lived in the vicinity of Ouargla, hunting and getting themselves into good health. Then they went back to Ouargla and robbed the Chaamba of twenty of their best camels, which they proceeded to drive off into an uninhabited region. There, hidden in the deep ravines of the desolate Tademait country, they lived for two years or more, moving out of their lair only to attack caravans that passed nearby. At length, apparently considering themselves invulnerable, they had the audacity to ride up to the very gates of El Golea and capture thirty camels from under the eyes of the Chaamba who owned them.

A Chaambi from Ouargla happened to be with the other Chaamba when the raid took place. He was one of those who had been willing to give Medagan wheat on credit. When he had finished telling the others that part of the story, the men determined to go in pursuit of the Tuareg. A few days later sixty men set out on fast *mehara*.

When Medagan and his sons arrived back to their hiding place they suspected that they might be followed, but they were fairly confident that the Chaamba would not venture into the maze of gorges and narrow passageways which characterize the terrain. Nevertheless, before lying down to sleep that night, Medagan prayed for a dream that could guide his behavior in the event the Chaamba did manage to catch up with them. In the morning when he awoke and realized with dismay that he had had no dream whatever, or none that he could recall, he conferred with his sons. They read this as an unfavorable omen, and agreed that if they were forced into battle they would seek *anaya*, throwing themselves upon the mercy of the Chaamba once again, this time definitively. Then Medagan sent off his youngest son, who was no more than a child, with some camels they had captured earlier, to sell them in El Golea. Since the group had just returned from there, this act would seem to indicate that Medagan foresaw the possibility of serious trouble, and hoped to save this son at least. In this he was successful, for the boy reached El Golea with the camels, unharmed.

The Chaamba meanwhile found the group with ease, and heard Medagan call out to them that Allah had advised him to seek *anaya*. Seeing that the Tuareg in truth were not even attempting to defend themselves, the Chaamba settled the matter by sending their black slaves against them. This ruled out the possibility of *anaya*, since a slave is powerless to grant it. The blacks cut the throat of each man, thus ending the saga of Medagan and his sons.

This took place in 1863, just as the French were making strenuous efforts to extend their hegemony southward into the desert. It marked the begin-

ning of a twenty-year period of excessive lawlessness throughout the Sahara. Bandit groups sprang up on all sides to sweep down on oases, plunder
passing caravans, and massacre voyagers. Some of this activity was legiti-
mate retaliation for French incursions, but the greater part was simple
outlawry, due no doubt to the breakdown in moral conventions attendant
upon the prolonged infidel presence.

A small group of the Mekhadema tribe having been attacked and mur-
dered in the same region of the Tademait where Medagan had met his
death, the popular imagination around Ouargla was quick to attribute the
raid to Medagan and his sons, who were declared to be wreaking vengeance
from beyond the grave in return for having been denied the possibility of
anaya by the Chaamba. Thereafter, as the raids proliferated, each new
razzia was attributed to the ghosts of the Medaganat, and the word fast came
to be a Saharan synonym for outlaw. Every petty thief, agitator, pillager,
renegade or highwayman was labeled a Medagani. Only the empty shell of
the word remained, its original and secondary meanings both having been
lost in the general confusion that existed in the region. The assaults became
organized and took on a more openly political character. Now it was the
Chaamba themselves en masse who decided to be outlaws, and who in 1871
adopted the name of Medaganat as their official designation.

In 1876 they boasted of killing the three French priests, Fathers Paul-
mier, Menoret, and Boujard. The French press reacted with hysteria: the
situation in the Sahara was utterly intolerable. Meanwhile the attacks
increased in number and violence. The Medaganat conducted raids along
the Tunisian border, in Libya, in Morocco, and throughout the Algerian
desert. It was only several years later, in 1883, when they were careless
enough to attack a group of Reguibat, that they finally met with an enemy
able to destroy them.

At the very beginning of the battle a good many of the Medaganat,
sensing likely defeat, defected outright to the Reguibat. The others, once it
became clear that they could not win, then tried like their original
namesakes to obtain *anaya*. But the women of the Reguibat, who were with
them in the camp, repeatedly warned their menfolk not to grant it. Thus the
Reguibat were obliged to chop the Medaganat into pieces with their swords
to prevent them from touching the folds of their capes. The women fur-
thermore insisted that even those who had surrendered at the outset be
slaughtered. This was a grave infraction of desert law, but to oblige them
the men cut a few dozen throats, and finally the women were quiet.

In this instance it is clear that neither *anaya* nor *istikhara* produced what
was desired of it, and yet the results were by no means the same as they
would have been had neither been practiced. To a Moslem, the failure of
Medagan's attempt at *istikhara* is implicit in the facts. One may pray, but if

one is not in a state of grace the prayer fails to get through. Once Medagan had betrayed his protectors, he was not in a condition which permitted contact with the Deity. And having construed his dreamless night as an instruction to seek *anaya*, by going out and requesting it immediately, without making even a gesture of self-defense, he doubtless helped to bring about his own defeat. To the Chaamba this behavior could only have seemed a proof of cowardice; the sending of slaves to despatch the bandits thus gave a flavor of contempt to their refusal. Apparently, Medagan and his sons were beyond the radius of normal functioning with regard to both *istikhara* and *anaya*. Many of the Chaamba Medaganat, however, would have been saved by *anaya* if the Reguibat had not happened to have their women along.

Thus there was no *istikhara*, no *anaya*, Medagan was not a Medagani, and the Medaganat had never heard of Medagan.

Tangier
1975

Things Gone and
Things Still Here

Tangier—if I were to move into the house at Ain Chqaf I should go to great expense to have the workmen install a fountain in the center of the courtyard. The water would fall into a marble basin and run out along marble troughs into a ditch. Running water, they say, rests the soul before the hour of prayer. On occasion, perhaps too much. An example: the familiar story of Hadj Allal, who came to grief through no fault of his own.

"As if he had stepped on a mine," explained one divinity student. "Only the mine was invisible and made no sound when it exploded. No one knew anything about it. He was there looking into the stream. Then he came into the mosque. For all of us he had been out there perhaps five minutes. But in the place where he had fallen two years had gone by. He tried to explain it to us. We took him home and told his wife to put him to bed and cover him up."

There is the tale of the fqih who taught in a local mosque some two centuries ago. No trace of his passage through life would remain now had it not been for an inexplicable psychic misadventure: the man must have stumbled upon one of those rare fissures in time—an open fault, as it were, in the surface of time—and fallen in.

Another fqih, this one in Hajra den Nahal, is said to have slipped between two instants and fallen into a deep well of time. The accident occurred while he was washing in the stream outside the mosque. As he squatted by the running water two tolba passed by on their way into the mosque to pray. They were having a conversation. Later the fqih stated that he had heard only one phrase: "in the twinkling of an eye." That seems to have been the signal. Everything around him stopped existing and he was in darkness.

In all versions the entry into this bubble in time is decisive for the protagonist. The two false years, according to the Nahali's story, were spent by him in India in a state of invisibility. During that time he did nothing but observe a famous goldsmith at work. When he was cast out of the time trap and returned to the stream by the mosque, he had brought with him all the Indian master's secrets, knowledge which he immediately put to use by becoming a goldsmith himself. His fame as a master artisan spread throughout Islam, so that the Indian goldsmith, on hearing of it, could not rest until he had visited Morocco and seen the designs himself. Unwisely, he traveled with his wife. The dénouement and meaning of the story for those who tell it is the Nahali's double victory. Not only did the Indian see all his own designs improved upon by the Moroccan, but he also lost his wife to him.

Another unfortunate fqih passed his sojourn in the time bubble as a woman, but returned to the world with greater wisdom.

A brilliant account could be written of the saga of the Haddaoua and their destruction. The patron saint sat smoking kif in a nargilah all day every day, it is said; even seven or eight years ago adepts could still be found smoking beside the ruined tomb. The brotherhood has been painstakingly eradicated by the authorities. Sometimes you see a lone man walking along the road wearing the dusty rags and wild hairdo of a Haddaoui, but since the cult no longer exists (and, perhaps more importantly, has no headquarters) such a man no longer deserves the respect which being a member of a brotherhood would give him, and so for most citizens he slips into the category of ordinary madman.

In the eyes of the government, the Haddaoua were not a religious sect at all, but an organized group of brigands to be finished off with bullets. Apart from their uncanny powers over goats, which made it possible for them to arrange the wholesale theft of these animals all over northern Morocco, and their use of magic spells as a threat in order to extort money from the rural populace, there would seem to be no valid reason for their persecution and extermination. Perhaps it was the fact that they built a fortress and kept a good many women shut into the cellars. They claimed that the women had come of their own volition and asked to be taken in as adepts. Whether or not that was the case, once the women had been present at the rituals they were not permitted to leave the premises, but were locked into the basement where they performed domestic duties.*

The Haddaoua placed great stress on food. Each meal was a banquet. This emphasis on eating may have been the result of the vast quantities of cannabis the men ingested each day, but the meals themselves were made possible by the easy availability of edible livestock. A Haddaoui could go out alone into the countryside and return in a few days with hundreds of goats following him in single-file formation. This alone was enough to strike fear to the hearts of the peasants. No one appears to know exactly how they

---

*This is the legend. A recent examination of the place, however, proved to me that there are no cellars beneath any of the structures in the sanctuary.

imposed their will on the animals, but all agree that it was a special art which took time and patience to learn. When you consider that the men learned the technique by lying down among the animals and conversing with them at night during their sleep, it does not seem so improbable. The Haddaoui lying in the Marrakech dust forty years ago "became" a goat while I watched, and there in front of me was a man's body with a goat inside it, as if the goat had been able to assume the visible form of a man, while at the same time it remained unmistakably a goat. Whatever it was that they stumbled upon in the way of esoteric knowledge, their misuse of it was their undoing.

For people living in the country today the djinn is an accepted, if dreaded, concomitant of daily life. The world of djenoun is too close for comfort. Among the Moroccans it is not a question of summoning them to aid you, but simply of avoiding them. Their habitat is only a few feet below ours, and is an exact duplication of the landscape above-ground. Each tree, rock and house has its identical counterpart beneath the earth's surface. The only difference is that there the sky is made of earth instead of air, and so it is totally dark. But since the lower world is a faithful reproduction of the upper world, it follows that the djenoun are perfectly equipped for life down there, and actually prefer it to our world. The trouble occurs when they emerge and take on human or animal form, for they are our traditional enemies, an alien tribe always on the lookout for an opportunity to infiltrate our ranks, and they do this merely by establishing contact with us.

Once a djinn has revealed himself to you your life changes. You can suspect his influence or presence whenever things have not gone as they should have, whenever there is a suspect or inexplicable element in a situation, whenever, in short, you are confronted with anything you don't understand. This is your warning; you begin to look for the djinn, and sooner or later you come across it and recognize it, no matter in what form you find it. What counts is your behavior and method of dealing with it at that point. Losing out in your struggle with a djinn can involve you in years of harassment or illness; it can also be fatal.

Above all you must guard against becoming emotionally involved with a djinn or a djinniya. There are many instances of miscegenation, but these are usually not discovered until after one partner has killed the other. "I watched her for months and I noticed that she never ate anything with salt in it. That was how I knew she was not a woman."

The open points along the frontier between the two worlds can conceivably occur anywhere, but exist generally in caves and under water, particularly under running water. If your itinerary involves crossing a stream, best have something made of steel (or at least iron) handy. City people often say there are no djenoun, not any more, or in any case not in the city. In the country, where life is the same as before and where there are not many automobiles and other things containing iron, they admit that djenoun probably still exist. But they add that the automobiles will eventually drive them all away, for they can't stand the proximity of iron and steel. Then it will be only in the distant mountains and the desert where you will need to worry about them.

Notwithstanding the rationalizations, djenoun continue to raise havoc now and then in the very center of the city by coming suddenly out of sink drains and attacking housewives. With this in mind, many women will not allow any hot water to fall into the sink, which means they must wash the dishes in cold water for fear of burning the possible inhabitant of the pipe. Djenoun have been known to be extremely vindictive in such cases, and commonly retaliate by causing paralysis in the offender.

If you go to the outskirts of any town, to where the fields begin and sheep are grazing, and dig in the earth under certain trees, you will come upon a knife. If you dig somewhere a few yards away from there, you may find another. There are many of them, all of the folding sort, and each one is clasped shut on a scrap of paper. Even though you open every knife you find, each time releasing a man from the spell of some accursed woman, still you are not going to spend all your time doing good turns for a whole group of men you have never known and never will meet. There would be no reason in the first place to go and dig for knives unless you suspect that a woman has shut a knife on you. Then, depending on who you think it might have been and where she would be most likely to go in order to bury it, you get busy and start to dig.

Sometimes you come upon other men digging, and when they see you they look ashamed and pretend to be looking for some change they have dropped. Often they stand up, shrug, and walk away. But if you go some distance and wait, they come back and start again to dig. Where is the justice in a world in which a woman with a simple folding knife can make so much trouble for a man?

"Twice I've found folded knives deep in the water at the bottom of the cliffs along the strait. The women who do this are even worse than the ones who bury them in the ground. They are willing to walk all the way to the cliffs so they can ruin the lives of the men they hate. There is not much chance of these knives being found and opened. And even if the paper where the curse was written has dissolved in the water, the man can have no sort of life again until the blade is opened. It's the shutting of the blade on the curse that keeps a man from being able to get hard. If I ever come across a woman burying a knife, she'll never get back home."

Tangier
1975

Allal

He was born in the hotel where his mother worked. The hotel had only three dark rooms which gave on a courtyard behind the bar. Beyond was another smaller patio with many doors. This was where the servants lived, and where Allal spent his childhood.

The Greek who owned the hotel had sent Allal's mother away. He was indignant because she, a girl of fourteen, had dared to give birth while she was working for him. She would not say who the father was, and it angered him to reflect that he himself had not taken advantage of the situation while he had had the chance. He gave the girl three months' wages and told her to go home to Marrakech. Since the cook and his wife liked the girl and offered to let her live with them for a while, he agreed that she might stay on until the baby was big enough to travel. She remained in the back patio for a few months with the cook and his wife, and then one day she disappeared, leaving the baby behind. No one heard of her again.

As soon as Allal was old enough to carry things, they set him to work. It was not long before he could fetch a pail of water from the well behind the hotel. The cook and his wife were childless, so that he played alone.

When he was somewhat older he began to wander over the empty table-land outside. There was nothing else up here but the barracks, and they were enclosed by a high blind wall of red adobe. Everything else was below in the valley: the town, the gardens, and the river winding southward among the thousands of palm trees. He could sit on a point of rock far above and look down at the people walking in the alleys of the town. It was only later that he visited the place and saw what the inhabitants were like. Because he had been left behind by his mother they called him a son of sin, and laughed when they looked at him. It seemed to him that in this way they hoped to make him into a shadow, in order not to have to think of him as real and alive. He awaited with dread the time when he would have to go each morning to the town and work. For the moment he helped in the kitchen and served the officers from the barracks, along with the few motorists who passed through the region. He got small tips in the restaurant, and free food and lodging in a cell of the servants' quarters, but the Greek gave him no wages. Eventually he reached an age when this situation seemed shameful, and he went of his own accord to the town below and began to work, along with other boys of his age, helping to make the mud bricks people used for building their houses.

Living in the town was much as he had imagined it would be. For two years he stayed in a room behind a blacksmith's shop, leading a life without quarrels, and saving whatever money he did not have to spend to keep himself alive. Far from making any friends during this time, he formed a thorough hatred for the people of the town, who never allowed him to forget that he was a son of sin, and therefore not like others, but *meskhot*—damned. Then he found a small house, not much more than a hut, in the palm groves outside the town. The rent was low and no one lived nearby. He went to live there, where the only sound was the wind in the trees, and avoided the people of the town when he could.

One hot summer evening shortly after sunset he was walking under the arcades that faced the town's main square. A few paces ahead of him an old man in a white turban was trying to shift a heavy sack from one shoulder to the other. Suddenly it fell to the ground, and Allal stared as two dark forms flowed out of it and disappeared into the shadows. The old man pounced upon the sack and fastened the top of it, at the same time beginning to shout: Look out for the snakes! Help me find my snakes!

Many people turned quickly around and walked back the way they had come. Others stood at some distance, watching. A few called to the old man: Find your snakes fast and get them out of here! Why are they here? We don't want snakes in this town!

Hopping up and down in his anxiety, the old man turned to Allal. Watch this for me a minute, my son. He pointed at the sack lying on the earth at his feet, and snatching up a basket he had been carrying, went swiftly around the corner into an alley. Allal stood where he was. No one passed by.

It was not long before the old man returned, panting with triumph. When the onlookers in the square saw him again, they began to call out, this time to Allal: Show that berrani the way out of the town! He has no right to carry those things in here. Out! Out!

Allal picked up the big sack and said to the old man: Come on.

They left the square and went through the alleys until they were at the edge of town. The old man looked up then, saw the palm trees black against the fading sky ahead, and turned to the boy beside him.

Come on, said Allal again, and he went to the left along the rough path that led to his house. The old man stood perplexed.

You can stay with me tonight, Allal told him.

And these? he said, pointing first at the sack and then at the basket. They have to be with me.

Allal grinned. They can come.

When they were sitting in the house Allal looked at the sack and the basket. I'm not like the rest of them here, he said.

It made him feel good to hear the words being spoken. He made a contemptuous gesture. Afraid to walk through the square because of a snake. You saw them.

The old man scratched his chin. Snakes are like people, he said. You have to get to know them. Then you can be their friends.

Allal hesitated before he asked: Do you ever let them out?

Always, the old man said with energy. It's bad for them to be inside like this. They've got to be healthy when they get to Taroudant, or the man there won't buy them.

He began a long story about his life as a hunter of snakes, explaining that each year he made a voyage to Taroudant to see a man who bought them for the Aissaoua snake-charmers in Marrakech. Allal made tea while he listened, and brought out a bowl of kif paste to eat with the tea. Later, when they were sitting comfortably in the midst of the pipe-smoke, the old man chuckled. Allal turned to look at him.

Shall I let them out?

Fine!

But you must sit and keep quiet. Move the lamp nearer.

He untied the sack, shook it a bit, and returned to where he had been sitting. Then in silence Allal watched the long bodies move cautiously out into the light. Among the cobras were others with markings so delicate and perfect that they seemed to have been designed and painted by an artist. One reddish-gold serpent, which coiled itself lazily in the middle of the floor, he found particularly beautiful. As he stared at it, he felt a great desire to own it and have it always with him.

The old man was talking. I've spent my whole life with snakes, he said. I could tell you some things about them. Did you know that if you give them majoun you can make them do what you want, and without saying a word? I swear by Allah!

Allal's face assumed a doubtful air. He did not question the truth of the other's statement, but rather the likelihood of his being able to put the knowledge to use. For it was at that moment that the idea of actually taking the snake first came into his head. He was thinking that whatever he was to do must be done quickly, for the old man would be leaving in the morning. Suddenly he felt a great impatience.

Put them away so I can cook dinner, he whispered. Then he sat admiring the ease with which the old man picked up each one by its head and slipped it into the sack. Once again he dropped two of the snakes into the basket, and one of these, Allal noted, was the red one. He imagined he could see the shining of its scales through the lid of the basket.

As he set to work preparing the meal Allal tried to think of other things. Then, since the snake remained in his mind in spite of everything, he began to devise a way of getting it. While he squatted over the fire in a corner, he mixed some kif paste in a bowl of milk and set it aside.

The old man continued to talk. That was good luck, getting the two snakes back like that, in the middle of the town. You can never be sure what people are going to do when they find out you're carrying snakes. Once in El Kelaa they took all of them and killed them, one after the other, in front of me. A year's work. I had to go back home and start all over again.

Even as they ate, Allal saw that his guest was growing sleepy. How will things happen? he wondered. There was no way of knowing beforehand precisely what he was going to do, and the prospect of having to handle the snake worried him. It could kill me, he thought.

Once they had eaten, drunk tea and smoked a few pipes of kif, the old man lay back on the floor and said he was going to sleep. Allal sprang up. In here! he told him, and led him to his own mat in an alcove. The old man lay down and swiftly fell asleep.

Several times during the next half hour Allal went to the alcove and peered in, but neither the body in its burnous nor the head in its turban had stirred.

First he got out his blanket, and after tying three of its corners together, spread it on the floor with the fourth corner facing the basket. Then he set the bowl of milk and kif paste on the blanket. As he loosened the strap from the cover of the basket the old man coughed. Allal stood immobile, waiting to hear the cracked voice speak. A small breeze had sprung up, making the palm branches rasp one against the other, but there was no further sound from the alcove. He crept to the far side of the room and squatted by the wall, his gaze fixed on the basket.

Several times he thought he saw the cover move slightly, but each time he decided he had been mistaken. Then he caught his breath. The shadow along the base of the basket was moving. One of the creatures had crept out from the far side. It waited for a while before continuing into the light, but when it did, Allal breathed a prayer of thanks. It was the red and gold one.

When finally it decided to go to the bowl, it made a complete tour around the edge, looking in from all sides, before lowering its head toward the milk. Allal watched, fearful that the foreign flavor of the kif paste might repel it. The snake remained there without moving.

He waited a half hour or more. The snake stayed where it was, its head in the bowl. From time to time Allal glanced at the basket, to be certain that the second snake was still in it. The breeze went on, rubbing the palm branches together. When he decided it was time, he rose slowly, and keeping an eye on the basket where apparently the other snake still slept, he reached over and gathered together the three tied corners of the blanket. Then he lifted the fourth corner, so that both the snake and the bowl slid to the bottom of the improvised sack. The snake moved slightly, but he did not think it was angry. He knew exactly where he would hide it: between some rocks in the dry river bed.

Holding the blanket in front of him he opened the door and stepped out under the stars. It was not far up the road, to a group of high palms, and then to the left down into the oued. There was a space between the boulders where the bundle would be invisible. He pushed it in with care, and hurried back to the house. The old man was asleep.

There was no way of being sure that the other snake was still in the basket, so Allal picked up his burnous and went outside. He shut the door and lay down on the ground to sleep.

Before the sun was in the sky the old man was awake, lying in the alcove coughing. Allal jumped up, went inside, and began to make a fire in the mijmah. A minute later he heard the other exclaim: They're loose again! Out of the basket! Stay where you are and I'll find them.

It was not long before the old man grunted with satisfaction. I have the black one! he cried. Allal did not look up from the corner where he crouched, and the old man came over, waving a cobra. Now I've got to find the other one.

He put the snake away and continued to search. When the fire was blazing, Allal turned and said: Do you want me to help you look for it?

No, No! Stay where you are.

Allal boiled the water and made the tea, and still the old man was crawling on his knees, lifting boxes and pushing sacks. His turban had slipped off and his face ran with sweat.

Come and have tea, Allal told him.

The old man did not seem to have heard him at first. Then he rose and went into the alcove, where he rewound his turban. When he came out he sat down with Allal, and they had breakfast.

Snakes are very clever, the old man said. They can get into places that don't exist. I've moved everything in this house.

After they had finished eating, they went outside and looked for the snake between the close-growing trunks of the palms near the house. When the old man was convinced that it was gone, he went sadly back in.

That was a good snake, he said at last. And now I'm going to Taroudant.

They said good-bye, and the old man took his sack and basket and started up the road toward the highway.

All day long as he worked, Allal thought of the snake, but it was not until sunset that he was able to go to the rocks in the oued and pull out the blanket. He carried it back to the house in a high state of excitement.

Before he untied the blanket, he filled a wide dish with milk and kif paste, and set it on the floor. He ate three spoonfuls of the paste himself and sat back to watch, drumming on the low wooden tea-table with his fingers. Everything happened just as he had hoped. The snake came slowly out of the blanket, and very soon had found the dish and was drinking the milk. As long as it drank he kept drumming; when it had finished and raised its head to look at him, he stopped, and it crawled back inside the blanket.

Later that evening he put down more milk, and drummed again on the table. After a time the snake's head appeared, and finally all of it, and the entire pattern of action was repeated.

That night and every night thereafter, Allal sat with the snake, while with infinite patience he sought to make it his friend. He never attempted to touch it, but soon he was able to summon it, keep it in front of him for as long as he pleased, merely by tapping on the table, and dismiss it at will. For the first week or so he used the kif paste; then he tried the routine without it. In the end the results were the same. After that he fed it only milk and eggs.

Then one evening as his friend lay gracefully coiled in front of him, he began to think of the old man, and formed an idea that put all other things out of his mind. There had not been any kif paste in the house for several weeks, and he decided to make some. He bought the ingredients the following day, and after work he prepared the paste. When it was done, he mixed a large amount of it in a bowl with milk and set it down for the snake. Then he himself ate four spoonfuls, washing them down with tea.

He quickly undressed, and moving the table so that he could reach it, stretched out naked on a mat near the door. This time he continued to tap on the table, even after the snake had finished drinking the milk. It lay still, observing him, as if it were in doubt that the familiar drumming came from the brown body in front of it.

Seeing that even after a long time it remained where it was, staring at him with its stony yellow eyes, Allal began to say to it over and over: Come here. He knew it could not hear his voice, but he believed it could feel his mind as he urged it. You can make them do what you want, without saying a word, the old man had told him.

Although the snake did not move, he went on repeating his command, for by now he knew it was going to come. And after another long wait, all at once it lowered its head and began to move toward him. It reached his hip and slid along his leg. Then it climbed up his leg and lay for a time across his chest. Its body was heavy and tepid, its scales wonderfully smooth. After a time it came to rest, coiled in the space between his head and his shoulder.

By this time the kif paste had completely taken over Allal's mind. He lay in a state of pure delight, feeling the snake's head against his own, without a thought save that he and the snake were together. The patterns forming and melting behind his eyelids seemed to be the same ones that covered the snake's back. Now and then in a huge frenzied movement they all swirled up and shattered into fragments which swiftly became one great yellow eye, split through the middle by the narrow vertical pupil that pulsed with his own heartbeat. Then the eye would recede, through shifting shadow and sunlight, until only the designs of the scales were left, swarming with renewed insistence as they merged and separated. At last the eye returned, so huge this time that it had no edge around it, its pupil dilated to form an aperture almost wide enough for him to enter. As he stared at the blackness within, he understood that he was being slowly propelled toward the opening. He put out his hands to touch the polished surface of the eye on each side, and as he did this he felt the pull from within. He slid through the crack and was swallowed by darkness.

On awakening Allal felt that he had returned from somewhere far away. He opened his eyes and saw, very close to him, what looked like the flank of an enormous beast, covered with coarse stiff hair. There was a repeated vibration in the air, like distant thunder curling around the edges of the sky. He sighed, or imagined that he did, for his breath made no sound. Then he shifted his head a bit, to try and see beyond the mass of hair beside him. Next he saw the ear, and he knew he was looking at his own head from the outside. He had not expected this; he had hoped only that his friend would come in and share his mind with him. But it did not strike him as being at all strange; he merely said to himself that now he was seeing through the eyes of the snake, rather than through his own.

Now he understood why the serpent had been so wary of him: from here the boy was a monstrous creature, with all the bristles on his head and his breathing that vibrated inside him like a far-off storm.

He uncoiled himself and glided across the floor to the alcove. There was a break in the mud wall wide enough to let him out. When he had pushed himself through, he lay full length on the ground in the crystalline moonlight, staring at the strangeness of the landscape, where shadows were not shadows.

He crawled around the side of the house and started up the road toward the town, rejoicing in a sense of freedom different from any he had ever imagined. There was no feeling of having a body, for he was perfectly contained in the skin that covered him. It was beautiful to caress the earth with the length of his belly as he moved along the silent road, smelling the sharp veins of wormwood in the wind. When the voice of the muezzin floated out over the countryside from the mosque, he could not hear it, or know that within the hour the night would end.

On catching sight of a man ahead, he left the road and hid behind a rock until the danger had passed. But then as he approached the town there began to be more people, so that he let himself down into the seguia, the deep ditch that went along beside the road. Here the stones and clumps of dead plants impeded his progress. He was still struggling along the floor of the seguia, pushing himself around the rocks and through the dry tangles of matted stalks left by the water, when dawn began to break.

The coming of daylight made him anxious and unhappy. He clambered up the bank of the seguia and raised his head to examine the road. A man walking past saw him, stood quite still, and then turned and ran back. Allal did not wait; he wanted now to get home as fast as possible.

Once he felt the thud of a stone as it struck the ground somewhere behind him. Quickly he threw himself over the edge of the seguia and rolled squirming down the bank. He knew the terrain here: where the road crossed the oued, there were two culverts not far apart. A man stood at some distance ahead of him with a shovel, peering down into the seguia. Allal kept moving, aware that he would reach the first culvert before the man could get to him.

The floor of the tunnel under the road was ribbed with hard little waves of sand. The smell of the mountains was in the air that moved through. There were places in here where he could have hidden, but he kept moving, and soon reached the other end. Then he continued to the second culvert and went under the road in the other direction, emerging once again into the seguia. Behind him several men had gathered at the entrance to the first culvert. One of them was on his knees, his head and shoulders inside the opening.

He now set out for the house in a straight line across the open ground, keeping his eye on the clump of palms beside it. The sun had just come up, and the stones began to cast long bluish shadows. All at once a small boy appeared from behind some nearby palms, saw him, and opened his eyes and mouth wide with fear. He was so close that Allal went straight to him and bit him in the leg. The boy ran wildly toward the group of men in the seguia.

Allal hurried on to the house, looking back only as he reached the hole between the mud bricks. Several men were running among the trees toward him. Swiftly he glided through into the alcove. The brown body still lay near the door. But there was no time, and Allal needed time to get back to it, to lie close to its head and say: Come here.

As he stared out into the room at the body, there was a great pounding on the door. The boy was on his feet at the first blow, as if a spring had been released, and Allal saw with despair the expression of total terror in his face, and the eyes with no mind behind them. The boy stood panting, his fists clenched. The door opened and some of the men peered inside. Then with a roar the boy lowered his head and rushed through the doorway. One of the men reached out to seize him, but lost his balance and fell. An instant later all of them turned and began to run through the palm grove after the naked figure.

Even when, from time to time, they lost sight of him, they could hear the screams, and then they would see him, between the palm trunks, still running. Finally he stumbled and fell face downward. It was then that they caught him, bound him, covered his nakedness, and took him away, to be sent one day soon to the hospital at Berrechid.

That afternoon the same group of men came to the house to carry out the search they had meant to make earlier. Allal lay in the alcove, dozing. When he awoke, they were already inside. He turned and crept to the hole. He saw the man waiting out there, a club in his hand.

The rage always had been in his heart; now it burst forth. As if his body were a whip, he sprang out into the room. The men nearest him were on their hands and knees, and Allal had the joy of pushing his fangs into two of them before a third severed his head with an axe.

Tangier
1976

Paul Bowles has lived for many years as an expatriate American in Tangier, Morocco. He is the author of four highly acclaimed novels: *The Sheltering Sky*, *Let It Come Down*, *The Spider's House*, and *Up Above the World*. He has also written several volumes of short stories, including *The Delicate Prey* and *The Time of Friendship*, and in 1972 Black Sparrow Press published his Selected Poems, *The Thicket of Spring*. In 1965 Bowles met the young Moroccan, Mohammed Mrabet, whose texts he has translated into English, the most recent of these being *The Big Mirror*. Bowles is also well known as a composer and is responsible for an important collection of native North African music gathered for the Library of Congress.

This volume collects all of Paul Bowles' stories, many of them long out of print and unavailable, written over a period of more than thirty years, and presents them for the first time as an entity.